D0400696

1

Selah crouched amid the towering pampas grass. Feathery seed plumes swayed in the breeze, pushing wisps of dark brown hair across her face, tangling her locks in the sticky seed pods. She blinked through watering eyes, stripped a rawhide lace from the bottom of her leather vest, and tied a haphazard ponytail. There'd be no falling asleep today . . . no chaotic dreams, no visions of the past to blur her resolve.

Her focus wandered to the beach as she fingered her favorite kapo. The throwing knife acted as a sort of touchstone . . . a feeling of security amid the present chaos.

Sometimes she felt such anger . . . No matter. Tomorrow on her Birth Remembrance, she would attain the eighteenth year of life and her rights as an adult, which included hunting. Determination swelled in her. Maybe if she could prove her worth. She'd just hang around awhile, and if the opportunity arose . . .

A smile pulled at the corner of her mouth. A rust-red rabbit lingered near the edge of the tender grass on the high side of the sandy beach. Twice she thought about impaling it, and twice it meandered behind one of the many ancient metal debris fields littering this section of beach. Why take out her anger on a helpless animal? Although it would make a delightful Remembrance meal.

Still, she wasn't here to catch rabbits. She hoped to catch a Lander. The odds of an arrival today, after what happened yesterday, were slim to none. Regardless of her father's refusal to allow her in the hunt, she'd show them all. In her mind it was one last act of defiance before she was shipped off to her death sentence.

A rustling sounded behind her. She turned to see her younger brother Dane wading through the waving sea of grass. Selah pressed her fingers against her lips and motioned to the nine-year-old. She pointed in the rabbit's direction. Dane loved following her because she tolerated him, whereas her older brothers badgered and chased him. Selah felt she owed him a huge dose of gratitude. Until he came along, she'd been the youngest and suffered the same indignities.

Dane grinned as he crept up beside her. "Mother said for you to come home right now!"

Selah ignored the message and concentrated on distracting Dane from gleaning her original purpose.

Crouching low, Dane used his stubby little fingers to part the curtain of grass and peeked through.

"Rabbit!" He squealed and darted forward.

Selah snatched the back of his leather tunic as his feet

launched into empty air. Jerking him back from the abyss, she thudded him to the ground beside her. Fear pounded her chest as she tightened her embrace on him.

"What were you thinking? You'd better thank Mother for stitching your vest so well it held when I grabbed you." Selah's arms shook as she thought about what could have happened. It would have killed her father to lose a son. "Do you realize you could have gotten killed pulling a stunt like that?"

Dane looked at her wide-eyed, sucked in a huge breath, and scrunched up his eyebrows. "What did I do? I wanted to see the rabbit."

Selah reached out and parted the thick wall of grass. "Do you see this? How many times have I told you to tread lightly on this part of the beach?"

Dane craned his head to look beyond her. His eyes widened as he stared into the deep pit obscured by the grass shield, one of the leftover vestiges of the destroyed city. "I didn't know that was down there."

"That's okay. You'll learn." Selah's anger faded as she retrieved her dropped kapo and slid it into its pouch. Dane was still too young to be responsible. She was thankful for her fast reflexes.

"You shouldn't be catching rabbits," Dane said. "I'm telling."

Selah sighed and attempted to hide a grin. His command of the language always included telling on one of them to their parents.

Unlike most others in the Borough who ate from their farm stock of cows or wild deer, her father and brothers ate food mostly from the sea. But it was better to let Dane think she

9

was trying to bag rabbits than to have him run home and tell Mother she was stalking Landers.

"You're supposed to be my soldier. You promised to keep my secrets." She tousled his yellow curls. His fair coloring took after their father's blond hair and brown eyes, as did her other two brothers, while she favored her mother's dark hair, olive skin, and green eyes. The boys turned fire-coal red in the sun while she acquired a delicious bronze.

"Father says rabbits have disease from the Sorrows, and we can't eat them." Dane shook his head as though it would emphasize his point. He had no idea what he was talking about, but it amused Selah that he imitated Father so well.

The Time of Sorrows had begun with a single spectacular flash in time, 150 years ago and two hundred miles to the north. Three devices called suitcase nukes had destroyed Washington, DC, leaving nothing but a big hole in the ground and radiation that spread for hundreds of miles, affecting all life. Animals surviving the radiation suffered genetic mutations, souring their meat, as her father called it.

But Selah had discovered a species of rabbit with sweet, clean meat. She refused to share the tidbit, or her abundance of game would rapidly grow scarce. When she caught a rabbit, she always skinned it and buried the evidence before taking the meat home. Father refused to acknowledge her prowess. He called her foolish. Yet she often wondered why he never stopped her or Mother from eating it.

"Do you think Mother or I would feed you something bad?" she asked Dane now.

He put his index finger to his chin, mimicking what Father did while thinking through a particularly daunting situation, waited a few seconds, then shook his head. *What a little man.*

Selah squeezed him again and watched the rabbit's tail bounce out of sight down the beach. Her gaze diverted from down the beach to across the water. On the horizon something bobbed in the sea. Her heart rate ticked up a beat. The only vessels ever to come by sea carried Landers.

Without looking back, she patted Dane on the arm. "Run home. Tell Mother I'll be along shortly." She knew at that very moment it was a promise she wasn't going to keep. But delivering the message would send him home. It looked like today might be her chance to join the family's second business.

"Mother said to come home right now!" Dane said again.

Selah turned and shooed him with a flip of her hand and a pretend fist. Dane grinned and scurried off in the other direction. Her promise quickly forgotten, she worked her way around the pits of concrete and steel rubble down to the shoreline. Gray-green waves slapped at the sand, then pulled back into the surf, leaving fingers of white foam that seemed to beckon her. Within the hour, another vessel would turn into kindling, smashing itself against the sunken remnants of the city once known as Norfolk, Virginia.

Selah climbed onto her favorite rock at the edge of the waves where the algae surface had begun to dry in the morning sun and low tide. She stood on the flattop and surveyed her world. In Dominion Borough, her clan controlled the prime sea fishing area out to the horizon in the east, south to the oil-drilling platform belonging to Waterside Borough, and north to the sea-bound wind farm belonging to Rolke Borough.

She turned from the sea and took a reassuring glance at the ruins of the Dominion building, the namesake of her Borough. Probably majestic in ancient days, the decaying concrete and rusted steel shell presented a sad commentary of the past. Nature had worked hard to obliterate man's ancient invasion. Kudzu vines twisted throughout the broken and missing windows, clinging to the porous surfaces, obliterating the building's shape, and turning it into a skyward mound of vegetation with the word *Dominion* as a capstone. Despite annoying brothers or the uncertainty of her future, this place made her feel safe.

She peered intently at the forested area around the building's base. Any of her family coming down to the sea for fishing would come from that direction. If her brothers didn't show up, she could catch this Lander on her own.

She jumped from the rock and walked to the edge of the receding surf. Seaweed-laden water slapped at the stone outcroppings along this section of the ragged shoreline, leaving behind soggy vestiges of the plant and sending up a misty spray that clung to her skin and wet her lips. She tasted brine and smelled fish tainted with a dose of rotting plants, while a gritty mixture of water and sand caressed her bare toes, enveloping them in warmth.

Seeing the boat bob in the sea made her chest tighten in anticipation.

It wouldn't take long for the swells to push the fragile vessel into the tangle of building carcasses. This protected cove had faced north until the tsunami washed away the land on its east side. And effects of the volcanic eruption had caused the sea to rise, encroaching on the cityscape and putting many buildings in permanent watery graves.

She judged the conditions—maybe a half hour or so. No sense standing here. She retreated to a rubble outcropping farther back on the beach, stabbed one of her kapos vertically into the soft sand to use for timekeeping, and went about the work of collecting clams. There would be seafood for dinner tonight. The thought gagged her, but it would please Father. She glanced up every few minutes to measure the boat's progress. If she could capture a Lander herself, Father would have to recognize her worth to the family business.

This would make the eleventh vessel coming ashore this moon cycle. The survivors were unconscious when they arrived, and waking them brought disorientation and later ranting of a final Kingdom. They each possessed a curious tattoo. It resembled a wing that started at their left temple and stretched up and over their eye almost to the center of their foreheads. On many Landers, after they'd spent a day on solid ground, the tattoo faded into oblivion. As the mark faded, so did the memories and their worth. Landers retaining the mark were the prized possession sought after by the Company.

The Company was a business entity squirreled away in an underground colony called the Mountain, forty-eight miles west of Washington, DC. They were rumored to be ancestors of the original government before the Sorrows, but no one remembered for sure anymore. People only cared about buying coal, oil, and gas and selling Landers. Selah didn't understand their value.

It took almost three quarters of an hour according to the movement of the sun shadow created by her kapo. The small boat finally slammed into a heavy metal beam that in ancient times had been part of a building. The wooden vessel cracked like an egg, spilling its contents. The male lay facedown in the sand with arms and legs outstretched. A soft breeze rippled his loose clothing, giving him the appearance of floating above the sand.

Selah dropped her bags and sat back on her haunches. Now what? She'd never been close to a captive. She watched for several minutes. Maybe this one was dead? Sometimes they were. Others acted vicious and combative, but most were docile. Father warned her to keep her distance and leave the hunting to the men.

She shook off the thought and stared. She was just as fierce as her brothers. It was her rightful place. But what was she going to do if he awoke combative? Better still, what would she do with him if he weren't? She had no weapons except her bag of kapos. She hadn't thought this through, hadn't even come prepared to ward off, let alone capture, a Lander. She finally understood what her mother meant when she said, "Fools rush in." Maybe she'd better get Father.

Something inexplicable stopped her from leaving. Curiosity won over caution, so Selah crept toward the figure. Her heart thudded as she looked him over. A white shirt and pants covered his sturdy frame. The material appeared similar to linen but of a much finer quality. It seemed to shimmer in the morning sun.

"Hey, wake up!" She stood four feet away and angled herself, trying to see his face.

Half of his face was pressed into the sand. Blond curls fell across the other half, covering his features. A mental stab caused her to jerk back. Pain. He felt *pain*. Better still . . . how did she know he felt pain?

⟡

Wet sand infiltrated Bodhi Locke's nostrils and mouth, but the fog in his head receded with each shallow breath. His fingers pressed into the warm sand. He couldn't feel the Presence! *What place is this?* He'd never had a time in his existence when he didn't feel the overwhelming mantle of . . . It shook his courage, leaving him feeling vulnerable and alone. *Think.* He remembered being taken to a tiny boat, and then . . . nothing. No memory of what direction he went, how long it took to get here, or where *here* was.

He did remember why. His stomach clenched, pushing pangs of guilt and remorse up his chest to stab straight to his heart. He'd been warned repeatedly. He needed to rethink his position, but now it seemed too late.

With his eye open a sliver, he watched a girl moving closer. He wanted to sit up and smile at her, pour on the charm, but caution won out. Even though she was cute with big green eyes, he needed to behave. This could be a trick, a test. After all, this situation mimicked his original troubles. He blinked back the last of the fog and formulated a plan.

⟡

Selah moved closer and nudged his hand with her foot. "Can you hear me? Wake up!"

Suddenly his hand shot out and wrapped tightly around her ankle. Her chest clenched, and she screamed and tried to back away. His iron grip raised her trapped ankle from the sand and jerked her toward him.

She screamed again and fell back as her hand scrambled for her kapo. Nothing. She clawed at the sand to get away. She'd been stupid to get this close.

Sand! She dug her fingers into the warm granules and slung a handful in his direction.

He dodged the spray with a hardy laugh and rose on all fours, crawling up to loom over her.

Selah gasped. She was going to die. She drew her hands to her face to protect her head from the anticipated attack as her breath came in ragged jerks. Her eyes locked in a stare with blue eyes rivaling the color of the sky on a clear, sunny day. Fear mixed with a tingling hot flash, filling her belly and rolling up to her shoulders. Her arms relaxed, then her hand darted out to slap him. He easily deflected the move, pinning her hand to the sand.

His eyes searched her face. Not hostile. Her breathing slowed to longer, deeper pulls of sea air.

Selah drank in his features—a strong chin and a straight nose with eyelashes that swept his high cheekbones every time they closed. And the mark. It was visible beneath shaggy blond hair that reached almost to his shoulders. Strong muscular shoulders that strained at the wet shirt fabric. A shiver rolled down her arms, tingling her fingertips.

She jerked her hand from under his and rammed her palms into his shoulders. "Get off me, you sea slug."

The Lander fell to the side and came up on his elbows with a grin. "Who are you?"

Selah stood and brushed the sand from the seat of her

coarse linen pants. "Since you arrived on my property, I think I'm the one who gets to ask the questions." She reached up and shook the sand from her ponytail.

The young man's eyes danced with amusement. "You don't look old enough to own land."

Selah jutted out her chin. "How old do you think I am?" This wasn't the demeanor she'd expected. Confusion gnawed at her. Was this a ploy to knock her off guard and attack her? What would she use to defend herself? How was she going to detain him now that she'd found him? She wanted to kick herself for the lack of planning. Maybe Father was right. She wasn't ready to be a hunter.

"About seventeen." He smiled and sat up, wrapping his arms around his knees as he drew them to his chest.

Her smile deflated. He'd guessed correctly. "Well, what's your name?" She knew the drill. He wouldn't remember much, and she would wind up with the upper hand.

He glanced off to the right, as though trying to remember something hidden. "Bodhi Locke . . . My name is Bodhi Locke."

Selah raised an eyebrow. He seemed very confident. She forgot her fear. "What else do you remember?"

He smiled. "I remember that I asked who you are, and you haven't answered."

"So you're a smart mouth too." She relaxed, drawn to his eyes. So blue. He seemed friendly, not at all like she'd been told, and close to her age, not an adult like her parents. "My name is Selah Rishon Chavez."

"That's a big name for a little girl." He flashed a grin, then raised a hand to his head and grimaced.

She recognized the superior attitude. He acted as bad as her brothers, so she refused to give him any more ammunition by responding to the taunt.

"Did you get hurt in the wreck?" Selah leaned over, pushed his hand away, and examined his scalp for cuts.

"No. Don't think so." Bodhi looked past her to the broken boat and then out to sea. "Is that how I got here?"

"Yes. Do you remember the trip?" Selah didn't find any cuts or bruises. She sat down on the sand a few feet in front of him.

He shook his head. "Last thing I remember? Being escorted to the launch."

"Do you remember where that was?" A rumble swelled from within her. Selah rubbed at her chest to quell the sudden disturbance.

Hearty laughter and a revving Sand Run echoed across the grassy dunes. SRs were single- or double-passenger four-wheelers with tall, fat tires for negotiating the beach. They were normally the main mode of transportation for inland people from Ness Borough to the West who were allied with Dominion. But if these boys were from Waterside, they didn't belong and were trespassing on this beach. Either way, her right to claim the Lander was being threatened.

Selah scrambled to her feet and pulled Bodhi up. She reached over and tousled his hair across his face, obscuring the mark.

His hand shot up to stop her.

She slapped his hand away. "Stop! Follow me." She dragged him by the shirtsleeve.

Bodhi stumbled along, trying to keep up with her. His

flat leather-type shoes couldn't gain traction, but his longer stride closed the distance.

Selah ran toward a disjointed rubble pile of rusted metal and broken cement populated with exposed rebar. She pulled to a stop, delicately ran her hands along the ragged metal edge, and ripped back the fake tin cover over the opening. Determination flashed through her like gas poured on a fire. She was not going to lose her first catch to her brothers or anyone else.

Selah looked back to see if they were visible. No one crested the ridge. She pushed Bodhi inside.

"Hey." He stumbled to a stop and turned. "What's this?" He glanced around at the exposed jagged metal edges and sharp objects in the dark, cavernous space and recoiled toward the opening.

She pulled in a long suck of air, trying to catch her breath, and pointed a finger at him. "Shut up and stay quiet. I'll tell you when it's safe to come out."

Selah slammed the cover against the opening and turned to move away from the pile. Her secret place among the ancient ruins had never been discovered by any boys in the Borough, so confidence helped to calm her welling jitters. She'd keep him hidden until tomorrow and hope the mark remained. He would be her first catch, and she wasn't sharing the honor.

Stooping to the sand, she feigned interest in a mutated starfish carcass lying among a clump of seaweed. Actually, it was interesting. She didn't often see them in this condition and she was sure her father hadn't either, or he might rethink the eating-from-the-sea thing.

From the corner of her eye she watched as two boys spilled

over the hill, about three feet to the right side of the pit where she'd crouched with her little brother. With a great screaming whine of its powerful engine, the Sand Run shot over the dune. The huge bulbous tires threw copious amounts of sand on the two running participants as it hit the beach and spun circles around them. Her brothers were not part of this group.

The Sand Run gunned its engine and approached. Selah feared it might run her over, but she held her ground and casually looked up. The boy on the four-wheeler wore ragged cutoff pants and carried a long bow slung across his back. He stopped short of her, released the handle bars, and dismounted.

"Hey, girl, what're you doing on this beach?" The taller of the boys, the one with a razor-smooth head, strolled over to her and used his long walking staff to kick sand on her hand and the starfish.

Selah glared at them, rose slowly from her crouched position, and shook the sand from her hand. She recognized them now. "I could ask you the same question. My family lives in this Borough. This is our beach." She jutted out her chin. "So what are you doing on *my* beach?"

Her heartbeat continued its upward tick. These boys were from Waterside Borough to the south, where the sea encroached on buildings. Waterside had no beachfront property to speak of, so their only claim to fame grew from their oil-drilling platform and their partnership with Ness Borough, which owned the remnants of the ancient refinery and vulcanizing operation that afforded their clans petrol and tires for such extravagances as Sand Runs.

The other two flanked her like guards, one on either side.

"Rude girl. You know who you're talking to?" The ragged-pants boy shoved her shoulder.

She lurched forward two steps but caught herself and swung around to face him. In doing so, she glanced beyond his shoulder. She saw an eye staring at her from the hiding place. After spending many hours hiding from her brothers, she knew Bodhi had full view of the happening. She frowned, wishing he'd retreat from the hole. He didn't.

"You'd better hope my brothers don't show up or they'll pound you into a sand stain." Maybe if she mentioned that they were due any moment . . . Or maybe draw their attention to something farther down the beach. Anything to get them away from the hiding spot.

Razor Head leaned forward on his wooden staff. He appeared to be in his midtwenties. He eyed her up and down. "Who're your brothers?"

"The Chavez boys," she answered, glaring at him. "Raza and Cleon." Her only weapon was sitting in the sand next to her clam bucket, too far away to be helpful. Maybe she could move them away from Bodhi and closer to her kapo at the same time.

The other boy, who had a missing front tooth, reached out his hand as if to touch her shoulder. "Wouldn't you like to come to the Side? We don't have girls cute like you."

Selah flinched and slapped his hand away before it made contact.

"Wait," Ragged Pants said. "If the Chavez boys are her brothers, she's Selah, promised in marriage to Jericho Kingston."

Missing Tooth's face contorted in rage as he grabbed her

by the wrist. "Don't care if she's going to marry our clan leader's son. All females should know their place and it's not slapping me."

The bones of her wrist ground together under the viselike pressure. A whimper escaped her lips, as much for the physical pain as for the mental pain of her father selling her hand in marriage for an endless supply of petrol that uniting her clan with these barbarians would bring.

She struggled, but resistance was as useless as Mother trying to get Father to relent on the nuptials. Her other hand pried at his fingers, unable to create an opening. She sucked the moisture from her mouth and spat at him.

He backhanded her across the face.

Tiny stars burst into her vision, dancing in front of her eyes. Selah tasted copper. Her tongue ran to the inside of her cheek, feeling the gouge her teeth had cut. She ran the back of her free hand across her mouth and came away with blood. The tin cover to the hiding spot began to move.

Her free hand darted out, fingers splayed. "No, stop!" she shouted, looking at the boy holding her wrist but addressing Bodhi. She shook her head to get a look at the tin without being noticed. It rested flat against the hole.

Ragged Pants stuck out his bow and whacked Missing Tooth across the wrist, forcing him to let go of her arm. "Didn't you hear her, stupid? Her brothers are the Chavezes."

Selah used the opportunity to back away from the other two.

"So what? They aren't marrying Kingston." Missing Tooth stepped behind her to stop her retreat.

"They killed Remo and Zimmer for fishing their beach,"

Razor Head said. He eyed Selah up and down with a long, slow look.

It felt like he was groping her. She winced and wrapped her arms across her chest to ward off his look and to hold back the thunder growing around her heart. What was this new feeling? She was ticked off, but she didn't fear him.

She knew her brothers often defended their territory, but she didn't know they'd killed anyone. One more reason she felt excluded when it came to her father and brothers. But she would change things. She would show her father she could equal his precious boys.

"I didn't know it was in this direction. Thought the Chavez boys were north of us," Missing Tooth said.

Ragged Pants shook his head. "This *is* north of us. When're you going to learn directions?"

Selah's confidence took an upswing. She was brighter than at least one of them. Could she lead them up the beach to protect her catch?

Maybe if she ran. She moved to the right but had a split-second hesitation as her feet gained traction and her toes dug into the sand. Her right leg stretched out for the sprint. Then the walking staff swung out in front of her, cracking into her left shin and sweeping her foot from under her.

Selah crashed chest first into the beach. The air rushed from her lungs. The sand that felt like cotton when walking on it turned to cement when crashing into it. She tried to cry out, but her remaining air expelled as a weak grunt. She fought to inhale. Her arms flailed, but the weight of a body pressed her deeper into the sand.

Bang!

Selah recognized the sound. The tin cover.

"Get off me!" She gasped for air. She thrashed about, trying to dislodge whichever boy was pinning her. A punch to the back of the head forced a whimper from her as her face was ground into the sand.

The weight on her back. She couldn't breathe. Sand invaded the openings in her face. She felt particles climbing to her sinuses. Her arms flailed. Granules clogging her tongue. No room to inhale.

The body holding her down was suddenly lifted away.

Selah flipped onto her back, gagging and coughing as she snorted out the sand blocking her air. Bodhi lifted Missing Tooth over his head. The boy's arms and legs flapped in the air. Bodhi body-slammed him to the sand. He stopped moving.

Bodhi turned to the others and lunged for the closest.

"Get him!" Ragged Pants drew his bow and nocked an arrow.

"Kill them both!" Razor Head shouted. His smooth dome reflected the morning sun as he swept the long staff over his head in a circle, advancing on Bodhi.

Selah crawled a few feet away, still struggling to reinflate her lungs.

Bodhi leaned over on his hands and swept his body in a sideways pinwheel. Razor Head was caught off guard, and it drove his feet out from under him as his staff flew toward the sea and he landed on his back. Bodhi delivered a fist to Razor's neck, and he went limp.

"Behind you," Selah yelled in a raspy voice.

Bodhi swung to face Ragged Pants' bow at the same moment the boy released the arrow.

As though time switched to slow motion, a sound came from somewhere near her toes, crashed up through her body and out her mouth. Selah screamed. The arrow spun toward Bodhi, who swung out his right arm and snatched it from the air.

Selah's mouth dropped open. Bodhi took a step forward, and his right leg shot out in a roundhouse kick that connected with the boy's face. He too went down. Bodhi pivoted on his side to deliver a crippling elbow slam across Ragged Pants' neck.

Selah suddenly felt panic. It had all happened in less than a minute. She tried to crab walk away from Bodhi, healthy respect and fear for the man rising to the forefront. Watching someone dispatch many enemies at one time went a long way to change a girl's perception.

Bodhi walked to where Selah sat in the sand. "Are you all right?"

Her mouth opened but words wouldn't come. Her lips trembled. She wanted to cry but refused to look weak and invite more danger.

"Let me help you." He held out his hand. She shrank back.

He looked at the arrow clenched in his other hand as though just noticing it. He threw it away and reached out both hands.

Selah tentatively reached up to him, and he easily pulled her to her feet.

"How did you do that?" Selah stammered over her words, her chest heaving. Ten thoughts were trying to rank themselves in her head all at one time. Surprise, fear, and excitement topped the list. She had to be losing her mind to find him thrilling. Maybe that punch in the head she'd gotten had shaken something lose.

Bodhi shook his head. "Don't know. Never did it before."

Selah stared at the bodies littering the beach. She still couldn't process the superhuman abilities he'd displayed.

He held up both open palms, turning them slowly to look at the backs. "There's a vibration in them."

Selah looked up from his hands and saw it coming. "No!"

2

A hunting boomerang slammed into the back of Bodhi's head. Selah heard the sickening crunch as wood connected with bone. His head jerked forward, his eyes went blank and fluttered closed, and he collapsed face forward into Selah's arms.

She grappled with lowering his limp body to the sand without dropping him as she searched the ground. The boomerang lay to her left. She recognized the intricate pattern etched on the L-shaped polished surface. It belonged to her brother. "Raza, you come out here right now! What's wrong with you? You could have killed me."

She scoured the rubbled landscape. Anger welled up as her hands began to shake. She wasn't sure whether it was because her brother had incapacitated her catch or had come so close to whacking her with his stupid stick.

Raza and Cleon scrambled over littered steel beam roofing and jumped to the beach. They could almost be mistaken as twins. Both blond and brown-eyed, both muscular, but Raza, at twenty-one, stood six feet tall and weighed about 190 pounds, while Cleon, two years younger, was five nine and about thirty pounds lighter. Both wore the dark brown double-weight linen pants Mother's business created specifically for farm workers. The only thing setting them apart— Raza liked short hair and button shirts while Cleon, with shoulder-length shaggy hair, preferred tunics.

"You could have hit me." Selah fisted her hands at her hips. It was more an act of disrespect to her well-being. Raza seemed to enjoy instilling fear in her.

Raza smiled broadly. He tousled her ponytail and rubbed her head. "I know how to aim, little girl."

She jerked her head away. Anger swelled, making her legs tremble. "I'm serious, Raza. I'm telling Father. You know what he told you about throwing near us."

Raza stood over the fallen form. He stooped, grabbed a handful of blond hair, and lifted Bodhi's head from the sand. "Good job, little sister. He's a Lander. You distracted him long enough for us to close the deal."

Selah ignored the little sister remark. This was not the time and it wouldn't get her anywhere. She lost focus when she allowed herself to get visibly angry, and he knew it. She peered over his shoulder, looking at Bodhi for a wound. No blood, just a big bump separating his hair on the back of his head. She winced. That was going to leave a mark.

She knitted her brow and thrust out her chin. "I wasn't distracting him for you. He's my catch. Not yours."

"Not today, little sister. My 'rang took him down and he's mine. It's five thousand credits if that mark is still there in the morning." Raza tied Bodhi's limp arms behind his back and proceeded to truss his legs.

Selah opened her mouth to protest. But what good would it do her? She knew Father would back the boys and ignore her attempt at hunting. Emotion stormed in her like a raging bull. She wanted to lash out. Scream. Stomp. None of it would help. They'd just laugh. She was so frustrated she could cry, but she refused to give them the satisfaction.

Cleon, carrying the staff, bow, and a few knives, returned from checking the other fallen bodies. "Sissy, it looks like you got yourself in a bit of trouble here."

Selah winced and gritted her teeth. Her brothers called her *sissy* to bug her. It was partially her fault for letting them see that it got to her.

"I did no such thing." Selah looked up the beach at her bucket and kapos, unwilling to admit she was defenseless. They'd never let her live it down. "I knew exactly what I was doing."

Raza tied the last knot and rose. "What's their condition? Anything we have to worry about?"

Cleon dropped the booty and shook his head. "No, nothing at all." He pointed at Bodhi. "This guy is a real bad one. They're all dead. Got to keep him tied up tight or there'll be trouble."

"He was helping me," Selah said, looking for any way to make them give her credit. Maybe if she could convince them that she'd charmed him, they might relent.

"Saw the whole thing." Raza pointed his finger at her. "You're stupid to get yourself in the middle. Hunting is not for babies."

"Tomorrow I'm a woman." She tossed back her ponytail and crossed her arms over her chest.

Raza laughed. "Yeah, saw how well you handled yourself. Couldn't have been worse."

Cleon lowered his head. To his credit, he wouldn't treat her this badly if Raza wasn't around. He was protecting his own status with their older brother.

Selah turned on Raza. "You saw it all? You were going to let those Waterside boys beat me up?" She glanced sideways at Cleon.

His cheeks turned bright red. His pale complexion always gave him away when embarrassed. "You weren't in danger. I was right here. Besides, the Lander seemed capable."

"That's not the point." Selah noted Cleon spoke only for himself. At least she could count on him in time of need. She turned and pointed at Raza. "Were you seriously willing to let them beat me to build your ego and prove I'm not fit to be a hunter? Or was it payback for my skill in thwarting your attempt to be my babysitter?"

Raza set his jaw and stared at her, then leaned over Bodhi's still form to check for a pulse. "Might teach you to do what you're told."

Selah's chest tightened. She'd never been close with Raza, but until today she'd never realized the depth of his ego. Or was the look on his face hatred? Was it directed at her? No, it couldn't be. He was her brother.

❦

Selah trudged the worn path from the larger of their barns down to the house. She'd spent the better part of the day trying to negotiate with her brothers to reclaim her catch. At least Cleon had let her ride to the barn on the back of his Sand Run. Raza carried the Lander on his, and would have left her to walk home. At the barn she'd argued over the unconscious Lander until Raza chased her out with the comment that Father would back him up. She knew he was right. All she could remember was how Father had defended Raza at the beach yesterday, and what she had seen happen there.

She looked down the hill and shivered. She was too annoyed to enjoy the beauty of the view out over the ocean. Ultimately the sea had caused her angst yesterday and today, but there was nothing that couldn't be fixed by going home. She hurried down the path and around the tree line to her right. The house came into view.

She bolted toward the house, remembering the time when she was about ten that Father had planted a corn crop on this side of the tree line. As she rounded the path that late summer, tall corn had obscured her view of their rambling, single-story home. She couldn't even see the slate-red color of the clay-tiled roof. She recalled her depth of panic, thinking home had disappeared. Charging through the sharp corn leaves willy-nilly cut up her arms and legs, but she had reached the house and safety. To this day she still possessed a long scar on her right forearm that she fingered when she was fearful.

Today the field lay fallow. It would be planted with winter flax for Mother's linen business.

Stomping into the house, Selah slammed the kitchen door behind her. The soft thunk of the heavy wooden door was not the satisfying sound she craved. Wrenching a chair away from the table created a squealing scrape of wood on wood as the legs dragged. That sound gratified her, mimicking what she wanted to scream.

Her mother, Pasha Rishon, looked up from the flour she was sifting. Her dark hair was piled on her head in unruly curls, and her olive skin, set against the backdrop of the pale yellow of her long linen jumper, radiated a beauty uncommon in other forty-one-year-old women in their community. "And what size pebble is stuck in your shoe? Or should I ask what have your brothers done to you now?" Her green eyes glowed with peace, creating a calming effect.

Selah's mood softened a tad. She found comfort in knowing her mother could read her so well. She knew lots of girls her age hated mothers snooping in their business, but Selah remained bonded to hers even as she reached the awkward age of accountability.

"I'm never talking to either of them again. They are so mean." Selah plopped onto the chair next to her mother and smacked her fist on the table. "It's my turn! I should be able to claim my own catch without them horning in on the action."

Mother's smile dissolved as she dropped the sifter, dislodging the last chalky remnants across the table. She grabbed Selah by the arm. "Catch? What catch? I told you to stay away from the beach today."

Selah froze. Should she lie or tell the truth? Mother hadn't been this angry since she'd gotten mud on the clean laundry. "I . . . there was a Lander who came in on the beach today."

Mother's face went pale. "Did you touch him?" Her grip increased.

Selah grimaced. What was the problem? She needed to think of something to get out of this trouble.

"Answer me!" She shook Selah. "Did. You. Touch. Him?"

Selah burst into tears. "No, I didn't touch him. I stayed far away, and then the boys came."

Mother emitted a strangled gasp. Her grip relaxed and her hand fell away. She reached out an arm to enfold Selah in a hug. "My sweet baby."

"Stop calling me that! I'll be eighteen tomorrow. I'm sick of everyone treating me like a child." Selah pulled away and crossed her arms. Tears slipped from her eyes and slid to her chin. Mother didn't mean it the same way the boys did. But if Selah ever expected them to stop treating her like a baby, she needed to stop whining like one.

She tipped her head down, then looked up and furrowed her brow. Something wasn't right. "Mother, what's wrong?"

No answer, but Mother pulled her back into her arms.

She felt safe, secure in her warm hug. Loved. *No.* Selah squirmed from the embrace. "I want to be treated like a woman. I want my right to hunt."

Her mother's attitude reverted to the calm it had been when Selah walked in the door.

"Ahh, I see. The hunt." Mother frowned and used her finger to tip up Selah's chin. "Must you follow the men in such savage practices? Dane told me you were trying to catch rabbits. Can't you just stick to that?"

The question brought a scowl. Should she continue the lie or face the consequences? She'd forgotten about the story to her little brother. "Well, that's another catch I lost." Her bottom lip quivered at the lie. "What's wrong with me? Why can't I do anything right?"

Mother opened her arms again. This time Selah leaned

in, resting her head on her mother's shoulder. She felt like a fraud lying to the one person who was truly on her side. But the disappointed look that would be in Mother's eyes was more than she could bear at this moment. Her insides hurt.

Mother stroked her hair. "If you want my true opinion, I think it's abominable to be hunting people, and you shouldn't start."

Selah sat up and looked at her. "Why do you say that? I've never heard you say anything negative about Father and the boys capturing Landers. How else would Father be able to afford some of the luxuries we have if it weren't for the extra income? I mean, look at our house. It's huge compared to some of my friends' houses."

"Yes, that's also what your father says, but I disagree." Mother glanced wistfully toward the window then turned back. "I guess I've kept some things to myself for too long. The thought of humans selling other humans into slavery is barbaric. There is a lot of ancient history about people on this continent doing the same thing hundreds of years ago. It was reprehensible then and is no less now."

Selah lowered her head. "But Father is selling me into marriage with the Kingston boy."

Mother emitted a strangled sob. "I have spent many hours trying to talk him out of this coupling. I'm sorry. Your father is the head of our clan, and his word is law."

"I've only met Jericho Kingston once, when I was about seven. We were at the farmers' market. He had a long nose, buck teeth, and was gangly like a stick bug. What if he's turned into a planter toad? Your grandchildren will spend their days chasing flies."

Mother tried to smile, but it came off as a pained expression. "My poor child, your drama precedes you. There's still six months of freedom. After your Remembrance tomorrow, you two can start courting. You may find out he's not a bug or a toad. With the abundant petrol that comes as a result of this clan marriage, maybe I can get your father to stop hunting Landers for income."

Selah had traveled this route before and all it ever did was add to her anger. Her father's last word on the subject revolved around the two clans joining forces. Her marriage would cement the bond, but he was forcing it and ruining her independence. And he wouldn't let her hunt, thus holding her up to ridicule. He was determined to wreck her life at every turn, so she couldn't envision him relenting on hunting Landers.

Selah shook her head. "I don't think he will ever quit. I've watched him talk about Landers. He takes on a whole different persona, like he's vengeful. He once laughed, almost sadistically, when he said the Company is being humane to give them medical care for their memory loss."

Mother chewed on her lower lip. "It's just a parade of more lost souls."

"Why do you say that?" Selah's chest started to tingle again. She rubbed at the spot.

"No one has ever come back from there. None of the Landers captured have ever been seen or heard from again in these parts."

Selah snickered. "I don't think they would come back this way. Think about it. These are the people who put them away in the first place. They're not exactly going to be friends."

Mother went back to stroking Selah's hair. "I guess you're right, my smart child. But I'd much prefer if you'd just take out your desire to hone your hunting skills on wildlife. Practice on the rabbits or something."

"That's not the problem! I'm a great hunter. I can catch rabbits better than any of them."

"Well, maybe that's because they never hunt rabbits."

"And they never will. They are so cruel. I refuse to share with Cleon and Raza which ones are safe to eat." Selah looked up at her mother and smiled. "Mother, are you sure I'm not adopted? They're so different from me."

Mother glanced away, then looked at the clock on the fireplace mantel. "Darling, don't talk so silly. You look just like me. You are definitely my child."

Selah heaved a sigh. "I don't know. Sometimes Father makes me feel second class with the way he fawns over the boys. He takes them wherever he goes, and he's never invited me along, not once."

"Your father just doesn't know how to relate to girls. He feels more comfortable with the boys because they act the same."

"Well, some days he makes me feel like I come from another world."

Mother laughed. "Dinner and a good night's sleep will help you see things differently. This day will pass and tomorrow will be the start of a whole new life."

Selah shook her head and pulled away. She propped her elbows on the smooth wooden surface of the table and rested her head in her hands. "I don't think so. I think I've made a mistake."

"What could you possibly have done that's so terrible?" Mother sat back in the chair.

"If I hadn't tried to capture Bodhi, he might have gotten away."

Mother raised her eyebrows. "Bodhi? Who's Bodhi?"

"The Lander I tried to capture. His name is Bodhi Locke."

Mother shot from her chair. "I thought you said you didn't touch him!"

"I didn't." It bothered her how easily the lie to her mother rolled off her tongue. "He saved me from a bunch of evil boys from Waterside Borough. They were going to kidnap me."

"Your father needs to know this! I want him to contact the Kingston clan and find those boys before this happens again."

"They're dead." The words slipped from Selah's lips in a whisper.

Mother stared at her. "What did you say?"

Selah tipped her head and a tear rolled down her cheek. "They're dead. Bodhi fought them to save me! Me, Mother!" She thumped a fist to her chest. "And then Raza and Cleon showed up. First I'm mad because they stole my catch, then I'm even madder because as a payback for saving my life, I let him get captured. What is wrong with me?" She put her head in her hands and wept.

Mother rushed to her side. "I know, baby. I understand. You were scared—"

"I was not!" Selah bristled at the thought. Her fingers absently traced the scar on her forearm. A tingling invaded her chest again, and she tried to ignore it. "I'm just as brave as they are."

Mother gave her a look bordering on sympathy. Selah wanted to get away from that look. She darted from the chair. "I need to be alone. Yell when dinner's ready."

"Your father went to Council and took the team and wagon with him rather than waste fuel, so as soon as dawn breaks one of the boys will have to take the AirStream to retrieve the wagon so they can transport their captive."

Selah calculated how long it would take Raza to pilot the hovercraft to Council and then drive the team and wagon back. AirStreams traveled only a foot above the road, so it wasn't like he could zip cross-country in a straight line. He was forced to follow the roads.

She shook her head. "They'll wait twenty-four hours from when they found him with me to see if he's still a viable catch. I hope for that poor man's sake the mark may be gone, and they'll have to set him free."

Selah drummed her fingers on the table surface worn smooth by years of polishing. She counted the hours in her head. Maybe she would have a chance to get him back while Cleon guarded him alone.

Mother turned back to the table. "Dinner will be me, you, and Dane. Do you want soup?"

Selah turned. "No, I don't want soup. I want my catch back. All I can think about are those eyes . . ."

"Don't you dare look like that," Mother said.

"Look like what?" Selah pulled back her chin.

Mother pointed at her face, making circles in the air with her fingertip. "That wispy, faraway look. I know that look, Selah Rishon Chavez! Don't you dare think of getting involved with a Lander. It will cause you . . . nothing but heartbreak.

And your father . . . well, I don't want to think about what your father would do."

Selah cocked her head. "That's an odd thing to say. I've never even seen one up close before. Why would you think I'd get involved with a Lander?"

Mother crossed her arms. "No reason at all. But you just keep it that way for your own good, young lady. You're betrothed."

Selah rolled onto her back. Her eyes remained closed but she detected radiant light filtering through her eyelids. She could hear birds outside her window singing their morning song. She'd made it to her Birth Remembrance! She didn't want to open her eyes. She just wanted to lie still and bask in the glory of being grown. As of yesterday she'd finished school. She'd be allowed to drive an AirStream. Her possibilities were endless . . . Well, not exactly, but she refused to think that far ahead. She would enjoy today.

She sighed and smiled so wide she could feel her cheek muscles heating. Even breathing felt different. She opened her eyes and sat up. The sun poured through thin curtains floating softly on the breeze that pushed its way through the open window. The air smelled fresher than she ever remembered, and the bird song . . . She could hear more birds than—

Selah cocked her head. Could she really hear the ocean waves lapping at the beach several blocks away?

Adrenaline coursed through her chest. What was going on? She scurried from the bed, entangling herself in the covers and plopping to the floor on her bottom. She burst out laughing. Well, that really looked adult. Maybe she needed to rethink the whole worldly shift that came with an eighteenth Remembrance.

Selah pulled the covers from around her. Still laughing at herself, she brushed the hair from her eyes and stood up. The reflection in the mirror caught her attention. What was that? Her hands flew to her chest. She looked down her nose at the mark as she moved closer to the mirror. She rubbed at it. Put her fingers to her tongue for moisture and rubbed at it again. But it remained. She stared into the mirror.

There was a small wing imprinted on her chest about an inch below her left collarbone. She tipped her head sideways. It looked like a smaller version of the mark she'd seen on the Lander yesterday. She stared. Could this be a trick? Her brothers had done this to her as a Birth Remembrance surprise. Well, surprise! She wasn't amused.

She ran to the bathroom and grabbed a washrag. Wetting it, she scrubbed at the mark. It didn't come off. In fact, it didn't even look applied. It appeared to be part of her skin.

Her hands started to shake. "Mother!" She didn't wait for an answer. "Mother!"

She ran for Mother's bedroom and pushed the door open. The heavily curtained room kept the sunlight at bay. Selah picked her way around a chair and small table and flung herself onto the sleeping woman.

"Mother, help!" she cried as she rubbed at her chest. The area had grown red from her scraping and digging.

Mother jerked awake, eyes bleary with sleep. "Selah, sweetheart." She yawned. "What's the matter? You act like the house is on fire."

Tears welled in Selah's eyes. "Worse! Look at this!" she wailed. "The boys must have done it as a joke while I slept." Although she couldn't figure out how they wouldn't have woken her.

Mother sat up and rubbed the sleep from her eyes. She glanced at Selah's chest, then did a double take. Her eyes opened wide, and she reached to touch the winged imprint. Selah could feel her fingers tremble.

"Why do you look scared? This is a joke, right?" Selah asked in a shaky voice.

"Um . . . honey . . ." Mother bit down on her bottom lip. A sob rushed from her throat. "I don't think this is a joke."

"What are you talking about? Of course it's a joke. This is the Lander symbol, and it's on me. I'm not a Lander!"

Mother's face turned crimson as she withdrew her hand. She turned her head away, and her voice became so small it was almost a whisper. "I thought you said you didn't touch the Lander."

Should she admit the lie? Selah fiddled with her fingers. How did Mother know? "I . . . It was just—"

Mother shook her head. "You have no idea what you've done." She wrapped her arms around her own chest, lowered her head, and began to rock back and forth.

Selah angled around her and looked up into her face. "Mother? You're scaring me."

Mother closed her eyes, tears cascading down her cheeks. Her arms trembled violently as she reached out and hugged Selah so hard the air rushed from her chest.

Selah pulled back and touched her shoulder. "You aren't saying anything. What's wrong? This has to be some stupid prank by the boys. They were really mad at me for arguing with them about my catch."

"No, my sweet child, I'm afraid not." She reached out and stroked Selah's cheek. "I have dreaded for years that this day might come, and now my fears have grown fruit. There is no choice. You must leave, and do it before your father gets back." She squeezed her eyes shut again. Her bottom lip quivered as she rocked.

Selah leaned away. Her jaw slacked. "Look, I'm sorry I told you a lie. I'll never do it again. Why do I have to leave?" That seemed a radical punishment for so simple a mistake.

Fear enveloped the tingling in her chest until it grew to full-fledged thunder. It felt like all the air had been sucked from the room. She struggled to breathe. "But this is just a joke."

Mother stared at the mark below her collarbone and shook her head. "No. This is no joke. Your father told me this might happen, but I only halfheartedly believed him."

"My father? I don't know what he has to do with it, but he can help figure this out when he comes home. He'll be back this morning."

"That's why you need to go away. Now."

"Mother, you're talking in circles. I don't understand."

Mother reared up straight and gripped her by the shoulders. "Your father is *not* your birth father. Your real father was a Lander."

3

The Mountain

Dr. Noah Everling sat at his wife's bedside. He leaned over to kiss her hand, careful not to scratch her delicate skin with the two-day-old stubble on his chin. Bethany would chastise him when she woke to his disheveled appearance. His gray and thinning hair growing south of his collar was not a complimentary look—neither was an unstarched shirt minus a tie. And since there were no evening walks, just haphazard meals he'd cobbled together, his stomach had ballooned over his belt. At sixty years old, Everling made every effort to hide most of his new normal under his lab coat.

His elbows rested on the mattress as he held her hand. Her translucent flesh showed every vein and artery. So cool to the touch. Almost like she wasn't alive. The constant blip and clack from the machines testified she indeed remained among the living. He watched her chest rise and fall, agonizing over every shallow breath. He was losing her. He needed this experiment to work.

As if on cue, a smattering of acid bile crept up his throat. He gulped it down and searched his pockets for an antacid, also a new element of his daily regimen. A heavy sigh escaped his lips, and the next breath drew in the antiseptic fumes of the room sterilizer. He'd counted during the night. Every fifteen minutes, the soft swish of the jets embedded in the ceiling cycled the release. A column of sanitizing mist flooded the room to eliminate bacteria. He'd opted for the mist rather than an ultraviolet light sweep. He held misgivings about the effects the light spectrum might have on Bethany's cancer.

Rubber soles squeaked on the tile floor. Someone tiptoed to his side and a hand touched him on the shoulder. "Dr. Everling."

Everling recognized the voice of his assistant. His head rose. "Yes, Stemple, what is it?"

Bethany had always referred to Stemple as "Mr. Tall, Dark, and Handsome." She'd tried to fix him up with several of the younger women, but her matchmaking skills couldn't seem to marry him off. At thirty years old, Drace Stemple declared his body fit and his bachelorhood permanent.

Stemple glanced at his arm crystal. His eyes flashed concern. "It's nearly 8:30 a.m., sir. You've been here all night. Your wife would not like that. You have an executive meeting in a half hour."

Everling relished his job as head of the Science Consortium. For the last twenty years his prime mandate had been to find ways to enhance the degrading genetic code of Mountain dwellers. He could readily command the necessary perks for his ailing wife because she was also a scientist. But his father's demise had made him the de facto leader of the Company. Recently, a group that wanted to take Company technology outside the Mountain had challenged his leadership.

A loathing for politics pulled at his chest. He didn't care about meetings, only Bethany's survival.

"I thought I asked you to clear my schedule today. I want to stay in the lab and work on the next set of tests." Everling struggled to his feet. His joints had stiffened from long hours in a seated position. At his age he shouldn't be this incapacitated, but the secret trial experiments on himself were taking their toll on his nervous system.

Stemple shrugged. "The operational staffers were attuned to your father's management style. They're expecting to get acquainted with you."

Everling shook his head. "No. I have more important work in the lab." He looked back as he walked away from Bethany's bed. He'd come back later and check. He might need another course of serum.

For his whole life and then some, his family had led the self-sufficient colony of ten thousand inhabitants as it grew to encompass twenty miles of underground cities and natural resource reclamation operations. Robo-mining and laser-traction allowed the Mountain to run itself without human interference. He didn't have the tenacity or the desire to oversee daily operations as his father had.

As he left the hospital and stepped into the street, the antiseptic odor lingered in his nostrils, mixing with the outdoor ozone smell tinged with floral scents. It created a wild assault on his senses that he always hated. He adjusted his eyes to the artificial sunlight as a MagLev train zipped through the clear tubular tunnel above the halo–tree line. He followed its silent trail through the cavernous space until it curved out of sight about a mile away and noted the far-off clouds meant an impending shower would soon wash the streets and freshen the air.

He sighed. It must be Tuesday, or were the showers a Wednesday event? Weather patterns were one of the ordinary events he didn't normally follow. But Bethany knew them all. She could practically tell time by the weather outside their living unit. And he was hard-pressed to tell time without her.

Stemple followed close behind as Everling crossed the smooth, nonporous surface of the rocrete composite roadway to his laboratory sitting less than fifty yards from the hospital. He should have been there working. But his irrational fear was if he didn't stay near Bethany, she would get substandard care.

Together the men entered the main lobby and worked their way through myriad halls to the lab section. Stemple smacked the metal access button and waited for the wide glass partition door to slide into the ceiling.

He turned to Everling. "I spent quite a bit of time trying to find you this morning." He lifted Everling's left arm and deactivated the mute setting on Everling's ComTex. "You really need to stop turning this off."

Everling released a sigh. The need to be with his wife was something a single man couldn't understand until his own world was being ripped from his grasp. The door lifted and they entered the lab.

"Dr. Everling, I'm sorry to interrupt you, but this oversight is unacceptable."

Everling and Stemple swung to face the voice.

"No, you're not sorry or you wouldn't have interrupted," Everling said, venom in his tone. He peered over his antique glasses at the bane of his existence—Charles Ganston III.

The portly man with a receding hairline barged through the doorway just as the glass partition closed.

Everling considered him a throwback. Ganston purposefully wore historical clothing like three-piece suits and bow ties that were as ancient as his desire to proclaim he was the fourth generation of his family. He emerged as part of a growing faction making noises about the size of the Company and its one-man ruling body.

Ganston slowed his charge but continued toward Everling. "Doctor, you have missed almost every meeting we've conducted since your father's death. We would really like to hear your feelings—"

"My feelings on what?" Everling bristled. "Dismantling my father's Company and creating a government to run the Mountain?" He pressed his lips together to avoid saying what he really wanted to. He and Ganston had been rivals since they were children in school. Nothing had changed. Ganston was still trying to take away his power as he had on Youth Council.

"I'm sure you're a man of reason. Just the fact you don't have time to come to a meeting shows how overwhelmed you are trying to run the Science Consortium and the Company. We're trying to shoulder some of your burden," Ganston said with a half smile.

Everling could feel his face warming. "You can't even say that with a straight face."

Ganston glanced at Stemple and shrugged before turning back to Everling. "I think you've been working too hard. Your creative imagination seems to have gotten away from itself."

"Do you think I don't know about your rabble-rousers wanting to move outside?"

Ganston's jaw slacked. "I, uh . . ."

Everling turned to Stemple. "This illustrious antique and his cohorts have convinced a group of businessmen they could filter commerce out of the Mountain and live on the surface again under the real sky and stars."

"And what's the problem with that?" Ganston recovered his composure. "There are almost ten thousand people living inside this mountain. It's time we moved back out into the world. People are tired of our controlled birth rates and limited occupational opportunities. There may be uncounted hundreds of thousands out there who could create a whole new age of growth."

Everling slammed his fist on a nearby desk. "You're all fools! Living in this protected environment has negated 99 percent of the diseases people suffered before the Sorrows. Do you want to infect our people with those outsiders?"

Ganston stared into Everling's eyes. "Being in the Mountain didn't protect your wife."

Everling lunged.

Stemple cut him off before he could reach Ganston. Stemple's youth overcame Everling's rage as he backed the doctor a safe distance away.

Stemple craned his neck toward Ganston. "You should leave, old man, before I let him loose on you."

Ganston hitched another half smile. He ignored Stemple and peered at Everling. "Drop the self-righteous anger. You've had the same act since we were teenagers."

Everling tried to force his way past Stemple. "Act? I love my wife more than any person in this Mountain, and I'd do *anything* to save her."

"Yeah, anything but remain faithful to her," Ganston said under his breath. Stemple turned to look at him again. Everling dodged past his outstretched arm.

His eyes bulged, burning like his brain was on fire. "Whatever you *think* you know, you'd better keep it to yourself. You hear me? Or I'll kill you."

Stemple flinched and reached out to restrain Everling. "You don't really mean that."

"I mean every word." Everling shook him off and continued toward Ganston, who retreated to the doorway.

Ganston whirled to face him from the safe distance. "We'd only like to help carry the burden of governing."

Everling raised a fist. "My great-grandfather single-handedly rescued this Mountain from total collapse. None of your kin were worth spit back then."

This time Ganston lunged.

Everling was not going to let Ganston accuse him of infidelity without being challenged. Stemple struggled to keep them apart.

"You old fogey!" Ganston yelled. "How dare you try to malign my ancestors. They came to this country hundreds of years before your relatives even climbed out of the pig troughs."

"Gentlemen, please!" Stemple pleaded. He was clearly trying to keep them from coming to blows. The incident was starting to gather an audience of nearby lab workers.

"How dare you call me an old fogey! You're the same age I am," Everling said.

A woman walked in between the flailing men and faced Ganston. "Mr. Charles Ganston, I presume."

Ganston stopped cold. His hands fell to his sides, and his face took on a flushed appearance. "Y-yes," he stammered.

Everling stopped jostling with Stemple and moved to the side, curious at the exchange.

"I think this laboratory is not the place to air your differences with Dr. Everling. Don't you agree?" She raised an eyebrow.

Ganston dropped his head, then shoved his hands into his pockets. He shot Everling an evil look. "No, I guess it's not the best place for a confrontation."

"Good. Then let's end this now. I will see you out." She took Ganston by the arm and led him back through the sliding glass door.

Everling looked at Stemple. "What just happened?"

Stemple shrugged and attempted to straighten his jacket. "I don't know, but I'm glad someone stopped you. I think it's a little silly for grown men to be coming to blows."

Everling muttered as he made his way into his private lab. For just a moment it struck him as odd that he would have actually relished knocking the snot out of Ganston. He hadn't thought of doing violence to another person in years. It was a good thing that woman had pulled Ganston away, the old goat.

Everling looked up from the report as Stemple rushed into his office. "Did we get the test results from the latest gene-splicing?" Good results would bolster his spirits right now.

Stemple lowered his gaze. "Sir, the testing was inconclusive. We have a bigger problem."

Everling spun in his chair to face him. "What could be bigger than the test run—"

"The donor has died." Stemple pulled his halo-tablet close to his chest as though using it as a shield.

Everling's face went crimson. "You let him die?"

"We didn't *let* him do anything." Stemple took a step back. "I sent the technician to harvest an additional sample. He was dead and in the process of desiccating like the others."

"Rank incompetence! Did someone start the timer?" Everling bolted from his chair, slamming it into the wall as he rushed through the doorway.

He stormed into the lab area. Several technicians veered from his path to avoid a collision. "Where's the body?"

"They moved it from the prison pod to Lab Section Ten." Stemple waved off people trying to stop him for conversation.

Everling swerved toward Ten. The sound of his leather shoes on the lab floor matched the staccato beat of his heart. He couldn't have lost another subject. How did this keep happening? He slammed through the magnetic doors and stopped to don a quarantine lab coat and headgear.

He needed more test subjects. He'd committed a secret

team of scientists to work on overcoming Bethany's cancer mutation. She'd fallen into a coma two months ago, and unless he pulled this off, she would be gone in another month.

Everling burst through the quarantine barriers. "Where's subject fifteen? Give me the time." His bellowing reverberated off the metallic resin walls.

"Subject fifteen had a name. He was called Joshum," Stemple said.

Everling expected Stemple to do his job well, but sometimes he was an annoyance with his attention to details. Everling turned on him. "I don't care if his name was—"

"Here's the subject, sir," a petite lab intern interrupted as she wheeled the sheet-draped body into the examination theatre.

Everling looked over his glasses at the young lady as Stemple helped him into the special gloves. This was the same girl who'd just dispatched Ganston. Her white linen pants and lab jacket were well pressed and crisp. "And who would you be?"

"Treva Gilani, sir. I'm the new lab tech." She flipped on the time monitor at the head of the table. Green numbers counted down as the visual slide moved toward the red zone. She folded her hands together and backed away from the body.

Everling stepped to the gurney and lifted the sheet. A gasp escaped his lips and he stumbled back from the wheeled table.

"Sorry, Doctor. I should have warned you about the advanced condition of this particular subject," Treva said. Standing five feet four allowed her long auburn ponytail to flop over her shoulder and almost reach the gurney as she attempted to cover the corpse with the sheet.

Everling composed himself. "Leave it. Tie back your hair better. It's distracting."

Treva blushed but used a complicated over-and-under hand movement to secure the ponytail into a bun at the nape of her neck.

Everling clicked together the two pieces of the antique magnifying glasses dangling around his neck by a cord. He glanced at the timer then peered closely at the shriveled skin. The desiccation was so complete the skin retreated from the face, exposing a macabre sort of grin on the open jaw.

Stemple pushed an examination tray of instruments and containers within his reach. Everling inserted the tip of a scalpel into the leathery skin between two ribs, sawed his way through what had been supple and soft flesh just an hour ago, and inserted a probe to measure moisture content.

He stared at the probe dial. It registered zero. He hurriedly scraped at a section of bone, attempting to collect a sample and remove it from the body in time.

Stemple stood on the other side of the gurney. "Five minutes."

Everling nodded. He knew what he was looking for, but finding remaining evidence often proved rare. His hands worked with deft precision, claiming bits of leathery tissue and cross-sections of wide bone.

"Two minutes," Stemple announced. He moved away from the glare of the theatre lights trained on the gurney and pulled peripheral equipment away with him.

Everling snatched up forceps and plucked out sliced-off samples of liver and kidneys that were shriveled to the size of dried-up fruit.

Stemple trained his gaze on the timer at the head of the table. The slide entered the red zone. "One minute!"

"I know, I'm working as fast as I can," Everling said. His hands delicately pried loose a section that looked like links of dried-up sausage and placed it in the collection pan on the rolling tray. He pushed the tray toward Stemple, who grabbed the handle and moved it to the other side of the room.

Stemple turned back. "Dr. Everling, five, four, three—"

"Clear." Everling threw up his hands and backed away.

4

S elah started to laugh. She clutched at the rumbling in her chest and expelled a huge gush of air. "Oh, Mother! I never knew you had such a scary sense of humor. You really had me going for a minute there."

"Your real father ended our marriage before you were born so he could protect us from the Company." Mother remained stone-faced. She slid from the bed, padded barefoot to the window, and drew back the drapes. Sunlight spilled into the room. She moved to a cedar chest in the far corner, squatted, and rummaged through the contents until she found a small metal box near the bottom. Holding the box to her chest with both hands, she turned to face Selah.

Selah watched her mother walk toward her as though she were going to the gallows. Her last few steps faltered, but she sat on the bed and opened the box with pale, shaking hands.

"This is no joke." She sat on the bed and placed the box between them. Yellowed folded sheets of paper came into view.

"What is this?" Selah reached for a paper.

Mother touched her hand. "You need to hear this from the beginning."

Selah shook her head and moved to leave. "No . . . you're scaring me."

Mother reached out to stop her. "Selah, you need to hear this."

Selah's mind turned to scrambled eggs. *No. No more words.* She tried to squirm free. Tears welled in her eyes. The rational part of her brain screamed for her to cover her ears and flee far away before her world crashed. But Mother's hand kept her rooted to the spot.

Mother used her free hand to open the top page with the kind of care usually reserved for handling her delicate pastries. "You've come of age, and unfortunately it's time you know the truth about your heritage."

Selah stared, afraid of what might come next. Finding out her mother had betrayed her father during their marriage was tantamount to murder in her book.

"You were conceived when I was married to Glade Rishon." Mother held out a yellowed document.

Okay, so it wasn't betrayal in marriage, it was another husband. Selah pushed her hand away. "I don't want to hear this. You're telling me the only father I've ever known isn't really my father, and you expect me to just stand here and calmly listen?"

"You have told us for weeks—no, months—that today you would be a grown-up. Actually, you demanded it. Well, these are grown-up problems. I'm sorry that it came to this, my darling, but you need to know the truth. Your survival will depend on it."

"Survival? And you called me a drama queen." Selah slumped to the bed.

A strangled sob pushed from Mother's throat. "You are now among the hunted."

Selah shook her head. "I am *not* one of them! This is lunacy."

"Your real father was one of them. He told me before he left this might happen to you, but I always gambled that it wouldn't."

The realization finally settled on Selah like a boulder. She jumped to her feet. "This is insane. Why are you trying to ruin my life?"

"I'm trying to save your life."

"I need to talk to my father." He would fix this. He always fixed everything, even when she sometimes didn't like his ultimate answer. He would not force her to leave home and never see the family again. She could explain. She hadn't meant to defy his order. It was an accident.

"You shouldn't do that," Mother said in a small voice.

Selah turned to leave again. She looked back to her mother. "Why? Why can't I talk to the man who's been my father for eighteen years?"

"Because he came here as a Lander. His mark didn't remain after the first day. He's hated other Landers since then, and he trained you and the boys to hate them. He's jealous and vengeful, and I can't help him with those feelings." She shook her head.

"But why would he take it out on me?" Her thoughts mashed into a jumble of emotions. Maybe this explained why he spent more time with the boys and seemed to ignore her now that she was grown. She'd felt it before. She really was adopted. It was more than fanciful imagination.

"You would be an extension of all that he hates."

"I-I would be . . . Are you telling me he doesn't know about my real father?" Her heart sank even further. He didn't know her father was a Lander, yet he treated her differently than his own boys. So his indifference was just because she wasn't his blood.

Mother buried her head in both hands. Her shoulders trembled, wracked with sobs. "There was just no right time to tell him. After he confessed his story and the disdain he felt . . . Well, then I couldn't tell him. I was afraid of what he might do to you."

Selah shook her head. "He'd never hurt me." She couldn't be sure of that, but saying it helped her to feel better.

"I couldn't take the chance. You've always said yourself he favors the boys over you."

Selah stopped in her tracks. Anger welled in her. "So what happened to my brothers? No, wait! They aren't my brothers, they're Father's sons." She slapped her palm to her chest. "Why didn't Raza or Cleon get this mark? Why did only I get it?"

Mother shook her head. "I don't know. But I do know that Glade's mark—er, your father's mark—remained on his forehead, so maybe that has something to do with why you got one and Raza and Cleon didn't when they turned eighteen. They also didn't come in contact with Landers the day before. Your father knew the possibilities, and we made sure to keep them at home. I don't know how he does it, but he has more information about the Landers than anyone in our clan."

Selah wiped her sweating palms on the hem of her nightshirt. Too much to process. Too many emotions trying to wrestle for the top spot.

Mother strangled another sob and shook her head. "You're just so headstrong. I tried to keep you home yesterday without tipping my hand to your father."

"Were you ever going to tell me he wasn't my father?" Selah started pacing the room. Mother had always prided herself on telling the truth, but this was the biggest lie of them all. She wanted to strike back and tell her mother all she had seen and heard yesterday, but her insides were collapsing. This was life-changing and earth-shattering.

"No, that was one of the conditions Varro Chavez set before we married. You were never to know that he wasn't your real father. But I vowed in my heart when Glade first left that I would honor my love for him all of my days."

"Is that why you kept Rishon and never took Chavez as a name?"

Mother nodded. "It's not unusual for women to keep their family name if they are the last offspring, so no one ever thought anything of it."

"But Rishon was your married name, not your family name."

"I'm sorry," Mother said. Tears streamed down her cheeks. She sat statue-still.

Father. Stepfather. Deception. Fear. All jumbled together. She didn't know why but she began to laugh. "And here I always thought I was adopted because Father seemed to love the boys more." The laughter turned to anguished crying. "It was the truth all this time. I'm such a loser that my own father left me behind."

She darted toward the door. She needed air. Time to think.

"That's not true." Mother rushed around her, blocking the way. She tried to wrap her arms around Selah but she pushed away. Mother grabbed her hand. "Please come back. Let me tell you the whole story before you decide how you feel. I know this is a lot for you to handle at one time. But we don't have the luxury of time."

Selah's head hurt. Too many things were trying to filter into her brain. Her chest hurt and she didn't understand why, which only added more fuel to the headache pounding in her temples. Her brain threatened to explode, but she reluctantly followed Mother back to the bed.

Mother sat and patted the spot beside her, but Selah didn't want to sit. Her mother busied herself rooting through the folded papers. "Your real father and I fell in love the day I saw him on the shore in Georgia. We were married for almost four years before I became pregnant with you, and we thought our marriage would be complete with a baby. Then they started the hunting."

"You mean no one hunted Landers back then?"

"No, there were whole communities of Landers and normals living together in peace. They didn't make the bounty announcements until I was about six months pregnant. We fled from Georgia because people went crazy at the thought of easy money just for capturing people who were different. Your father, Glade, felt we would be safer if he left us."

"But didn't you fight to stay with him?"

"Glade was a very stubborn man, and he frightened me with stories of what they might do to you since you would be a hybrid. He took me to our Borough Council and they pronounced the marriage ended. I let him leave, but then I had a change of heart and tried to follow."

"You never found him?" The pounding in her temples began to subside.

"No, after three months of traveling I made it here before I went into labor. Your stepfather was traveling through the area and found me along the road. His wife had died giving birth to Cleon during their travels to escape the plague. He was so out of his element with Raza as a three-year-old and Cleon as a baby. But he helped me through your delivery and offered to let me stay with them if I'd help with the children."

"And you never went back to looking for my father?"

"I couldn't take a new baby on the road. It was a very hard life. The only reason I escaped attack from marauders for the three months I was on the road was because I was hugely pregnant and none of them wanted to tackle that problem."

"So you just gave up?"

"Yes. Your stepfather was so caring and gentle during that time that I eventually learned to love him. He felt we needed to marry right away so I wasn't looked upon as an unmarried woman with child. And since we were both new to the area, no one would be the wiser. We spent all the credits we possessed between us to pay the Borough official to marry us and keep it quiet that we arrived with children and unmarried."

"You never found out what happened to Glade?" Saying his name out loud pushed a warmness into her chest. Selah felt a strange calm wash over her.

"No, I couldn't risk it with a child, and as I said, I eventually came to love your stepfather. I felt my time with Glade was lost. He did leave me several letters he'd written over time and never gave to me. I want you to have them. Maybe you'll interpret some clue I may have missed and it will help you find him." She quickly placed the letters back in the box, pulled a small leather bag from the drawer in her side table, and shoved the box into it, then pressed the bag into Selah's hands.

Selah clutched the brown drawstring bag to her chest. This was happening too fast to process. She felt like she was standing outside the house looking in a window. Maybe this was really a nightmare. She pinched her arm and pain shot up to her elbow.

Thunder rolled through her chest again. Her hand slid up the center of her ribcage as her heart pounded with a vengeance. No, not a nightmare. Real. But this time the thunder brought peace. She didn't understand why.

"Why do I have to go? I could hide the mark." She rubbed at her chest. It didn't distress her as much now.

"It took several years before your stepfather admitted he'd been a Lander. He has some kind of strange sense about the mark. He knows when there's one nearby and he'd figure it out. I'm afraid of what he'd do, and I'm torn because I do love him."

"You would choose him over me?" Her mouth went dry.

"No, never, but we've got Dane to think about. He's so young and he loves his father. Do you want him to lose a father the way you did?"

"No," Selah said. "But this isn't fair. Why do I have to suffer?"

"I'm sorry, but we have no choice. I can't take Dane from his father. None of this is his fault."

"So it's my fault?" Selah stared. It seemed like she was always giving in so the boys could be treated better. Hadn't this been the reason she'd felt adopted in the first place? Don't mess with the precious boys' psyche, but rip hers to pieces and then throw her away.

Mother squeezed her eyes tight. "If only you had listened and not gone—"

"Okay, I get it!" Selah pounded her fist into her other hand. *If only* covered it all.

"If I want to keep you alive, you have to leave." Mother put her hands over her eyes.

Selah's eyes darted about, landing no place in particular. "Where would I go?"

"Glade talked about traveling north. He said there were other Landers in that direction, but that's all I know," Mother said. In the morning light her face took on a worn and haggard look that Selah had never noticed before.

"We know all captured Landers wind up at the Mountain," Selah said, thinking out loud while she still had Mother's advice to guide her.

"You've been to the Mountain with your—with Varro and the boys. So you know how to get that far. I've got maps and drawings hidden away that Glade saved. You can take everything." Mother scrambled to her dressing table and pulled out one of the long, narrow drawers at the top. She pressed her palm on the bottom. A false panel slid away and folded papers fell out.

Selah stared. She had never known of her mother's secrets and now there seemed to be so many. "Where did that come from?"

Mother hurried back to the bed and shoved the papers in the leather bag. "Glade built that for me when we were married. It was the only thing I brought from Georgia in my small wagon. It made me feel close to him, being able to lay my hands where he laid his."

Selah watched her mother. Did she really know this person of secret drawers and furniture, of memories?

"I will give you all the credits I've saved from my sewing and weaving," Mother said.

Selah snapped out of her thoughts. "But those are *your* savings. What if you need them?"

Mother took both of Selah's hands in her own. "Nothing is more important than your safety. I just wish I could help you more, but I don't know what to do."

"Well, I'm not taking your bio-coin. I can survive on my own. I think. Is it all right if I'm afraid?" She was having trouble breathing. She didn't know if it was fear squeezing her lungs or the rumble invading her chest.

Mother brushed the stray hair back behind her ears. "Yes, my sweet. It is fine to be afraid. It will help keep you safe."

"I don't know if I can bear not seeing you." The words caught in Selah's dry throat. Who would love her? Offer her advice? Hold her hand when things were tough?

Mother placed her hand on Selah's chest. "Follow your heart. I will always be with you."

Selah smiled weakly. It was easy to say but so hard to put into practice. She patted her mother's hand. "When I woke this morning, I wished for a whole new life and a chance at independence. I just didn't know it was going to happen this way."

"I always knew there was a possibility. I just hoped this day would never come. But I'm confident I've prepared you for a life in this world, with years of lessons on plants, weapons, maps, and survival. You're a strong woman, Selah. You've learned well. I know you can survive." Mother nodded.

"I'm not feeling very strong." Selah rubbed a finger across her scar, then fisted both hands on her hips as her legs trembled. The leather bag dangled by the rawhide strings. "I'm feeling scared."

⬧

Selah swung the backpack from her shoulder and let it fall to the ground. Like any other day, the birds twittered and she heard an occasional screech from the pair of hawks that made their home in the huge tree next to the larger barn. She would never hear them again. She would miss watching the nest grow in size every year, but maybe someday . . .

She slid onto the boulder at the end of the dusty road leading to their storage barns, pulled her knees up to her chest, and leaned back on her hands to drink in the scenery, wanting to commit every detail to memory. She stared at the east field. It was only June, but in a few more months the field would be sown with the flax that supported Mother's linen business. The sun sat low in the morning sky, creating long shadows along the tree line in the field. It looked like a line of soldiers. Were they watching over the body from yesterday? Her shoulders tightened at the thought. Her hands pressed onto the irregular surface as her fingers rubbed the rock. This would be the last time she could ever be here.

Her teeth began to rattle so she shut her eyes and clenched her jaw. Today should have been a day of celebration about coming of age. No school, the possibilities of joining the family business, and a whole host of adult endeavors she'd always relished the idea of doing. Well, all except getting married. A smile creased her lips as she guessed that plan was now off the table. The one bright spot in this mess.

Now she owned her freedom. Actually, she probably fit the category of fugitive better. Her hand went to her chest, fingering the reason. Looking down, she could see the leading edge of a wing peeking out below the scooped-out neck of her sleeveless top. The spot still sparkled with feeling, sometimes pounding like thunder. How could one single act like touching a stranger have caused this?

Tears welled in her eyes. Selah squeezed her eyes shut again and swallowed the lump forming in her throat. It wouldn't help to cry.

Bodhi Locke sat on a bale of hay in the darkened stall, watching the morning sun filter through the weathered barn boards. It created vertical shafts of light on the hay-strewn dirt floor, reminding him of containment bars. Jail. Seemed like that was working out to be his lot in life lately. His hands and legs were shackled, but he knew he could be free if he chose. Other than a very sore spot on his head, which he healed by concentrating on it, he didn't feel an immediate threat.

Last night he'd feigned unconsciousness and listened as the two men talked. If he let them carry him north before he escaped, he would be closer to finding others. He didn't understand all of what was going on. There were still fuzzy parts to his thinking process. The girl from yesterday had shown him how he got here, and he was almost certain he understood why, but now he needed to know how to get home.

Bodhi cleared his mind and watched the dust filtering through the sun streams. He could feel others, a few close, others far away, and some very strange. The vibrations weren't always friendly and were at times even sorrowful. Like a beacon, they pulled him, guiding him in their direction. But it was not the Presence. *What kind of place has others but no Presence?* In all his years he had never heard of such a land.

A scraping on the door cut into his thoughts. Bodhi looked up. Bright light streamed into the barn as the door swung out. One of the men from last night entered, looked at Bodhi, and strode around him to the other side of the stalls. He eased onto a bale of hay and pulled himself up to sit cross-legged directly across from Bodhi.

"You normally treat strangers like this?" Bodhi scowled and held up his shackled hands.

The man looked down at his own hands. "Sorry 'bout that, but you're not to be trusted."

"Not to be trusted! You don't even know me!" Bodhi yelled.

The man flinched. "We know your kind. They all act the same."

Bodhi bolted to his feet but was jerked back to the bale. He hadn't noticed the end of the chain tethered to the wall. "What do you mean, *my kind*?"

"Landers."

"I don't know what a Lander is, or where I am."

"I do," the man said in a low voice.

Bodhi glared at him and sat forward. "What do you know?"

The man pulled away from the front of the bale. "Everything."

"Are you going to tell me or do I have to bodily harm you?" Bodhi asked, raising his voice.

The man scrambled from the bale and ran for the door.

Bodhi softened his tone. "Wait! Come back." He ground his lips together. He didn't have a clue about being diplomatic. That wasn't his style.

The man slowed to a stop in the open doorway.

Bodhi tried to remember how to act contrite. "I'm sorry. That's rude of me. What's your name?"

The man looked back, seeming hesitant to return.

"Please. Come back." Bodhi feigned a smile, lifted his shackled hands in a submissive palms-up gesture, and pointed at the bale across from him. "Maybe we can trade information."

The man cracked a smile, pulled the door shut, and walked back to where he'd been sitting. "What more can you tell me about Landers?"

"First, introductions. I'm Bodhi Locke. Who're you?" He knew the civility of common people, and although he'd never found a reason to need to practice it, it would come in handy now.

The man lowered his eyes. "I'm Cleon Chavez. You saved my sister yesterday from those rowdies from Waterside. Thanks. They're known for kidnapping young women, and captives don't come back."

Bodhi thought for a second. "I got knocked out and trussed like an animal as a thank-you."

Cleon grimaced. "Sorry, that's our brother Raza."

"Why?"

"For the bio-coin." Cleon shrugged.

"Bio-coin?" Bodhi pulled back. "You talking about money?"

"Yes, there's a large bounty on your kind."

Bodhi stared. "Why?"

Cleon shrugged. "Don't know. The Company up north pays good for Landers keeping that mark on their foreheads." He gestured at Bodhi's head.

Bodhi rubbed his forehead. "There're people like me *without* the mark?"

Cleon nodded vigorously. "Sure are, they're not worth spit. We're supposed to wait twenty-four hours and see if the mark stays put before we take 'em in."

Bodhi's chest clenched. It had never occurred to him anyone could lose the mark of the Presence. Suddenly he grabbed his forehead. His breathing became labored. "Is mine still there?"

Cleon nodded. "Yep. It's right there. You'll make Raza real happy when he gets back with Father and the wagon."

"They're not here?" Bodhi put on his best face. Testing the waters for later when they were closer to his objective. "Could I bribe you to let me go?"

Cleon chuckled. "It would make Raza powerful mad. Couldn't risk it."

Bodhi grinned, trying to befriend him. "You're afraid of your brother?"

"Yes. He hates me as it is."

That wasn't the answer Bodhi expected, but he decided

to take it further. "Never heard of brother hating brother. Why is that?"

Cleon looked down at his hands. "Not something I want to talk about with a stranger."

Bodhi sat forward. He needed to work the friendship angle. The loop on his chains jangled on the floor, reminding him this wasn't one of his games. "Fair enough. Tell me more about the people like me. Do you know where we came from?"

Cleon leaned forward and put his hand near his mouth as if to shield the words. "I heard one say he came from the Kingdom, and he was sorry for the transgressions that got him sent here. Said he was going to spend the rest of eternity trying to atone for them."

"Why are you whispering?"

"Because the guy sounded nuts and my father hates you people. I'd get a whippin' if he heard me talking about Landers to a Lander."

Bodhi felt like he'd been punched in the chest. *Transgressions.* What had the man done? Why was he willing to atone? Bodhi knew what he'd done but didn't feel the need to beg for forgiveness. He figured there'd be some other way to get home than bow and scrape. It was his life and he was going to live it on his own terms.

Bodhi tamped down his anger. There was time enough for that later. Right now he needed to figure out how to get away once they got closer to his target. His head was getting clear enough to think, but it distressed him feeling others who were scared. He'd never felt them in fear before. "Did the guy say where home was?"

"He said across the ocean."

"Ocean! Pacific or Atlantic?" Bodhi's head jerked in the direction of the door.

Cleon looked around and then back at Bodhi with a questioning look. He hopped up from the bale. "Someone's coming."

5

The Mountain

Everling tensed, arms still raised.

As though it sneezed, a puff of dust rose about eight inches high along the full length of the desiccated body, then collapsed back in on itself. The body turned to a pile of dust.

Everling turned toward the examination tray and relaxed. All was accounted for. He'd learned by trial and error that tissue and objects moved from close proximity could survive the reclamation process. He sighed. There probably wouldn't be any better data from this subject than from the last few in this batch. He needed to dispose of the leftovers and get a new set of subjects right away. The serum trials on himself were netting results. The cure for Bethany's cancer was close.

He looked down. Some of the dust filtered from the table and onto the front of his shoes.

Treva Gilani returned. "Should I take it now, sir?"

Everling nodded then knocked the dust from his shoes. His head throbbed. He couldn't figure out how to stop this process from claiming subjects. "Yes, dispose of the dust and get these samples catalogued and into my lab."

"Do you think you can re-create the sampling?" Stemple tapped some numbers into the virtual keyboard of his halo-tablet, and a 3-D model of the body appeared above its surface. He aimed the tablet at the samples on the cart. They appeared above the original image with laser leads showing where they came from in the body.

Everling stripped off his gloves. "Why didn't they call me when the subject first died? I lost precious time."

"The attending intern stepped out for ten minutes to help in another lab," Stemple said.

The doctor averted his glance. "I'm sorry for being short with you. I had such high hopes for this group. I know there are a few left, but we're going to have to start over." He shook his head. "Do we have any new arrivals to cull DNA?"

Stemple waved his hand across the halo-tablet. The 3-D model faded and charts took its place. "All we have left are originals. They're just not compatible for creating sample groups."

"Increase the bounty. There have to be more Landers around. Those idiot peasants need monetary encouragement." Everling started to pace.

"I've researched our claim payments. Most of the incoming subjects are being located in Boroughs to the south of us." Stemple held out his tablet.

Everling walked back to look at the screen. "Can you overlay a map?"

74

Stemple clicked something, and the human captures showed up as yellow dots on a topical map. The livable area outside the Mountain was nothing more than a ragtag band of settlements dotting the extreme East Coast from north to south.

"Orient me," Everling said, waving a hand. Science was his field, not geography. He had no interest in what was left of the outside world.

Stemple rotated the map. "We're here. All the subjects we've gathered in the last fifteen years have come from this area." His finger highlighted the yellow dots going south from the Mountain's position, approximately forty miles west of Washington, DC.

Everling studied the map. "Why are there none to the left of the longitudinal line?"

"Those are mountains. There aren't any settlements on the western side. Or at least we don't think so. Too much ash from the volcano over there. Historically it looked like an alien landscape. No one's ever gone back."

The Sorrows had happened 150 years ago. Everling rarely thought back to his youth forty years ago, let alone to the Sorrows. His ancestors had been government workers who remained safely locked in Weather Mountain as the country's population succumbed to the ravages of the environmental catastrophes. Left to their own devices and without national leadership, most of the people outside perished, but his family had prospered in this closed environment.

Thinking about the events and the hundreds of millions of lives lost in one week's time brought no emotion. He could do nothing about the past, but he would control the future. His longstanding project of enhancing the DNA signature of Mountain people had been set aside to focus on securing a future for his wife, but the results of one could help the other.

Everling stared off into space. "Have we tried using any more of our own patrols to capture Landers?"

"No, sir," Stemple said. "Very ineffective. Last year we spent several months with AirStream units stationed at the beach areas most frequented as landings. A week after we suspended the patrols, peasants caught a Lander and turned him in. Remember the one who changed?"

Everling nodded. "Yes, that was the first time we learned the tattoo wasn't permanent on all Landers. To find that out after all these years was quite shocking. How many others have we missed?"

"You have to admit it was quite brilliant of the peasants to figure out they could get paid and be gone before the Lander's mark disappeared."

"I believe it was just dumb luck. Those peasants were new to the hunt and didn't know any better. Acquiring the Lander right away gave us a chance to observe his change overnight."

"I must admit it was surprising to find their DNA reverted to the same as ours after they lost the mark," Stemple said.

"Agreed, and having no mark makes them useless." Everling walked to the data board and pulled the data Stemple had just inputted. "The premise is very disconcerting, though."

"What premise, sir?"

"That they could be among us and we can't tell the difference."

Stemple looked up from his map, a frown etching his eyebrows together. "That *is* very disconcerting. There might be Landers in the Mountain and we'd never know about it."

"Don't worry. We've never been infiltrated. Our lineage is very pure."

Stemple pushed his eyebrows up. "If you say so, sir."

Everling tweaked some figures in the data. "Notify the AirStream units traveling the area to up the rewards by 25 percent."

Stemple's eyes widened. "That much, sir? We've never offered anywhere near that kind of compensation for Landers. How should we divide the payments?"

"Give them 25 percent bio-coin and 75 percent energy credits," Everling said.

Stemple ran his palm over the data board's controls to activate the panel next to Everling's work. A list of comparisons flashed on the screen. He waved his hand across the panel to change the view to new orders.

"Hold on there." Everling moved over to the screen. "What was that?"

Stemple ran a hand across his brow. "Just some calculations I was making on genetics."

"I'll be the judge of what's important." Everling gestured to the screen. "Put the data back up, please."

Stemple drew his lips tight. His hand hesitated. A split second passed before he recovered his composure and called the data to the interactive screen.

Everling walked the length of the calculations, tweaking data on the screen. He clapped his hands together and spun to face Stemple with a broad grin. "You're brilliant! It's right here in your third section. You've defined the missing progression between their DNA and ours."

"I could see it, but I didn't understand why. We've genetically engineered farm animals and food grains with no problems." Stemple ran a hand across his hair. "You're saying we need something to bridge the gap."

Everling smiled. "A union."

Stemple looked confused. "I'm not sure I understand."

Everling stared at the board. "We need a child from a Lander."

"Well, since that is obviously not possible I suggest—"

"Oh, but it is possible." Everling rubbed his chin. "Never had a clue they'd be this important to my work."

"You know where there are Lander children?" The color drained from Stemple's face.

"Get me a security team. I'll key in the biometrics and location of the subject," Everling said as he tapped out the details on the halo-keys.

"What kind of team—JetTrans or AirStream? How far are they going?" Stemple asked as he manipulated the security screen to order a team.

"AirStream. They're going to Dominion Borough." Everling moved to the far side of his lab and stared at the screen as the scanning microscope read the samples and built a 3-D model on the work surface.

"Doctor, I've done this experiment two dozen times. The telomerase in the Lander sample degrade when I introduce our DNA," Stemple said. He flipped the test results onto the counter with a hint of frustration.

Everling kept his eyes on the layering model. "I've told you our only recourse is—"

"I won't accept it as the only recourse. We need to have other options." Stemple ran his hand through his hair and paced.

"Then solve the Hayflick Limit. In the meantime I'm offering a bigger bounty for Landers and sending a team to claim the child."

"Hayflick can't be solved. Telomeres only divide maybe a hundred times," a female voice said.

Everling and Stemple swung in her direction. Treva Gilani stood near the doorway leading to the confinement quarters with her hands shoved in her lab coat pockets. Her auburn hair was still tied in the tight bun at the back of her head.

Everling looked over the rim of the glasses slipping down his nose. He figured a first-year lab worker was only as good as their experience time. "What do you know about telomeres, young lady?"

Treva squared her shoulders and stepped forward. "What do I know? I know the Hayflick Limit is the number of times a human cell will divide. I know the end caps on those cells are called telomeres, and every time the cell divides, those end caps get shorter until they die—thus bringing about the Hayflick Limit, which by human standards is about a hundred replications per cell. That's why we age. And I know that in Lander DNA, telomeres replicate forever."

Everling took off his glasses and laid them on the counter. "Aren't you the lab tech who brought in the body? And the one who ushered away Ganston?"

Treva cleared her throat. "Yes, sir, I'm Treva Gilani. I have a bachelor's degree in genetics and I'm about to complete the same degree in microbiology. I could be an asset to your project." As she flipped her head, the ponytail started to slip. She quickly maneuvered it back into the bun.

Stemple moved closer, his expression blank. "I haven't cleared you for those experiments."

"As my professor used to say, it doesn't take a rocket scientist to figure out what you're doing." The young woman stepped closer. Her hand rested on the computer table as she fingered the holographic keys. Several files opened, and she flicked her finger to virtually push the pages up to the screen on the wall.

"You're studying laminin, which holds organisms together." She tapped the keys, opened another folder, and moved it up to the wall screen. "This experiment is for the telomerase enzyme to add DNA sequence repeats and keep those pesky telomeres from shortening themselves into extinction. When you add the two of them together, well, you're trying to find the proverbial fountain of youth." She appeared proud of herself.

Everling balked. She was exceptional. With a scornful expression, he looked to Stemple.

"She can be trusted. I vetted her well before bringing her on board," Stemple said.

Everling scowled. "When were you going to tell me about a microbiologist on staff?"

Stemple shrugged. "You've been so busy lately I've hardly time to tell you about work, let alone staff."

"Sir, I could be an asset." Treva crossed her arms and stood confidently.

"How old are you, child?" Everling asked.

"I'm twenty, sir." Treva pressed her lips together.

"And you've already got your bachelor's degree?"

"Yes, sir, I was a child prodigy. I've been in college since I was thirteen."

Everling took off his glasses. "Really? What is your IQ?"

Treva shrugged. "Last time they checked it was 165."

Everling's eyes widened as he turned to Stemple for verification.

Stemple nodded.

"Well, young lady, we're not exactly looking for the fountain of youth. My wife has a form of radiation-induced cancer, and it will prove fatal in a very short time. I'm trying to extend her life until I can develop a cure."

Treva thought a second, nodded, and moved back to the computer table. "I guess you've missed the latest papers by Borsen and Manhurst." Her fingers slid through rows of university files she'd called up on the surface.

"The geneticists?" Everling moved toward the computer.

"Yes, their research shows certain cancer cells can be realigned by telomerase." Treva closed the original files on the screen and inserted a new one.

Everling put on his glasses to study the research paper.

"So you can literally solve both problems if you can overcome Hayflick." Treva brushed her bangs back from her eyes, looking satisfied.

Everling turned to Stemple. "Remind me to give you a raise for finding this child."

Stemple's shoulders relaxed and a slight smile crept across his lips.

Treva furrowed her brow. "Sir, could you forgo calling me a child? I think in this day and age, twenty is old enough to be considered a woman."

Everling studied the research paper. "Yes, and don't call me *sir*. *Doctor* will do."

⚭

Treva stood with her hands in her pockets. She knew she'd overstepped the boundaries Stemple had mandated, but he was wasting too much time.

Stemple motioned her to follow him. She glanced in Everling's direction. He'd returned to studying the screen.

Outside the Lab Section Ten confinement area, the reader scanned Stemple's palm and right eye, then beeped. The frosted glass panel slid into the ceiling, then closed with a soft whoosh once they entered.

He turned on Treva and snatched her by the arm. At five eleven he appeared menacing, towering over her five-feet-four frame. "What was that all about? I told you to lay low."

Treva refused to be intimidated. She wrenched her arm free from his grip and rubbed at the spot. "What's your problem? You wanted me to get the job as his lab assistant, and I'm pretty sure I just accomplished the task."

"That wasn't the point. Do you know how many ways it could have gone wrong?"

"Well, it didn't, so let's get on with the job. I can use the extra bio-coin." She knew just the right bit of knowledge to add to the equation to deem herself an asset, and she'd picked correctly with the genetics report. She hadn't been ready to start her plan this early, but when the rare job opening in this section had come up, she jumped on it.

"Is that all this job means to you—monetary advancement?" Stemple stood toe-to-toe with her.

Treva screwed up her bottom lip. No, that wasn't all the job meant to her, but she couldn't tell him. There was no possibility of trusting Stemple with her real objective. "What else? Do you really expect me to give a hoot about those aliens they capture?"

Stemple furrowed his brow and glared. "They're human beings just like we are. And they deserve better than your loathing."

Treva stepped back. Maybe it was worth testing him. It would be helpful to have an ally. "Well, aren't you just the champion of the downtrodden."

Stemple frowned. "I have no interest in the captives other than scientific. But I've seen the notations about suspected illegal alien interactions in your full life records."

Treva's shoulders dropped. "Suspicions are not facts." She needed a look at those records to see what might be in there. Embarrassing data wouldn't help her long-term goal. "I didn't know full life stats stayed in your records after university."

"The records are forever."

She mentally calculated what it would take for her to hack the system. "I thought parts of it were sealed."

Stemple raised an eyebrow. "Are you worried about something?"

Her eyes darted up and to the right. She'd never been good

at lying, but she needed to put on her best innocent face. She flashed a smile. "I guess not. You hired me."

"That I did. And we're going to get off to a better start once I lay out the ground rules."

"Like not eating your lunch out of the cooling unit?" She figured light teasing might put him at ease faster than being standoffish.

"No, like your interaction with the Landers."

Treva lowered her gaze, hoping he wouldn't ban her from the necessary interaction. "Landers—as in plural. How many are left after the one that just died?"

Stemple's cheeks reddened. He hesitated then recovered. "Several, but a Lander child is being brought in from Dominion Borough."

"A child? How did they get a Lander child?" Treva's heart rate ticked up. This couldn't be happening. Not now.

"I don't know. Everling got the data." Stemple looked at his halo-tablet and pulled up several reports. "Why?"

"I'm just curious," she stuttered.

He stared at her. "I just bet you are."

"Listen, I'm not too fond of the way you seem to be treating me. Maybe it was a mistake for me to take this job."

Stemple rubbed his chin. "I'm sorry. I was being rude. You just threw off my schedule by plunging in like that. I wanted to talk with you first about the ground rules for the job before we approached the doctor. The paramount rule is nothing gets outside of this lab. Nothing about our work, our conversations, or anything you observe."

Treva smiled. Okay, back on track with work. "That's a

pretty basic rule of confidentiality for an experimental lab environment."

Stemple shook his head. "I don't think you understand the ramifications of this gag order. This means absolutely no one other than you, me, or the doctor knows exactly what we're processing."

Now it was Treva's turn to raise an eyebrow. Test the water. "What if one of the Politicos calls me for questioning?"

Stemple's look drilled holes in her. "Then you know nothing."

"Well, I should probably tell you Charles Ganston was a friend of my father's. He's like an uncle to me." She figured he'd find it in the records before she could alter them. And it would give them a small secret she could use to see if she could trust him.

Stemple perked up. "That's why he let you lead him out of the lab. I thought it was a little strange he became docile so quickly."

Treva grinned. This might just work.

Stemple clenched his teeth and pointed a finger. "If you want to keep your job, never mention him again, especially to Everling. They are childhood rivals."

Treva opened her mouth but then closed it without a word.

"Now you're getting the idea," Stemple said. "Let's see if we can come to terms on everything else. You'll take over this job monitoring Landers that I normally oversee."

He walked to the console and tapped the green button for the first pod. The plascine composite wall changed from opaque to translucent then slowly became transparent. This new material fascinated Treva. It had the strength of steel but the fluidity to allow unfettered views as though it were glass.

She glanced at the cell interior. A private water closet stood in the far left corner against the wall, displaying a virtual screen with a pastoral scene of mountains, a waterfall, and several deer frolicking among meadow flowers. The rest of the room consisted of a slab bed with a thin mattress, coverings that slid from the wall diagonal to the screen, and a small table and chair this side of the water closet.

At the table sat a subject. He never glanced up or made any movement to acknowledge that the wall had become clear. He sat perfectly straight in the chair with his head down. Long dark hair fell over his eyes, obscuring his face. She guessed by the length of his torso he probably stood about six feet tall.

Treva stared at the Lander. "Is the wall two-way? Does he know we're here?"

"Yes. He has very distinctive abilities we have to control." Stemple crossed his arms and backed up a step.

Treva averted her eyes from the dark-haired man and glanced at Stemple. "Is there something wrong?"

Stemple frowned and dropped his arms. "No. Why do you ask?"

Treva smiled. "Because your body language tells me differently. Have you ever had a run-in with him?"

Stemple jerked his head back. "No! Why would you think something like that?"

The man sitting at the table slowly turned his head in their direction and lifted his chin until he was staring eye to eye with Stemple. His hair fell back, exposing a handsome face with a chiseled jawline and olive complexion. He carried the standard forehead-and-temple marking of a Lander. His lips parted in an almost imperceivable smile.

Stemple stumbled back, shook himself, and regained his composure. "I'm late for a meeting." He looked everywhere but at the cell.

Treva shrugged. "I have to finish gathering the samples for the test station."

Stemple smacked the wall panel and stormed from the room.

Treva leaned back against the near wall and watched Stemple leave. What had gotten into him? There was fear in his eyes. She turned back to the man staring holes through her. It didn't make her nervous, but it did make her curious. She'd been waiting for this. She picked up the control module and walked toward the wall while maintaining eye contact.

"Hello."

He didn't respond. Treva reached out to touch the clear surface of the cell, and a mellow vibration radiated through her fingers and into her wrist. She jerked her hand away and rubbed the tips of her fingers together. He continued to stare at her. She knew full well that plascine walls didn't vibrate. Maybe she was imagining it. She reached out again.

Her fingertips rested gently against the surface, and warmth radiated outward from them. She tipped her head to the side. "Are you doing that?"

She didn't pull back this time, but the warmth subsided as she stared at her hand. The change felt like a loss she couldn't explain.

"What if I am?" the man asked in a baritone voice.

Treva opened her mouth to speak, but what was she going

to say? Stemple had left without any explicit instructions. "I assumed the drugs were disabling your abilities, or at least that's what I was told. Why are they drugging you?"

"Do you really care, or are you just making conversation?"

Treva bit down on her lip then released it. "I really care."

The man cracked a smile, lowered his head, then looked up at her with a devilish grin. "Once, long ago, I slammed Stemple against a wall."

"You've been physically violent?" Adrenaline flooded her body. She felt the urge to flee.

"No."

Her legs trembled. "You don't think throwing someone against a wall is violent?"

"I never touched him."

Treva's eyes widened. "Then how?"

"I thought it."

Her brain became an instant jumble of thoughts all bombarding her at the same time. She laid her palm against the wall. "You did it with your mind?"

He smiled broadly. "Yes, and I've let them think they're controlling me with the drugs."

Treva looked down at the controller in her other hand. "What is your name?"

His head jerked toward her. He stared at her with smoky green eyes. "Glade Rishon."

Her heartbeat pounded in her ears. She wondered if he could hear it. "Are you planning on hurting me?"

"No, but why would you believe my answer?"

Treva tipped her head to the side. This was illogical, but other than excitement, her emotions were calm. She needed to start this operation somewhere. "I can't tell you why right now, but I do trust you." She fingered the controller and the clear door slid up out of the way. Treva slowly stepped inside the cell, conscious to stay by the opening. "If you still have abilities they can't control, why are you letting them keep you in this place?"

6

Selah tipped her head to home in on the sound. Wagon wheels. Horses. Sliding from her perch, she snatched up her backpack and sank behind the boulder. It took a good ten minutes for them to arrive. How had she heard them that far away? And what else could she do out of the ordinary? Smells. She could smell the horses before she saw them. Could she really smell Father? The familiar mix of his body scent and her mother's special-made herbal soap was unmistakable.

The team came into view, pulling a wagon. She'd recognize those bay horses anywhere. The one on the right was a light copper red, the left one a dark mahogany. Both horses tended to pull to the side, so Father had trained their manes to lay in the direction they pulled. The horses were positioned with their black manes toward the center between them to draw them toward each other, thus moving in a straight line.

Father manned the reins, Raza beside him. The AirStream was lodged in the bed of the wagon. Raza must have left to get Father right after she'd quit arguing with him yesterday. Her opportunity to speak to Cleon alone had evaporated. The wagon passed by the boulder and stopped about halfway between her and the barn.

Father stood up from his seat and looked around. Selah pressed herself into the ground.

"What's the matter?" Raza scanned the bushes.

"I don't know," Father said. "Something's not right. I feel like there's a Lander nearby."

Selah shrank away from the rock. Her mother had told her this could happen. At least knowing Mother was right helped to bolster her resolve.

"Cleon has him in the barn. Good, he must have kept the mark. I didn't wait to see, fearing I'd miss you at the Borough meeting."

Father shook his head. "No, it doesn't feel quite right."

It took until this very moment for Selah to realize she and the boys had never questioned how or why Father had honed the perfect ability to track Landers. Funny how one piece of information connected so many pieces of the puzzle. She saw so many things clearly now.

"You're out of practice. We haven't caught one in a couple months."

"I don't think so, but you may be right." Father patted Raza's back. "I'm proud of you. You're becoming quite the hunter."

Selah balked. Raza probably didn't tell Father she'd actually done the hunting and all he did was the stealing.

"Are you going to accompany us up north to the Mountain?"

Father sat and signaled the horses forward. "No, I have other business. You two boys will be fine. This isn't your first time alone."

Father looked back over his shoulder one last time. Selah pulled her head back but peeked at him through the bush without so much as twitching a muscle.

"Goodbye, Father," she mouthed.

Selah had never needed a devious nature in the past. Well, she didn't count getting one over on her brothers. But this new mode felt foreign. She'd never have time to free the Lander here. She'd have to follow and grab him while they slept. But how could she keep up? They were traveling by wagon. *Think.*

She watched as Cleon waved and darted back in the barn. Father and Raza unloaded the AirStream and directed it to the storage bay beside the barn. She thought about taking it but knew Father could electronically trace its whereabouts if he noticed it missing. Granted, he wouldn't be able to signal the boys, but he could take the other machine and catch up to her, so that wouldn't work.

Bodhi came into view, hands and legs shackled to allow him only tiny steps. He didn't deserve that kind of treatment after saving her. She made a mental note to slip into the barn after they left and grab the spare set of keys for those shackles.

Bodhi shuffled slowly, kicking up little puffs of dust from the worn hardpan surface in front of the barn. It looked as though he were taking extra-small steps just to annoy Cleon, who urged him on by prodding him in the shoulder. Father stepped in front of him. Bodhi glared. Father looked him over and inspected the mark on his forehead. No words were exchanged.

Seemingly satisfied, Father patted Raza on the shoulder, unhitched the horses, and directed them into the barn. When he finished grooming and feeding them, he'd head past the barn to the lane leading up to the house and Selah would never see him again.

She could hear their conversations two hundred feet away as though they were standing next to her. She'd have to learn to use these skills to her advantage.

"Come on, move it! I don't have all day." Cleon pushed Bodhi's shoulder again.

Bodhi tripped forward. As he caught his footing, he looked right at her.

Selah froze. Was she visible? No, she couldn't be. The foliage on the bush had grown lush with the constant rains this summer. Yet he'd looked right here.

She didn't know anything about Landers. Another blank spot in the learning she should have acquired before deciding to hunt them. Since Mother had explained about her father's—correction, her stepfather's—abilities, she guessed all Landers had the same discernment. She hitched a half smile. Wait till Bodhi got a look at who he was sensing. Or could he tell that it was her? Her smile faded. Would he be angry at her for causing his capture? There was no expression on his face to give her a clue. She'd seen his fighting abilities. What if he wanted to hurt her?

Too many questions and not enough answers.

Raza and Cleon hauled Bodhi up into the wagon and loaded supplies in behind him, probably to make it more difficult for him to slip out unnoticed. They lifted several short cage crates covered with loose tarps into the back end.

What were they? Maybe food for the trip? No, neither of them ate meat and they wouldn't carry fish in a cage. Maybe they carried big snakes to sell to the tanner on the way to the Mountain. Both anacondas and Burmese pythons were rare this far north, but on occasion a traveler would lose one or two at a Company station en route and it would take up residence, decimating the local small game population.

Next they rolled out an RU. The Reclaim Unit would convert moisture in the air and give them fresh drinking water for the trip. Neither Raza nor Cleon would drink stream water. They were so much like Father. He'd invested much bio-coin to buy the unit several years ago. It cost precious amounts of fuel to operate, but Father felt it was a necessity for travel so they didn't have to drink from unknown water sources.

That gave her an idea. The horses and wagon, with three people and the supplies, could probably get to the Mountain in several days depending on how much they pushed. They'd have to follow about two hundred miles of meandering roads around the rubble and ruin of ancient cities and towns, but she knew where they'd settle in for the night. The areas were full of good pasture and streams for the horses. If luck was on her side, Selah could cut across land and travel straight as the crow flew, beating them there. Granted, she might have to traverse some large kudzu-infested areas, but she felt confident she could stay ahead of them at any of the stations.

Her heart pounded against her ribs. What made her think she could do this? Doubt crept into her mind, making her hands shake. She smashed them to the ground. *Stop it!* Selah bit her bottom lip hard enough to make herself yelp and taste blood. Her mother's words rolled through her head loud and clear: *Okay, that's enough with the self-destruction. Get on with the task at hand.* She needed to plot a travel route.

She planned the first leg of the trip in her mind while she watched Bodhi. With his head hung low, his blond hair fell across his face, masking his rugged features and sea-blue eyes. The first time those eyes stared at her, she'd hyperventilated. At the time she'd convinced herself that it was his sudden awakening that had startled her, but now, with time to think about it, she felt a stirring deep within her better left untouched.

She shook her head to dismiss the visual of those eyes, then looked up to see Raza reach over the side of the wagon and rip Bodhi's shirt from the back of his neck.

Selah rose on her haunches to stop him, then huffed under her breath and pulled back. She couldn't give herself away or she'd be of no help. Her brother tore Bodhi's linen shirt to shreds and laughed. Raza used a remnant of the fine material to wipe the sweat from his brow, then threw the fabric to the dirt and ground it into the road with his heavy work boot.

She seethed. Captive or not, Bodhi would sunburn and need salve and extra water to keep him alive until they reached the Mountain. Logical reasoning was the one skill she held over her brothers. They were crude and basic and acted on any whim, while she had spent her time learning the lessons Mother diligently drilled into her. *Patience is a virtue.*

She tried to tamp down the anger. Mother said hotheads made stupid choices. She glanced from Raza to Bodhi and her breath caught in her throat. Bodhi's arms and torso possessed the well-defined muscles of a fighter. And although he didn't appear to be expending the energy it took to sweat, moisture glistened on his fair skin, radiating a glow from the sun overhead. It compelled her to stare.

His skin looked close to translucent after the protective linen was stripped away. Selah averted her eyes as a tingling crept up her chest and settled in her throat. A gulp pushed it back down. She reminded herself that this was not about his looks but about the condition he'd be in after hours in the unrelenting sun.

Bodhi lifted his head. The hair fell back from his face. He opened his eyes and turned to stare in her direction again. She swallowed another invading lump. He couldn't possibly see her.

He smiled . . . and winked.

Her world screeched to a halt.

Selah's eyes widened as her hand flew to her chest. Not sure why, maybe to see if her heartbeat was still there. He smiled again.

Selah squinted. It was as though he could read her thoughts and was responding.

Raza came around the side of the wagon carrying more supplies. He turned back to the barn and glanced up at Bodhi. "What're you grinning about?"

Bodhi shut his eyes and hung his head without answering. He seemed calm, almost too calm. She would have been rabid with rage at being trussed, but he seemed to have moved beyond his physical state. He sat erect, eyes closed most of the time. It unnerved her that every once in a while his eyes opened and he would calmly look in her direction.

Even though she sat still, sweat dripped from her temples and slid down her chest. The sun crept toward its noonday high. Raza and Cleon were beginning to show large wet spots under their arms and down the backs of their shirts as they loaded the wagon.

Selah remembered shorter trips than the normal several days' ride because they were afforded the opportunity to hop a Company AirStream at one of the stations. Those jet-propelled hovercrafts traveled near the ground but averaged fifty miles an hour.

A thought slapped her. If they arrived at a station at the right time and hopped a Company AirStream before she could rescue Bodhi, what was she going to do? She would have no recourse left to stop them or catch up.

Having no recourse was not an option. She'd not thought that far ahead. Maybe the sun was getting hotter, but she felt a sudden flush to her skin. Was it fear?

It took another half hour for her brothers to hitch up the spare team and head out. The dust had barely settled back to the road when Selah grabbed her backpack. She tiptoed to the barn and peeked inside, hoping her father had already left through the back door. He had.

She grabbed the keys from the nail inside the door and scraped the soft flesh of her thumb on a jagged piece of timber. She yelped. A trickle of blood oozed from the slice. She brought her thumb to her mouth to clean away the blood. Great. First blood and she wasn't even out of the barnyard.

She trotted across the tall-grassed hayfield to the left of the barn and disappeared into the tree line at the break in the encroaching kudzu where the animals normally grazed. For her, it would be about a two-hour journey to the first travel station, where her brothers would bed down for the night. The wagon and team would take the better part of the afternoon to get there.

It felt good to trot. For most of her life, Selah had enjoyed running. Mother had encouraged her to depend on her feet instead of mechanical forms of travel. She felt they made people lazy and fat. Seemed another one of Mother's lessons was proving fruitful.

Selah's backpack hung firmly cinched to her body, offering no resistance to her movements. She'd keep up this pace until she got tired and then stop at her favorite stream for water and a short break.

She used the compass Mother had given her for the tenth Birth Remembrance. Funny how so many things she'd learned now seemed important when at the time they'd felt useless and so out of place. The emerging culture of most Boroughs grew dependent on Mountain technology, and the old ways were slowly disappearing. She remembered scowling and tossing the compass into her box of dolls, which were much more important to her at the time. Now she silently thanked Mother and headed due north.

Normally she'd have to be right on top of the pig farm before she knew to veer off to the right to find the stream, but the stench reached her nose long before the large oaks, apple orchard, and curing sheds told her to turn.

There were several Boroughs raising and eating pigs. Pork was one meat that Mother would not let her eat. She said pigs didn't sweat, so any impurities they ate were kept in their meat. But Selah loved the smell of cooking slab bacon. The heavenly aroma caused her stomach to rumble with hunger . . . until the day Father came home from a Borough meeting and told Mother the farmer they usually bought apples from had died while feeding his hogs, and the animals ate him as an extension of their meal.

Selah forever gagged at the smell of cooking pork, thinking about the poor man becoming part of the meat. The tale haunted her to this day. She was glad to give wide berth around the farm without seeing any animals.

The clear, swift-moving stream was a welcome break after less than an hour of travel. She'd gotten here much faster than normal but suffered no fatigue—in fact, she felt invigorated as though she could run for hours. Strange. Selah plopped to the ground at the edge of the water, pulled off her pack, and shimmied on her belly to the edge. A few handfuls of the clear, cold water refreshed her. She wandered to a nearby apple tree, plucked a huge, dark red specimen, and bit into it.

She could afford to rest for fifteen minutes. She stooped beside the stream as she ate. The sky was beautifully clear and the sun warm. It felt good considering it could have been a rainy, damp day, forcing her to travel wet. She amused herself watching the minnows dart in little side pools where the current stayed at bay. A hawk played chicken with a group of three tiny birds, swooping and diving as the three annoyed little ones tried to chase him away.

Maybe she wouldn't linger here. She'd never noticed the pig smell to be this strong near the stream. Usually it was only this rank near the fields being plowed and rooted by the swine herd, and those fields were easy to spot by the turned-over clumps of root, no grass, dark soil, and fallen trees. She sniffed the air again.

Off to the left and behind her, a twig snapped. It came from a safe distance away, but Selah rose, spit out the apple seeds, and leisurely picked up her pack. Her heartbeat started its ramp-up to a pounding. She began walking north away from the sound. The place shallow enough to cross to the other side was still about a half mile upstream.

The bushes in front of her rustled. Selah took a deep breath. A free-range sow weighing at least two hundred pounds plowed through the brush and grunted her displeasure. Selah stopped in her tracks. On her right came the playful grunts of a litter of piglets in the high brush near the stream. She was between the sow and her babies, which never ended well. Her legs began to tremble but she forced herself to back up. Getting out of the middle would improve the situation.

Selah darted back the way she'd come. A boar ran from the tree line, considerably larger than the sow and bearing four tusks that looked five inches long and sharp enough to poke holes in her that a fist could pass through. She skidded to another stop. A wall of pork hurtled at her.

Trapped between the two, she swung her backpack. The boar impaled it on a tusk and tried to jerk it from her hand. Selah yanked back. For a moment, a virtual tug-of-war ensued. He dropped his head and the bag slid free. In the process of trying to pull it back, Selah lost her balance and stumbled backward. She recovered just as the boar charged again.

Selah took her only option. She clutched her pack to her chest and flung herself into the stream, landing in a crouch. Water covered her head and sharp rocks on the bottom tore at her knees and elbows. Struggling to her feet in the slow current, Selah coughed and spit out water invading her lungs. She swung around. The boar looked uninterested in climbing down the embankment. Selah exhaled a huge sigh and coughed up more water as she slogged to the other side and scrambled her way up the slippery bank. Her feet squished in water-logged travel shoes as she headed off across the field. She really hated pigs now.

⟐

Selah raised her hand to shade her eyes and peered at the sun in the afternoon sky. She had run twenty miles. In her usual regimen she would gain a second wind, as her mother liked to say. The endorphins would kick in and flood her body with happy juice, making it easy to push on. But today . . . was it her imagination, or could she have traveled another twenty miles? Whatever she felt, there was no need to go farther today. The travel station sat less than a hundred yards away.

She crossed the field to the road, followed it around the bend, and jerked to a stop. A Company AirStream sat on the landing pad in front of the building. Its occupants were coming out of the station.

Selah muttered to herself and backed into the bend. She'd beaten her brothers here and now would be bested by a stupid Company transport.

While she ranted to herself about her misfortune, the officers climbed back into the vehicle and lifted off. Selah dashed into the protective cover of the tree line. With a soft hum, the AirStream rose above the road and disappeared around the bend.

"Yes!" Selah charged toward the station. She peered in the window. Empty room. She quickly entered, the cool interior of the rocrete and stone composite building offering welcome relief from the sweltering heat. Her clothes had dried at least an hour ago, so heat was no longer being drawn off her body. She'd sit here for a few minutes before setting up a hiding place.

Selah dropped her backpack on a bench along the far wall and spied a poster on the Company bulletin board.

Attention: By the order of the Company, bounty on Lander subjects shall be raised by 25 percent. Total bounty will be paid as follows: 25 percent in credit, 75 percent in energy.

Her stomach lurched. Selah wanted to tear the poster to bits. She reached out.

"What do you think you're doing?" a male voice said.

7

Selah spun to face the door.

The man straightened after picking up a small case leaning against the open doorway. He wore the uniform of Company security. Behind him she saw the AirStream on the landing pad.

"I-I'm just trying to read what it says," Selah said with a wide smile. She could feel her face getting red but hoped he didn't notice in the low light. The transport, nearly silent, had returned without her hearing it. She needed to learn to stay alert.

The man sauntered forward. He looked around the empty room and gave her a sideways glance. "You wouldn't be trying to steal the notice so no one else sees the new bounty, would you?"

Selah shook her head. "No, sir. I'd never do that."

The officer motioned her forward. Selah froze. He unhooked the small biometric scanner from his utility belt.

"What is your name, young lady?" The officer held out the scanner.

Selah hesitated. Was her stepfather looking for her already? Unfortunately, the hesitation put the officer on alert. His expression went from friendly to stony. He cocked a finger, beckoning her forward.

Selah swallowed hard and slowly walked toward him. There was nowhere to run. If she got out the door, the other officer sat in the AirStream. She held out her arm.

"I asked for your name," the officer said as he scanned her arm.

"Selah Rishon Chavez," she said in a barely audible voice, as though the quieter she said it, the less it would register.

The officer raised an eyebrow as he ran a finger over several spots on the scanner. Selah tried to keep her breathing in check. Seconds seemed like minutes. He looked up. Her heart skipped.

"Okay, you appear clear. No run-ins with the Mountain is a good record for a citizen."

Selah started to give a smart remark. Outside the station the panel on the waiting AirStream began to lift.

"Did you find the case?" the officer piloting the transport asked.

The officer continued to stare at Selah. "Yeah, I got it."

"Let's go! We still have at least an hour's travel time before we get close enough to the Mountain to get duty updates. I'm really hoping to be in my own bed tonight," the pilot said.

The officer turned on his heels without so much as a good-bye, climbed into the transport, and it disappeared from sight.

Selah let out a huge huff of air and ran to the doorway.

The AirStream rounded the bend for the second time. This time Selah watched for them to return. Several minutes went by before she was satisfied they were gone for good.

She scanned the trees surrounding the station for the most advantageous spot. It wouldn't do to get caught here, not after she'd skirted two potential problems today. She knew where the boys would bed the team for the night and where they'd set up camp. She'd stopped at this station before when the boys accompanied her and Mother to sell her woven linens.

Rather than climb a tree, she stayed at ground level because heights were not among her favorite things. Although she was on the road to self-discovery, she didn't feel the need to accomplish it all at once. She searched out a spot with good cover beside a couple of large trees surrounded by lush bushes. Plopping her bag to the ground, Selah dug out her water cylinder and navigated across the road and through the dense foliage behind the station to the stream on the other side of the tree line. They'd get water for the horses from here.

This stream had already become her friend, both saving and refreshing her today. She filled her container and drank deep, noticing that on this side of the bend the streambed widened and deepened, looking more like a little river. The liquid cooled her from the inside out and refreshed her resolve.

Her confidence had grown in her travels today. Mother's voice audibly played over and over in her head. So many times she'd wondered why Mother drilled such lessons as self-reliance into her and in secret even taught her how to hunt animals. Those curious bonding instances were now perfectly clear examples of Mother preparing her for this future.

As if on cue, thunder rolled across her chest. The anxiety

of these strange vibrations and unsettling fears had passed in a few hours. She felt different after each rumble, as though new connections were coming together inside her. It gave her an odd sense of confidence. Her fears of being on her own . . . they weren't the normal things she'd expected from being pushed out of the nest like a baby bird learning to fly. Selah pressed on the spot, rubbing her hand over the impression. Instead, she felt comfort, like she wasn't alone.

She filled the cylinder again and headed back to her hiding spot to eat some jerky Mother had packed. With her hunger and thirst satisfied, Selah leaned back against the tree, lulling herself with the sounds around her. Birds flitted among the trees. Quick little breaths sounded like rabbits, the chatter like squirrels.

Selah needed to rest her eyes for a few minutes. The last thing she noticed was how dark the insides of her eyelids could be in the daytime.

8

The Mountain

Stemple ran through the rain to retrieve a chart Everling
had left in Bethany's hospital room. He never understood
why Mountain weather needed to mimic the outside world
since everyone knew they were faux weather simulations. He
grabbed a deflector, pulling the covering over his shoulders
and raising the hood as he traipsed through the lobby and
out into the street.

Stemple jerked at a flash of lightning and rumble of thunder. He slogged across the wet road, avoiding the tiny streams
running down both sides, where the water diverted to the
irrigation system for the farming section.

The hospital door slid open and Stemple shook himself
from the covering. He felt a surge of excitement at getting an
opportunity to look at Bethany close up. He'd found a serum
plan about an hour ago that led him to believe Everling was

conducting experiments on her. Why would the man risk his wife? Had he gone rogue? What result was he expecting?

Stemple approached the door to Bethany's room. He stopped, took a deep breath, and pushed the door pad. The door slid out of the way with a slight whoosh. Stemple stepped inside, turned to the left, and froze.

Bethany's bed was empty. The covers were pulled back, disheveled. The machinery keeping her alive was turned off. Stemple glanced around the room. Where was she? Everling hadn't mentioned her being moved. If she had succumbed, he surely would know by now.

Stemple spotted the chart. He grabbed it up as though it would protect him from Everling when he asked about Bethany. Maybe they'd taken her for some kind of testing. He faded into thoughts of what had happened and didn't hear the door open behind him. A hand came to rest on his shoulder.

Stemple jumped at the touch, spun around, and backed into the bed. His mouth fell open as the chart clattered from his hand.

"How are you, Mr. Tall, Dark, and Handsome? You look like you've seen a ghost."

Stemple's chest constricted tightly enough to cut off his air. This couldn't be possible. He was looking at a very animated and awake Bethany Everling. His mouth opened. What came out resembled babbling more than English.

"Mrs. Everling, er, uh, Bethany. When did you wake up? *How* did you wake up?" Stemple took in her appearance. She looked ten years younger than she had mere hours ago. Maybe it was a trick of the lighting or he hadn't looked close enough when he was here this morning.

"It's simply astounding, isn't it?" a male voice said. "I'm sorry I sent you over here, but I couldn't resist seeing the surprise on your face."

Stemple swung around. Everling stood in the doorway, grinning.

Bethany waltzed to Everling's side and gave him a peck on the cheek. "Hello, my darling."

"Surprise? A Birth Remembrance party is a surprise. This is . . ." Stemple couldn't think of appropriate words.

Everling nodded. "You could say this is a party of sorts. We're getting younger by the hour."

"I-I don't understand. How is this possible?" Stemple bent and picked up the chart. There were no cancer cures that could promote this kind of cell regeneration.

Everling closed the doorway and strolled to Stemple. He slapped him on the back. "I did it, my boy. I broke the code."

"The code for what?" Stemple could only think of her cancer. It wouldn't explain the age regression. All this time he'd thought he was Everling's confidant. Their work together had never touched anything so far-reaching.

"Longevity. I've discovered the fountain of youth using Lander DNA," Everling said. He gently cupped a hand under Bethany's chin and turned her face side to side. "Isn't she lovely?"

"You're also looking quite well, my dear." Bethany gazed into Everling's eyes.

Stemple searched Everling's face. Wrinkles and signs of aging were gone. His hair had started filling in the thin spots. The skin had tightened like that of a man ten years his junior.

"How did you do this? Our experiments never progressed

this far. In fact, none of our work was even directed—" Stemple cut himself off as the thought took hold. Treva was right after all. She'd called this and he'd ignored her talk as foolishness.

Everling nodded. "True, but I was doing experiments of my own. I didn't want any deliberations on whether I should be using myself as a test sample for the injections."

Stemple jerked up straight. "We need controlled studies of long-term effects you've obviously ignored. Experimenting on yourself . . . have you lost your mind?"

Everling narrowed his eyes and set his jaw. "I'm going to forget you said that to me."

Stemple refused to remain silent. Fear emboldened him. "This is absurd. You don't know what might happen. There could be cell collapse, organ failure, or a hundred other maladies."

"I can see the results on my wife and myself. They get better by the hour."

"What? It's continuing? Are you still taking the drugs?" Stemple started to pace.

Everling cast his eyes downward. "No . . . I stopped both of our injections when Bethany awoke."

Stemple glanced at Bethany. He would have to temper his questions now that Everling's wife was back in the picture. She had always presented herself as a friendly woman when she wanted something, but an authoritarian taskmaster as a boss, and she didn't like having her judgment or her husband's questioned.

"Was there a control on this to stop or slow the process when you reached a certain stage?" Stemple said, treading lightly with the questions.

"At the time that wasn't my goal. I just wanted to stop Bethany's cancer."

"Has it stopped the cancer?"

"I took needle biopsies. The tumors are shrinking." Everling looked hopeful.

Stemple ran a hand through his hair. "We need to start monitoring this. Do you have anything to slow or stop the process?"

"That was not my immediate objective. I was going to tell you we'd start the next phase forthwith. But as it stands now, I've achieved my goal." Everling wrapped an arm around Bethany's waist and pulled her close to nuzzle her neck.

"How do I get access to the samples?" Stemple asked. "The damage could be fatal."

"There will be plenty of time. Right now I want you to start dismantling the Lander project. I no longer need test subjects," Everling said without looking away from his wife.

"Dismantle the project? Doctor . . . this has been going on for years. Why would you shut it down?"

"I've gotten everything I need. And getting rid of them will give the Board one less thing to harp on about going forward."

Stemple watched his reaction closely. "You couldn't care less about what the Board thinks. What's the real motivation here?"

Everling looked at the floor again. His jaw clenched.

Bethany motioned with her thumb and forefinger. "We're this close to discovering immortality. Maybe he used the wrong word saying *dismantle*. Let's say we're revamping the program to the next phase."

"Are you still getting rid of the Landers?" Stemple asked.

"Yes," Everling said.

Stemple got the feeling this wasn't Everling's idea.

Bethany held up a hand. "I'd like to do one more set of experiments on the test set we have now. But we need to get the gene-splicing started right away."

Everling turned to Bethany. "I've sent a team to retrieve the child."

"The Lander child? I never asked how you obtained the information." Stemple gritted his teeth. Using children for experiments . . . This was not what he had signed on to do.

"I know where Glade Rishon's family has lived all these years. Leaving them alone was the condition of his cooperation. Now it's time to break the deal. I need his child. He would never cooperate if he knew I was bringing her here, so he needs to go," Everling said.

"What do you want us to do with Glade and the rest of the prime project? Let them go?"

Bethany spun around to face Stemple. "Are you crazy? You can't release those . . . subjects into the world. They're dangerous. It could come back to haunt us. They're a violent sort, if you remember the riots a decade before the drug therapy began. Destroy them."

Everling turned away from the conversation with his head down.

"Excuse me, Doctor. I don't think I understand what you're saying," Stemple said, numb with shock. He refused to address Bethany on something this important.

Everling's shoulders squared and he turned back. "The Landers are no longer useful. I want them all destroyed. They're my property."

"They are not your property! These are living, breathing people." Stemple's voice rose even though he was trying to control himself. He couldn't be a party to murder. Already his mind had shifted to possible scenarios for getting the people to safety.

Everling peered over the edge of his glasses. "When did you turn into such a bleeding heart?"

"What's a bleeding heart?"

Everling raised a hand in a dismissive gesture. "Just a phrase from before you were born. But anyhow, this is business. Their destruction is an acceptable loss."

"How do you possibly think you could spin people's lives into a business loss?"

When had Everling become so indifferent to killing?

"We have everything a society could want. We've eliminated poverty, most disease, war, famine, and every other imaginable friction to everyday living. Only lack of longevity remains as a deterrent to happiness, and now we've solved it," Bethany said.

Stemple stared at her. He knew continued questions would put him in dangerous territory with her, but he had to understand. "You used Lander DNA to create this longevity. Why do you need to involve their children now?"

He could see trouble coming.

Bethany's eyes narrowed and her lips pinched before she spoke. "I—we—don't owe you an explanation since you are merely an employee, but since you have been loyal to this point, I will humor your curiosity. The gene-splice to create longevity did not require a progression to make it work. It was just a code insertion. Where we want to go now requires a step from our DNA to theirs. A child who is a product of them and us carries that progression."

&

Charles Ganston III sat behind the antique oak desk, rubbing his finger in the groove worn smooth in the weathered surface near his right hand. Generations of Ganston men had spent their time pondering at this same spot.

He stared at the large expanse of halo-screen on the far wall displaying an image of the outside with sunshine and trees, and he imagined the fresh air. Not this recycled air inside the Mountain, scrubbed and infused with psychologically calming compounds. There was just enough substance to keep the populace from going stir-crazy but not enough to affect performance. Over the years the drugs had become a normal part of Mountain reality.

Ganston, while in his forties, had discovered what effect the drugs had on the people's DNA—high mortality of newborns . . . now accepted as a fact of life.

The Mountain's dirty little secret.

Neither the life of relative ease, the lack of poverty and adversity, or the absence of disease could coerce a growing faction of the younger generations to remain inside. They wanted out of the Mountain.

His intercom sounded. He waved a hand across the panel. "Yes."

"They're ready in the conference room," his assistant Jax said.

Ganston passed his hand over the link. He practiced patience and plodding in his plan, so as to miss no details. The

3-D machinery was procured to erect the buildings. Food and animal herds were sequestered. And he even added his own element of insurance.

He moved through the side door and took a seat at the head of the slate-gray conference table. The polished stone surface lay bare except for the tray in the center containing a clear flask of drinking water and a group of empty glasses. Flanked by his three trusted Politicos, Ganston pushed back the nagging doubt of a major misstep in his personal vendetta against Everling. He planned to rectify it very soon and just hoped no other anomalies cropped up because of it. He felt enough guilt over Bethany Everling's cancer. He pushed aside self-recrimination that he was no better than Everling and thumbed through the day's agenda.

"Sorry, Charles. I was having problems with Everling's lab," Lilith said. The redheaded researcher swiftly took her seat at the other end and slid her long legs under the table.

Ganston ran his finger over his halo-tablet, opening two new data points. "What's the latest intel on that project of his?"

Even though each person at the table remained loyal to his cause, Ganston required them to carry out projects that would put them on the wrong side of the Company if ever exposed, thus assuring their allegiance to him.

Lilith shook her head. "Not much, I'm afraid. He keeps it boxed up tight."

"I expect more from you. I need information that can give us the upper hand in our negotiations. Over the last 150 years the DNA gene pool inside this mountain has degraded to the point where two or three generations down the line, there will be no saving this colony. Everling's job is supposed to be finding a cure. I want to know what detaining these Landers has to do with it!" He slammed a fist on the table and the water in the flask vibrated.

Lilith flinched. "I know he's doing experiments on Landers. But that's not common knowledge, and you have to be part of the project to get inside. I don't have clearance."

Ganston looked around the room. "Does anyone else here find slavery repugnant?"

The participants nodded their heads.

"Then why are we as the Political Council allowing it to take place?"

Byron, the bald man to Ganston's right, raised a finger. "Because it's been going on for years. I remember when it first started eighteen years ago. They said the program was to help rehabilitate these vagrants with their memory loss."

"They disappear, but none have ever been released that I know of," said Hurst, the long-haired man to Ganston's left. "None of the common people in the Mountain even know Landers exist. Everling has kept the populace in the dark all these years. That's the first clue this is wrong."

"Everling labeled them as a danger to the general public," Lilith said.

"Since when did he care about the people outside the mountain? This will be a case in point when we come out openly against Everling's leadership. He is spending millions in bio-coin to maintain a system of slavery." Ganston played his words carefully. He was planning a Council showdown, and it would bolster his plans if more factions expressed discontent and came on board with his plan for the outside colony.

"Has anyone ever seen or interacted with any Landers? Are they as dangerous as he says?" Ganston looked at each person in turn.

They each shook their heads.

"I saw one male subject last year. He was a young guy about twenty or so. He didn't look or act dangerous." Lilith shifted in her chair. "As a matter of fact, I saw him again this year, and he didn't look like any kind of threat then either. But at the time he was sitting in a holding cell, so that could bring about a docile demeanor."

Ganston set his jaw. "You're letting me down! I need specific information that makes Everling look bad."

Hurst chuckled. "Everling is looking pretty good lately."

Ganston slowly turned his head in the man's direction.

He recoiled. "No, I really mean it. Have you seen him? I don't know if he has a woman on the side since his wife took sick, but he's looking refreshed and renewed. If I didn't know better, I'd say he may even be dyeing his hair."

Ganston growled his displeasure and stabbed a finger at his notes.

Lilith sat up straight. "I do know there have been a large number of unexplained missing subjects in the Prison Unit."

He stopped taking notes. "How do you know this if you can't get in there?"

"His logistics filter through my science procurement department when there are changes for food, clothing, bedding, and such. Even the number of synthesized meals has decreased radically. I'd say they're losing subjects at the rate of four or five a day."

"Could he just be starving them?" Ganston rubbed his chin.

"No. There's no profitable reason to starve test subjects. Fit and healthy is always more desirable than weak and sick," Lilith said, leaning back in her chair.

"Could they have been released?"

She shook her head. "There haven't been any authorized transports. Besides, Everling never released a test subject in all the years I've been at the helm of procurement."

"Could there be deaths in the program?" Ganston tapped his chin. This program of Everling's seemed to be taking on a more sinister tone.

"There have been sporadic deaths in the past. I've seen the records. But if this is a rash of deaths, he must have them stacked up in there like cordwood, because there sure haven't been any requisitions to dispose of them," Lilith said with a look of horror.

Ganston leaned back in his chair. "I think I know where I can get some answers."

Bethany stared at the pile of dust on the gurney. She ripped off the filter mask and threw it at the biohazard can. The mask missed the opening and skittered across the floor like an upended turtle. She pursed her lips. Her husband had lost four subjects this week and they were still no closer to solving the instability than six months ago before she became ill.

Stemple and Noah stepped from behind the bio-shield.

"We've done every variation imaginable on those samples, Dr. Bethany—uh, Dr. Everling." Stemple's face went crimson.

Bethany had never noticed Stemple so flustered. She smiled wryly. "Bethany will do."

120

"Excuse me?" Stemple said.

"Just call me Bethany. You can drop the Dr. Everling. There's only one of him," Bethany said as she smiled fondly at her husband.

"Thank you, ma'am—uh, Bethany. I still don't know why the subjects won't hold together." Stemple's expression was filled with panic.

Noah glared at Stemple then turned to Bethany. "Do you, my lovely partner, have anything intelligent to add to this conversation?"

Stemple looked as though he'd been slapped.

Bethany fingered some calculations on her halo-tablet. "Well, part of our accelerated maturing process seems to be triggering the same acceleration of Hayflick. We have the last test group coming online in two days. We've reworked the enzyme sequence to slow down maturation."

Noah smiled. "I'm glad to have you back in the lab. With you helping me, we can solve this."

Conflicting emotions roiled inside her. Bethany was sure she'd known the proper procedures to bring this project to fruition, but Noah had been a hindrance since day one. If he'd listened, she could have secured samples of the child's DNA long ago. She could have been breeding a Mountain of immortals by now and the cancer might never have happened in the first place.

Deplore her husband's inaction or herald his solving her cancer?

☙

Charles Ganston sat facing the virtual window in his office as he waited for his niece. It reminded him of the area outside the Mountain where they were secretly building the community.

The door to the outer office slid into the wall, and Jax hurried into the office. "Mr. Ganston, we've secured five more 3-D tooling machines."

Ganston smiled. With the raw materials they'd squirreled away and the full manpower roster, he could literally build the whole basic town. "We can get everyone into the new town in less than a month," he said.

"Sir, do you think we should push it that close? We don't know if there'll be any structural or geological problems."

Jax was one of the younger generation. He'd started out enthusiastic about the secret project, but as launch time moved closer Ganston noticed the young man's enthusiasm taking a sharp turn. The building blocks of downfalls. Jax might need to be replaced.

"I've done mountains of due diligence, if you don't mind the pun. Everything is on schedule," Ganston said. He tapped his fingers on the desk.

Jax glanced over to the model layout spread across the eight-by-eight-foot table area on the other side of Ganston's office. "You haven't discussed how this is all going to run. I know the finances to support this project are coming from your family inheritance and the group you've put together. Are you going to create an organization to compete with the Company?"

"No one organization should ever be the absolute ruler without people having a say. We can learn from past mistakes and avoid those pitfalls. We will have an elected government. Those specific points will be part of our New World Constitution."

"New World Constitution?" Jax scrolled through the files on his halo-tablet. "I don't seem to have anything about that particular proposal in my notes."

Ganston walked over to the community model. "I was planning on introducing it here." He pointed to the building at the center. "This will be the center of our new government."

Jax frowned as he looked at the model. "What do we need a government for? We don't have one here and everything works fine. When there are problems the Company solves them."

"But the Company will not be a part of our community. The old structure from our history before the Sorrows will be a wonderful pattern if handled correctly." Ganston smiled as he glanced over the model.

Jax moved to stand at his side. "What does 'correctly' look like?"

"Basic points, my boy. To start with we will be isolationists. We will mind our own business and keep everyone out of ours. And no infections!"

"Infections?" Jax asked. "You mean diseases?"

Ganston turned to face him, his hands clasped behind his back. "No, I mean foreigners. Historically they came here and infected our founding generation with ideas and cultures that were counterproductive. They won't be allowed in our new country. Only people born and bred here and their progeny can be citizens."

Jax knitted his brows together. "What happens to the Landers that have come here? As I hear it, many of them suffer from some sort of amnesia and the Company created a program to help rehabilitate them. It must be working because none of them stay in the Mountain."

Ganston frowned. "Landers will—"

The intercom beeped. He moved to his desk and ran his hand over the sensor embedded in the surface next to the halo-screen console. "Yes?" He glanced at his wrist and tapped the clock interface. Perfect timing.

"Your five o'clock appointment is here, sir," the receptionist said.

"Send her in." Ganston smiled as he stood. He pushed a button on the operating panel of his desk, the model lowered, and the cover closed, creating a table-like surface.

"I need to talk to my niece alone," Ganston said to Jax.

Jax nodded. He swiped the sensor and the office door slid open for him to exit.

Treva strolled in. She and Ganston met in the center of the room and hugged.

"Uncle Charles, I haven't seen you in weeks, and what's the first thing I need to do? Separate you and my new boss from coming to blows." Treva cuffed him in the elbow.

Ganston smiled. "The old coot is just lucky you were there to save him."

Treva shook her head and chuckled. "I'm sure you didn't bring me here to trade combat stories. What's going on? I'm in the middle of a rather large project. I've only got about five minutes to spare, but you said it was urgent, so I came."

"I am finally ready to show you my next project," Ganston said. A grin crossed his face.

"So we both have new projects," she said.

Ganston pointed toward the table as he pressed the button to retrieve the model. "I present the city of Stone Braide."

The tabletop parted in the center and the sides folded down

Bonnie S. Calhoun

into the frame. The model rose with the soft whine of a servomotor and locked into place. Treva moved toward the table, and Ganston watched with amusement as she studied the miniature buildings and businesses complete with streets, scenery, and homes.

She turned. "Where'd you get the name Stone Braide?"

Ganston gestured. "Do you see the image on the sandstone-colored building at the center of the model?"

"Yes." She moved closer and bent over to peer at the structure, reaching out to touch the symbol above the front doors of the tiny building. Three pointed ovals were woven together at the center, with a larger circle overlaying the three as though they were intertwined like a braid.

"That's a curious symbol. It has a certain energy to it. Where did you get it?" Treva straightened up and faced Ganston.

"You know my passion for collecting antiques. This is a replica of a large stone image uncovered a few years ago in an area close to the Mountain." He smiled. "Look closely at the model."

"To laser out a town of this size in the Mountain is going to take years," Treva said as she studied the landscape from all angles. "I'm not an engineer, but I see a few things I know they couldn't manage in here."

Ganston put his arm around her shoulder and drew her close. "That's why this town is outside the Mountain."

Treva backed up and sat down next to his desk. "Outside? Are you crazy? Everling will have a stroke. He'll bring you up on charges. You could spend the rest of your life in detention."

Ganston sauntered to his desk and looked at his ComTex.

"He's the least of my worries. I want you to think about coming outside with us. I'm going to give you time to let this sink in, and I'll have my assistant message you a package of data, but you must keep it to yourself."

Treva's eyes widened. "But sending me data is dangerous. It could get intercepted."

"We've got that covered," Ganston said. His intercom beeped. "Send her in." He turned to Treva. "She's right on time."

Again the door slid open and Ganston set his sights on Mojica. Using only one name like the rest of the members in her clan, she stood six feet tall, with an ancient Amazon warrior build of sinewy muscles and flowing black hair that complemented smoky dark eyes and heavy lashes. Make no mistake about it, any man who challenged her position as the head of security found himself on the ground looking up.

Ganston motioned her to a seat, then looked at Treva. "I would like you to meet Mojica. She's head of Mountain security."

Treva looked nervous. She started to rise. "I don't think—"

"Easy, my child. She's on our side. She's leaving the Mountain to be our head of security in Stone Braide," Ganston said with a wink. "Mojica, this is my niece Treva Gilani."

Treva wrung her hands but sat back down.

Mojica held out her hand. "Just call me Mojica. And don't look so scared. I'm not going to arrest you for imprisoning Landers."

Treva's eyes widened. Her face drained of color.

Mojica turned to Ganston. "She's a nervous one, isn't she?"

Ganston leaned over and patted his niece's hand. "We need

to know what information you can give us on the Lander project."

She swallowed hard. "Uncle, that's dangerous business. There are so many ways we could get caught if I told you anything."

Mojica batted her thick lashes. "My elite force is from my own clan and completely loyal to me. There will be no slipups with information."

Treva's ComTex chirped and she looked down at it. "I'm being paged. I'm needed in the lab." She rose to leave.

Ganston stood with her. "One question. Do you know where the test subjects are disappearing to?"

Treva started to walk to the door. She turned, pressed her lips tight, then shook her head. "This is against my better judgment to tell you . . . but they're desiccating."

"What?" Ganston asked. "What does that mean?"

"They're turning to dust. Poof. Gone—and so am I." She ran her hand over the panel button and the door slid open. She hurried out.

Treva strolled into Lab Section Ten and seated herself at the desk opposite the retainer pods, her hands shaking. She remembered what Stemple had said about the gag order. She couldn't jeopardize this job, not when she was so close to putting her plan into action.

She glanced at the plascine wall across from the desk. It looked like an ordinary gray-white wall with five widely spaced doors. To the uninitiated it just led to an assortment of plain storage rooms.

But when the control panel on the desk activated, the wall became a different world. She stared at the buttons. Many of them she never used, but she knew the purpose of each.

On the top row, one green button correlated to each of the five pods and turned the plascine wall of the pod transparent, exposing the interior living area.

The next button controlled the virtual wall. Each pod came equipped with a VW that afforded stimulation from outside scenery. It could be raised into the ceiling for solitary confinement status or lowered to reward compliant behavior.

The next row of black buttons controlled doors. The pale blue buttons were intercoms.

The bottom row of shield-covered buttons terrified Treva. With a bright shade of fire-red, they meant just that. In times of emergency, someone could lift the cover and hit the button, unleashing a firestorm inside the pod. Blowtorch-like jets in the ceiling, walls, and floor would incinerate and sterilize everything in the room.

Treva had heard stories. Her head jerked, probably more of a shiver than anything, but it helped to dismiss the agonizing and horrific thoughts. She pressed the green button for the first pod. The plascine wall changed from solid to translucent then slowly to transparent, allowing her an interior visual.

Glade Rishon seemed to be sitting in the same location each time the room materialized. Treva wondered if he did that on purpose. She'd never thought of looking at the interior camera ahead of time because it felt like she'd be invading his privacy.

She used the code and accessed his chart on her halo-tablet to finish her work.

Glade sat at the table with his back to her, staring at the virtual screen. She knew from past experience he realized the wall behind him had changed, but he refused to play the game by turning to greet the intrusion to his meditations.

Treva opened the intercom. "Hello, Glade. How are you today?"

"The same as I've been for the last eighteen years. That question holds no meaning any longer, and I feel you're humoring me by asking it," Glade said without turning from the screen.

Treva bit her bottom lip. So much for polite conversation. "I didn't mean to insult you. I just—"

"You just what?" Glade slid around to face her. His forty-ish good looks and chiseled features always took her breath away, especially his eyes, green with gold flecks that seemed to increase in number when he smiled.

Right now he wasn't smiling.

Treva averted her eyes, regrouped her thoughts, and looked back at Glade with a broad smile. "I need the required weekly tissue sample, and I have another injection for you."

Glade narrowed his eyes. "Since you came, I've started feeling better, more normal. What are you doing to me?"

Treva's heart ticked a staccato beat. Her eyes searched the lab, looking for others, then she turned back to him. "You must never talk like that again. No one must know."

9

Bodhi tested the shackles. He could feel the metal links give way as he flexed the muscles of his forearms. No need to free himself at the moment. Just knowing he could satisfied the urge. There'd been no opportunity to test his range of skills. He'd experienced increased dexterity with Selah on the beach but didn't know if the physical advantages would last once his mental abilities returned in full force, or even if his mental abilities would return. Mental impressions with others seemed to be getting stronger, but they didn't feel the same as communication skills at home. Here thoughts were deeper, harder to make connections. The only thing he knew for certain—the direction. North. He'd free himself when this pair of boys lost their usefulness.

The strange mix of ancient ways and modern technology amused him. During the travels north by horse and wagon, they had passed four-wheeled machines like he'd seen on the beach. They were distastefully noisy and propelled by an acrid-smelling petroleum product that burned the inside of his nostrils. Fossil fuel use at home was ancient and a bane to the environment.

He'd also viewed top-line hovercrafts zipping over the trees and a low type of craft hovering above the ground. Neither craft trailed a smell so he surmised they used anti-matter or fusion propulsion. It interested him seeing them all mixed together . . . the Elite and Mundane living in harmony.

He came from a world populated by immortals and non-immortals called centorums. While immortals lived forever, barring catastrophic physical harm, a centorum lifespan consisted of one hundred years. The two races didn't mix—actually, interaction was illegal, which was part of the reason he had wound up in this forsaken land.

Among those two races, people were classified as Elite or Mundane depending on their economic status. The girl Selah probably fell among the Mundane. Her people seemed to be those who worked the dirt. He found her cute and she appeared flattered by his attention. She could prove useful.

He didn't know why he could generate communication with her. He'd seen her face clearly and she was not a Lander. He'd sensed her back at the barn and now in the tree line when her brothers set up this camp a few hours ago. Her rhythm was quiet and undisturbed. Probably asleep. He decided to nudge her. A test opportunity. Could he wake her with a few thought jabs?

⚭

Selah tossed and turned. The ocean shattered. *Thump.* The people on shore shattered. *Thump.* Fear. *Thump.* Sound invaded her sleep, soft at first, then a growing intensity pushing away the pleasant dreams of home. Her eyes flew open. Disoriented. Her mind had been enjoying the ocean, now she stared into darkness. Where was she? She looked at the stars through the forest canopy. A sigh escaped her lips. The Company station.

She must have slept at least three hours. Darkness had fallen. She could have been caught. She'd devise a better plan, but right now she needed to get her bearings.

Selah focused on the sounds. Her brothers' voices drifted to her as she tiptoed forward. They had pastured the team and were enjoying a roaring fire. She reminded herself how foolish she'd been. It was pure luck they'd never found her. She crept through the tree line parallel to their camp.

In the glow of the crackling fire she saw Bodhi, still shackled, sitting on the ground propped against a tree. Her hopes soared. She could sneak behind the tree when the boys were asleep and free him with no problem. A perfect plan.

She watched Raza and Cleon eat. They didn't offer Bodhi anything, not even water. Stupid boys! They had never been forward thinkers. If he died before they got to the Mountain, what good would that do?

As though Cleon heard her thoughts, he threw a hunk of bread at Bodhi. "Here, enjoy it. That and a cup of water are all you get of our supplies."

Bodhi stared down at the bread, not attempting to retrieve it.

"You idiot," Raza said. He cuffed Cleon on the side of the head. "His hands are shackled behind him. Do you expect him to pick up the bread with his mouth? Go fix it!"

Cleon looked sheepish. He scrambled around the campfire and retied Bodhi with a tether leashing his hands and feet together. It gave him enough room in a sitting position to reach his hands. He bent forward to chew on the bread.

With his head down, his eyes looked in Selah's direction. They sparkled in the light of the campfire. Selah's breath caught. Once again he knew she was here. This time he smiled. At least he didn't appear angry. She owed him an apology and hoped he'd accept.

She drank in how bronzed he'd become from a full day under the sun. The firelight danced on the golden sheen covering his muscular shoulders. A tingle rolled up her back.

Selah leaned back against the tree. She could do this. The boys would bed down an hour later. She spent the waiting time using her new hearing skill to distinguish sounds of the forest. A hiss. Two opossums rustled the undergrowth over a dead mouse. A raccoon passed, probably on its way to the stream to wash the leaves he carried. Owls hooted and a night bird twittered.

She would watch for fifteen more minutes to be sure they were asleep. Raza began to snore as usual. Cleon never snored but he had a disgusting habit of drooling. Sure enough, ten minutes later the glistening rivulet of liquid began to slide from the corner of his mouth onto the sleeve where his head rested.

Selah snuck her way around to the trees behind Bodhi. Just as she was about to break through her undergrowth covering, she glanced to her right.

Two large green-flecked eyes stared back at her. A scream welled in her lungs and she slapped a hand across her mouth to stop it. Backing up in fear, she toppled over. A small hand put its dirty finger to a pair of lips, motioning her to be quiet.

Selah nodded. She didn't know if this was friend or foe. With no chance of getting away, she decided to comply. The foliage parted, and a thin girl dressed in rags emerged. She pointed toward Bodhi and shook her head.

Selah didn't understand. Did the girl not want her to rescue him? She started through the bushes again. The girl grabbed her by the arm and vigorously shook her head.

Selah backed up and whispered, "What's the problem?"

The girl pointed past Bodhi to the other side of the trees. She leaned over and whispered in Selah's ear, "There are four men camping in those trees. I heard them tell these two they would stand watch half the night if the two boys would look out for bandits the rest of the night. I snuck around them. They're awake and watching."

Selah leaned back against the tree, banging her head a couple times. Another mess up. If she'd been awake when they arrived, she'd have seen the other group. She owed this child a big thanks.

Her spirits sank. She wasn't going to rescue Bodhi here, so she needed to move on to the next station and hope her luck held. She peered through the foliage. She couldn't signal him. His head was down, his eyes closed. Was he sleeping? Silently she wished him peaceful sleep and told him she would try to get him free tomorrow night. She motioned the girl back into the trees and they moved in the opposite direction.

Selah stared at the girl's dirty, disheveled appearance. "I was trying to free my friend," she said as they sorted their way among the trees.

The girl led the way toward the sounds of the stream. "I saw you make eye contact with him, but I wasn't sure you saw the others."

Selah saw the stream come into view, glistening in the moonlight. Suddenly something grabbed her around the neck. A hand thrust across her mouth. She clawed at the fingers and tried to stomp on the feet but the grip on her throat cut off her air. She felt herself becoming lightheaded.

"Be quiet or I'll snap your neck," the gruff voice said.

She could smell tobacco and alcohol. Fear squeezed her chest. It wasn't her brothers. Panic set in and her limbs started to shake.

"What do you want? I don't have any bio-coin," she managed to croak through the grip on her neck. It wasn't a lie. Her leather pouch was hidden in her backpack, on the other side of the Company station.

A snorting exhale fluttered the hair close to her ear. Every time she struggled, the large meaty hand increased the clutch on her windpipe. Stars swirled before her eyes. Selah thought of the horrors that befell Borough girls when they ventured too far away from home at night.

Where was the little girl? It was a stupid thought, but the only thing that felt real at the moment. Had the child run away?

On the verge of tears, she imagined the marauder, grimy and unshaven. *Please stop.* No, this couldn't happen to her, not now. She blinked, trying to hold the drops at bay. Did she see the child behind that tree? Yes. The child motioned her to back up. Selah didn't understand. The girl motioned again.

Selah stepped backward into her assailant, throwing him

off guard. He stumbled another step back, pulling her with him. She heard a rope slip and a tree rustle, followed by a great whooshing sound.

"I want you to be nice to me," came the voice behind the sour breath. "I think we should move to—"

A sickening crunch of flesh and bone. Something rough crossed her back, making her stumble forward and fall to the ground. A short scream and a huge splash. Selah jerked up on her hands and scrambled away.

She wheeled around. A large log swung back and forth on two ropes like a sideways swing. The dirty little girl scurried out from behind the tree and grabbed Selah's hand. "We have to get away in case the others heard him hit the water."

Selah gaped. The current carried the flailing man downstream. The stream on this side of the station joined with another stream to become more of a river. The water had saved her again.

The two girls ran through the rest of the trees, stepped from the soft forest floor to the pressed hardpan of the well-traveled and rutted road, and crossed to the other side. Selah stopped and leaned over, hands on her knees, trying to catch her breath. Her mind conjured visions of what could have happened. Her knees shook. She needed self-defense skills. There would probably be many more lecherous men between here and her father. After she'd skirted the Waterside boys, why hadn't that entered her mind? Now her arms trembled too. *Stop it. Not now.*

Selah hugged the child, who struggled to get away. The embrace helped to stop the tremble in her arms and legs and reminded her of Dane. She thought of him on his own at the age of nine and it scared her to death. What if there was an accident and her family died? Who would help Dane? Could she wish for someone like herself to help her brother?

"You saved me again. How did you do that?" Selah asked with a laugh as she released the squirming child.

The girl made the same funny faces Dane usually made after getting free of her hugs. "It's a tree trap. The older boys made it. Sometimes they get chased by Company soldiers. I can't let them know I tripped it because they get real mad at us kids for messing with their stuff."

Selah looked around. "Are there more of you?"

The girl nodded. "I'm usually by myself but there are others that hang around. Least ten. Sometimes more. Depends on who's passing through. They travel a couple of Boroughs. The neighbor lady calls us miniature marauders. What's that mean?"

"Never mind. You did good today." Selah sat on a downed tree. "Thank you for saving me. Who are you?"

The girl plopped to the ground at her feet. "Amaryllis."

"Amaryllis? That's very pretty. My name is Selah Rishon. What's the rest of your name?" She realized this was the first time she didn't say Chavez.

Amaryllis shrugged. "Don't know. Don't remember."

Selah touched the girl's head and removed a small twig entwined in the snarled mess that used to be called hair. It looked like it hadn't seen a comb in years. She foraged for several other protruding stems. The child reminded her so much of Dane. It must be the traits of their age group. There had always been refuse in his hair after he'd crawled through the underbrush watching rabbits.

"Why don't you remember? Where are your folks?" Selah continued rooting for stems.

The girl sat cross-legged as Selah cleared the roughage from her hair. "Ain't got folks. Momma said Poppa got killed in a wagon tip-over when I was five. I don't remember it. Momma died of the sickness thirty-six moons ago."

"Thirty-six moons?"

"Yeah." Her hand traced an arc. "When the moon comes up full in the sky at night. I been counting the big full ones."

Selah gasped. The girl had been on her own for three years. "Do you know how old you are?"

Amaryllis put a grimy finger with a dirt-encrusted fingernail into her mouth. Selah gagged. She wanted to snatch the girl's finger from between her teeth but feared scaring her. Still, it made her queasy thinking about what was going into the girl's mouth.

"Best I can remember, Momma made a little Birth Remembrance cake." She held her fingers together in the shape of a cupcake. "I was nine, and that was the month before she died."

So she was now twelve years old. It broke Selah's heart that the girl had no parents. She was learning to deal with that feeling herself. "Who do you live with now?"

"Nobody. I live in the woods and in my hidey-hole in the city."

"What city?" Selah didn't remember ever seeing any cities along this road, and she'd come this way many times with her mother.

"The city all broke down in the ground. That way." She pointed off down the road and through the trees to the east.

Selah looked back in the direction of Bodhi and sighed. Her backpack was back there, but there was no going for it now. Better luck tomorrow. She took the child by the hand. For a split second she imagined Dane beside her.

The girl pulled away. Her eyes widened.

"I won't hurt you," Selah said in a soft voice.

Amaryllis shrugged, but the right side of her lips raised in a grin. Just like Dane. She thought about it for a second. "Okay."

They walked down the center of the road with the moon behind them as a companion. The long shadows they cast added to the eeriness and strange sounds. Selah couldn't remember being alone outside this late at night, but she worked at identifying every sound.

An owl screeched from a nearby perch. She heard crashing and rustling as it swooped down and grabbed a tiny squealing prey from the forest floor. Sounded like a mouse, or was it a baby rabbit?

The owl screech must have unnerved Amaryllis. She slipped her hand into Selah's and increased her grip. About a quarter mile down the road, Amaryllis stopped and stared into the forest on their right. She gestured with her free hand.

"You lead," Selah said. She took notes of the twists and turns through the forest in case she ever needed to come back this way. They broke through the trees near the remnants of the forgotten town. In the moonlight it seemed to have been plopped in the middle of the forest. There were no roads, just overgrown vegetation and big trees. Time and travelers passed it by.

The girl skipped ahead, pulling Selah. She would have let

go but she feared losing the child and having her fall in some great chasm where she'd be injured or killed. Dane's escapades came to mind.

"Come, I'll show you where I sleep. It has magic light."

"Magic light?"

"Yes! It's friendly. It always knows when I come. It likes me." The girl slithered out of Selah's grasp and dodged into a pile of rubble behind a huge pine tree.

"Wait!" Selah reached for her but missed. "Don't run ahead. It might not be safe."

She felt her way along the maze of stone pillars and tumbled boulders. Suddenly there was light streaming through the jumble of roots and kudzu vines invading the rubbled cavern. She could see where she was going now. Her heart pounded. What manner of light could be this bright? What had the girl found?

"Amaryllis? Come here, please. Where are you?" Her voice echoed as she maneuvered among the debris. She could tell by the change in her echo that the narrow tunnel opened into a large hollow area.

Selah found Amaryllis standing on a jumbled pile of benches and tables. The child grinned broadly, her arms held wide.

"The light is happy to see me! It gets bright when I come." She twirled around on the flat area of the pile, laughing and giggling.

Selah scrambled into the cavernous room and peered up at the walls. She stared in awe. High above, on a two-foot-high marble slab, were engraved the words "City of Hampton, Public Library."

Buried in the rubble of time, a library had survived the Sorrows. Now she knew the name of the city. Her father rarely knew the original names of the places they passed through unless they found an old sign or met an aged resident of the Borough.

The cavernous room rose about three stories tall. Cobwebs hung from every available beam and pillar. The shimmering curtains of floss reflected the light emitted by the glowing ceiling. Large, leafy kudzu pushed its way through cracks in the ceiling and crept along the surface in a few areas.

Row after row of stacked glass columns marked by engraved plaques covered the perimeter walls. Mother had taught her to read them. The markings were called a Dewey decimal system—a catalog that survived the ages. Selah gazed at the thousands upon thousands of glass crystals representing digital renderings of books. Her years of education had been accomplished with handed-down paper books, but occasionally she'd been graced with the use of these crystals by one of Father's traveling friends.

Amaryllis pulled a slingshot from her pocket and reached down to grab a small rock from the litter on the pile. She took aim at one of the stacks on the wall. "Listen to the music."

"No! Stop!" Selah scrambled to climb the pile but was too late.

The crystal column exploded with a pop and a shower of tinkling shards of glass, creating a lilting melody as it rained down three stories onto a large pile of previously destroyed crystals.

Selah scrambled to the girl's side and snatched the slingshot from her. "What are you doing? Stop it! Those are books you're destroying! No one will ever be able to replace them."

Amaryllis shrank back. Her eyes widened and she began to cry. She crawled down from the pile and threw herself onto the corner of a bench, her head in her hands.

Selah closed her eyes with a sigh. She sometimes yelled at Dane with the same result. Would she ever learn not to scare children? The girl didn't know what she was destroying. She barely knew her own name.

Selah bit her bottom lip and slowly approached. "I'm sorry for yelling."

Amaryllis scrambled from the bench, crawled underneath, and hid her face. "Stay away! You're mean."

"Please come out." Selah softened her voice and lowered to her haunches. "I was trying to stop you before you destroyed more books."

Amaryllis uncovered her eyes and sniffled a few times. "What's a book?" She looked up as tears created clean trails through the dirt on her face.

Selah balked. She'd heard about people who didn't school their children. Her mother said if the parents weren't taught, their children couldn't do much better. Mother named lack of education as the number one reason that society languished and had never recovered from the Sorrows.

"Did your mother teach you any schoolwork?" Selah asked.

The girl softened her cry. Selah needed to gain her trust again—after all, she owed the child a debt. Amaryllis nodded but then shook her head. "Momma taught me some numbers and the alfbit and how to read some words she wrote on a slate, but then she got sick and we didn't do it no more."

"Alphabet. Your mother taught you the alphabet. That's great." Selah smiled. "So you know some words. That's what all of these are." She raised her arm and waved it around the room.

Amaryllis crawled out to the edge of the bench. She looked up at the walls. "I don't see no words, just glass, and it makes a pretty sound when it breaks. It's like music. I come here a lot to make music. I was just trying to show you."

"I understand now. You didn't know." Selah reached out to pat her hand.

Amaryllis flinched and pulled back. She shook her head. "I don't see no words. You must be wrong."

"Let me show you." Selah stood and walked around.

The interior of the building was in adequate shape. Apparently no raiders had ever found it because all of it would have been stripped out for salvage and the power source drained and confiscated. She glanced up at the LED lighting. Somewhere in this building or beneath it there was something nuclear, probably a cold fusion power source with a working motion detector. Selah silently thanked her mother for cramming knowledge into her, even when she fought tooth and nail to resist learning things she was sure she'd never use. Once again Mother was right.

"These aren't just pieces of glass like in a windowpane. They're called quartz data glass." Selah walked to a stack and carefully removed one of the one-inch-square, wafer-thin pieces of clear crystal. She held it up to the light between her fingers.

"Come see." She motioned Amaryllis over. The girl shook her head and stayed put.

Selah carefully replaced the square in the stack and navigated around various piles of rubble. She glanced at the large heaps of crystal shards. So much knowledge destroyed. She searched for a reader, lifting several chairs and an overturned bench, until she spied a rack pinned beneath a pile.

"Come help me." She attacked the pile, throwing off chairs and pushing aside benches and racks. How did the furnishings wind up in piles like this when the stacks were mostly untouched?

"What are you looking for? There's nothing under there. I've been everywhere here." Amaryllis inched forward. Selah turned to her, but the girl backed away again. Selah continued digging.

"It's something very special." Selah mimicked the girl's interpretation of the automatic lights. "I want to show you more magic."

Amaryllis smiled. "Magic? There's magic in there?" She inched forward again, peering into the space Selah was creating.

"Here, help me with this." Selah took one end of the bench, figuring if she could get the girl engaged, her fears would subside.

Amaryllis gripped the other end of the bench and helped Selah push it aside. Selah strained to reach into the mess. She grabbed a grayish-black metal rectangle about two inches wide and four inches long with a narrow slot across the leading edge. The back side had a molded finish for easier gripping. She brushed off the dust and cobwebs and blew dirt from the slot. Now, if only it worked. She pushed the button indentation and felt the hum in her hand.

She turned to Amaryllis. "Go to that stack and bring me one of those glass chips. Hold it by the edges with your fingers like you saw me do."

Amaryllis scrambled to the wall stacks. She returned, walking slowly as she looked at the piece of glass between her fingers. She grinned and handed it to Selah. "Did I do good this time?"

"Yes, you did very good." Selah loaded the quartz glass into the reader slot, and a beam of light shot from the leading edge of the reader. Selah aimed it toward the closest surface, a tipped-up table covered with 150 years of dust.

The surface came alive with a three-foot-square screen featuring pictures labeled "Life in the Sahara Desert." Selah remembered reading about this place in a country called Africa, but she had never seen pictures. Oasis watering holes with camels, men dressed in colorful robes, fig trees, palm trees, and women picking olives graced the screen.

Amaryllis squealed with delight and clapped her hands. "Are there pretty pictures on all of those? How does that happen?"

Selah chuckled. "Yes, all of those little glass squares have pictures on them. You use a reader like this to see them."

"I'm sorry." Amaryllis lowered her head and her bottom lip trembled.

"Sorry for what?" Selah touched the child's shoulder.

"For destroying so much of it." She looked at the piles of glass near the wall.

"That's all right. You didn't know. Come over here and enjoy these."

Selah laid the reader on the edge of the bench so Amaryllis could watch the screen, then turned and sat on the floor next to the wall. She shouldn't leave this child here alone. It would feel akin to abandoning Dane.

What could she do? Obviously no one had offered to take the girl. Selah chastised herself. She didn't have time or knowledge of the area to find a home for a stray child.

Maybe Amaryllis would solve the problem and run away while Selah slept. She had survived for three years by herself and seemed better equipped than Selah. But on her own, sooner or later she'd be snatched by marauders. Selah didn't want to think about her in their hands.

According to Amaryllis, Raza and Cleon had consented to the second watch. At dawn they'd get back on the road. She needed her backpack and to head for the next station before her brothers.

She pursed her lips. That was her only mission. As for the girl . . .

10

Selah jerked awake. She looked around. *Please let it be a dream.* She cleared the sleep from her eyes and focused. No dream. She was still in the library, among a pit of data glass rubble. With a heavy sigh, she dropped her head back to her arm and closed her eyes.

A feeling of warmth registered against her side. Maybe she'd attracted an animal in the night. Scared to move again, she opened one eye. Relief. In her fog, she'd forgotten about the girl. Amaryllis slept curled up against her.

She peered around again. The lights had turned off. She glanced up at the ceiling. A tiny shaft of light peeked in near the place where she'd spotted the kudzu. It wasn't a large area but she could see daylight through the slit.

Selah sat up and stretched. Amaryllis awoke.

"I have to leave today, and—"

"No! Don't leave." Amaryllis grabbed her hand and squeezed it. Selah could feel the tremble in the girl's arms.

Selah shook her head. "I'm sorry. I have to go. You saw my friend last night. Those bad men are going to do something evil to him if I don't get him free." Strange twist of events, identifying Bodhi as her friend and her brothers as bad.

Amaryllis started to weep. "I like you. I'm lonely. You made me feel safe."

Selah's heart softened. She'd been lucky to have loving parents and even brothers. It was still up in the air how loving the brothers were, but they were hers. She had never been alone in her entire life until now, and she didn't like it very much. Knowing how a twelve-year-old child must feel, she squeezed her eyes shut. All she could see was Dane standing there on the verge of tears. There was no way to avoid this.

She patted Amaryllis on the head, removing another twig. How many things were hiding in this girl's head? She grimaced. Sidetracked again.

Selah took a deep breath. "Would you like to come with me?" The child had saved her grief twice. She couldn't bring herself to just abandon her for the kindness.

Amaryllis stopped in mid-cry. "Come with you? Where?"

"I don't know where. I'm heading north. I doubt if I'll ever come back this way."

"Never?"

Selah shook her head. "No. I can't come back."

"Can I stay with you forever and ever?"

Selah chuckled. "Well, for however long forever and ever is." The words caught in her throat. She'd never dreamed of a time she would have to leave her own mother or go out on her own.

"But what about this?" Amaryllis motioned to the room.

Selah pursed her lips. "We'll always know where it is, and since I know the power in the reader will outlive us, I think we should gather a library of chips in case we need them."

She almost choked on the words. Who was this person that had taken over her body? She was consciously thinking of something to entertain the child—what was the world coming to? This was probably the least important thing on her mind right now. But she was sounding more like her mother by the minute. Well, more like a big sister. She had always wanted a sister. Mother had laughed after Dane was born and told Selah he was her last chance for a sibling. She sighed, missing Dane.

Selah searched for one-inch carrier cubes to fit several dozen data chips apiece. She found several virtual catalogs embedded in the walls, but only one of them powered up. She was limited to searching one section, but she filled half a dozen cubes with enough material to keep Amaryllis busy for quite a while. It felt odd planning ahead when she didn't know if she'd be alive next week. *Hope springs eternal*.

Maybe she could find a good family along the way, or maybe the girl would take off. Either way, she needed to get back on the road and avoid more distractions.

Selah followed as Amaryllis squirmed her way among the roots and vines, twisting through the boulder-strewn cavern. Outside the library, she used the sun for time. Six in the morning. The boys had been on the road for at least an hour.

Selah looked for a landmark so she'd have an idea of where the library was hidden. A landslide had blocked the original road with a new mountain, and a pine tree grew up directly in front of the library opening. Unless someone knew the opening was there, they'd never see it. The building had a domed roof, but covered in kudzu, it looked like a hill of vegetation. She took note of the single tree. That was how she'd find this place again.

Amaryllis slid her hand into Selah's. Another father and a little sister, all in just a few days. What was next?

"Take me to the station. I need my backpack, then we head north," Selah said.

"I've never been north," Amaryllis said. "Is it a nice place to live?"

"I don't know. We'll find out after I save my . . . friend." The word brought a trickle of warmth to Selah's chest. This time she didn't dismiss the thought but embraced it.

"I'm hungry." It looked like a storm cloud was forming over Amaryllis's eyes.

Selah smiled. Dane made that same face when he was hungry. "What do you eat?"

Amaryllis shrugged. "Nuts, berries. I sometimes dig up farmers' potatoes or carrots or raid their other vegetables."

"Do you eat meat?"

"When I can but I'm not a good cooker." The girl scrunched up her mouth like she tasted bad medicine. She grinned. "But I know which birds are good to eat."

Birds? Selah didn't have any birds in her Borough that were food-worthy. Most were carnivores like blue jays, crows, and hawks. "You find the birds and I'll cook them."

Amaryllis pulled Selah by the hand. "There's quail birds by the station."

Selah thought it would be safer if they reached the next station first or even waited until she freed Bodhi. "We need to go north before we hunt."

As they broke from the forest at the same place they'd gone in, Selah noted the felled tree leaning against two others.

"Is that where we're going to save your friend?"

Selah opened her mouth to say yes and realized she had gained a partner. How much trouble could this lead to?

The whine of an engine. She heard it long before Amaryllis and pulled the girl back into the woods.

"What's the matter? Why are we going back?"

Selah put her fingers to her lips. "We've got company coming."

Amaryllis craned her neck. "Who?"

Selah pulled her back again as two Sand Runs passed by. They gunned and revved their engines, lifting a spray of dust that coated the immediate area and caused Amaryllis to cough. Selah covered her nose.

"How did you know they were coming?"

Selah looked down at the sputtering child. "I've got good ears."

When they reached the station at Hampton, Selah retrieved her backpack. She pulled some jerky and fruit from the bag and handed them to Amaryllis.

"You eat these for now, and when we get to the next station, I'll let you do the hunting."

Amaryllis smiled and bit into the pear.

Selah checked her brothers' fire pit, running her hand over the coals. Still slightly warm. The boys must have broken camp a short while ago. She looked at Amaryllis. "We are off to the north."

Amaryllis started for the open road.

"No, not that way. This way." Selah pointed to the open field on the other side of the tree line.

"That's all tall grass. What if there's snakes or animals hiding in there?" Amaryllis asked, wide-eyed.

Selah pressed her lips together to stifle a laugh. "Then your tromping through the tall grass will scare them away."

Amaryllis didn't look like she believed her.

"This is the shortcut to get us to the next station before my brothers."

She still didn't look convinced.

"I'll walk in front of you," Selah offered.

The child smiled and ducked into the field behind her.

Using the sun, Selah guessed it was about an hour before noon. It took an hour longer than she'd anticipated to reach the second station. Amaryllis dawdled like most children, especially after she'd lost her fear of the tall grass. Still, they made good time. She figured the boys were still two or three hours behind. This time she wouldn't be taking any naps.

She checked the station, destroyed a poster announcing the increased bounty, then scoured the area looking for a good vantage point.

"Can I go hunt now?" Amaryllis bounced around on legs that acted more like springs than appendages.

Selah figured she couldn't get in too much trouble if she stayed near the station. She'd call her back if she heard anyone coming. "Sure, go ahead. Maybe you'll get lucky." Selah wasn't sure she could catch anything, but at least it would keep her busy.

⬦

Selah glanced at the sun's movement on the tree shadows. Amaryllis had been gone the better part of an hour. Her heart began to race. *Where'd that girl get to? The boys might be coming soon.* She rose from camp and crossed to the tree line, ducking into the woods.

"Amaryllis!" she shouted. No answer. She traipsed farther in. She could smell moss and moisture. There must be a swamp nearby. She navigated through thick brush and vines as the ground turned spongy.

"Amaryllis, girl, you answer me!" Selah's breathing ramped up. Where was she? If she'd known there was swamp back here she wouldn't have let Amaryllis go alone.

Still no answer. Selah stopped to listen. Nothing.

Her steps quickened, but was she going in the right direction? She checked bushes for signs of disturbance and watched for footprints in the soft forest floor.

She stopped and screamed at the top of her lungs. At this point she didn't care who heard her. "Amaryllis!"

A faint sound. Not a forest sound. She scanned the trees and spaces between them.

"Amaryllis!"

Another sound. This time it was closer. Muffled. High-pitched.

Selah ran in the direction of the sound. It stopped. She yelled again.

The same sound. Selah sprinted through the trees, calling

the girl's name. She almost ran past it, but skidded to a stop and screamed.

The boxes on the skin were unmistakable. A Burmese python had coiled itself around Amaryllis. There was blood everywhere.

Selah jumped on the snake, pounding it with her fists. One of the girl's arms was free and thrashing about, digging at the snake, but it didn't seem to affect the python.

The snake's head hovered at the girl's feet and the tail coiled around her head. Selah pried the tail off to find Amaryllis's eyes wide with terror. Her face trembled as her mouth opened and closed, trying to gasp air. The python covered her whole body, preventing her from breathing. Her lips were turning blue.

The snake's head bit down on Selah's boot. She jumped and nearly tumbled over backward. Leaning in on the coiled snake, she stomped on the snake's head again and again with her other foot.

Amaryllis's eyes rolled back and her arm fell limp.

Tears pooled in Selah's eyes, blurring her vision. Her heart pounded her ribs. "Amaryllis, hang on!" she screamed.

The snake released Selah's boot but went back to wrapping around the girl. Selah got another coil of the tail off Amaryllis, exposing her neck, but the tail swung back around as fast as she removed it.

She dug in the side pocket of her pants for a throwing knife. With both hands, she plunged it repeatedly into the tail, stabbing and slashing until numerous wounds dripped blood. The coil flopped away.

Selah grabbed another length and forced it to unwind.

The head rose to attack her and she stabbed her knife into its right eye. The snake thrashed about and bit into her hand. Pain radiated up her arm but now she had a good opening. She stabbed the snake in the other eye.

The snake let go of her and the coils loosened as it tried to get away.

Selah, emboldened by her rage, threw herself on top of the fleeing snake and slashed it until entrails oozed from the gaping gash.

Suddenly she regained her focus and scrambled from the writhing snake to Amaryllis.

The girl lay silent and still. Selah grabbed her up in her arms. "Amaryllis, please open your eyes." She cradled the girl's head in her arms and wailed. The girl's head flopped from side to side as she shook her. Selah put her ear to her chest. Nothing. No heartbeat. No breath.

"Mother, help me!" she screamed. "What do I do?"

She rocked on her knees as she knelt in front of the pale, lifeless body covered in blood. She heard her mother's voice in her head. *Pound.*

She'd seen it done before. She clasped her hands together and brought them down on the girl's chest. "Breathe!"

Nothing.

She raised her hands again, tears streaming down her face. "Amaryllis! Breathe!" She thumped her clenched hands onto the girl's chest again. Amaryllis's torso jerked up as her mouth opened in a gasp and then another. Her arms flailed as she coughed.

Selah grabbed her and continued to cry, this time for joy. She did it! Amaryllis opened her eyes and whimpered as she clutched at Selah's arms. The color slowly poured back into her face.

"Girl, don't you ever scare me like that again." Selah tried to smile through the tears but her trembling arms were giving her away. She hadn't failed. The boys were wrong. She wasn't useless or a child anymore.

Amaryllis smiled weakly. "You saved me."

Selah managed to carry Amaryllis back to camp. The girl lay weak and disoriented. As Selah washed off the blood she discovered several puncture wounds in the child's foot and hands.

Amaryllis managed to tell her the snake had surprised her while she lay in wait to shoot a quail rooting in the under-brush. Once the snake bit down on her foot, Amaryllis tried to pry its mouth open. Her hands earned puncture wounds from the sharp teeth. The snake was faster at winding than Amaryllis was at getting away. Then Selah arrived.

Selah figured the snake had been stalking the same bird. That was the last time Amaryllis would hunt alone. She wondered if Mother ever thought about Dane falling into this kind of trouble. She'd never mentioned it. Suddenly Selah wanted to go home and warn her.

With her wounds cleaned and bandaged, Amaryllis snuggled down next to Selah to sleep. Feeling the girl's breathing against her chest gave Selah a feeling of peace that she didn't quite understand. Was it about the girl or herself?

She'd expended a lot of energy and craved rest, but she was determined not to fall asleep again. As she thought through the events and what she needed to accomplish, she heard the familiar sound of a wagon approaching the station.

She scrambled to the lookout point and peered through the trees. The first person she spotted was Bodhi. Her heart fluttered. He looked sound and no worse for the travel. In fact, he looked remarkably bronzed and fit, as though he'd spent the day exercising and playing in the sun.

On the other hand, her brothers looked like they'd ridden hard. Both boys were sweaty and their clothes dusty. Selah wrinkled her nose. She could smell their sweat. They both needed a bath and a change of clothes, which wouldn't happen anytime soon. She wondered if it was possible to smell them before she heard them coming. A giggle escaped her lips but their camp was far enough away to be safe.

Bodhi raised his head. She gasped. That same response had happened several times now. She was sure he could hear her. Dare she test it?

"Can you hear me?" She spoke in almost a whisper.

He nodded. Her eyes widened. It had to be a fluke.

"Do you know who I am?"

He nodded again. Her mouth opened in surprise.

"Are you hurt?"

He shook his head.

"What are you shaking your head about?" Raza hopped up in the back of the wagon and grabbed Bodhi by the shackles, dragging him out of the wagon by his feet.

Bodhi didn't answer, but was able to keep his torso in an upright position as Raza dragged him to the end of the wagon bed.

Cleon hopped in the wagon behind him and pushed him to the ground. Bodhi landed on his feet. Selah wanted to pummel those boys for the way they were treating him, but she admitted her behavior might have been as bad several months ago. She wondered about others she'd helped send to their doom. Would she be called to answer for it someday?

Too many questions and not enough answers.

Selah lay in wait and watched them unload supplies and build a campfire. She feared talking to Bodhi and agitating her brothers. She was so close to putting her plan in motion. Better leave well enough alone and not create problems.

She watched Bodhi as he ate. She watched him when he closed his eyes. She could have closed her own eyes and still seen him. She memorized his eyes, those long lashes, his hair, and the way he breathed. She shook her head to dismiss the thoughts. Not part of the plan.

Amaryllis stirred. A soft moan escaped her lips.

Bodhi looked in her direction, concern etched on his face.

"It's all right," Selah whispered.

He put his head back down, and she scrambled away from the lookout to tend Amaryllis, who was sitting up rubbing her chest. Selah hugged her. The girl moaned again.

Selah released her. "Are you okay?"

The girl grimaced. "My ribs hurt. That stupid snake tried to squeeze the life out of me."

Now it was Selah's turn to make a face. Part of the pain was probably from her pounding on the poor girl, but she wasn't going to bring that up. Let the snake take the credit.

"My brothers have set up camp, and my friend is still with them. I'm going to get him free as soon as they go to sleep."

Amaryllis stuck out her chin. "Those boys are your brothers? Why don't you just tell them to let your friend go?"

"It doesn't work that way. I'll explain it to you someday."

"But they're your brothers. Don't they love you?"

"Of course they do . . . sorta. Well, it's a long story. I promise to tell you but not now. We need to get ready." There were so many things she wanted to wait to talk about. Maybe waiting would make the hurts not so fresh, and she'd have more logical answers. And maybe she just wasn't ready to talk or think about them.

Twice Selah nodded off but fierce determination overrode the chronic need for sleep. The blue sky had dissolved into blackness, exposing the stars. The boys had bedded down. The closer Bodhi's freedom came, the more her heart pounded. She felt the same high from running.

Energy surged through her body, filling her chest with thunder. She caught herself rubbing her scar.

The fire crackled and danced, sending off tiny embers that floated on the air currents like fireflies. She watched her brothers' faces in the shadow of the flames. Both had fallen into their regular pattern of sleep. It was time.

Selah pulled the single key from her pocket and held it tightly in trembling fingers. She crept forward. The roaring fire burned through a knot in a piece of wood and flames popped.

She flinched as a trail of embers exploded from the spot and floated away. One landed on Cleon, who slept too close to the fire. She gasped. *Please don't let it set his cover on fire.* The ember winked out.

Selah didn't realize she was holding her breath until she

exhaled. She continued the slow move forward. Reaching the last tree, she paused. She was about to step into the open. Were the boys really asleep? Or were they lying in wait? She had no choice, it was now or never.

She put her foot forward. An owl screeched. She froze.

11

Selah's heart pounded against her ribs. A rabbit screamed as the owl claimed its prey. Now that every nerve stood on edge, Selah got a burst of adrenaline, and it might carry her through this operation without her hands shaking.

She set her sights on the tree and concentrated on stepping lightly. As she approached, Bodhi raised his head. At least she wouldn't startle him.

Selah crept up behind the tree and pressed her back into the bark. The boys were still asleep. They normally slept like the dead, and she hoped tonight was no exception. Lowering herself to the ground, she reached to unlock the shackle holding Bodhi to the tree.

He looked around the tree at her and smiled. The muscles in his shoulders flexed as his hands closed into tight fists and turned outward. The center link in the shackles stretched as he pulled, until the shackles separated and the chains fell away.

Selah gasped, furrowing her brow. Why was she trying to

save him when he could do it himself? She tossed the key to the dirt.

Bodhi quietly pulled apart the loops holding his ankles and gathered the open ends in his hand. He laid the shackles gently on the ground. Selah motioned him to follow. They tiptoed away and disappeared into the trees.

She led him back to Amaryllis. Happy to see the child where she'd left her, Selah beamed. Not too bad for her first plan. She'd feared she'd get Bodhi's part of the action completed only to find Amaryllis dead or dragged off by marauders.

He looked down at the girl and knelt. "She's hurt."

"A python attacked her this afternoon," Selah said. She waited for him to chastise her like her parents would for letting Dane get injured. Apparently he didn't care.

"Can she travel?" he asked. He stood and looked around the woods.

She bristled with annoyance. He could have at least asked about the girl's condition. "Yes, but she can't travel fast. We need to get away from here before the boys call in Mountain security to help find you. And another thing! If you could break the chains, why didn't you get away before I had to spend all that time trying to get you free?" she asked, hands on her hips.

"I was letting them carry me north since I don't know the landscape," Bodhi said. "Why'd you want to free me anyway? You wanted me as a prisoner too. But I'm having impressions of you and they don't seem to make sense."

Selah raised a hand. "We'll have time for that later. We need to move." She had wanted to claim her rightful catch, but now, since she could never go back to prove her prowess to Father—well, her stepfather—the catching part had lost its appeal. Rather than needing this man to appease her stepfather, she needed him to find her real father.

"I'll go away. You'll be safe."

"No!" Selah panicked. "No, I won't. I need your help."

He stared at her. "Is this a trick? I noticed you don't have any means of confining me."

"Trust me. Please. This is no trick. We have to be far away by the time the boys wake up. Then I'll have time to explain this very long story." Selah scrambled to snatch up the few items laid out around Amaryllis. She stuffed them in the backpack, handed it to Bodhi, and helped Amaryllis struggle to her feet.

The girl's legs wobbled like those of the new colts Selah used to watch at home. She put an arm under Amaryllis to give her support.

Bodhi looked at the backpack in his hand and shoved it back at Selah.

Selah huffed as she struggled to hold the bag and the girl. "Well, I at least thought you would help since I set you free."

Bodhi glared at her, reached down, and scooped Amaryllis up in his arms. Both girls gasped.

Bodhi tipped his head. "Where can't they follow?"

Selah thought a minute then pursed her lips. "It's not the direction I wanted to go, but we'll be safe until Amaryllis heals."

⚜

Bodhi carried the child with no effort, even for the fast pace Selah wanted to travel. She seemed rather agile, and he liked watching her movements. But he didn't like her leading him back to the south. Why should he trust her? He decided to play along since she didn't seem strong enough to present a threat. Although it could probably get him in more trouble. Her seeming innocence had gotten him in this trouble in the first place.

He'd heard Selah telling her brothers he was her catch. He bristled. He was an Elite and an immortal, but he wasn't anyone's *catch*.

He'd shaken off the lethargy of the voyage but still operated at a loss. Normally, when he threw open thoughts, it brought a flurry of responses or walls where thoughts were blocked. But there were zero responses, and the two times he'd felt any mental kickback had been first from Selah's father and second from Selah herself. But neither of them were Landers. Very strange place indeed. He tired of trying to make contact with others.

Bodhi figured the more interaction with these Mundanes, the more information he'd glean on what kind of world nonimmortals could throw and receive thoughts in. It might be advantageous to stay with this girl for a while.

He looked to the sky. "Why are we going south? I need to go north."

Selah walked along the edge of the woods. "Amaryllis is hurt. She needs time to heal before I can force her into a long trek. Your needs are not important right now, and neither are mine."

He glanced down at the child in his arms. She was seriously injured—he could feel her broken aura seeping into his arms. He wondered if a banflux would work here. He stopped.

Selah was walking a few yards away but turned and hurried back. "What are you doing? We need to keep moving. My brothers could come anytime."

"Your brothers were interested in bio-coin for the animals in crates. They will continue north."

"Animals? What animals? Their main business was turning you in for the bounty."

"Rabbits. Vicious ones at that." Bodhi had never seen animals so deadly. Some of the rabbits had fangs an inch long.

Selah squinted in the sunlight. "You're lying. Neither of them would have anything to do with rabbits. They won't even come near them when I'm cooking them."

"No reason to lie," Bodhi said. He hadn't heard any other details and he didn't care if she believed him or not. This relationship would be short-lived. He'd probably run across a half dozen others like her on his quest to find answers.

"Let's move, mister," Selah said. "We still have a ways to go, and we're burning daylight."

Her way of talking amused him. She sounded bossy, but he could feel her frightened thoughts. He'd never noticed centorums to be such a contradiction. But then he'd never had the ability to read their thoughts either.

"I need to concentrate," he said. He pressed his arms tightly to his sides.

Selah stared at him, hands on hips. "I said we—"

Bodhi's arms began to shimmer like a heat illusion. He watched as the shimmer slid down his arms and engulfed the child sleeping in his arms. Yes, this could work.

"What are you doing to her?" Selah charged him. As she touched the shimmer, it threw her back. She stumbled but regained her footing and stared, wide-eyed. "Bodhi, answer me. Please don't hurt her. She's only a child."

No answer. Her hand went to her mouth and she started sobbing. "Bodhi, let her go!" she screamed.

Broken bones. Bruised organs. A small internal laceration from constriction. None life-threatening. Bodhi expended the energy to knit the healings. The glow faded. He pulled in a long breath of air.

"She'll heal faster now," he said. He wasn't turning into one of those do-gooders like at home. He just did this to advance his own cause. He figured the sooner he could get them moving in the direction he wanted to go, the better off he'd be.

Selah pulled back and waved her hand in a circle. "What was that? We need to talk about . . . whatever that was . . ."

"She needs time to absorb sullage." Bodhi looked at the child. Her breathing had leveled from short, halting pulls of air. She slept quietly in his arms.

"I've never heard of you people doing all this strange stuff." Selah paced, running her hand over the top of her head.

"Stop calling us 'you people.' It sounds rude. Besides, it was just low-level healing. Among us there are different sets of abilities."

Selah rolled her eyes. "Oh, is that all. What other abilities—" Her head perked up. "I hear a wagon coming."

Bodhi glanced at her sharply. "I heard it, but how did you?"

"That's another one of those conversations for later." She led them down the slope and onto the road.

"Why are we on the road? Could it be your brothers?" Bodhi asked. He looked up the road to the north. The wagon would be here in a minute.

Selah stopped. "You said my brothers were continuing north. Have you changed your mind about that bit of information?"

Bodhi lowered his head. "I'm not used to people questioning me. I thought we were traveling near the forest edge to use it for cover. Now you hear a wagon and you're on the road. I'm trying to understand."

"The wagon sounds heavy and the horses' gait is too long to be my brothers'. And it's going in our direction. We could use the ride. I'm tired of walking."

Bodhi watched her. After a couple hours of walking with her, he'd grown accustomed to her voice. The tone was pleasant, even when she was angry. And her posturing, all fire and ice, made her desirable. But he needed to back off those feelings. This could be a test. Did he want to toe the mark to get home, or act on his feelings?

He and Selah turned toward the sound. A pair of draft horses trotted around the bend, pulling a wagon with two large wine casks strapped in the back.

Cleon flopped onto his back, yawned, and rubbed the sleep from his eyes as the sun pushed over the horizon. He rolled to face the tree.

Bolting upright, he searched to his left and right. He just knew somehow this was going to be his fault. "Raza! Where's the Lander?"

Raza mumbled something indistinguishable and pulled his covering over his head.

"Get up!" Cleon gave Raza a kick in the leg and scrambled to his feet.

Raza jerked awake, flailing to escape his blanket. He scrambled to the tree and searched the underbrush. Curses filled the air.

"I told you to check him one last time before we went to sleep. This is your fault." Raza glared at Cleon.

Cleon yawned again, stretching his limbs to wake up. Good. He felt sorry for the guy. He had been heroic in saving their sister, and they'd rewarded him by capturing him. "I did check him again when you fell asleep. He couldn't have gotten away. Did he just pull himself and the chain around behind the tree?"

Raza held up the two ends of the shackles. "Does this look like there's anyone on the other end?"

"No, I guess not. What happened?"

"I don't—" Raza spewed out another curse and bent to the ground. His face turned crimson. He lifted his head and screamed, "Selah, I'm going to kill you!"

Cleon's eyes widened. He stared at his brother. "Why are you blaming Selah?"

"Because of this." Raza held up a key to the shackles. "This key should be in the barn at home." He pulled the other key from his pocket. "Here's our key."

Cleon shuffled to Raza and lifted the shackles. "They weren't unlocked. The link is broken." He glanced at the ankle pair lying on the ground and pointed. "So are those."

Raza bared his teeth. "I don't care what deception they've made up. This is still the other key from the barn. Selah was here!"

Cleon grimaced. "Maybe she's madder than we thought about us taking her catch. I told you we should've let her come along."

"She's a girl, not a hunter, and I don't care if she did turn eighteen two days ago."

Cleon slapped his forehead. "I forgot to say anything to her. She's going to be awful mad by the time we get home."

"She didn't go home." Raza paced. Cleon could tell his teeth were grinding because his ears were twitching.

Cleon stood and stretched once again. "So you really think she stole the Lander to claim him as a prisoner herself?"

Raza ran his hand through his hair. "I don't know what she did. But that would be her smart choice."

"Am I missing something? What are you talking about?"

"Nothing." Raza dropped the shackles back to the ground and kicked them.

"What's wrong with you?"

"I'm sick of everything about Selah. At least I'll get the bio-coin."

"Did something hit you on the head while you were asleep? What does bio-coin have to do with Selah?"

"I know Father let me take this assignment for extra bio-coin to keep me quiet." Raza motioned to the crates in the wagon. "He knew he was wrong. I'm the oldest. I'm his first son. It should be about me, not about her."

"What about her?" Cleon swiped up the blankets and loaded his belongings into the wagon.

"It's always about Selah. That's why we were following her the days before her Birth Remembrance. Father wanted to know everything she did."

Cleon averted his eyes. "Do you know why?"

Raza dragged the shackles to the wagon.

"Raza? You didn't answer me." Cleon wondered why Raza didn't know. Strange. After all, he was the firstborn.

"No more talking. Get the stuff in the wagon so we can leave. I want to beat her to the Mountain. She doesn't have a wagon, so we should be able to catch up. I want the Lander back."

"What if she doesn't go to the Mountain?"

"Well, we're still going to the Mountain. I need to deliver those rabbits."

"I saw empty crates the last three times you came back from the Mountain with Father. What are you up to? We don't eat—"

"It's none of your business. Father let me make the deal and I'm getting good money, so I'm not giving it up."

Cleon raised both hands. "I wasn't asking you to give anything up. You're so secretive about stuff. I just thought—"

"You just thought you'd horn in on my bio-coin. Well, that's not going to happen. Find your own income."

Raza threw the shackles into the back of the wagon. They skittered across the plank floor and came to rest against the tarp-covered crates. A low growl filtered out from the covering.

Cleon opened the bin of vegetable matter. "Here, you feed those things. I'm not going near them. Helping carry them was close enough."

Raza curled his lip at his brother and snatched a couple handfuls of field lettuce and wild carrots. "You act like a child. They're just feral rabbits, not wolves."

He flipped back the tarp. The black, white, brown, and rust-red rabbits pressed themselves to the back of the cages.

Raza opened each of the staggered crate tops and dropped in a clump of food.

Rabbits charged forward, baring razor-sharp teeth. The growling intensified as they tore into the vegetables.

Cleon watched with disgust. "Why would anyone pay for these diseased mutations?"

12

Selah relaxed against the wagon's side rail as it rolled along. She appreciated the ride, and the beautiful draft horses were mesmerizing. No one in her Borough owned this kind of horse. She thought Father would be excited to have horses such as these for heavy work. And Dane—well, he would adopt one as a pet right away. She could picture the look on Mother's face at Dane leading one of these great beasts into the house on a leash like he once did with a lamb from the shearing pen.

The wagon hit a bump. Her head bounced off the cross rail, loosening the leather tie on her hair. She winced and rubbed her head as her long hair spilled over her shoulders. She noticed Bodhi watching her.

"What's the smile for?" Selah maneuvered the tie back into place. She was positive he'd lied about her brothers having rabbits, so she knew not to trust him, no matter how sweet the smile. Besides, she'd seen how easily he'd killed those three from Waterside. Now he'd done some kind of hocus-pocus on Amaryllis. She knew girls who fell for bad boys with sweet smiles. But she still needed him to reach her goal.

He cocked his head and smiled. "You look good with your hair down."

Selah furrowed her brow. He looked so innocent complimenting her. Granted, she didn't have a lot of experience with boys, but this one worried her. Weird thoughts plagued her, like someone was speaking in her head.

Amaryllis lifted her head from Selah's shoulder, stared at Bodhi, then glanced at their surroundings. "This is where we get off," she said in a small, tired voice.

Bodhi looked at Selah for confirmation. She shrugged. The path to the library lay farther up the road. No telling where Amaryllis wanted to go.

Selah leaned forward and tugged the sleeve of the wagoner. "Excuse me, sir. You can let us out here."

Speaking softly to his horses, the man pulled back on the reins. He turned in the seat. "You folks sure you want out here? There's not a homestead for miles in these parts."

Selah looked at Amaryllis. The girl gave a weak smile and a nod.

"Yes, sir. We're sure. Thank you for your kindness." Selah helped her from the wagon as Bodhi grabbed their gear.

She figured it was easier to backtrack to the library where Amaryllis lived until she healed. Maybe find someone to leave her with. They stood on the dusty road amid the long shadows as the sun continued its climb to midday. Strange, she felt safe here.

"This way," Amaryllis said. She pointed to the overgrown

area between two aged maples then limped in that direction. Selah marveled. Her condition had dramatically improved in the last few hours.

Selah wondered if the girl might be disoriented by her injuries. This wasn't the direction to the library. "Are you sure you know where you're going?"

Amaryllis turned and gave Selah a sour look. "I lived here all my life. I'm pretty sure I know where my house is." She continued into the tall grassy weeds. A cloud of gnats and pollen rose from the disturbed vegetation.

"I thought we were going to the library," Selah said. She plowed her way through the weeds. Bodhi followed. It had never occurred to her the child actually lived in a home.

"We can stay at my house during the day and go there at night so the magic lights come on." Amaryllis pushed through the tall grass, walking backward to face them.

The hidden library was the safest place. Selah opened her mouth to protest but choked on several swarming gnats. She coughed, spitting them out and gagging in the process.

Bodhi gave her a playful tap on the back. "That'll teach you to walk through bugs with your mouth open. Cough them up."

Selah shot him an evil look. Just as smart-mouthed as her brothers, but easier to look at, so she'd give him a half pass. She was beginning to wonder just how much he knew about being in the wild. He acted like the Borough guys who stayed in town and never got their hands dirty. She glanced at Bodhi's hands. The nails were clean and trimmed, certainly not a farm boy's hands.

Amaryllis snickered and continued her limp into the brush.

Selah finally spotted the path, a lane leading out to the road, but now overgrown and snarled with weeds including the perennial kudzu. On closer inspection, she could make out the roof of a small house in the distance.

Amaryllis hobbled to the dilapidated door and pushed. It gave way at the top while the bottom remained stuck. She threw her shoulder against it, whimpering in pain at the unyielding wood.

Selah reached the door. "This is your house?" Aghast that anyone would live in such awful conditions, she didn't want to offend the child.

Amaryllis nodded. "This is where I lived with Mother before she died."

Selah cringed. "What did your mother die from?" Some illness her mother had taught her about left behind germs that could continue to kill if a person wasn't careful.

"She died from brain fever. She went blind first." The girl's head dropped. "Then she forgot how to move or talk and finally how to eat. She's buried over there." Amaryllis pointed to a spot between the house and a large rickety-looking shed.

Selah felt a measure of relief. She had feared the girl's mother was still in residence and had become varmint food. A few years ago, Mother had taken her along on a visit because a certain Borough woman hadn't been seen in a while. The woman had died in her bed and wild dogs smelled the decay. Selah squeezed her eyes shut. She still remembered the look of the woman's scattered bones, gnawed and stripped of flesh.

Amaryllis tried the door again. This time Bodhi put his shoulder into it and forced it open. The large single space smelled musty. A tattered curtain of bug-eaten holes separated the back quarter, creating a sleeping area. A dusty, torn, and partially unstuffed mattress lay haphazardly across a rusted bed frame. The girl ignored the blight, pushed the mattress straight, and crawled up in the corner against the back wall.

Selah took in her surroundings. Dirt and cobwebs galore. Opening the door had disturbed dust from several surfaces, filling the air with luminescent particles. Loose boards in the plank walls let daylight filter through, and the few remnants of lace curtains didn't do much to keep the bright sun pressing on the grimy windows from spreading into the room.

She saw the signs—of living cut short. Grimy plates on a sideboard shelf, a battered lantern next to dust-laden cups and utensils set on the table, the blackened kettle on a rusted gray metal stove.

Selah looked to Bodhi for some sort of help. "Should we stay here?" She really wanted him to argue, giving a reason to leave without hurting Amaryllis's feelings.

"I think rest, and then something to eat," Bodhi said.

Selah could only interpret the look on his face as disgust. She wasn't feeling much better, but safety ranked higher than comfort.

"There's still some of Mother's canned food in the root cellar. I never liked fruits and vegetables much, so I only ate them when I was starving," Amaryllis said.

"What do you eat besides bird meat?" Selah asked. She knew the girl liked the jerky and biscuits Selah had shared, but her meager supplies wouldn't feed three of them.

Amaryllis shrugged. "Bread from neighbors when I look real sad."

Selah shook her head. "You mean when you hustle them."

The child had used those same faces on her. She knew all the angles from Dane's behavior.

"Well, that too." Amaryllis was acting more animated now. Being home seemed to bolster her spirits.

"Why have you never stayed with any of them?" This was the first she'd heard of neighbors. Maybe she could talk one of them into taking the girl. Then she'd get back to taking care of herself—although Amaryllis had proved to have her own skills.

The child's face turned from shock to fear. She backed farther into the corner and shook her head. "No, no . . . the man! I won't. I'll run away! I'll never come back."

"Okay, calm down. You don't have to." Selah's stomach twisted at the way Amaryllis said "the man." Something sinister lurked in the story. She wouldn't push the topic.

The girl trembled. Later Selah would say it was at that moment she decided. She would not be leaving Amaryllis in Hampton.

Selah changed the subject. "Where's the root cellar?"

"The flat door on the back side of the shed." Amaryllis curled up in a ball and began rocking herself to sleep.

Selah moved to the door. Bodhi stood his ground with arms crossed.

She looked back. "Are you coming?"

"Why?"

"Well, man of few words, I might need you to help carry food. Or whatever else I find that might be useable. We could do with a shirt for you." Maybe it was a guilty pleasure, but his chest remained a looming distraction to her resolve.

Bodhi rubbed a hand over his bare midsection and grinned.

Selah swallowed hard. It bothered her when he acted like he knew her thoughts.

Amaryllis lifted her head. "There are some of Father's clothes in the shed. Mother could never bear to get rid of them."

Selah led the way to the shed. This would be a good place to confront Bodhi about the occurrences of the last few hours without frightening Amaryllis with her tirade.

Bodhi followed. "Listen, I have to find people who know what's going on and can help me get home."

Selah spun and poked him in the chest. "This situation is your fault in the first place." She'd never admit her defiance had caused the problem. Mother said behaviors bore consequences. She was always right.

Her anger made easy work of the door. She pulled hard, yanking it loose from the dirt and vegetation claiming the bottom edge, and entered the darkened space, slowing to let her eyes adjust to the dimness. Along the narrow back wall, wooden pegs held shirts and pants. Below them in a neat row were several pairs of heavy work boots.

Bodhi stood in the open doorway. "I met you a few days ago for about a half hour. Your brothers beat me in the head and shackled me. How's this my fault?"

Selah decided to avoid the subject. How do you tell someone you've turned into one of them when you're not sure what "one of them" is? Since freeing Bodhi last night, a constant thundering had rolled over her heart with the weight of a boulder, and she still couldn't bring herself to read Mother's letters. The way forward included Bodhi Locke, whether she liked it or not.

She walked to the wall. Maybe if she covered him up, she wouldn't feel so vulnerable to his looks. She grabbed a shirt. Making a face at the musty mildew smell, she shook off the dust. A gray cloud rose from the material to hang in the airless room like a silver fog.

She waved a hand to disperse the particles. "You probably should shake this outside. It needs washing before you put it on."

Bodhi fingered the coarse linen material. "You want me to wear this?"

"No," Selah said, but she wanted to scream, *Yes, cover yourself so I'm not all flustered every time I look at you!* "Civilized people wear clothes, but you could continue to act like a heathen and broil in the sun."

She averted her eyes. Why did Bodhi have to be so good-looking? She had spent her life in the Borough and could pick only a bare handful of guys who had affected her like him. *Bare* . . . Even her thoughts were betraying her. *Cover him up.*

"You didn't answer my question. How's it my fault?" Bodhi crossed his arms without taking the shirt. He planted his feet wide.

Selah had seen the same pose when Raza balked at doing tasks Father assigned. She held out the shirt. "Listen, we'll find you something better, but for now this will have to do."

Bodhi didn't take it. "You still—"

"Well, what do we have here?" She pushed the shirt at his chest and let go.

He scrambled to grab the shirt as it fell to the floor. Selah walked past him to the side wall covered in knives of all sizes and shapes, some rusting or severely nicked, several sharp and clean other than a patina of dust. One in particular caught her eye, a machete with a fourteen-inch blade, a wide tip, and a full-sized handle ending in a bulb shape.

She carefully lifted it from the pegs. The machete balanced well in her hand, like the one belonging to Father had. She'd used it on a regular basis to clear brush and kudzu encroaching on the back hay field. She swung the machete a few times.

Bodhi stepped back. "I remember you had small knives at the beach. Is that your weapon of choice?"

Selah searched for the sheath. "Yes. I need a bigger knife after the hard time I had killing the snake with those little things. I never thought I'd come up against something so large."

After some trial and error she found the right sleeve with a belt loop on each side. Selah rooted through dusty piles of rags and equipment. There surely was a belt to fit or at least one she could alter the way Father had taught her.

Bodhi coughed from the dust. "Are you done in here? I can't breathe." He put the shirt up to his nose, but apparently the smell became too much and he lowered it. "This is as vile as the smell of the dump at Geh—"

"Then go outside, you baby." Selah continued to root around. She'd said the wrong thing. Now she was treating him the same way her brothers treated her. Why'd she do that?

Bodhi clamped his lips shut, held his ground, and glared.

She could see she'd hurt his feelings, the same way the boys hurt her. She'd never been intentionally mean to people. What had changed?

She found a horse harness in one pile and stripped out a

leather belt with a buckle. The belt fit snugly into the sheath loops, and she positioned it like a sash across her chest, measuring where the ends met in front. Then she pulled off the belt, grabbed a rusty nail and a mallet, and pounded a hole in the leather.

Bodhi watched as she cinched herself into the carrier and inserted the blade behind her back. "Where did you learn to do this?"

"I've hung out with Father on the farm since I was big enough to sit on a milking stool." She practiced drawing the blade. The movements felt sleek and powerful, bolstering her confidence. "He taught me a lot."

"Now you've answered a *new* question, so how about answering the old one? Why is this my fault?" Bodhi asked.

"I was waiting to get you alone." Selah did another quick slice with the blade, brandishing it at an unseen foe. He just wasn't going to let up.

Bodhi broke into a broad smile and moved forward. "Is that so?"

"Back up, mister!" Selah stuck the blade out in front of her about an inch from his bare chest.

Bodhi raised both hands. "I surrender. You got me."

"That's the problem," Selah said, making another little stabbing gesture close to his chest. "I touched you."

His smile faded. "You're talking in riddles."

Selah huffed out a breath and plopped onto a plank bench. The old wood squealed at the new weight but held. "First I want to say that I'm really sorry I ever tried to capture you. It was foolish of me to treat other people like property. But I guess the joke's on me."

Bodhi furrowed his brow. "Okay, apology accepted . . . I think. But what joke?"

"Sit, please. I'll try to explain."

Bodhi hesitated. He walked back and forth a few times before sitting next to her.

She traced the outline of her boot on the dirt floor with the knife. "Apparently when we touched on the beach, it started some kind of physical reaction in my body."

Bodhi jumped from the bench, index fingers pointing like weapons. "Wait! I don't know what you think you can blame on me. I didn't do anything to you."

"You don't understand. That's not what I meant." Selah rubbed her forehead. Her words were coming out in incomplete thoughts and her brain ran six steps ahead of her tongue. Her brothers often liked to fluster her so they could watch her babble talk like this.

"I understand perfectly. This isn't my first time in the game. You're trying to say I molested you or something." Bodhi backed toward the door.

"No, that's not what I meant. We have to read the letters to understand." She needed to face this, and he could help.

Bodhi looked suspicious. "Understand what?"

"You have a symbol on your forehead, right?"

Bodhi absently fingered his forehead and smoothed his hair over it. "Yes, of course, I've had it my whole existence."

"Well, I didn't have one until the day after I touched you." As if on cue, Selah's chest thundered.

Bodhi squinted and looked at her forehead. "That's impossible. It doesn't happen that way. I don't see anything."

"This." Selah carefully pulled down just the edge of her

top to expose the imprint hiding an inch below her collarbone.

⬦

Bodhi gasped as the wing came into view. "How'd that happen?" Immortals and centorums having children together? Could it actually happen? Had it ever happened at home? Or was this among the things purged from their memory? Why did he have to come to this place to get the answer?

Selah's eyes widened. "Are you hard of hearing? You touched me!"

Bodhi had seen females on the edge—they were apparently the same everywhere. He knew to back off.

He tried not to stare at the mark. What happened to these half-breed people in the Kingdom? He didn't remember ever knowing any. But they'd have been of a lower class and not necessarily among his circle of influence. Probably one of the many examples of his self-centered existence that didn't include the regular world around him.

Was this some kind of illusion? He reached out to touch her mark.

Selah jumped. "Back up. What do you think I am?"

Bodhi jerked back his hand. "I'm sorry—I didn't mean . . . Is it real?"

His eyes traveled past the mark. She was a beautiful young woman and stirred thoughts that weren't exactly gentlemanly. He chastised himself for choosing this moment. He could see her fear.

"Of course it's real. Do you really think I'd choose to become one of the hunted just for fun?" Selah rolled her eyes and curled her lip.

Bodhi glanced down. Insensitivity was one of his biggest challenges. Looking back from this new position of banishment, he lamented the sense of empathy he now needed to cultivate. This would probably be a good place to start, but could he really be serious?

He shook his head to dismiss the invasion of conscience. "I don't understand this hunting season on my people. I listened to your brothers as we traveled. Why are we being sold into slavery?"

Selah's eyes widened again. "Because the Company gives huge sums of credits to anyone bringing Landers to the Mountain."

"That doesn't answer the question why," Bodhi said. What were they after? All of these questions were a sensory overload. He needed to get away to think, but unfortunately that would probably prompt more questions. Maybe she was a key to the answers after all.

Selah's eyes filled with tears that threatened to stream down her cheeks. "It's always been that way. I don't know why. This isn't my fault."

Her sad eyes tugged at his heart. Bodhi wrapped his arm around her. The soft material of her shirt slid across his arm, creating pinpricks of electricity. He pulled her close. For a moment she leaned into him and sobbed. Her body heat seeped through her clothes, warming his flesh, and she shivered. His own heartbeat mixed with hers and pounded in his head.

Selah pulled away and tapped him on the arm with her

fist. "Your heart is pounding like a drum. Are you trying to take wanton advantage of my tears?"

Bodhi broke into a wide grin. He threw up his hands to fend off her playful blows. "Ouch! Take it easy. I've been beat up more in the last two days than I have been in the last hundred years."

Selah stopped in mid-punch and stared at him.

Bodhi looked at her and grimaced. "What now?"

"You said more than you were in the last hundred years."

He tipped his head up, looking at nothing in particular on the ceiling. *Do I remember that long? Yes, I do, and longer.* "Yes, that's what I said."

"Well, old fella, you don't look a day over twenty." Selah grinned. "Good joke."

Bodhi raise an eyebrow. "Old age is a disease we don't suffer. The only ones I've ever known to die were from physical catastrophe." He'd heard about others but saw only one immortal expire. An earthquake had dislodged a massive block of granite from a city building, and the man was crushed beyond repair.

Selah sat up straight. "You're not kidding?"

"No. I have no reason to lie. I'm stuck here regardless."

"Where do you come from?"

"The Kingdom." An internal conflict kept him from explaining. Preservation. Or maybe things were just too muddled. There seemed to be blurry spots in his memory. He could reach out to touch the thought but then it would slip through his fingers like sand.

"Where is this Kingdom?" Selah turned to face him.

"I don't know. I mean, I know it's not near here." Bodhi

waved an arm around. "The sun is different, even the air is different. Here it smells like dirt and salt mixed together. And I no longer feel the Presence."

Selah stood up. "My mother mentioned that word *Presence*. My father wrote to her about it. What is it?"

Bodhi hesitated, grasping for the thought. It escaped. He shook his head. "I can't say."

Selah slapped her hands together. "We have to read the letters."

"What letters?"

Selah darted from the shed. Bodhi moved to the open door and glanced out. She came running back carrying a small wooden box. The tie had slipped from her head again and the rhythm of her running tossed the hair back and forth across her shoulders. She was a natural beauty, fresh and uncultivated, not pretentious like the women he was used to.

She scrambled back into the shed, breathless. "Amaryllis is sleeping. I think we should keep this secret just between us."

Bodhi nodded. He didn't really care, but if it pleased her he didn't mind.

Selah took her seat on the bench and set the box between them. She rubbed the intricate design on the lid several times and looked at Bodhi.

"What's the matter?" Bodhi asked.

"I put off reading these. They're going to change my thinking and I don't know if I'm ready for it." She opened the box, retrieved the pile, and with a deep breath began reading the yellowed papers.

Bodhi stood and ran a hand through his hair. He looked down at Selah. She lifted her head and tears streamed down her face. He gulped. He hated it when women cried. Right about now he'd be ready to agree to anything she asked. All he wanted was for her not to cry.

Still, he was impatient to get answers. "What did you find out?"

"My real father loved Mother and me more than life itself." Selah sniffed back more liquid threatening to add to the mess already running down her face.

"Does the letter say anything about why this happened to you? Or where he was going?"

"It's the most romantic thing I've ever read. He said she was the mate he'd searched for his entire existence and he'd finally learned sacrificial love." Selah wiped the back of her hand across her eyes and sniffed again.

Bodhi wanted to poke himself in the eye with one of the knives from the wall. All of this touching romance was making him nervous. But something about one of the phrases got his attention. He returned to sitting beside her. "What did he mean by 'sacrificial love'?"

Selah shook her head and turned over the page. "I don't know, but back here he says it's his turn to protect the others. He told her to kiss their daughter." Tears spilled from her eyes in great rolling trails. "And he said to tell her he loved her with all his heart. How did he know I would be a girl?"

Bodhi stared at her. "I don't know, but why the big tears?"

"My mother never told me about my real father, or that he loved me." Her head went into her hands and she wept uncontrollably.

Bodhi fidgeted. Watching a crying girl was the absolute worst thing he could think of. How had he gotten into this mess? He felt like punching himself because he knew exactly how he'd gotten into this mess—by being selfish and immature in his life choices.

He nervously slid his arm across her shoulder and patted it a few times before pulling back. He grimaced. There had to be a way out of here.

Selah raised her head. The tears diminished. She folded the paper carefully and placed it back in the box as she removed another. She scanned it and lifted her eyes to Bodhi. "Okay, so I believe you about the age thing. My father says he was 132 at the time, which would make him 150 now." Selah's eyes widened. "How could you all be 150 years old? You couldn't have all been born on the same day. Were you born a grown-up? Do you remember?"

Bodhi ran a hand across his mouth. He did remember. But how much was he allowed to tell her? "Counting our age started—"

A bolt of searing pain shot through his skull. He screamed. He doubled over, clutching the sides of his head.

Selah dropped to her knees in front of him and put her hands on his shoulders. "What's the matter? I knew Raza hurt you with that stupid boomerang. Maybe you have a concussion."

Bodhi broke out in a sweat that ran down his neck and onto his chest. That answered his question—he couldn't tell her about their age. He regained his composure. "I'm good. It's not a concussion, just an old injury flaring up." The best lie he could think of quickly.

Selah seemed satisfied. "Sorry. Now, you were saying about your age?"

191

Bodhi shook his head. "My mind is still a little confused. Sorry, I don't remember."

Selah stared at him for a minute as though she didn't believe him. Bodhi scrambled to think up another answer that wouldn't stab him in the brain. She rose and sat back on the bench.

He relaxed and tried to steer the conversation. "A hundred and thirty-two years here and he didn't find a way out?"

Selah pointed at a spot on the page. "He says any of the ships they made seaworthy were supposed to cross the horizon and then come back. None ever returned and after a couple years of trying they gave up. He also says something about sending out flights with airplanes too. I'm not sure what those are. Seems I remember from history that they were big air machines that carried hundreds of people at a time back before the Sorrows. But because of the ash in the air for so many years after the volcano, the use of those engines became obsolete."

"They?" Bodhi perked up. "He found others?"

"Yes, at one time there were hundreds of them. They migrated north. Father stayed in Georgia because that's where Mother wanted to live." Selah leaned back against the wall and sighed. "Such love. He said he waited a long time to find the right one."

Bodhi was getting antsy. "Is that all?"

Selah sighed, placed the paper back into the box, and removed the last one. She read down the one-sided page and then refolded it. "He said something about novarium. The only problem—"

"Stop!" Bodhi shot up straight. Novarium? This couldn't be happening. He only knew the term from the ancient readings, but why would an awakening happen in a place like this? "What did you say about novarium?"

Selah shrugged. "I don't know. He must have spelled the word wrong or something. I've never heard it before." She slid the paper into the box.

"Read it out loud. I need to hear the words." Bodhi's voice rose an octave. His hands started to shake. His touch had caused an awakening? No. No. Why him? His actions were too careless for such a responsibility. This needed someone else. A lump formed in his throat.

Selah scowled and pulled away. She slowly retrieved the paper.

"Read it!" Bodhi demanded.

She flinched, tossing the page at him. "Read it yourself!"

Bodhi's hands began to sweat. He rubbed them together and then wiped them on his pants. He mumbled through most of the unimportant stuff but read aloud when he reached the mandate.

Rest assured, my darling. I love you more than life itself, and to that end I will spend every waking hour keeping you and our precious child safe from the evil overtaking this world. I will come for you if it is at all ever possible for you to be safe at my side.

Remember, my love, this girl child of ours is special. She is the awaited novarium. She brings forth life and hope for this world. I know it will be a hard thing for you because she will then belong to the ages, but you must be sure she has contact with a Lander on the day before she turns eighteen. The right one will come.

Bodhi released the page, watching it flutter to the ground. What form of punishment was this? He'd been a rebel his whole existence. He wasn't cut out to be someone's protector. The bond was closer than . . . No, not him. He needed to find the others. Pass this duty on to someone more responsible. If he left immediately and followed the impressions he felt, he could send someone back to guide her.

"What does novarium mean?" Selah asked. She looked frightened.

Bodhi squeezed his eyes shut then opened them. "It means . . ." He waited for a stabbing pain. None came. "It means you're special. Novarium happens only once every hundred years."

Selah's eyes widened. "Once every hundred years! I don't understand why I would be part of this. I'm nothing special. I'm pretty much a mongrel. At the moment I don't even have a father. Why me?"

"Unfortunately I was never much into the humanities, so I know very little. *Novarium* means 'new,' or a 'new thing.' It could mean an ability never seen before, or it could mean waiting for the proper opportunity to do a new thing. And I don't even know how someone is picked, or who or what picks you."

Selah looked down at her hands. "Mother must have known. She didn't want me on the beach that day so she wouldn't lose me. If I had listened, none of this would have happened."

Bodhi nodded. "You're probably right, but it may have taken your father another generation to sire another daughter for novarium. As for my part . . ." Well, he didn't want a part.

Bonnie S. Calhoun

"I have to find my father," Selah said. "I'm scared of messing something else up."

"Your father will know what to do. He'll come for you." She looked so sad. Right now he was trying to make her feel better, but he didn't know if he believed it himself. He was even trying to reach out to other immortals, but there were only vague impressions, not actual contacts. How was he going to deal with this situation without more information?

"If my father comes looking for my mother, he'll never find us. We're not in the same place he left her."

Bodhi pulled from his jumbled thoughts. "He can find you." Why did he know that the man wouldn't be present for her awakening?

Selah jerked to face him. "What do you mean?"

Bodhi bent and rested his elbows on his knees. He felt too careless to be trusted with this. "Don't you feel it?"

"Feel what?"

"The connection. The awakening would probably start with a rumble in your chest."

Selah's hand slid to the collar of her shirt. "Like a thunder."

He felt an impression, as if covering the mark was a way to restrain the feelings trying to burst from her.

Bodhi nodded. "Guess you could call it that. The right side of your brain is waking up and connecting to the left."

"What in the name of the moon and stars are you talking about?"

He stared at the floor. "Have you heard voices yet?"

Selah looked down at her hands. She folded the paper and slid it carefully back in the box. "Yes, I have," she said in a small voice. Quite a few times she'd thought she was hearing her mother's thoughts, but the voices were audible, even if only in her head.

Bodhi touched her hand. She flinched but didn't pull away. "That's the awakening. Thousands of years ago it was normal for people to *talk* with their minds, but the ability was lost. Since then, in most people, the left side of their brain is dominant, and the right does hardly anything. In us, the Landers your people despise, both sides function. It makes us telepathic."

Selah tipped her head. "So that's why I smell and hear better." Her head jerked in the direction of the door.

Bodhi also heard it. The scream belonged to Amaryllis.

13

B odhi scrambled from the shed behind Selah. Had the child found another snake, or had marauders found the child?

They burst through the ramshackle door of the house. Amaryllis lay curled in a ball on the bed, screaming. Bodhi halted. No visible threats. Screaming children were not part of his understanding. He backed up, the sound hurting his ears.

Selah rushed at her. "Amaryllis, wake up!"

The girl jerked awake, her arms and legs flailing. "Snake! Snake!" She scrambled back against the wall, wide-eyed, with legs pumping to beat an invisible foe. Her eyes slowly registered recognition, and she pulled the threadbare tattered blanket up to her chest.

"It's okay. I'm here. You're not alone." Selah softened her voice and slowed her forward motion. The fear left the girl's face as she woke fully and recognized Selah.

Bodhi's patience was on the down side of agreeable. He

needed food, not all this girly emotional stuff. "Since the child is awake, can we eat?"

Selah swung her head around and gave him such an evil stare he felt glad she didn't have a weapon in her hand.

Bodhi raised both hands, palms out. "I just figured it's getting late, and maybe you girls needed something to keep up your strength." Plus his stomach was growling in protest.

Selah continued to glare at him. "Why don't you take that smelly shirt down to the water and wash it while I get some dinner together. You don't want to sit at the table with no shirt."

"Why not?" Bodhi glanced at the dirty and decrepit condition of the table. Not having a shirt on might improve the view.

Selah narrowed her eyes. "I don't know about where you come from, but here in civilized society, we don't come to the dinner table with bare chests."

"Where I come from, dinner tables don't look like that." Bodhi knew the look on her face and wanted to smile. He knew he wasn't going to win. "Where did you say the water was?"

"Follow your ears. Can't you hear running water when you're outside?" She turned back to Amaryllis.

Bodhi marched back to the shed, snatched up the dust-encrusted shirt from the floor, and loped off in search of the water. It gave him time to think without Selah in his head. She was worming her way into his thoughts, getting to him. Bad situation. He was never cut out to be someone's protector. Accountability was not among his strong points.

North. He knew the direction.

He homed in on the sound of water. It was larger than a stream. He pushed through the underbrush of the forest behind the house. About two hundred feet farther into the trees, the brush opened onto a gently sloped bank leading down to a wide, slow-running river.

He worked his way down to the water's edge and dipped the shirt in, rubbing the material together several times. Dirty water drained from the shirt, taking the dust and crustiness with it. The material began to soften in his hands. *This might not be so bad when it's clean.* As Bodhi scrubbed, he looked upstream. Four hundred feet away a bridge crossed the river.

He looked back at the woods in the direction of the house. What if he just crossed the bridge and kept going? As far as he could tell by the position of the late afternoon sun, the bridge headed north. How long would it take him to decipher the impressions he felt, find an immortal, and send them back to watch over Selah? There must be someone who understood her purpose. Novarium came for many reasons. He wanted to kick himself for not paying more attention.

Bodhi wrung the water from the shirt and shook it out. It looked more inviting now, and he slipped into it. The wetness gave cool and welcome relief from the afternoon sun. Leaving the shirt open to dry faster, he picked his way along the bank. The bridge opening came into view.

He continued looking behind him, expecting Selah to pop out of the woods any moment. He felt drawn to her, but independence pulled even stronger.

He moved closer to the bridge. A young boy sat on the railing close to the center of the structure. Bodhi climbed up the brush-covered hill as the boy watched him.

He reached the bridge. One last chance to turn back. He clamped his lips tight and shook his head. She'd be better off with someone more responsible. He'd find someone. *Goodbye, sweet . . . goodbye, Selah*. He began to jog across. It felt good to run.

His legs took on a rhythmic pumping and the breeze parted his hair and pulled the sides of the shirt away from his body. The boy sitting on the railing stared at Bodhi. As he ran closer the boy's eyes opened wide and he pointed in fright. "Lander!"

Bodhi tensed. *Not again*. He was not going to be captured again. He ran flat out, passing the boy. The boy's scream faded. Bodhi looked back. Gone. Another scream and loud splashing.

Bodhi slowed, moving to the railing to look over. The boy slapped at the water below as the slow-moving current carried him downstream. He yelled for help. Bodhi thought this would be a great time for Selah to show up. She could save another child and he could get away.

The child slipped under the water. Bodhi pounded his fist on the railing. Wasn't there anyone to hear the boy?

The child came back up, flailing. "Help!"

If Bodhi waited any longer, the boy would be too far away to catch. His heart pounded. He wanted to get away. He turned to leave, took two steps. A stabbing in his chest. He turned back to the railing then ran for the center of the bridge.

Bodhi hauled himself over the railing. He perched on the edge, trying to calculate the depth and speed of the water. *Go now or he'll be too far away to reach*.

"Help! I can't swim!" the boy screamed. The current pulled him under again.

Bodhi executed a perfect dive, slicing through the water with the ease of a fish. The instant cold created a marked difference to the heat he'd felt moments before. He broke through the surface of the water ten feet from the boy. Swiping the water from his eyes, he expertly stroked to the child's side.

As he approached, the boy went under again. Bodhi dove. He opened his eyes in the murky water, and the sunlight at the surface created enough contrast for him to spot the boy and pull him to the surface.

The child inhaled water and fell unconscious. Bodhi flipped him on his back, grabbed him under the chin, and side-stroked toward shore. Adrenaline pumped. He expelled several large breaths and spit out some water fighting the current, but he made it.

Bodhi heaved the boy's limp body to the shore. Slamming him to the slope expelled some of the water in his lungs. The boy sputtered.

A hand reached down.

Bodhi looked up.

Selah planted her feet for leverage and helped haul the boy up the bank and onto the forest floor. She knew he'd be okay when his sputter turned to a cough. A stream of water poured from the side of his mouth as he gagged.

"Lander!" the boy yelled between gasps.

She reached back down and yanked Bodhi up the bank. They collided, and he wrapped his arms around her to steady them.

Selah looked at his chest and then up into his eyes. "This

could be trouble. We need to get you out of here before he brings the whole Borough down on us."

Bodhi watched the boy scramble away in the opposite direction. He turned back to her. "You're right."

Selah felt his breath on her face. His arms were wrapped tightly around her waist. The water on him seeped through her clothing, drawing in the warmth of his body as his chest heaved great gulps of air.

She looked up. He gazed into her eyes. He gently lowered his head, inching his full lips toward hers.

At the last second Selah turned her head away and pushed off from his chest.

Bodhi grinned.

Selah punched him in the arm. "I pour out my heart out to you and what's the first thing you do? Leave!" She pulled loose and scrambled the rest of the way up the bank with him following.

She stomped through the trees toward the house. A moment of weakness and where did it get her? She almost kissed him! Why didn't she? He was right there.

She held her breath. She'd never let on, but she secretly hoped for another time. Would she rebuff him again or actually kiss him? *Breathe.*

"I saved the boy. What seems to be your problem now?" Bodhi rushed behind her.

"I watched the whole thing. If you hadn't run across the bridge, the kid wouldn't have been scared into the water in the first place."

Bodhi grabbed her by the arm and spun her around. "You watched the whole thing?"

Selah jerked her arm from his grasp and kept moving. After she spent all this time saving him, he'd just deserted her. Didn't he understand she was scared without him?

Typical male behavior. Men in the Borough called the shots for their women, like her father did about her hunting and giving her away in marriage, while the women were supposed to stand by and be happy for the scraps they were given. Well, no more. She deserved respect and a thank-you, not a kick in the teeth.

"Wait! Why didn't you jump in and save him?" Bodhi dodged a tree limb. The next one slapped him in the forehead. A mist of water droplets shot from his wet head.

Selah bit down on her lip. She wanted to laugh but was too angry to let him off the hook.

"I wouldn't have let him drown. I'd have jumped in when he floated down to my spot," she said. She thought about saying that if she'd jumped in Bodhi would have kept going and left her and Amaryllis in the dust.

She stormed across the yard to the house.

"So you saw him fall in the water and you did nothing," Bodhi said as he hurried to keep up. His clothes were plastered to his wet body, showing off his physique. Selah tried to focus on his nearly deserting them.

She turned to him. "Blah, blah, blah. I watched you scare the poor kid into the water and I also watched you almost keep going. Don't give me any of your high-handed talk."

"Well, excuse me for—"

Selah looked down at his one bare foot. "Where is your shoe?" She let out an exasperated sigh. "How can you not notice you're walking without a shoe?"

His wet blond hair still plastered to his head, Bodhi looked down sheepishly and wiggled the exposed toes. "I guess I lost it in the river. My feet are sort of numb from the cold water, so—"

"Go to the shed and get a pair of work boots. You can't walk around in bare feet. There's too many nettles." She shook her head as she watched him gingerly pick his way among the stones and prickly plants to the shed. She seemed to be losing the ability to get mad at him and was finding it necessary to pretend she was. But why? She didn't need an addled boy-brain like the silly girls at school had. They seemed to lose all sense when they trained eyes on a boy. Besides, if she acted nice he might try to take advantage.

She shoved the door open. "Amaryllis, get ready. We have to get out of here now!"

"But I'm hungry. Are we going to eat?" the girl asked.

"Later, when we're safe for the night." Selah grabbed her backpack and an old bag Amaryllis found. She looked the bag over. A solid canvas material, it looked ragged around the edges but still sturdy. Bodhi entered, carrying a pair of well-worn leather work boots.

She jammed the bag into his chest. "We'll load this with food. We'll each carry one."

Bodhi dropped a boot as he grabbed the bag. "You know, this is the second time you've done that. You're quite bossy about shoving bags into my chest."

Selah spun around to face him. "Well, it always seems to be that we're in a hurry because of you. So excuse me for trying to keep us from getting caught."

☙

Selah could hear Amaryllis squeal with delight as the lights came on. She felt better in this safer location. Light flooded the tunnel, making their travel easier as she pushed through the roots and vines, scrambled over the last of the boulders, and squeezed her way into the opening of the library.

Bodhi climbed his way in behind her and touched her shoulder. "Where is the light coming from?" He moved away into the room.

She could still feel the warmth of his hand on her shoulder. "Amaryllis found an ancient library buried under the rubble. It must have a fusion generator or something because the interior light still works. It's quite remarkable. We'll be safe here overnight."

Amaryllis twirled in the center of the room. Selah was glad to see her recovery despite the severity of her injuries. They would be able to travel without losing time.

Bodhi walked to the walls of stacked data crystals. He gazed at the columns. "I know this technology. It's old-fashioned but still serviceable in some of the poorer districts at—"

"You remember that kind of detail about your home?"

Bodhi looked off into space. "Yes, unfortunately I remember quite a bit. I'm sorry about a lot of it, but apparently that won't get me out of here."

Selah slid onto the bench she'd righted the last time here. "I'm not sure I understand."

She watched as Bodhi ran both hands through his hair. The dried clumps separated into blond ringlets that bounced down around his face, obscuring the mark. The loose curls made him look innocent, but at the same time he was standing here admitting some sort of guilt.

She wondered what he'd done.

"Let's say I didn't exactly follow the rules." Bodhi appeared to be measuring his words.

Selah understood rules and that kind of deception from growing up with brothers. Odd—he'd responded to what she was thinking. Had she said it out loud?

She snickered. "And for this you were banished from your country? Was everyone who came here sent for the same reason?"

He sat beside her, his elbows resting on his knees and his head in his hands. "Probably. I've never known another expelled person."

"How could you not know someone? Many have come here over the years."

"They're purged from our memory."

"Selah, help!" Amaryllis yelled.

Selah spun. "Where's Amaryllis?"

Bodhi hopped up and gestured to the back. "She headed in that direction."

The child's voice echoed in the cavernous room. Selah couldn't pinpoint a direction. "Rylla, where are you?"

Bodhi listened intently as the shrill echo bounced around. He pointed toward the section with the loose "Reference" sign hanging by one old rusted hinge. "The other side of that pile."

Selah scrambled up the jumbled mass of broken furniture and office equipment piled along the right side of the room. Clawing her way to the top, she teetered on the unstable mess. Wooden furniture buried in the pile creaked and cracked under her weight, shifting the jumble and causing it to slide.

Bodhi maneuvered around the edge of the pile and wedged into a small clear area close to the wall.

Selah steadied herself and spotted Amaryllis pressed into a doorway farther down the other side of the pile on Bodhi's side of the wall.

"Rylla, what's wrong?" Selah asked.

The child turned, her eyes registering terror. She screamed again—one of those shrill child screams that can cut through your brain like nails on a school slate. She pointed at the corner, and Selah's eyes followed her finger. Bodhi craned to see past her. In the corner of a side entryway sat a large rust-colored rabbit.

Selah slid the machete from her back case. On second thought, she put it away and whipped out a kapo. She took aim and pegged the rabbit to the wall by its neck. The back legs shuddered a couple times and stopped moving.

Selah let out a victory whoop and raised a fist in the air. The pile shifted to the left, propelling her to the right. For a moment she was airborne.

"Selah, watch out!" Bodhi yelled. He reached out but he wasn't close enough to grab her.

She tumbled into the mass of furniture with a sickening thud. Chairs rolled down the pile toward her and a tabletop with legs pointed in the air slid over her position as though to close a door. The pile completely swallowed her.

Bodhi grabbed the wall to steady himself and picked his way along the pile to her last location. She had to be all right. *Please let her be all right.* He'd felt something when they'd held each other. Didn't know what it was, but he wasn't leaving her till he figured it out. He scrambled up the pile.

Amaryllis started to wail. "Selah, don't die. Don't leave me."

A muffled voice drifted from the mess.

Bodhi gingerly skirted the pile on the low side and began to rip it apart, flinging chairs and racks out of the way. "I'm coming. Hang on."

Another muffled sound.

Furniture, benches, and book stands flew in all directions. His breathing ran labored and short, and he stretched his muscles to their limit. He slid a table from the pile and pushed it the other direction. Selah appeared with her arms covering her head. Relief flooded his chest.

He reached in and pulled her out, wrapping her in his arms. The pounding of her heart reverberated with his own. She relaxed into his embrace.

"Are you injured?" he asked. She rested her head on his chest. He breathed in the scent of her hair, the faintest hint of perfume or a flower.

She raised her head, long lashes resting on her cheeks. Her eyes opened. Her lips parted. He looked into her green eyes and suddenly felt vulnerable.

Amaryllis squeezed between the two of them and wrapped her arms around Selah's waist.

Selah laughed and gave a mock gasp. "You almost squeezed the air out of me." She released Bodhi and smoothed the girl's unruly hair, patting her on the back. Raising a hand to her head, she looked up at Bodhi. "I was trying to tell you I wasn't hurt, just trapped. I think my pride is the only thing injured. But I got the rabbit!"

Bodhi's telepathy received clearer impressions of Selah— her strengths, her weaknesses. She was developing an affection for Amaryllis but still held a longing for her brother Dane.

Bodhi chuckled. "Girl, I've met cats with fewer lives than you."

Selah scrunched her eyebrows. "What did you say?"

"Never mind, it's an old saying." Bodhi turned to look at the wall. "Yes, you got the rabbit. Good throwing. Remind me never to get on your bad side." He steadied her as she stumbled over the tangled mess of chair legs, racks, and tables.

Selah strode to the corner, unpegged the rabbit, and held it up by the ears. "We've got meat for dinner!"

Amaryllis shrank back, tripping over a couple chairs. She caught herself and stumbled backward again. "No! You can't eat that. It killed my mother." She started to cry.

Selah dropped the rabbit and rushed to her. "No, honey, it's all right. This rabbit is good for food. Do you remember what color rabbit your mother caught?"

Amaryllis sniffled back tears and wiped her eyes on her sleeve. "It looked like a baby deer, brown with white spots."

"I'm going to teach you one of my hunting secrets. See how this rabbit is rust-colored?" Selah retrieved the rabbit again and held it out.

Amaryllis shied away from a closer look. "It looks like dried blood."

Selah lifted the carcass. "You're right. I never noticed. It's a good way to remember. The ones that look like blood are safe to eat."

Amaryllis shook her head, pushing Selah's hands away. "No . . . death."

"No, life, and good eats. Come here and I'll tell you my secret story." She dropped the carcass and took Amaryllis by the hand, leading her to a righted bench. "When I was about fourteen, a family came to my beach from Ness Borough, a place much farther inland. I saved one of their children from drowning, and as a reward, the family shared their clan secret on hunting rabbits. At first I was like you and didn't believe them, but watching them eat and not get sick convinced me it was safe to eat rabbits with the same color fur as the rust-covered beams embedded in the ground near the beach."

Amaryllis listened, glancing at the carcass several times. She made a face when Selah finished the story. That was probably the best Selah could ask for at the moment.

"I've got to skin and gut that thing." Selah grabbed up the rabbit and headed outside.

Bodhi righted a table and found several metal chairs that weren't too bent or rusted while Amaryllis retrieved their canned supplies. He tried to coax her to join him outside, but the child didn't want anything to do with the animal she blamed for her mother's death.

He eased through the rubble-strewn opening of the buried library and perched on a fallen tree to watch Selah. He'd never known anyone like her. She certainly could take care of herself.

Selah sat on a log beside a small fire she'd built inside a rock circle. She rotated the rabbit on a spit fashioned from a green tree branch as she sprinkled something on the meat from a small pouch. Fat drippings made the fire dance and pop.

Bodhi watched, intrigued by her expert hands. This clearly wasn't the first time she'd cooked game. The sun set behind her, filtering through her hair, creating a halo around her head. It softened her features and caused an ache in his chest that felt unfamiliar. He continued to observe, transfixed by the strength radiating from her.

His thoughts wandered. He didn't notice she'd finished and covered the fire with dirt until she approached him with the spit of browned meat. The aroma made his stomach growl.

Selah held up the game. "Ready to be amazed at my cooking skills?"

"Smells great. Hope it tastes as good," he said. He rose from the tree and followed her into the library.

Bodhi had never spent time around children, but he enjoyed watching how Selah handled the child. First she tried to encourage her, and when that didn't work, Selah dropped the matter and went about eating her own meal. Once Amaryllis saw Selah eating, the savory smell pulled her in. She tried a little bite then another, and eventually they were all enjoying a sumptuous meal of meat with canned vegetables and fruit.

After the meal Amaryllis curled up in a corner with a reader Selah pulled from their belongings. The child had developed a fascinated interest in ancient buildings, especially castles.

Bodhi sat with Selah at the table, watching her. Good food and pleasant company gave him a moment of peace.

"If I didn't know better, I could almost picture this as a happy family," Selah said.

He got a fleeting impression. She longed for her mother's touch or voice. Things she'd always taken for granted were now a thing of the past. Strange—he felt her loss.

Bodhi fidgeted with his hands. "I've been on my own for so long I don't have any family times to remember." He'd never stayed in one place long enough to build a family. Now he was feeling invested not only in the responsibility to a novarium but in the girl. For how long? Did these people live as long as centorums?

Selah watched him for a minute. He felt her judging him about his lack of relationships.

Bodhi suddenly felt as though a stone rested on his tongue. He wanted to know how she felt about him but refused to take impressions from her private emotional thought place. He did have the barest minimum of scruples. This girl seemed to be pulling things from him he didn't know he possessed.

Selah clasped her hands together. Her cheeks flushed red. Bodhi pressed his lips together to keep from smiling. Was she thinking about their near-miss kiss?

"Let's pick a new subject." Bodhi rested his hand on hers. He didn't want her embarrassment associated with him. He felt her instant relief.

Selah surveyed the room, looking at the crazy pile of furniture and debris. "I wonder what happened here that all the furniture wound up on only one side of the room."

Bodhi glanced around nonchalantly. "That must be from the tsunami." He picked up the water pack and gulped from it.

Selah stared at him for a second and looked over the mess again. "I guess it could have. I've seen the wrecked parts of the coast where people don't live anymore. How would you know it was a tsunami?"

Bodhi shrugged and gulped more water. "A tsunami was part of the Sorrows, along with the bombs, earthquakes, and volcano."

Selah sat up straight. "That was 150 years ago."

"There are some things I have vivid impressions of and I remember like yesterday."

Selah started laughing. "How can you remember that if you weren't here?"

Bodhi looked down at his hands. A sigh pulled on his chest. She would sense it as soon as her abilities started to mature. He might as well tell her now.

Selah tipped her head to look in his eyes. A nervous smile played at the corners of her lips. "Did you hear me? I asked how you could remember that."

He chewed on the side of his lip. "I heard you and . . ."

"And what? You're making me a little nervous." Selah scraped back her chair as she moved to get away from the table.

Bodhi reached out to stop her. "No, I don't mean to scare you."

Selah slapped his hand away and pulled out a kapo, brandishing it in front of her. "I don't know what your game is, but I'm not liking the feeling I'm getting from you at the moment."

Bodhi raised both hands in surrender and sat back down at the table. "Fair enough. Because of your mark, the new synaptic connections are letting you tune into my impressions, and you're feeling the deceit."

Selah's hand moved to her collarbone. She'd tried ignoring the mark. If she didn't acknowledge it then it really wasn't there and ruining her life. Now that he'd brought it up, she felt as though it were an appendage. He was right. When she concentrated, an emotion from him came through loud and clear. Deception. Now the feeling was easing.

She looked up at him. "What just happened?"

"Your strength is growing, and I was lying. Well, I wasn't exactly lying, but I wasn't telling you the truth, and you sensed it."

"What weren't you telling me?'

"About the tsunami. I remember when it happened."

Selah plopped back onto the chair and started laughing. "Okay, that's funny, ha-ha. So you're still not going to tell me the truth."

"Concentrate on the impressions you're getting. I *am* telling you the truth. I remember when it happened." Bodhi dropped his head to his hands. "I remember no one knew it was coming until it was too late. The water, mass panic, millions dead."

Selah scowled. "For you to remember that kind of detail, you would have to be here."

Bodhi shook his head. "I can't explain it. I can see . . . I get bits and pieces."

Selah's eyes widened as her mouth dropped open. "I thought you were joking before!"

"That's not something to joke about."

Selah grabbed his arm. "Tell me what you remember."

"It makes me tired to concentrate, to probe those places where it hides."

"Try, please."

Bodhi sighed. "Nuclear bombs, then an earthquake that triggered . . ." He squeezed his eyes tight and gripped his forehead.

"Triggered what?"

"The Canary Islands. A dormant volcano on La Palma collapsed because of the earthquake, sending the left flank into the Atlantic Ocean. The wave was 160 feet tall and traveled more than five miles inland from Canada all the way down to Brazil."

Selah stared. "Where are these places you're talking about?"

"Countries that were once populated on or near this continent."

Selah looked down at her hands. "I'm sorry."

"Sorry for what?" Bodhi chuckled. "The tsunami?"

Selah shook her head. "For being so mean to you before at the river, and for smacking you. I was . . . my feelings were hurt that you'd act so nice and then desert me."

Bodhi stared at her. "I was a jerk, as usual, trying to avoid responsibility. I didn't really want to leave you. I'm just leery of the responsibility."

She looked into his eyes. He was being truthful.

His face edged closer. Their breaths mixed together. She inhaled him. Shiver. She lowered her head and his lips brushed across her forehead.

Selah swallowed hard. So close, he was so close she could . . . She slowly lifted her head. His lips were still in the same place her forehead had been. She held her breath.

Her throat went dry and her hands grew wet. Now if she

could just get that moisture to her mouth without sticking her fingers to her face. Selah inhaled.

His lips touched hers. Soft, gentle. She leaned into the kiss. He pressed his arm into the small of her back to bring her closer. She felt his heartbeat pound against her chest. Her head too heavy for her neck to hold up, she swayed, relaxing in his hold.

Bodhi gently touched her face with his hand. He slowly pulled away. "I'm sorry."

Selah's lips were still where his were a second ago. She opened her eyes slowly. "Weren't we just around this same bend? Now what are you sorry for?"

"For taking advantage of you."

She'd wanted that kiss but couldn't let him know that, not yet. She tried to think of an appropriate flippant answer.

Bodhi suddenly gripped his head tightly. "Must stop. Pain."

Selah jumped. Her only experiences were vicariously through her girlfriends. This was the first time a boy ever ended a kiss that way.

Bodhi slumped to the side and slid to the floor. He lay on his side, arms barely able to push him to a sitting position.

Selah scrambled to his side. "Did I do something wrong? Are you all right?"

"It's not you. It's an avalanche of thoughts opening up to me. I'm beginning to feel others."

"Well, leave them alone," Selah said with a nervous smile.

Bodhi tried to smile but it turned to a grimace. His head jerked forward. He grabbed his forehead with both hands, then looked up with wide eyes. "Glade Rishon."

14

Cleon knew the two hundred miles of scenery from their Borough to the Mountain. It was peppered with deserted towns of ghostly rotting storefronts amid rolling hills of reclaimed forest, and ruined cities with row after row of crumbling building shells separated by overgrown streets dotted with rusted vehicle skeletons infiltrated by kudzu. The countryside hosted wide fields of shoulder-high corn and other summer crops.

Cleon breathed a sigh. They'd arrived.

With Raza stretched out in the back, Cleon guided the horses off the rutted, packed dirt road of the Borough and onto the smooth, maintained road surface leading to the Mountain. He often wondered why the last mile was maintained when no one living in the Mountain ever came outside. Father said it allowed merchants and traders the time to lose the dust from their travels before they reached the Mountain. Cleon didn't understand why they cared.

He was hopeful they'd arrived before Selah and he could get Raza headed home before she showed up. But he feared he wouldn't see her again. He knew Father and Raza talked about her. They didn't let him listen, but he knew secrets about Selah that they didn't. He wasn't sure what she was going to turn into or if he'd be able to tell, but he couldn't let Raza take her back to Father, who would be furious.

"I haven't seen any evidence of Selah, have you?" Raza asked. He moved to sit beside Cleon, using a slingshot to pick off an occasional varmint.

Cleon scowled. "No. She's probably not coming, but we can't wait around for days. We don't have enough supplies. And I don't like the way you're talking about our sister, like she's the enemy or something."

"She is the enemy! She stole from me."

Cleon dared a smirk. "The Lander was her catch first. I've listened to you whine about her stealing him for the last few days. The woe speech is getting old."

Raza glared at him. "It's just like you to take her side."

"What did she do besides make you look foolish?" Cleon feared the way his brother talked. This wasn't his normal harassment of their sister.

"Father wanted us to follow her the other day for good reason. That's why we're going to take her home and let him sort it out."

Cleon couldn't let that happen. "How do you plan on doing that? You're not going to hurt her, are you?"

"Of course not." Raza smiled. Something in his voice told Cleon that wasn't the truth.

Cleon pulled the wagon to a stop at the fence, and they

hauled the crate to the entrance. The cargo growled, swiping through the wooden bars at the hands holding the rope cords. Heavy steel bars spaced five or six inches apart created the gate, which was nestled in a tall link fence with a top covering of razor-sharp protrusions.

Raza ran his hand across the sensor on the post to the left of the gate.

Cleon glanced around. "This is beautiful country. Why don't they come out here and live?"

Raza raised a hand for silence and ran his other hand back and forth across the sensor several times. He cursed under his breath. "No one's ever in the security booth to answer these stupid gates. I want this deal done so I can get out here for Selah."

Cleon smiled. "I guess they don't expect many visitors."

"Merchants and buyers of fuel are here every—"

"State your business and insert your pass," said the monotone voice coming from the speaker mounted on the gate.

"Delivery for Ganston," Raza said. He fished the identacard from his pocket and pushed it into the slot below the sensor.

The gate buzzed and slid back on its track.

Raza huffed. "About time." He led the way through the gate to the entrance about fifty feet away and ran his hand across the door sensor. The polished steel door automatically opened.

They traveled down a wide rocrete hallway. The coolness of the corridor was in direct opposition to the heat outside. It soothed Cleon at first, but soon he began to sweat from hauling the crate of growling, darting animals.

A light ribbon running down the center of the ceiling provided subdued but sufficient illumination. Raza pushed another button at the end of the long corridor, and the door slid open, sending them in a left-handed ninety-degree direction. Raza stopped inside the doorway and lowered his end of the crate to the floor. Cleon followed suit.

"I didn't realize how heavy these things could get. Next time maybe we shouldn't feed them on the way," Cleon said, hands on his hips to stretch the muscles in his shoulders.

"They'd probably be dead by the time we got here," Raza said, breathing heavily.

So much the better. Cleon lifted the cover to peek. He detested these things and didn't understand why they were selling them or anyone was buying them. "They're all moving. Let's get this over with."

They picked up the crate and continued down the hall and through another access point. The contrast was noticeable. Inside this hall the walls were adorned with large colorful posters. Cleon gawked at each as they passed by. One stated rules for merchants and peddlers. Another listed contraband items not allowed in the Mountain, while another listed violations that could get you a stint in detention.

They came to an open area labeled Security, where merchants checked in. Cleon noticed directional signs to the market area. Raza passed it by.

Cleon looked in. "Don't we have to go in here?"

"No, that's for merchants. We're making a delivery," his brother said. He ran his hand over the next wall sensor. The last door opened and they stepped inside the Mountain.

After the subdued light of the corridors, Cleon shielded

his eyes from the bright sunlight inside—or outside, as it seemed. He gazed around in wonder. He'd never been into the town. Sunshine, clouds, and even a breeze mimicked the outdoors. He could smell rain but the scent was odd. Small streams ran along the sides of the drying streets, emptying into rectangular grates.

They set down the crate, and Cleon moved toward the street intersection. People moved about just like in the Borough. Wheeled vehicles and AirStreams operated in the same paved spaces, in separate lanes. Cleon walked toward a tree that looked to be maple. An alarm sounded, shrill and annoying.

"Warning, you are entering a restricted zone. Please return to the area registered to your identa-card user or face detention," the monotone voice said.

He looked around, bewildered. He'd never been inside before. Where was he supposed to go?

"Get back here! You don't belong on the streets," Raza yelled.

Cleon hurried back to the corridor. "I'm sorry. We haven't seen a single person since we got here. What'd that voice mean?"

Raza held up the identa-card from his pocket. "The *recording* said because we registered with this card we can't stray from the path it designates, or they'll come after us."

Cleon moved back to the crate. He wasn't fond of the smell or the feel of this place. "Can we get this over with?"

Raza nodded. They passed many numbered or labeled sections—some were recessed hallways and others were flush with the corridor. Cleon needed rest. He was hungry and thirsty.

They stopped at a door labeled Area Twenty-Seven. Raza

221

passed his hand over the sensor. Several seconds later a portly man with a receding hairline opened the door.

"Mr. Ganston, I've brought the next delivery," Raza said with a nervous smile.

Ganston motioned them in. Leaning out the doorway, he looked up and down the corridor before closing the opening. "I expected you yesterday. I appreciate people who are prompt."

Raza looked down. "Sorry. It won't happen again. Where would you like them?"

Cleon watched with interest. He'd never seen Raza so passive.

Ganston led them down a corridor into a kitchen. Raza put on the heavy steel mesh gloves attached to the crate. He pulled the rabbits out of the opening by their ears and deposited them in a wire enclosure beside a stainless steel counter. Cleon peered into the container. Black and white ones, brown ones, rust-colored ones, all agitated and trying to claw their way out.

Fear zipped across his chest. Shiny steel appliances and immaculate countertops went on for as far as he could see. They were putting these dangerous diseased animals where people prepared food.

"Sir, uh, Mr. Ganston, these rabbits are not meant for food. I think it's dangerous, even unsanitary, to have them in this area," Cleon said.

Ganston glanced at him, then at Raza. "Who is this person you brought?"

Raza grabbed one rabbit with both hands, jockeying for control as it tried to bite through the steel mesh of the glove. "He's my brother, sir."

"Well, he needs to understand this is a very private deal with you alone, and he cannot talk about this with anyone."

Raza glared at Cleon then looked back at Ganston. "He understands that, sir."

Cleon wondered what kind of "deal" Raza had negotiated. He assumed the evil little animals were going to someone who wanted the hides. But this wasn't a place for collecting or curing hides. The hairs on his arms felt disturbed like when a mosquito tried to land on him.

Raza wrestled a belligerent rabbit into the container. Cleon backed away. The animal might get out. He wondered what he'd do other than hop on a table to get away from it, but that seemed like something a girl would do. Raza would never let him forget it.

Ganston walked to a wall panel beside the doorway and pulled an indentation. A tall closet doorway opened, exposing several weapons. He chose one with a shape similar to the antique guns Cleon's father sometimes refurbished for people in the Borough, except it was fatter, shinier, with a barrel opening about an inch across.

"Stand back," Ganston said. He walked toward the container as he dialed a setting on the side mount.

Raza moved to stand beside Cleon. Ganston aimed the weapon in the direction of the container and pulled the trigger. A shimmering heat wave, almost invisible to the eye, traveled from the weapon to the container. Instantly the rabbits went quiet.

Raza approached and peered into the container. "What did you do to them? Are they dead?"

Ganston stretched out the hand holding the weapon. "Yes.

They will be used immediately, so there was no reason to keep them alive. It's a pulse disruptor, a high-velocity energy beam that disrupts cellular structure with no muss, fuss, or visible damage."

"So you *are* going to use the pelts!" Cleon chuckled. "You made me worried there for a minute. I had the crazy idea you were using these for food."

Raza started to laugh. "Well, that was stupid. Why would anyone be so foolish?"

Ganston's ears reddened. He returned the weapon to the closet, slammed the door shut, and turned. "I'll get the payment. Please stay here and don't wander."

Raza watched Ganston leave. He crept to the front of the closet.

Cleon followed, whispering, "What are you doing?" His fear came through loud and clear. He glanced to the doorway Ganston had gone through as he pulled on Raza's arm.

Raza jerked free. "I want one of those. Keep your mouth shut and watch for him to come back."

Cleon hesitated. "What if their sensors know you took it?"

"I'll worry about that if it happens." He popped open the closet, grabbed the weapon, and shoved it in his waistband under his shirt.

Cleon ran back to the counter where there was a clear view of the doorway. He couldn't distinguish footfalls from the blood pounding in his head. "You're stealing. Don't you think he'll notice?" His hands trembled. He'd never stolen. Theft was *not* one of the morals Mother had ingrained in them. And Raza didn't have a need for that kind of weapon.

"Shut up! We'll be gone by the time he figures it out," Raza said.

Ganston returned a moment later. He looked at the brothers then held out a scanner to Raza. "Here's your bio-coin."

Raza extended his wrist with the modified ComTex for bio-coin payments. Ganston ran the scanner over it. The payment sounded with a blip and registered on the tiny screen.

"I'm sure you're anxious to get out of the Mountain." Ganston stared over his glasses.

"In more ways than one," Cleon said. He glared at Raza, who acted nonchalant.

Ganston led them to the exit. "This is the last shipment I need. The deal is done. Do not come back."

Raza turned to protest and Cleon noticed the outline of the weapon protruding from his shirt. If Ganston averted his gaze he would surely see it. Cleon snatched his brother by the sleeve and pulled him through the doorway.

Ganston strolled back to his office after overseeing the culinary integration of his last specimens. About a year ago a fluke demonstrated how virulent the diseased rabbits could be on second- and third-generation Mountain dwellers. Granted, there were several unfortunate deaths he attributed directly to the infused matter in the executive-level food line, but he considered them acceptable losses for the cause.

The cause. The operation hadn't gotten the desired results. Everling was still alive.

Ganston frowned. Nevertheless he'd be leaving in a month. Case closed.

Sitting at his desk, he called up a family album on his halo-screen. His fingers tenderly touched the images. If his great-grandma's wish of freedom wasn't granted by him, there would be no heir to take up the mantle. The love of his life had died forty years ago in childbirth. No wife. No children. The beginning of the Mountain birth rate decline.

A knock sounded on the half-open door. Ganston glanced up as Jax leaned in.

"Mr. Ganston, your security woman, Mojica, is here. She demands to speak with you even though I told her this wasn't an appropriate time." Jax looked flustered.

Ganston wanted to smile but feared the poor fellow might cry or do something equally unmanly. "Show her in. I have time before the meeting."

Jax turned out of the doorway, and Mojica, dressed in all black resembling leather, barged past him into the office, closing the door in his face.

Ganston sat back in his chair. She was quite a spitfire, all six feet of her. Reminded him of himself at that age. Her exuberance would build a mighty army. "What can I do for you now that you've completely unnerved my assistant?"

"Well, the little pea-head should recognize Stone Braide's head of security needs unlimited access to you."

Ganston paused. Hearing the town name uttered in a conversation gave him a certain measure of pride and a dose of reality. It was finally happening. "I will see to it for the future. So was this a test of your authority?"

Hands fisted on hips, she tossed her long black mane of

hair out of the way and furrowed her brow. "Yes. No. Well, probably. It's like commanders not having access to the general in a war campaign."

Ganston leaned on the arm of his chair and rested his chin between his thumb and forefinger. It helped to mask the smile. His own Amazon woman. "And what do you know about war at your age?"

"I'm very well read on the art of war. Apparently this ancient society and its citizens fought with every country in the world at one time or another." Mojica moved to lean on the corner of his desk.

"Did you come here to discuss the merits of war?"

"I'm concerned about the security initiative for Stone Braide. Reading your directives, I get the distinct impression you want me to create an army."

"Do you have a problem with that plan?"

"No, not at all," Mojica said. "I'd much rather have precision forces than the doodlebug squad we have here."

"What's a doodlebug?"

Mojica plopped into the chair beside his desk. "It's my great-grandma's saying. It's wood lice, I think. They have shells like a lobster, roll up in a ball to hide, and are said to have an unpleasant taste similar to strong urine. I have no idea who would have ever tasted urine to know that—"

Ganston raised a hand. "I get the point." He noticed that of all the chairs, she sat in the one with the same height as his desk chair. She apparently was not about to be intimidated by the need to look up to talk to him.

"Obviously you don't or we wouldn't be having this conversation." She rested the heel of her boot against the top of his desk.

He stared at the intrusion to his space and used the back of his hand to move the shoe away from the surface. "Are you talking bugs or armies? Explain, but please make it brief. I have a meeting."

"The Mountain security force is laughable. They couldn't navigate their way out of a JetTrans if you shut them up in one. There hasn't been anything or anyone to challenge them in decades, and even watch shifts aren't functional. People come and go when they want to on no particular schedule. There are times when I literally have to hunt down the personnel of a given area!"

Ganston pursed his lips. "This could be a problem. We don't know what types of outlaws we'll face out there. We should probably plan for the worst and hope for the best."

"We're going to need weapon drills, combat training, specialty forces—"

"Okay, I get the message. Put together a plan and submit it to Jax."

Mojica jumped from her seat. "I'm supposed to turn in a major security initiative to *him*? And when will it be acted upon? When he has a spare moment between getting your dinner and making your appointments?"

Ganston ran his hand over the link for Jax. He could tell he'd been listening at the door because instantly the man opened it and popped his head in. "Yes, sir?"

"Jax, take a memo. Along with Mojica's responsibilities as head of security for Stone Braide, she now has complete control over the security operation."

Jax straightened up and entered the room. "Sir? Does this mean—"

"It means just what I said. She has the ultimate authority over security. She gets what she wants, when she wants it. Understood?" Ganston put on his stern face.

His assistant recoiled. "Yes, Mr. Ganston." The door closed behind him.

"Is there anything else you need?" Ganston asked nonchalantly as he folded his hands in front of him.

"Yes. I've identified several hundred for our initial security force—"

"That many? If I'm not mistaken that doesn't leave many in the Mountain."

Mojica shrugged. "The Mountain doesn't need these people. I've culled them from my clan. They're top notch in combat and defense operations."

"Oh really. How come these *experts* aren't currently part of Mountain security?"

"Let's just say they needed discipline initiatives to motivate them."

Ganston understood—she assembled rebels. Occasionally the Company quelled uprisings among those groups. Usually they vanished into the untamed furthest reaches of the Mountain interior—the areas given generations to equalize flora and fauna growth before population inhabitation. "I see, and the ones you are taking from actual Mountain security—will they leave the Mountain vulnerable?"

Mojica grinned and shook her head. "There are only so many ways in and out of this place. They've always been overstaffed. Security duty pays well, and Politicos get their cronies assigned for easy jobs. They'll never be missed."

"How did you assemble this group so quickly?" Ganston worried she'd been at work on some other subversion without his knowledge, maybe as a mole for Everling.

"It's no secret that many in security are dissatisfied with the ways things are handled. Quite a few have returned to the private sector and are more than happy to join our new endeavor. We need to start training."

"What kind of training?"

"I want to take them to the wilderness at the other end of the Mountain. We need intensive exercises in a number of areas including combat."

"When do you want to do this?"

"Right away. I'd like to start moving them out today. If you want us to be ready with boots on the ground in a month, even this is cutting it close."

Ganston nodded. "Do it."

Mojica smiled and hustled out of the office.

Ganston tented his fingers and lowered his head. He found comfort in her ability and initiative, but was putting her in charge the right choice? Could he be sure before it was too late?

Was this an Everling trap?

◬

Stemple left his quarters and headed across the road to the lab. The rain cycle had finished and the faux sunshine baked the streets dry. The halo-projections on the far-off walls gave the illusion of mountains, forests, and sky. Right now the sun was climbing toward its noontime high. How could such peacefulness mask so much evil?

As if on cue, the MagLev train slid silently into the station above the tree line next to the Corporate Lab. People filtered from the station down to the street, and the magnetic rail train slid off through its tube traversing the Mountain. Stemple dreamed of getting on the train one day and never coming back. He'd relieve himself of all the evil he'd accumulated here.

He slipped into the lab and slowed to a stop. Which direction should he go? To Everling's lab to start prototype testing the new serum, or to the containment labs where the prisoners were held? Stemple gritted his teeth. *Dismantle* . . . Everling's choice of a singular nondescript word for the process of killing numerous people outraged him. And with Bethany Everling back in the lab, the situation was worse. She was more driven than Dr. Everling.

Stemple turned toward Everling's private lab, approached the door, and raised his hand to the scanner. This wasn't right. He needed to help the Landers before it was too late. He strode down the corridor to Lab Section Ten.

Stemple keyed his ComTex to locate Treva. It showed she was in the Lander confinement section. He hurried through the palm and retina scans and the door opened.

Treva stood before the transparent plascine wall talking to Glade Rishon. Stemple halted. She shouldn't be that close to a Lander. Glade looked toward him.

A few years ago he'd felt a burning sensation whenever he came near Glade. It unnerved him so he avoided contact. Not fearful, just prudent.

Treva looked up. He didn't miss her hands moving behind her as she turned to face him.

"What's going on?" Stemple approached warily.

Treva cocked an eyebrow. "Just working. Why, is something wrong?"

Stemple tried to look behind her. She evaded his glance to her hands. He furrowed his brows. "What's in your hand?"

"Nothing, why do you ask? Is this a game of ten questions?" She placed both hands into her lab coat pockets.

Maybe it was because of Everling, but at the moment Stemple wasn't feeling very trusting. He reached for her left arm and removed it from her pocket.

"Release her!" Glade's ear-splitting voice boomed.

Stemple flinched, his ears ringing. He stared into the slit eyes and pinched mouth of Glade Rishon seething with rage. He backed away from Treva.

"I need to talk to you outside," Stemple said. He turned and hurried from the lab.

He pulled on his ear a few times, the ringing still evident. How did Glade do that? He thought the new injections Everling had ordered eliminated those kinds of episodes. Why had they returned?

He mulled over a new formulation. The dismantle came to mind. No more formulas. Either he was going to help the Landers go free or he was going to kill them. Time was of the essence before one of the Everlings took charge of the dismantle.

The door swooshed open and Treva exited the confinement area. Stemple grabbed her.

"What have you done?"

Treva jerked from his grasp. "Don't you put your hands on me again, or I'll report you."

"How was he able to project pain on me?"

"You must have sensitive ears. It was only sound."

"Stop avoiding my question." Stemple grabbed at her lab coat pocket.

She pulled back. The material tore loose at the top corner with an audible rip.

Treva looked down. "I can't believe you did that. I'm reporting you." She stormed away.

"Wait!" Stemple yelled.

She spun around. "Wait for what, for you to physically assault me again?"

Stemple let out a sigh and raised both hands as if in surrender. "I'm sorry. Come back. We don't have time for this. I was just unnerved by the piercing sound in my head."

Treva stopped. "I didn't even notice."

"We gave them a drug cocktail eliminating their communications and higher-decibel sound abilities. But there's a lot we don't know because Everling never cared to explore the possibilities, just his own agenda. What were you doing in there?" Stemple wanted to ask why the sound didn't affect her, but he didn't want to appear sensitive to Lander sounds. It made him look weak. He rubbed his ear again.

"I don't know what you think I was doing, but—"

"Listen, no more games. You were right about Everling." Stemple knew they needed to act fast. No time for personalities or arguments.

Treva tipped her head. "You're not making sense."

"You asked him about the fountain of youth. He did it.

233

Wait till you see him *and* his wife. They've regressed at least twenty years."

Treva's mouth fell open. "Are you serious? How? The data has to be phenomenal."

Stemple shook his head. "No time to study it. He wants me to dismantle the Lander project."

"What does that mean?"

"Get rid of the Landers."

Treva grinned. "They can finally be let go!"

Stemple hung his head. "Everling wants them all dead."

"No! You wouldn't. They're not lab animals. These are human beings." Treva's bottom lip started to tremble.

"I admit I had no problem holding them for the experiments because I thought we were using them to cure cancer. But not this. Some lunatic proposition of living forever. And now he's going after children. I've changed my mind."

"What do you mean, *children?*"

"He's destroying the Landers because he's going after their children in some insane quest to find immortality. I think it's more his wife Bethany's idea than his, but he's going along with it. I have to figure out how to get the Landers out of here before Everling catches on." Stemple could feel the stress tightening his neck.

Treva wiped at her eyes with the back of her hands.

The outer door opened and Everling stepped in.

Treva looked at the younger, fresher version of the doctor, now possessing a full head of hair. Her mouth dropped open.

Everling motioned to Stemple with a look of dissatisfaction. "I need you in my lab. Bethany wants the latest projections on dismantling."

Stemple nodded.

"Now!" Everling barked. He turned and exited. The opening slid closed.

Treva turned to Stemple with her mouth still hanging open. "I'm sorry I doubted you. I'd give my eyeteeth to study that research."

"That's part of the problem. He didn't do extensive research or testing. He experimented on himself and his wife. I have no idea what the consequences will be. Already I'm seeing personality changes."

Treva shook her head. "Stupid actions have consequences."

Stemple started for the opening. "Speaking of that, please, no more surprises."

15

Treva darted back into the unit and over to Glade. "What did you just do to him?"

"I protected you." Glade rose from his chair and walked to the wall.

"I can take care of myself."

Glade paced. "I feel like I owe you more than I could ever repay. I'm feeling normal again. I can communicate with others—so much pain, so much anger. It's like sound waves that ebb and flow. I can't concentrate. Thoughts jumble together. Emotions make no sense."

Treva nodded. "Your system is still flushing years of chemical depressants."

Glade stopped. He pressed his palms to the wall. "Something feels strange. Different. Someone else. I've never felt an impression like this before. My aura is bouncing back. A reflection." Glade cocked his head to the side. His eyes widened. "It couldn't be. How?"

"Glade, is it pain? You look pale. Do you need another shot?" She turned to retrieve an injection. Her secret project. A nootropic to stimulate Glade's nerve growth and oxygen supply. He'd been on Everling's suppressants the longest and likely suffered the most damage.

His eyes sparkled with moisture. "My daughter! My daughter is near."

Treva stopped short. "How could that happen? Is she a prisoner? Does Everling have anything to do with this?" Her face paled. Had Everling retrieved the child that fast?

"No, Everling has nothing to do with this. That much I know. She's coming closer." Glade slammed his fist into the wall.

Treva jumped. His face didn't register pain. Was he becoming psychotic? Maybe Everling was right about his drug cocktail. Too late now. This wasn't working like she'd expected. Glade cooperated but Landers below were becoming unmanageable and rowdy. This could push up Everling's dismantle plans.

"Where is she? Can you integrate her into your thoughts?"

Glade's agitation heightened. He shook his head. "I've lost it. I can't find the thought. Others are pressing in around it. More voices from below. They won't listen to be calm. They want out."

"I gave them the last course of shots this morning. They need to rest. Let the detox complete."

Glade held his head. "I need a direct line of sight to affect them."

"How do I do it from here?" Treva headed back to the console and laid the syringe gently in the drawer tray.

"Get a halo-comm open to that level. I can channel on the wave and calm them."

Treva scrambled to dial the prison level. What was her reason for calling? *Think fast.*

A sentry answered the comm. "Level Three Confinement, Saylor speaking."

Treva put on her best smile. "Saylor, this is Treva Gilani in Lab Section Ten. I'm looking for data sheets that seem to have been misplaced in the transfer with the last Lander body."

"What Lander body?"

Treva pulled back. How could he forget the body that had come up just a few days ago?

"Three days ago—the dead one. Are you working double shifts down there?"

The tech's face lit up. "Oh, now I know what you mean. We don't call them Landers."

That was odd. Treva wondered what they called them down there.

A high-pitched vibration now drifted through the connection and hummed in her ears. Treva shook her head, turning to look at Glade. He was deep in concentration. She hoped he'd hurry. The sound was hurting her head.

The sentry put his hand to his ear. "What is that humming?"

Treva steeled herself to the sound. "I'm not sure what you're talking about. I don't hear anything."

The sentry winced. She feared he'd break the connection.

"Can you please check on those sheets? This is really important." She looked beyond the screen at Glade. He finally slumped to his chair and nodded.

The sentry returned to the screen looking apologetic. "I'm sorry but I don't see any extra material here that did not make the transfer with the clo—er, body."

"Thanks then, maybe they just got misplaced." Treva broke the link. She opened and closed her mouth to get the vibration out of her ears.

"Did you get through?"

Glade nodded. "I forgot, it's been so long. Their senses are sharpening and it's frightening them. I don't know how long I can keep control of them."

<hr />

Everling leaned back in his chair, watching Bethany work on new sample batches. She was a vision that brought tears to his eyes. Her graying hair had reverted to its blonde luster, and her worry lines had filled in. They had always bothered her—well, no more. The cancer had disappeared and the beautiful, radiant woman of his younger years had reappeared. All they needed were a few tweaks to stop the process continuation.

His mind kept wandering. It was hard to think.

"Did you hear what I said to you?" Bethany asked. Her pale green eyes flashed.

Everling shook off his thoughts. "I'm sorry, my love. What did you say?"

Bethany looked agitated. "The patrol we send to Dominion is reporting in. They met with your contact but the girl is not there. Her mother says she must have run away. She was slated to get married and didn't want to."

Everling shot straight up in his chair. "How could they

lose a young girl? And why has it taken two days to get me this answer?"

Bethany shook her head. "It's your fault. I told you before we needed a better communication grid outside of the Mountain."

"No! It's a waste of valuable resources to build a system out there," Everling said. He started to get irate. Why waste money when they'd never go out there to get any use out of it?

"Well, in a case like this, it would have been handy. We've lost a whole day trying to track her. That's not going to be very effective with AirStreams." Bethany slapped her halo-pad on the counter and turned away from Everling.

"I will not put resources into anything that could be used by those peasants out there."

Bethany turned back and slammed a fist on the counter. "Suit yourself. Since the JetTrans can't travel that far, we sent AirStreams, and they were required to return within twenty miles of the Mountain before we could communicate with them."

He knew she was right but didn't want to admit it. In her youth, her father had been head of Mountain security. Her destiny had been the next security head, but being a child of the Elite put her with other Elite offspring. He'd met her and fallen in love, and she followed him into research. But she could still run a security operation with her eyes closed, and her forward thinking on communication systems was something he needed to take seriously. When this present situation had ended.

Bethany stared at him, waiting for an answer. "We're losing days."

241

"She has a bio-signature. Tell them to start from where she lived and scan until they find her." He began an agitated tapping on the surface of his desk. "Rank incompetence. There are not many roads down there. She'd have stayed on one of them. Set up a security grid with AirStreams. They can interface at twenty-mile intervals. Send a dozen if you have to. Sweep from there to here. And get a JetTrans grid set up outside the Mountain perimeter to check as far south as they can travel."

"What about south of Dominion?" Bethany asked.

Everling shook his head. "Conditions are more dangerous farther south, so if she's going anywhere, she's coming this way. Find her."

⊛

Selah leaned back against a pile of wooden crates as the wagon bumped along the well-traveled road. She tried not to think about home, or Dane, or Father, but Mother's voice kept coming to her, quickening her heart. She'd never been away from Mother. She desperately missed her and her counsel on how to do things right. She needed to talk about a boy, and about kissing, and about what to do next. Funny, they'd never talked much of this rite of passage. She'd expected "the talk" before her upcoming marriage, but before now there was no use for it.

Bodhi sat facing her on the other side of the wagon bed, his blond curls bouncing in the breeze, falling across his closed eyes. It annoyed her that he seemed to sleep so much, oblivious to their dangers or her ruined life. She wanted to be mad, but Mother had taught her and the boys about personal responsibility for their actions. She always said transferring the blame to someone else never taught the intended lesson. How could she be mad at Bodhi when she hadn't known about her change either?

If she'd known the consequences would she still have tried to capture him? She truthfully couldn't say she'd have played it safe. By nature she tended to be daring—one of the reasons her mother had said she'd be fine on this journey. She didn't want to accept it, but she had to admit, she'd worked beyond the fear and embraced the adventure. She made herself a promise—she would see Mother again. The thought gave her courage.

As if on cue, Bodhi opened his eyes and smiled. The air around him seemed to glow with the radiation from those lips. She worked to restrain her thudding heartbeat. *Even breaths.* This was not the time, and besides, sometimes he acted arrogant and she didn't like it.

"I'm sorry," Bodhi said softly. His eyes looked so caring.

Selah balked but her heart melted. Why did he always seem to answer what she was thinking? "What have you done to be sorry about this time?"

He stammered, lowered his eyes, then raised his head with a sheepish look. "I feel I'm the reason for your pain."

Selah glanced down. "As of this minute, I'm letting go of that. I'm trying to learn to focus on what I'll gain, not what I've lost." She pursed her lips. "You have no idea how many years I fretted about being adopted because my father—uh, stepfather—never seemed to care for me, only to have this happen."

"Did you find any solace in your mother's letters?"

Selah shrugged. "Yes and no. I'm not brave enough yet. I can only let so much sink in at one time." There were personal pages Mother had written for such a time as this, and those made her cry. She only read small sections at a time.

"But we're getting closer to where your father is. I got that definite impression before of Glade Rishon, and I can feel a group of them, you know. It's like they've gone through some kind of awakening. It's all jumbled thoughts and impressions. You could feel them too—just concentrate."

Selah sat up straight. "Really? I could feel them too?" Her heart quickened for a better reason now. Her father. Her real father. Thinking of touching his thoughts for the first time made her prickle with excitement. But she just sensed empty space.

She shook her head. "I can't. I don't hear anything."

"It's not like an actual sound. It's more of an impression. Try. Clear your mind."

Selah went quiet for about three seconds. "I don't feel anything."

Bodhi smiled. "You're too noisy. Be quiet and listen. It's a still, small voice far away."

Selah huffed, closed her eyes, and crossed her arms. The wagon came to a jarring stop. Her eyes flew open. "What's the matter?"

She glanced at the front where Amaryllis sat with the driver, a middle-aged man the color of tree bark, with a heavy southern accent and arms the size of water barrels. He practically exploded from the cutoff sleeves of the worn shirt plastered to him by the sweltering weather. A gargantuan man, but the wide straw hat and handmade pipe made him appear friendly.

He looked back. "I'm stopping for something to eat and drink for me and my horses. Y'all are welcome to join us."

"We'd love to, but I don't want to put you out with three more mouths to feed," Selah said. They'd walked for hours before he'd come along and offered a ride to the Mountain, and they'd already used a good bit of their rations.

"My missus packed plenty of vittles for the trip—too much for just me, but the woman's got intuition. She must've known I'd have company."

The man hopped down off the wagon, tied the horses to the nearby tree, and walked around back to grab their feed buckets. "She has these things she sees. Just knows stuff. Don't know how she does it. We've been married nigh on thirty years, and she's always done it. So I just accept and don't try explaining the stuff."

Bodhi looked at Selah. She shrugged and grimaced. Amaryllis scrambled over the seat, climbing over the canvas sacks and crates and into the wagon bed. She nuzzled next to Selah, who wrapped her arms around the child.

"What are we going to eat?" Amaryllis asked. "There's things I don't like."

"Rylla, that's not polite. The man has invited us to lunch with him. We watch our manners, young lady." Was that *mother-speak* coming out of her mouth? It probably wouldn't have happened if not for the revelation that a man had tried to harm the child. Mother had once told her these days were coming. It made Selah want to protect Amaryllis—and beat the man to a pulp. She'd finally found something to make her fiery brave.

"That's no problem." The man laughed. "I raised a passel of children myself, got quite used to their honesty and wisecracking."

Amaryllis wrinkled up her nose and pointed. "What's in those sacks? They smell funny."

The man pulled the food satchel from the wagon. They followed him to a shade tree.

"Well, young lady, those are snake skins," the man said as he opened the food satchel and handed out thick slices of homemade bread.

"Eckk!" Amaryllis yelled, wrinkling her nose and waving the air like snakes were slithering in front of her.

"What kind of snake skins do you sell?" Selah asked, thinking of the field varieties of snakes at home.

"Big ones. Complete pelts are quite worthy of their high price." The man smiled broadly.

Amaryllis backed away. Her hands trembled. "Like the snake that tried to eat me?"

The man furrowed his brow, looking at Selah.

Selah bit into the sweet-tasting bread and nodded. "It was a huge one, at least twelve or fifteen feet. Never seen one that big up close."

The man pulled out a vegetable paste and passed the container for them to dip their bread. "I've heard some folks trying to grow them here in the North. Sometimes they get free by accident. Rest assured, when the temperature gets below freezing for a spell it will kill them off."

"Do you hunt them for a living?" Bodhi asked. He pulled pears and apples from the bag he carried and passed them around.

"Yes, sirree. I'm from down Georgia district way. There's

good money selling the skins. They make fine boots, belts, and I even seen clothes in snakeskin."

Bodhi munched bread and fruit. "Isn't it dangerous to live around them?"

The man threw back his head and snorted a laugh. "These big boys live down Florida way. People don't live there anymore 'cause of too many big snakes. They tend to eat people when they get that size."

Amaryllis nodded vigorously, pointing at her chest. Crumbs fell everywhere. "Me! Me! I know. One tried to eat me."

"You're right lucky, young lady. You sure could've been a meal. Even small game is migrating north. I've seen a lot of the birds from down that way, and as I'm travelin' north, I've started to see the rabbits too. That makes me happy. I'll have good eats while I'm up here."

Selah stiffened, testing him. "Rabbits? What do they look like?"

"They're cinnamon rabbits, bred for meat, great eating. Guess the snakes feel the same."

Selah looked at Bodhi and Amaryllis in turn, puffing out her chest. "Are they sort of rusty-colored and some have a fleck of gray?"

"Yep, that would be them. Have you ever tried one?"

Selah raised the right side of her mouth. "We ate one for dinner last night."

Bodhi reached across Amaryllis and handed Selah the vegetable paste. Her fingers brushed his. Adrenaline freshened her nerves, running electricity up her arm. She looked into his eyes with those long lashes. His nose crinkled and his eyes sparkled as he broke into a grin.

Amaryllis jumped from between them, breaking their finger contact. "Ugh! You two need to kiss face and stop making cow eyes at each other."

Both Selah and Bodhi sat back. Neither said anything. Selah felt her cheeks warming.

The snake man broke into a chuckle. "So, young lady, you telling me they aren't a couple? I sure thought y'all act like a family."

Amaryllis did the girly hand-on-hip thing. "She likes him and he likes her, and they—"

"Rylla!" Selah said. "We do not like each other!"

"Do too," Amaryllis said.

"Do too," Bodhi chimed in with a wide grin.

Selah sat back. She smacked her palm to her forehead and pointed at him. "You're reading me! That's why you're grinning." She slapped him on the arm. "You sea slug!"

Bodhi threw up both arms to fend off her blows and leaned back in laughter. "You could stop me anytime you want to. Concentrate."

Selah scrambled to her feet. "Ugh. You are the most insufferable . . . ugh."

Amaryllis turned to the snake man. "See what I mean." He nodded and continued eating.

Selah stomped her foot and turned to storm away. Both Amaryllis and the snake merchant grinned.

Bodhi grabbed his head and moaned.

Selah turned back. "Don't think I'm falling for that, mister."

He doubled over into a ball, still holding his head.

She moved closer. "Bodhi?"

Cleon sat beside Raza as the wagon rumbled away from the Mountain and down the maintained portion of road.

"What were you thinking, stealing that weapon? Have you lost what little sense you were born with?" Cleon expected a squadron of JetTrans to descend on them at any moment.

Raza gritted his teeth and urged the horses forward using the tips of the reins. "Shut up! I know what I'm doing."

At the end of the Mountain road he pulled the team into a field. Guiding the horses across knee-high grass, he steered behind a wide stand of oak trees near the rocky base of the Mountain.

"Why are you stopping here?" Cleon asked. He watched Raza jump from the wagon. The sun sat high and a breeze rustled the leaves. A nice day but they were still several days from home. He was hungry and tired of being with Raza.

"We're waiting for Selah," Raza hissed. "Mr. Ganston said no new Landers arrived yet, so she's on the road somewhere. This is the easiest place to catch them. They'll have to come this way."

"Let Selah have him. She bested us, and she did it well. Maybe it's time we let her join the hunt," Cleon said with a dismissive flip of his hand.

Raza walked toward the road. "I know what I'm doing. Watch and learn, little brother."

"You're being foolish. I thought I'd lose my mind when you hid his weapon under your shirt." Cleon vowed he would never act like his brother.

"But I have the weapon and you don't." Raza sneered and patted the weapon.

Cleon didn't care about that. He plopped onto a fallen tree. "How long are we going to wait here? I want to go home."

"Stop whining! You're driving me crazy. Next time you stay home and I'll get one of the Borough boys to help me."

Cleon lowered his head. "I'm just tired of traveling for—"

"Shhh!" Raza crouched behind a bush and motioned to the road.

Horse hooves clopped along the road. A wagon slowed to a stop at the end of the paved section. Voices drifted into the trees.

"If you pull that kind of stunt again I'll really make your head hurt," a woman said.

"I truly did feel pain, but it diminished as fast as it came," a man said.

"I don't believe you," the woman said.

"That's obvious. We've been arguing about this for an hour. Can we change the subject?" the man asked. He sounded exasperated.

"Okay, then stop invading my head."

"I'm only trying to make you stretch. Regardless of how you feel, the mark makes you novarium. You have to explore your abilities."

"Well, excuse me. Since when did you become my boss?" the woman asked.

"Would you two stop bickering? You sound like my parents," a child's voice said.

The talk grew louder. Cleon thought he recognized Selah's voice, but the tone seemed deeper. He didn't know the other two.

Raza grabbed him by the arm and pulled him into the trees as the voices moved closer.

"You need to focus your energy," the man said.

"And what if I don't want—"

Raza stepped out of the trees.

16

Selah skidded to a halt and let out a yelp. Not marauders, only her brothers. Amaryllis darted behind her, grabbing her shirt as Bodhi moved in front to protect her. Typical tricks. Trying to scare her to death. Her heart thudded. She pushed Bodhi's arm aside and stepped up beside him, facing off with the boys. She liked Bodhi's protectiveness, but these two she could handle. "Well, I figured we'd run into you somewhere along the line."

"Hand him over or face the consequences," Raza said. Venom dripped from his words.

Selah blinked. She didn't know this person so full of hate.

"Hi, sis," Cleon said, his head down. "Sorry I forgot to say happy Birth Remembrance the other day."

Selah saw a hint of color on his ears. Poor guy was embarrassed. "That's okay—"

"Shut up, both of you!" Raza screamed. "I'm tired of your

incessant whining." He drew the weapon from under his shirt and aimed it at Bodhi. "The Lander is mine."

Bodhi put his arm out, attempting to shield Selah. Her eyes widened. She glared at Raza.

"You don't mean this, Raza. Think about what you're doing. And where did you get a weapon?" She lowered Bodhi's arm and slowly moved toward Raza. He was her brother. He acted bossy, but this was just for show, for Bodhi, to intimidate him.

"He stole it. Be careful, Selah. Stay away from that thing," Cleon said. "This wasn't supposed to happen this way."

"It's all right, Cleon. Raza's not going to hurt anyone. Are you, Raza? But I can't let you have him. He has to help me," Selah said.

"Stand back or I'll fire," Raza said. He clamped his jaw. "He's a Lander. He's an alien in our country. They're an infection that needs to be erased."

"No, you don't understand. They're people like us. If you're going to shoot him, you'll have to shoot me." Selah figured that would break him from this tantrum and he'd start thinking straight.

"I can arrange that real easy." Raza spat out the words.

Selah's throat went dry. Suddenly she couldn't swallow. Her brother had threatened to shoot her? It must be just bluster. Her mind wouldn't allow her to think he was serious. Not her brother.

Cleon jerked his head to Raza. "What're you saying? Don't be stupid. Put that down."

"I could shoot her just as easy as I'd shoot him. She's a half-breed one of those." Raza motioned with the weapon toward Bodhi.

Selah's mouth fell open. She took a step forward. "You knew? How? I didn't even know."

Raza backed away. "Father told me years ago. And he warned me this week to be on the lookout for you getting close to these mongrels. That's why we watched you at the beach."

Selah's face flushed. "So you knew what would happen if I touched him and you just *let* me do it? Just *let* me ruin my life? You're my brother. Why?"

Raza threw back his head and laughed. "Easiest way to get rid of you, wench."

"Wench?" Calling her names was the end of being nice. Selah charged at him.

Raza raised the weapon. "Stop or you die."

Selah's steps faltered. "You wouldn't." Her mind ran through past episodes. School. The beach. Years of insults thought to be just sibling torment. The picture cleared. Yes, he would hurt her, and he'd probably enjoy it.

Cleon stepped in front of Raza. "You wouldn't. She's our sister."

"You're as worthless as she is." Raza pushed Cleon from between them. He tripped and slid across the stony road. Selah watched gravel bite at the palms of his hands.

"What's the matter with you? Have you gotten heat stroke or something? What have I done to you?" Cleon brushed off his hands and stood.

"I'm perfectly sane for the first time in a long time," Raza said. "Do you really think Father or I can ever forgive you for taking Mother from us?"

Cleon froze, his mouth fell open, and then his face went red with rage. "Mother died during childbirth."

Selah stood frozen. Was this the same family she'd lived with? Her feelings of being adopted made sense after finding out all the things she hadn't known about her own family.

Raza spit on the ground. "Yes, and if you were never born she'd still be alive."

"Well then, blame Father for creating me," Cleon said. Tears filled his eyes. He clamped his lips and clenched his fists as he moved toward Raza.

Raza turned the weapon on him. "Back up! Don't make me hurt you."

Cleon backed away to his left. Selah moved forward again. "Raza, you need to calm down. Let's talk this over—"

Bodhi pushed past Selah. "I don't know you, but I know you must love your sister—"

"She's not my sister. My father married her mongrel of a mother," Raza said.

"Don't you dare talk about Mother like that!" Selah yelled. She darted around Bodhi and rushed Raza. The words stung more than anything they'd ever done. Mother loved them.

Raza raised the weapon and pointed. He pulled the trigger as Cleon tackled him.

Selah heard Amaryllis scream as the weapon flew from Raza's hand and landed in the tall grass. Selah and Bodhi rushed to restrain Raza as he and Cleon hurtled to the ground.

Cleon landed on top of his brother, and Selah heard a great rush of air push from his lungs. He scrambled off. Raza was limp, his eyes closed.

"Come on, Raza, get up," Cleon said. There was no response. He knelt beside Raza and shook him. Nothing.

Thinking the air was just knocked from him, Selah knelt as well and touched his arm. "Raza, are you all right?"

Cleon reached his hand behind Raza's head to lift him. A strangled sob pushed from his chest as he pulled back his hand. It was covered with blood.

Selah screamed. Her hands flew to her mouth to stifle the sound. So much blood. He couldn't die. She hadn't finished being angry at him. He needed to finish the argument so she could win fair and square. Not this way.

Bodhi walked Amaryllis away from the scene. She struggled, calling for Selah.

Tears welled in Selah's eyes. *Please don't let this be happening.* "Is he . . . dead?"

✤

Cleon stared at his hand covered in Raza's blood. So dark red. The acrid smell of copper lurched his stomach. He swallowed the taste of bile. This was an accident. He rubbed his hand in the grass over and over, not wanting to get blood on Raza's clothes. He'd be mad.

He leaned over and put his head to Raza's chest, expecting to hear something. Breathing, a heartbeat, any sign of life. Cleon heard his own heartbeat pounding in his head. *You. Killed. Your. Brother.*

He nodded to Selah. Tears splashed the front of his shirt and soaked into Raza's body.

Selah fell to her knees, sobbing. Her hands shook as she reached out to Raza. She pulled back, bit her lip, and then reached out again. Her fingertips hovered over his body, then she nudged him onto his side. His head had landed on a large rock. A matching depression in the back of his head held blood and tissue, brains and bone fragments mixed in a surreal collage.

Cleon stared. His knees began to tremble. His stomach lurched again. He flung himself to the side and disgorged his stomach in great heaving belches that made him feel like his stomach lining was coming out. The acrid liquid dripped from his nose and mouth, burning the tissue in his nose and throat. Leaning on shaking arms, he tried to breathe, tried to get air in his lungs without sniffing in the bile lingering in his nose. The pain overwhelmed him.

Dead.

Selah looked at him with teary eyes and spoke softly. "Cleon, this was *not* your fault."

He glanced up, wiping a sleeve across his mouth. "Whose fault was it?" His family was dissolving before his eyes. He'd lost a sister, now a brother. His father had lost a son.

"Raza did this to himself. You prevented us from dying," Selah said. "I wonder if Mother knew how Raza felt about her. If she did, it must have broken her heart. She always gave him nothing but love."

They both turned to look at Raza.

"What do we do with him?" Cleon asked in a strangled voice. He'd never dealt with a dead body before. Or was this one of Raza's tricks? Was he really dead? His body was still warm.

Selah wiped her eyes. "At home he'd be cremated, but we can't do that here, so we're going to have to bury him."

Cleon moved back beside Raza's body. Did he see movement? He closed his eyes then opened them, half expecting

Raza to sit up. Nothing—all he could think of was nothing. He turned to Selah. "What happens when you die?"

Selah hunched her shoulders. "I don't know. What do you mean?"

"I mean what happens when you die? You stop breathing. You get hard and cold for a long time. What else?"

"I don't know. I've only ever seen people cremated on the Borough pyre. They turn to dust and smoke and float off in the air. Dead is dead. The end," Selah said, her stare blank.

"But if we put him in the ground, won't the worms and maggots get him like they do the dead animals?" Cleon stared at his brother's body. Even though Raza had tried to kill him, was this a fitting end for him?

"There's nothing else we can do, other than you take his body home."

Cleon hung his head. "If I take him home, how do I tell Father I killed him?" In his head he kept saying over and over, *You killed your brother.*

"You don't. Father would banish you, or worse. Raza was clearly his favorite, especially after what he just said."

"Maybe I could lie. Say he died in an accident. He really did." He had to convince himself or his heart would pound him to death.

"You still feel in your heart that you killed him. I can see it in your eyes. You can't go back either," Selah said.

His head shot up. "What do you mean?" *Never go back home. An outcast. You killed your brother.*

She squinted. "You've never been able to lie convincingly like Raza. Father will know the truth as soon as you open your mouth."

His shoulders slumped. He rocked. He wanted his life back, the one before Landers. "I know you're right, but I want to go home."

Selah rose and walked around the body to help Cleon to his feet. She wrapped her arms around his waist and laid her head on his shoulder. They hugged tightly. "I want to go home too, but I can't go back either."

Cleon pulled away. "Why can't you come home with me?" She would make things better. Mother would listen to her explanation even though Father would be devastated.

She shook her head. "I don't want you to hate me," Selah said in a small voice.

"You're my sister and I love you. I would never hate you. What's the matter?" Cleon looked into her eyes.

She gulped. "Raza was right. I'm a half-breed. My real father was a Lander, and now I've touched a Lander and been marked."

Her hands trembled as she pulled back her top to show him the wing below her collarbone. She searched his face. He knew she was looking for revulsion in his face.

Cleon smiled sheepishly. "I've known about that since I was about nine years old." He'd never cared. His love was unconditional for his sister.

Selah balked. Her hands flew to her hips, and she leaned forward with a scowl. "How did everyone else know this when I was in the dark?"

Cleon sighed. "I used to sneak in our parents' bedroom and snoop. One day I found Mother's little treasure box and I read the letters from your real father."

Selah slapped him on the arm. "You've known all this time and never said anything!"

"What was I supposed to do, admit I rummaged through our parents' things? If I'd told Raza, he'd have blabbed to get me in trouble." His head dropped. "Now I know why he always acted like he hated me. He did, and apparently so does Father. It explains a lot."

"It's dangerous if you go back. Stay with us," Selah begged, holding his hand in hers.

Cleon looked over at Raza's body. Words stuck in his throat. "How are *you* feeling right now?" To save his sanity, he needed her to convince him this wasn't his fault.

Selah looked down at her hands. "Right now I'm numb. It will probably hit me later. But my first thought?" She looked up at him. "You can never tell anyone. Mother would have to forgive me . . . but my first thought was, *My tormentor is dead*."

"I'm sorry he made your life so miserable and Father never defended you."

Selah shook her head. "That's all over now."

"We'll have to find a spot to bury his body," Cleon said in a low voice.

"I've done a lot of things in the past couple days I thought I'd never do. This just adds another to the growing list," Selah said.

※

Bodhi refused to let Selah help Cleon bury their brother. He'd spent a lot of his existence acting with deliberate disregard for other people's feelings, especially women's, but he would not stand by and let her be responsible for helping to dig a grave and push a body into it. He cared for her too much. He made her stay with the child at the wagon as he helped Cleon haul Raza into the trees and bury him.

It was a strange experience. He'd never handled a dead body, and it was still slightly warm. Felt strange to put a person in the ground and cover him up. He'd never done that before either. Cleon didn't seem to like him much, so the job went quickly with them both digging and no talking. Cleon stood at the freshly covered hole, talking to himself. Bodhi watched for a minute then took the shovels back to the wagon, figuring he wanted privacy. Darkness settled but a full moon lit the night sky, making it easy to see in the eerie glow.

Selah looked up as he came out of the trees. "Is it done?"

"Yes. I think you need some sleep. You look like a raccoon with those dark circles under your eyes," Bodhi said. He slid the collapsible shovels into the wagon and gave them a push to the back.

"Well, thank you for the compliment. It's from crying," Selah said.

Bodhi sighed. Wrong thing to say. She felt bad enough. *Never disparage a woman's appearance.* "Look, I'm sorry. I didn't mean—"

"It's fine. I'm fine." Her voice started to break and her lip quivered. She raised a hand in aimless circles, tears flowing down her cheeks. She turned and leaned against the wagon.

He cursed under his breath and clamped his jaw shut as he reached for her shoulder. He hesitated, rubbing his fingers together to be sure they were clean after digging, then gently laid his hand on her shoulder. "It will be all right."

Selah spun into his arms. Bodhi, caught off guard, stood with his arms outstretched.

She buried her head in his chest, sobbing. "It will never be all right. Why did it have to happen this way? Why couldn't he have left us alone and gone home? Cleon can't go back now either, so Father lost two sons today. His heart will be broken."

She clutched at his shirt. Bodhi slowly wrapped her in his arms and rested his chin on top of her head. He felt the jerky heaving of her chest as she cried. "I'm sorry." The only thing he could think to say. He needed to find a new word of apology. That one was getting old.

He rocked her back and forth as her body was wracked with sobs. He'd felt her brother needed to die before he killed someone, but Bodhi would never say that to her.

Amaryllis sat on the ground viewing one of her quartz crystal readers, but hearing sobs brought her scurrying to Selah's side. She also started to cry. "What's the matter with Selah? Did you hurt her?" She clutched at Selah's shirt.

"No, I didn't hurt her. She's sad because her brother died," Bodhi said softly.

Cleon emerged from the woods. With head down, he slowly walked to the wagon, grabbed his bedroll, and headed toward the trees on the other side of the clearing.

Selah pulled herself together, sniffed, and turned to the child. "It's been a long day, and we need some sleep. Grab our covers and make a bed near the trees by Cleon."

Amaryllis shook her head. "I don't want to sleep on the ground. There may be snakes."

Selah rubbed the heel of her hand across her eyes to dry them. "Bed down in the wagon then."

"Will you come with me?"

Bodhi was amazed at how fast the child had stopped crying.

Selah sighed. "Yes, I'll come with you, but I want to talk to Bodhi."

"Then I'll wait," Amaryllis said. "I don't want to be by myself."

"Let's sit in the wagon so the child can get to sleep," Bodhi said. Selah looked like she needed rest too. She needed her wits about her for what they were going to attempt tomorrow.

Bodhi climbed up, pulling Selah up after him. Amaryllis scrambled over the edge and wrapped herself in her blanket on the left side while Selah sat near Bodhi on the right.

She dropped her head. All the fight had gone out of her, and Bodhi sensed her sadness. He wrapped his arm around her shoulder and pulled her into his chest. She didn't protest, but it seemed to trigger tears again.

She cried softly into her hands as she pressed against him. "What can I do? This can't be fixed. Raza is dead in the ground."

"Well, the first thing you should do is talk to Cleon—"

"I don't want to hear solutions," Selah cried.

Bodhi grimaced and moved to disengage. He felt like he was making matters worse. He'd wait until she made more sense. "I'll let you go to sleep."

Selah gripped his shirt. "Just hold me."

Bodhi leaned back against the crates. Selah rested against

his chest, his arm encircling her shoulder, and cried herself to sleep.

❂

Selah awoke to the sounds of birds and gentle sunlight filtering through the trees. She glanced around with blurry eyes. Bodhi was gone. He must have slipped away after she'd fallen asleep. She couldn't explain it, but for the first time since leaving home, she felt safe. She leaned her head back. Beside her, Amaryllis stirred. The child had snuggled with her the past several nights, reminding her that someone counted on her for security. She rubbed the pack Amaryllis was using as a pillow. Her mother's letters in that pack substituted as her own security.

She turned on her stomach and stared at a crate. A large clump of rabbit fur was lodged in the slat lock on the crate. She sat up, plucked the fibers from the crate, and rolled them in her fingers. Bodhi had been telling the truth.

Selah ripped the cover off the crate. Empty. Her brothers had sold rabbits in the Mountain. Had their father condoned this? He must have. He'd allowed them to use the wagon and team for the trip. But maybe he thought they were only delivering the Lander.

Voices drifted through her thoughts. Bodhi and Cleon.

"We need to find a way in there today. I'm getting strong impressions of anxiety," Bodhi said.

"What are you talking about, *impressions*? You can't just waltz into the Mountain. It's a fortress, and your people are prisoners," Cleon yelled.

Selah sat up and looked over the side of the wagon. The

265

two men had obviously just woken. Neither had fixed their appearance, and both had unruly hair spikes like baby birds just out of the shell. She rolled her eyes. They sounded like a pair of fishwives arguing in the sea bass stall at the wharf marketplace back home.

"It's a travesty anyone would be hunted or held as a slave. What kind of a country is this?" Bodhi said.

"Well, if you didn't come to our country—"

"Stop!" Selah jumped from the wagon. "You two need to start acting like adults."

"Well, he's crazy. I was there yesterday with Raza. The chances of getting in unnoticed are next to none," Cleon said.

Selah held out the rabbit fur. "That's what I want to talk to you about. What were you doing selling rabbits in the Mountain?"

Cleon rubbed the back of his head. "It wasn't my idea. I was just along for the ride to help deliver the Lander." He flipped a hand in Bodhi's direction.

Selah got in his face. His breathing grew heavy but she wouldn't break eye contact. "Responsible or not, tell me what you did with the rabbits."

Cleon turned away, avoiding her stare.

She grabbed him by the shoulders. "You thought all rabbits were poison. Why did you sell them here?"

Cleon shrugged off her hand. "Because the man named Ganston wanted to buy them. Raza set up the deal. He made deliveries here every month for a year." His voice rose. "I wasn't part of it. I tried to stop him when I found out. He wouldn't listen."

Selah threw down the fur and started pacing. "Here I

thought Bodhi was lying about you two, but no, you have to be selling contaminated rabbits to the Mountain for who knows what purpose. Meanwhile I'm not trusting him, and he's not trusting me—"

She stopped in mid-sentence. Bodhi and Cleon stared at her as though she had two heads.

"Don't look at me like that, either of you," she said, waving a hand. "We came north for two reasons. Bodhi's looking for other Landers, and I'm looking for my father."

"Failure is not an option," Bodhi added.

"Your failure was coming here." Cleon glared at Bodhi.

Selah jumped in between them. "Knock it off! We have to work together."

Cleon backed up. "Why do I need to do anything with *him*?"

She could understand her brother's animosity. He had been taught his whole life to hate Landers. She softened her tone. He'd experienced enough change for a lifetime, and she wanted to slide him into this new world with the least amount of confusion. "He can help me find my father. He gets stronger impressions than I do. I'm just learning how to translate thoughts."

"That's the second time someone's said that. What are you talking about?" Cleon asked.

No one in the Borough ever knew the extent of Lander abilities. Would it put them in danger for *normals* to know? She wanted to trust her brother. If not him, who?

"Landers can read minds. There's interference with Bodhi hearing the ones inside the Mountain," Selah said. She searched his face for a reaction.

Cleon didn't say anything at first. He looked at the ground. "Anyone's mind? Am I walking around here with him snooping in my head?"

"No, just other Landers. We're telepathic," Bodhi said.

Cleon set his jaw and narrowed his eyes.

Bodhi smirked.

Selah raised hands. "Stop. Cleon, over there!" She pointed at a fallen tree.

Cleon started to argue then turned and stormed off. He sat on the log with his hands clasped and his head down. Selah moved to sit beside him and reached for his hand. He pulled away. She lowered her head and looked up into his eyes. It unnerved her to see puddles of moisture in his eyes.

A tear slid down his cheek. She reached out again, and this time he didn't pull away. She held his hand, feeling the warmth pass between them.

"We've lost Raza. Neither of us can go home. You need to stay with us."

Cleon nodded. A teardrop splashed onto her hand.

"I will always love you, Cleon. We are sister and brother forever."

Selah sniffled. They wrapped their arms around each other and cried. She felt Cleon's shoulders tighten as they held each other until no more pain washed out.

Bodhi hurried toward them. "I think we have a problem."

The whine of a squad of JetTrans filled the trees overhead.

17

Selah flattened herself on the ground underneath a bush. "Rylla, hide till the hovercraft are gone!" Amaryllis was probably the only person she *wasn't* worried about at the moment. She knew the child was savvy enough to understand the threat. She glanced around. Bodhi and Cleon lay camouflaged in heavy underbrush.

The whine seemed to go on forever. Through the tree canopy she watched the five JetTrans come into formation one by one, arriving from the Mountain platform on the other side of the tree grove. The center JetTrans in the triangular formation hovered directly over her head. What were they doing there so long? Nerves took hold. Had they been spotted?

She lowered her head to think and simultaneously the hovercraft charged their jets and took off. Selah huffed out a huge breath.

They gathered back at the wagon. Selah didn't know what she expected, but breaching the Mountain was not on her list. Yet Bodhi could feel Landers in there, her father among them. What were the choices?

"I was inside with Raza yesterday. We never saw a single person until we reached our destination," Cleon said.

"Do you know how to get where they're holding the prisoners?" Selah asked.

"He doesn't need to," Bodhi interrupted. "I can feel which way to go once we're inside."

"We've seen the kind of weapons they have." She held up Raza's pulse weapon. "We can't compete against this with knives or machetes."

"So then stay out here. I'll go in," Bodhi said.

Selah jumped to her feet. "No you won't." He wasn't going to treat her like the boys did. "I go or none of us go."

Bodhi pulled back his chin. "Since when did you become boss?"

"We're a team. I got you where you wanted to go, and you promised to help me."

Cleon stared at them. "What's this plan between you two? I assumed you were bringing Bodhi as a prisoner. What's your part in this, Selah?"

She kicked at a stone with the toe of her boot. "I'm pretty sure my father is in there."

Cleon gaped. "You mean your *real* father could be inside the Mountain?"

"Yes. I came with Bodhi hoping to find a Lander colony so I could pick up a lead. Mother said Father went north, and she tried to follow him until she gave birth to me." Selah looked toward the Mountain. "There's something terrible going on in there. Bodhi tapped the energy and I'm able to feel it. Don't ask me to explain."

Cleon looked like he didn't believe her. "We should think about this."

"I'm telling you from the impressions I'm getting it is paramount we go now or there will be dire consequences. You go with me or I go alone," Bodhi said.

Selah rubbed her hand across her forehead.

Amaryllis leaned up against her and slipped her arms around Selah's waist. "Are we going into the scary Mountain?"

"No, you're not," the other three said in unison.

Amaryllis's bottom lip quivered. "What if something happens to you? I'll be all alone again."

"Nothing will happen. You'll be fine right here while we're gone. I know you can take care of yourself. You've got to trust me, we'll come back," Selah said.

Amaryllis chewed on her thumbnail. "I don't want to be alone."

"We have to go now." Bodhi grimaced.

Cleon stood beside him. "The sooner we get started, the faster we can be done with . . ." He looked at Bodhi but said nothing more.

Selah gently extracted herself from the child's tight embrace. "You stay here. Promise me."

Amaryllis dropped her head and mumbled.

"Is that a yes?" Selah asked. She knew the evasion drill from Dane. She'd never realized how much all children acted alike.

Amaryllis nodded.

Cleon pointed to the machete. "You may need that. The overgrowth closer to the Mountain is almost impassable."

Selah strapped on the sheath. A feeling of dread slid over her like clouds covering the sun. Something felt wrong. Was this a trap?

⬥

Stemple tried to avoid Bethany and Everling today. They had both taken on this strange aura of agitation. Everling kept repeating himself, and Bethany—well, she ran unfettered by common decorum. She'd already yelled at two male lab techs enough times that they ran and hid from her, and she'd reduced more than one female assistant to tears in the last few days. Stemple wondered if it was some kind of psychosis involved with their regeneration injections. When he was required to be in the lab with them, he kept his head down and worked.

"The JetTrans squad took off to hunt the girl," Bethany said. "If you'd listened to me we wouldn't have any future delays in the system."

Stemple looked out the corner of his eye without turning his head. Everling sat at a lab bench fingering test tube samples. He mumbled something but kept working.

"Noah!" Bethany yelled. She slammed her open hand on the countertop.

"Can't you see I'm busy? What do you want now?" Everling asked. He'd turned into someone Stemple didn't recognize.

"I said you need to listen to me about adding distance to the JetTrans to speed up searches and avoid costly delays in reporting," Bethany said. "This squad can only search up to a hundred miles from here. It's going to be sheer luck and not science that finds her."

"No, no, no. Too big a cost. I own this Company. Sometimes I think you only want my money. Did you ever really love me or was it all just for the power?" Everling asked. He stood, wobbled a few steps, and headed for Bethany.

Stemple moved swiftly in the other direction and left the lab.

⟐

Selah chopped their way through the barrier of kudzu overgrowing the grove of trees closer to the Mountain. In many places the weight of the vines left behind snapped and ragged stumps of stalwart maples and pines being enveloped in the monster growth.

She hacked a path inside the mound. There wasn't enough breeze to refresh the stagnant air trapped inside the greenery. They pushed through the humid air, and Selah wiped away the moist tendrils of hair clinging to her face. They exited the foliage near the fence surrounding the utility entrance to the Mountain. Chopping and hacking made her arms feel like fifty-pound weights.

She needed rest and air and longed for her hiding place in the barn where she could be near the horses and hear Mother working in the garden. She stripped off the leather sheath and swiped the moisture from the machete onto her pants.

Dew clung to the foliage on the path to the gate, creating a jewel-studded appearance in the bright sunshine. It beckoned like the sparkling entrance to a fairyland, looking as

273

deceptive as the gentle ocean waves that hid riptides below the surface in her fishing inlet at home.

Cleon showed where to stay out of camera range among the bushes. Apparently, some of the trips he and Raza had made to the Mountain were for more than just deliveries, but he usually remained outside. Selah didn't want to know. The facade was already ruined.

"That's the keypad we pushed to open the door. The one on the left opens the gate to get back out." Cleon pointed to the brushed metal rectangles on either side of the doorway.

They surveyed the area inside the fence. It continued to the left and right of the opening. Large tubular bays with rectangular stone pads in front were cut into the Mountain at equal spaces as far as they could see. The area became hidden in the trees as it proceeded to the left. Selah saw no other gated entrances, and she wasn't willing to explore the fence line.

"It looks easy, but maybe too easy," Bodhi said. "How do they secure the entrances?"

Cleon grinned. "Technically, they're very lax. They assume no one can skirt their gates. They don't care about merchants trying to buy or sell goods. It took us quite a few tries to get anyone to answer the gate. The guards only answer when they're in their posted areas."

Bodhi stared at Cleon. "You sound like you've done this before."

Cleon stared back. "Everyone has their secrets."

Selah wondered if she needed to keep these two separated. "It can't be this simple. Did anyone notice there's no clear way over the fence? How do you propose we get to the keypad on the door?"

"We used the identa-card Raza carried," Cleon said.

"We buried it with him," Selah said. "It wouldn't have helped anyway. It was coded for his genetic material. I remember from our school lessons about commerce with the Mountain." She turned to Cleon. "You've been here numerous times. Have you heard of any merchants faking an identacard, or do you know how?"

Cleon shook his head. "A coal merchant tried to buy a black market identa-card to get more product but they caught him. The biometrics didn't match well enough."

Selah walked forward and stared at the gate. "So faking credentials won't work."

"It also registered me on Raza's card. Once inside it caught me when I left the approved pathway. We'll have to bypass the gate registration altogether," Cleon added.

Selah flopped back on her haunches and covered her head with her hands. The black bars on the ten-foot-tall fencing were a coated iron product spaced four to five inches apart. A wide razor lip attachment that leaned out away from the Mountain completed the top.

She suddenly realized that assessing situations felt normal now. Was this one of her new abilities? Or was she just developing what Mother had taught her now that she was out of the boys' shadows?

"That's a good space between the bars," Bodhi said.

Selah swiveled to look at him. "I'm small but not that small."

Cleon sighed. "Maybe we ought to get that kid—"

"No!" Selah said. "I will not put her in danger to help us."

"Even if it means getting to your father?" Bodhi asked.

Selah chewed on her bottom lip. Maybe if they waited for another merchant to come by, they could sneak in using his wagon as a shield. It didn't seem efficient, but at least Amaryllis wouldn't be at risk.

"Hey, look!" Cleon pointed at the fence.

Selah lifted her head. Amaryllis had run up to the fence and squeezed between the bars six sections from the gate.

Selah scrambled to her feet. "No!" Unlike with Dane at the abyss, she wasn't close enough to save the girl from the foolish move.

Cleon clamped his hand over her mouth. "Don't make a sound." He pointed at the laser cannon mounted on the side of the Mountain. "I've seen them disintegrate bandits lying in wait for merchants."

Selah wrenched free from his grasp, all the while keeping her eye on Amaryllis. "Why didn't you think to tell us about the cannon last night?"

"I forgot." Cleon shrugged.

Selah's head snapped in his direction. Who was this person that knew these kinds of details? "You forgot?" She felt ready to punch him.

"Stop fighting. She did it," Bodhi said.

The child slithered through the bars, darted to the panel, and slapped the brushed metal pad. The gate slid open.

Suddenly the sky was alive with sound. A humming sound intensified as though a million bees were descending. A steady downdraft agitated the dust, creating a cloud that billowed out like a pillow and rolled like a scroll.

Amaryllis scurried to the doorway and pressed herself

276

against the side wall, out of the JetTrans' viewing-portal range.

The gray bullet-shaped hovercraft made an unsteady descent, wobbling and jerking as though it were having navigational problems. The pointed nose whacked the fence near the open gate. It left a noticeable mark on the craft and bent part of the fence outward. Landing gear appeared with a sharp whine and the craft slammed to the ground with a shudder.

Selah watched the Mountain entrance on the other side of the craft, willing Amaryllis to stay put. The door panel on the craft slid up and two arguing men emerged.

"I told you it was handling badly when we left this morning. You should have listened to me," the younger pilot said, his sun goggles resting on the top of his head.

"You're always complaining about something. Usually it's to get out of work. How did I know it was a real issue this time?" the other pilot said. He looked old enough to be the younger man's father but was more likely his trainer. The younger man didn't wear pilot wings.

The older man walked toward the front of the craft. "You've really done it. That deep gash could compromise the battery pod. We're going to hear about this."

Selah spotted Amaryllis dashing from the doorway to the back of the craft. The child must have panicked. Selah slapped a hand over her mouth to muffle a yell. Her heart pounded and she clenched her teeth. If Amaryllis was injured she'd never forgive herself.

The younger pilot inspected the damage as the older man

walked to the bent section of fence. "We'd better call maintenance to fix this before the undesirables notice."

The younger man muttered something Selah couldn't hear. She watched Amaryllis, her feet evident under the craft.

"We'd better taxi to the pad and not try to lift off again," the older man said.

They entered the craft. The loud whine seemed to scare Amaryllis and she ran back to the doorway. The craft taxied out of view and the sound dissipated.

Selah hadn't realized she was holding her breath. Pinwheels floated in front of her eyes as she let it out. She ran through the fence with Bodhi and Cleon and scooped Amaryllis into her arms.

"What do you think you were doing? I told you to stay at camp. You promised."

Amaryllis hung her head. "I didn't promise. I just mumbled."

Selah grabbed her in a hug. "We're going to talk about you obeying, young lady." Her words reminded her that this whole adventure had started because she'd disobeyed her own mother just a few days ago.

Bodhi touched Selah's shoulder. "No time to chastise her now. Let's get inside, fast."

Cleon moved Selah and Amaryllis toward the doorway.

"Wait! She's not going inside," Selah said.

"Halt!" came a voice from behind them. "Turn slowly and raise your hands."

They turned to face the two pilots with pulse weapons drawn and armed.

"I told you they didn't know we saw them," the younger pilot said, smiling broadly.

"Well, at least you were right on something today," the older man said as he dialed into his ComTex for perimeter patrol help.

Selah glanced at Cleon and Bodhi. Bodhi gave an imperceivable shake of his head, which Selah took to mean "don't try anything." He looked worried for her safety. She shouldn't have let that sway her judgment. He was still virtually a stranger. But he'd never lied to her about her brothers. She trusted him now.

She cleared her throat to get Cleon's attention. He was staring at the two pilots as though he wanted to fight. He looked her way and she gave a slight shrug of her shoulders.

"You two, no communicating," the younger man said. He walked closer to Selah.

She raised her chin in defiance. Amaryllis clung to her. Selah wrapped a protective arm around her shoulder.

"Step apart, you two," the pilot said gruffly.

"Leave my sister alone." Cleon stepped toward him.

"Whoa, farm boy," the older pilot said. He moved in Cleon's direction. "Just hold your step or I may have to set you down with a pulse."

Selah stepped in front of his weapon. "He'll listen. Please don't hurt him."

Amaryllis chose that moment to dart behind Selah, between Cleon and Bodhi, and scramble out the open gateway.

The younger guard with his weapon trained on Bodhi tried to lunge in her direction.

"Let her go." Bodhi slammed his left shoulder into the man, propelling him backward into the older one, who discharged his pulse weapon.

The charge slammed into the ground between Selah and Cleon, throwing up a sudden burst of grit and stones. Amaryllis disappeared into the trees.

The entry to the Mountain slid open. Four guards charged, holding weapons.

The younger pilot hurried to the gate. "I'll get her."

"Forget it," the older one said. "One less problem for us to worry about."

"But, sir," the younger one said, looking at the tree line. "She's a fugitive who tried to compromise the Mountain."

The older guard shook his head. "You've got a lot to learn, my boy. She's a child. How subversive do you think she could be?"

⊛

Ganston looked up from his report as alert sirens beeped then wailed across the security halo-screen mounted on the wall of his office. Jax hurried in.

"Did you hear? They've caught interlopers trying to break into the Mountain."

"The sound's too intrusive to remain unnoticed." He ran his hand across the control on the right side of his desk to mute it. "If they've caught them, they could abate that infernal racket. There's no reason to broadcast it after the fact. Just another Everling power ploy."

Jax scooted around the desk and pushed a series of buttons to give Ganston a view of the criminals in the first level holding area. Being an executive member gave him unfettered access to activities considered top level.

Ganston stared at the group. "Is that a girl with them?"

280

Jax nodded. "Yes, it is. Nothing like this has ever happened before. It's quite exciting."

Ganston tuned him out. He used the roller on his focus to zoom in on the detained group.

"Get me Mojica." He sat back in his chair and rubbed his chin. This could be a big problem.

18

G anston watched as Mojica strode into his office with Jax hot on her heels. Jax could never get her to wait in the outer office until summoned, and it amused Ganston that he still tried to restrain the woman with the Amazon-like stature.

"What's the emergency, boss-man? I was at the other end of the Mountain conducting training exercises. If you want us to be ready next month we need—"

"Have you seen the alert about infiltrators in the Mountain?" Ganston asked.

Mojica plopped in the chair in front of him and lifted both feet to rest her boots on the edge of his antique oak desk. "I'm head of security, remember. Nothing escapes my notice. They're just a bunch of merchants. No big deal. I'm sure the alert is an overreaction."

Ganston frowned and made a flicking gesture toward her

boots with his right hand. "Well, this one could cause a few problems."

She lowered her feet to the floor. He motioned to the halo-screen. Mojica turned in her seat and came face-to-face with Jax's chest. Using her left arm, she brushed him out of the way.

"That will be all, Jax," Ganston said. Jax backed up a step and moved his arms behind him to rest in a military at-ease position.

Ganston stared at him. "I said that will be all. You can leave now."

Jax huffed out of the office while Mojica smiled. "He keeps track of your every move."

Ganston ignored the comment and directed her attention to the screen. He enlarged the frame with the three interlopers and zoomed in on Cleon. "This man is my person of interest. I need to know what he's being charged with and what he's said."

"Why?" Mojica sat forward to get a better look at him.

"He was doing some . . . work for me that I'd like to remain private," Ganston said. He hadn't thought he would have to impart this level of trust to her so soon. The concept felt as foreign as entrusting someone else to prepare his food, which was something he'd stopped doing years ago.

"What kind of work?"

He cleared his throat. Even Jax wasn't privy to this level of his business.

Mojica leaned in toward him. "I'm your head of security. That's like being your doctor. You don't keep things from me."

"And I would expect that you don't keep anything from me either." One of Ganston's spies had reported she sometimes spent inordinate amounts of time in the secure biometrics records. When questioned, she passed it off as scanning for a specific warrior gene of behavioral aggression in her new forces.

Mojica sucked her teeth and wagged her index finger back and forth like the antique metronome in Ganston's music collection. "Of course, but as I said, I need to know what I'm dealing with if you expect me to protect you from consequences of your actions."

Ganston dropped his head. He could feel his hands getting moist. Could he trust her? He didn't have much choice. "He was one of the men who brought a *delivery* yesterday."

Mojica sat back in her seat, stared at Ganston, then rose. "If you're not going to be straight with me, then we have nothing to talk about. Take care of it yourself." She headed for the door.

"Wait!" He sighed and ran a hand across the back of his neck. The stress felt palpable. He lowered his voice. "He and his brother brought me a shipment of wild rabbits."

Mojica turned back to face him. "Wild rabbits . . . as in diseased, do-not-eat rabbits?"

"Yes." Ganston ran his hands down his pants legs to soak up the moisture.

Mojica strolled back to her seat. Her voice lowered as well, as though speaking out loud was a crime. "Why would you do something like that? What did you do with them?"

Ganston's breathing increased. His heart pounded in his ears. He was about to rest his survival in a veritable stranger's hands. "I incorporated them into the food service that feeds Everling's inner circle."

Mojica started to laugh. Ganston sat stone-faced. She stopped and her mouth fell open.

"You're serious? You deliberately poisoned people?" She rose again. "What's wrong with you?"

Ganston bolted to his feet and pounded a fist on the desk. "I made the hard decisions. I'm doing what I have to do to protect the people in this mountain from that megalomaniac. If there are a few unforeseen consequences to the process, then so be it."

"How many?" Mojica clasped her hands together and rested them on top of her head as she looked up at the ceiling. "How many people have you killed?"

"Everling's father carried the corrupt gene in his system at the time of his death, and tests show that his wife Bethany has the gene present in her cancer."

"So someone in the lab knows about your misguided plan?"

Ganston set his jaw. "No, of course not."

"Then how are you getting these test results?"

Ganston sat back, a little relieved the question was easily answered. "As a member of the Board I can look at all data on every resident of the Mountain. You just have to know what to look for."

Mojica shook her head. "So what you're telling me is you aren't even an effective murderer. You take numerous chances at getting caught. Involve people that you can't control. And you don't even get a plausible rate of return on your investment. I'd say your plan was not well thought out."

Ganston's bluster deflated at hearing her assessment. It had seemed so perfect. Only Everling's food source had been

contaminated, and Ganston expected an almost immediate death similar to that of the four Mountain residents
who'd inadvertently eaten a contaminated rabbit while on
an expedition a few years ago. The men had died agonizing
deaths within three weeks. He'd been trying to rid himself
of Everling for years, and this had looked like the perfect
plan at the time.

Ganston stared straight ahead. He shook his head then
rested it in his hands. "Why did it take you to show me that?
Maybe I just thought doing something constructive was better than doing nothing at all."

"I think your plan of moving people out of here is a much
better one, and I would suggest that you let this rabbit plan
die a natural death. How many people were involved in salt-
ing the food service?"

"Just one. I can trust him implicitly," Ganston said. He
rocked back in his chair and closed his eyes.

"Good. Now let me get down there and take care of this
one. What's his name?"

"Cleon Chavez. He came with his brother Raza, who I
paid for the shipment."

Mojica shook her head. "You've left a lot of loose ends
that could come back to haunt you." She sauntered to the
door. "Stay available in case this goes bad."

&

Everling could hear the sirens. They hurt. He sat in his
lab clutching his head. *Make them stop. Turn them off.* Why
were pains shooting through his head? This wasn't normal.

He banged his head on the desk. *Make them stop.* Where was Bethany? She'd help.

Finally the sirens stopped. He breathed heavily. Peace. He dropped his hands from his head and looked at them, turning them over and then back again. His fingers looked too long, too straight. Were they really his hands? He could actually hear his fingernails growing.

He must stop being distracted. He had a mission and he was boss of the Mountain. Why had the alarms sounded? He might need to identify spies. They were everywhere, trying to steal his research.

He went to find out.

⟁

Mojica strode into the L-shaped security area on the first level, entering from the short end that contained the check-in stations for out-of-Mountain merchants and their wares. The walls, awash in earth tones, held posters and banners telling merchants what was legal and illegal to sell.

She made her way through the noisy crowd to the security station at the corridor where the holding cells and inspection stations were located. It functioned as a temporary jail for unruly or inebriated miscreants coming into or leaving the Mountain.

The holding area was composed of neutral-colored rocrete walls and composite plascine dividers defining cell spaces that could turn transparent. Several bench surfaces projected from the outer wall near the security station.

Her boots clipped along the patterned tile floor. She noted the well-worn patterns, in contrast to the pristine confinement areas for Mountain citizens. To their credit, the officers manning the security station recognized Mojica out of uniform and saluted her as she approached. She returned the gesture. "What do we have with the three interlopers?"

The officers seemed nervous to see their commander. The one sporting a fresh crew cut stepped forward with a halo-tablet. "Commander, we didn't know you'd be here for such a minor infraction. We'd have completed a more detailed report."

Mojica fingered the screen. Incompetence didn't surprise her these days. "What's been left out of the report?"

The officer conferred with his partner, an overweight man who was obviously embarrassed. Mojica made a mental note about physical exercise as a requirement of service to the Mountain. "Well, ma'am, the video feed shows there was a young child with them. She squeezed through the gate and activated the entrance. A hovercraft was involved in an incident with the fence. The pilots caught the interlopers and at some point the child slipped away. The pilots didn't pursue or initiate a record about her."

Mojica looked up from the tablet. "Has that gate been secured? And who were the pilots?"

"Yes, ma'am, the gate's been secured. It's been sealed off until repair can be initiated. Merchants will be directed in and out via Unit 3. They'll have a slightly longer walk to get over here, but that's the way it goes." The crew cut officer looked relieved he knew answers. "The pilots were from Recon 5."

Mojica knew that to be a pilot training unit, meaning they were fresh new faces and not the swiftest pilots. It was probably a miracle they'd caught and detained anyone. "Tell me about the interlopers. Have they been interviewed or scanned?"

All outside detainees were supposed to be bio-scanned. It was a throwback to when Everling had started bringing in Landers eighteen years ago. He'd expected incursions to free them, but no plot ever materialized and over the years scanning fell to hit and miss.

The officers exchanged glances. The crew cut guard addressed Mojica. "We haven't done a scan in years."

The overweight officer flushed. "We didn't know it was still required. We'll start it right away." He scrambled to the panel, pushed a few buttons, and ran his hand over the delivery screen. "Uh, ma'am? We've got an anomaly."

Mojica looked up from the tablet she was reading. "Well, tell me."

"The first subject was here yesterday to see Charles Ganston."

Mojica had come prepared for that response. The crew cut officer stepped forward. "We've already put in a summons for him to come here."

If they weren't so overzealous, she could have talked them through it. She would have to hope Ganston's demeanor didn't set off any alarms. She turned to face the three people behind the transparent wall. Her gaze locked with Bodhi's and threads of adrenaline coursed through her chest. Mojica cursed under her breath. "Stop the scan."

Both officers snapped to attention. "Ma'am?"

It occurred to her that Ganston might have left out other details that could be uncovered, or security could start asking about the missing brother. "You're probably correct. Don't waste the energy for three scans."

At that moment Ganston barged into the area, looking frazzled. Mojica hurried to his side. "All they know is Cleon was here yesterday. I made them stop before anything else showed up."

Gaston pulled back. "Like what?"

"Like where the other brother is. You apparently didn't contemplate there could be another person running around inside my Mountain while you're worried about keeping your secrets," Mojica said through clenched teeth.

He raised an eyebrow. "Indeed." He turned to the officers. "Please separate the young man who met with me yesterday into private containment. I wish to talk to him alone."

The crew cut officer opened an enjoining doorway with the containment cell and ushered the man into it.

Ganston sauntered into the room with his hands clasped behind his back. Cleon stood near the doorway. A half smile of nervous jitters played at the corner of his mouth.

"Well, young man, what do you have to say for yourself?" Ganston asked. He moved closer. He didn't want the boy creating any more of a problem.

Cleon lowered his head. "I'm sorry, sir. It's a mistake. Our little sister was playing around the fence. We went to get her, and—"

"Who are these people and where is your brother Raza?" Ganston peered through the doorway, then back at Cleon.

Cleon averted his eyes from Ganston and motioned. "These

are the rest of my family. My brother . . . he was set upon by marauders last night. They killed him and stole his ComTex with the payment you made. I was coming back to see if you could help." He swallowed.

"I'm sorry to hear of your loss," Ganston said. "I'll rescind the payment so the thieves will get nothing. Do you have a ComTex?"

Cleon shook his head.

Ganston walked to the doorway. "Officer, I need a payment chip."

The two security officers looked at each other as though he were speaking a foreign language. The crew cut one turned to Ganston. "Sir, we don't have those here."

"Then I suggest that one of you *get* me one now," Ganston barked. He wanted this boy paid off and gone from here as soon as possible.

The overweight officer scrambled from the office, hurried down the hall, and disappeared around a corner, the echo of his heavy footfalls receding. Ganston stared at Cleon. He'd always dealt with the older brother and didn't have a relationship with this younger one. He didn't know what would intimidate him into silence.

Ganston turned and looked at Mojica, motioning for her to move the other guard out of earshot. She moseyed to the office and busied the officer with a data station in the back.

He turned to Cleon. "I'm increasing the payment by 10 percent for your troubles. But when you leave this Mountain there will be no more deliveries. And I never want to see you again. Am I understood?" Ganston stared. He could feel the twitch in his left eye betraying his stress.

Cleon nodded vigorously. "Yes, sir, you are perfectly clear. We will not return."

He appeared relieved. Ganston had never anticipated that—he'd thought this was some sort of power play. He felt his shoulders relax. It was time to go before someone from Everling's circle spotted him. He turned to leave.

19

S elah stood at the clear plascine wall of the cell and watched the man walk away with the woman. He was obviously agitated about Cleon being here. Dare she try to coerce him for help? A clumsy plan had gotten them inside thanks to Amaryllis, but now they had to find her father before they were thrown out—which in some ways wouldn't be too bad because she was worried about how the child was faring out there by herself.

A growling moan interrupted her thoughts. She spun on her heels. Bodhi leaned against the wall, clutching both sides of his head. His knees buckled and he slid to the floor as his face turned crimson. She knew the drill. He'd made contact.

Selah rushed to his side. "Where are they? Have you found my father?"

Bodhi moaned again, lifting his head to meet her eyes. Tears welled and slipped down both his cheeks. "There are many. I wasn't prepared," he whispered. "I feel them all. Fear. Pain."

He pressed his fingers to her temples. A spider-like feeling scurried up her spine. She'd never seen him so debilitated by impressions. She felt only random connections. Nothing strong enough to provoke an emotion.

A hum invaded her brain. Low, but growing in intensity like a swarm of bees.

She jerked away from Bodhi. "What was that?" The feeling subsided like dissipating bubbles when heat was removed from a boiling pot. Her brain cleared.

"It's time for you to join," Bodhi said softly. He winced and pressed his eyes shut tight.

"Join what?" Yet she knew without asking. Her first instinct was to step away from the fire rather than rush in. But this would lead to her father. She touched her collarbone, deciding to embrace her heritage.

Bodhi smiled through his pain. "To come into your full rights as our next generation, as a novarium. They are all around us now. I can feel our people here in the Mountain." He staggered away from Cleon and motioned her to follow.

She moved with halting steps. Her palms moistened. "Is this going to hurt? The buzzing was trying to consume me."

Bodhi reached out and gently put his right hand to her left temple. "Open your mind like I taught you." The warmth of his fingers sent pin prickles of anticipation up her back. His eyes locked on hers. Selah's skin tingled with layers of goose bumps.

She closed her eyes. "I'm afraid."

Bodhi slowly brought his left hand up to her right temple. "I'm with you."

Calm washed over her at his touch. She felt safe.

"She said she was afraid. Back away from her," Cleon growled. She heard him jerk from his seat.

Her eyes flashed open. Selah raised a hand to halt him. "It's okay, Cleon. Don't interfere."

He plopped to the metal surface. His feet shuffled as he mumbled under his breath.

Selah blocked the intruding noise and let her eyes glide shut. There was comfort in the darkness. The buzzing bees were coming closer. Bodhi was right, it didn't hurt. Anticipation was the fear—or was it being so close to Bodhi? Her temples were on fire at his touch. Her knees buckled and she started to slip. Bodhi grabbed her under the elbows for support. She felt his closeness, a vibration in the empty space between their bodies. Her mouth went dry. She ran her tongue over her lips for moisture.

Cleon lurched to his feet again.

"Sit down," Selah said without opening her eyes. She heard him comply. She knew many things without visuals. Heightened awareness. Sounds of breathing.

She felt *him*.

Her eyes opened wide. She looked into Bodhi's eyes and grabbed his hand. "My father, my real father is alive! He's here." Her eyes darted around the area. "He's reaching out to me. Warning me to get away from here while there's still time. Help me find him."

"We need to get out of here first," Cleon said.

⚛

Mojica passed the chip over her ComTex, transferring the bio-coin to the device. She glanced at the balance. Her eyebrows rose. Subversion paid very well. She must remember that for future endeavors.

She strolled to the confinement area and keyed the panel to activate the opening. Cleon stood up and she flipped him the chip. He caught it with both hands.

"I'll be letting you out of here as soon as they finish the pilot interviews," Mojica said.

"We told you we didn't do anything," Cleon said in a whiny voice. Mojica disliked weak men. She'd have preferred him to act belligerent.

"I know, but it would be disrespectful to our pilots to let you go before they finished giving statements. Be patient," she said.

Her ComTex vibrated her arm, tickling the bone in her elbow. She raised her wrist and turned from the cell. "Mojica here."

"Commander, we have a major event developing in the Lander containment area of the prison section. Be advised, we think you need to get there ASAP," a male voice said with a hint of panic.

"On my way," Mojica said. Another weak male. She'd need to rethink the ratio of male to female security personnel in her new command. She darted from the security area.

❦

Treva scurried down the corridor into Lab Section Ten containment. She pushed the intercom and ran her hand over the comm panel, turning the wall to Glade's cell transparent. She heard him before she saw him.

"I will kill him! He's broken our agreement. Never again! I

will destroy this Mountain and everything he's ever touched!" Glade screamed.

The white wall turned to mist and evaporated. Treva's eyes widened. She walked toward his cell with hands raised as though in surrender. "What's the matter? Calm down. Talk to me." She worried her drug formula was creating side effects she couldn't control.

Glade stormed to the clear wall and slammed both hands on the surface. "He lied."

She jumped back. "Who? About what?" For the first time she was happy there was a barrier between them.

"Everling! I'm positive this time. She is not just nearby. She is here in the Mountain."

"Who?" Treva wondered if she should give him a shot to calm him down, maybe one of Everling's drug cocktails.

"My daughter. She is here." He stabbed a finger at the floor. "She is in this Mountain. I can picture where she is. It has light walls, a containment area like this, and two security guards. There are others with her."

Treva mentally traced the places she knew. "It has to be a security outpost for the outside. They wouldn't bring outsiders farther into the Mountain unless . . ." She smiled. "Everling must not have anything to do with this. When he brings Landers in, they bypass security." She furrowed her brow. "Stop. Focus on her. Is she frightened?"

Glade turned to the side, resting his head against the wall. "No, she isn't feeling fear, more like apprehension. She can feel me." His head jerked up. "There's a Lander with her?"

Treva rocked back on her heels. "Oh no. That's not good.

The bio-scan will pick up Lander DNA and send an alert to Everling." It was imperative for her to get down there.

He looked stricken. "You have to do something. He can't find her. Please help me."

Treva pointed with her index finger. "I think I can do this." Her mind raced. This would be a test of how fast she could think on her feet.

Glade stared. "What are you going to do?"

"Do you trust me?" She didn't know if she trusted herself right now, but she still must try. Maybe her plan could go into action now.

He swallowed hard. "I've only known you a matter of days."

Treva fisted her hands on her hips. "That was not the question. I asked if you trusted me. Think very carefully before you answer because it may dictate how far I'm willing to stick my neck out for you."

He ran both hands through his dark hair, leaned back against the wall, and tucked his hands behind him. A nod. "Yes, I trust you."

She stood thinking for a moment, then she smiled and nodded. "I believe you." She backed up to the comm panel, ran her hand over a few sensors, and flipped a couple switches. "I've turned the system off just in case a bio-alert comes through here, but I can't stop it from reaching Everling's lab, so I'll just have to be fast enough to cancel it down there."

"How are you going to do that?"

"I don't know. I'm not there yet." Treva scurried to the lab door.

◬

Ganston was nearly to his office when he got notice from the security officer that he forgot to sign for the payment chip. He tried to argue that Mojica could sign for it, but she had left. He found himself making the trip for the third time today, and he'd have to do it again to get back to his office. His back hurt and his feet were burning. The most exercise he accomplished in a normal day entailed walking a couple hundred paces from his living unit to his office.

He made a mental note to design everything he needed in Stone Braide to be within a reasonable walking distance. He could feel the ache in his hip growing as he turned the last corner. The security office sat at the end of the open area.

"Uncle Charles, is that you?" a soft, playful voice said.

Ganston whirled. He scanned the numerous merchants standing in the waiting area and spotted Treva hurrying toward him. He smiled broadly as she threw herself into his arms. The noise of the crowd faded as he embraced the bright spot in his life.

"What are you doing down here?" Treva asked.

He kissed her on the forehead and held her chin in the palm of his hand. "I signed some paperwork for a merchant."

They moved to the side for a product cart layered with snake skin to pass by. With a clear view of the station, Ganston spotted the crew cut security officer. The officer noticed him and approached with a halo-tablet. He scrolled through some pages and handed it to Ganston, who signed for the chip and then shooed the man away.

"I didn't ask you what kind of research you're doing in Everling's lab. I was so sure you'd stay with the plants you loved as a child." Her parents had been associates of his, helping with his archeological digs. When Treva was born he took on the roll of a sub-parent. In historical times before the Sorrows, the position was considered a godfather.

Treva grinned. "I'm into cellular biology now."

Ganston heard security tell arguing merchants to lower their voices or they'd be leaving. He frowned. He hated coming here when it was busy. The noise bothered him.

Treva suddenly seemed more interested in something at the other end of the hallway. Her glance darted to the side and then to the floor.

"Treva-a," Ganston said, wagging his finger at her. "I know that look. You're about to tell me something I won't like."

She glanced down the hall one more time then grimaced. "You know me so well, I might as well tell you. Sort of like ripping the bandage off all at once."

Ganston hugged her again. The fresh smell of her hair made him remember her youthful innocence. "You're stalling, young lady."

She lowered her head. "I'm working on Dr. Everling's Lander project."

Ganston released her and backed up a step. "You're doing what?" He felt the air being sucked from his lungs. In his peripheral vision he could see Stemple standing at the southeast corner of the corridor. What was he doing here?

"I understand your years of history with him and I know you don't approve, but it was a job I really wanted," Treva said. She gave him the pleading look she'd used as a child when there was a special sugary treat she wanted that he knew would ruin her appetite for dinner.

Ganston ignored her act, focusing on Stemple. Was the

man watching him? Or was he watching Treva? He decided to test the theory. He wasn't overly paranoid, but it was better to understand the man's intentions.

"Uncle, you seem distracted," Treva said as she rubbed the sleeve of his jacket.

Ganston looked at his ComTex. "I'm very late for an appointment, but I want you to promise me that you'll come by my quarters for dinner. We need to talk about this job, and my project."

Treva unfurrowed her eyebrows and smiled broadly. "I'll call and we can make a date."

"Promise it will be in the next two weeks."

Treva pulled back her chin and narrowed her eyes. "If that's what you want. What are you up to, Uncle?"

"Yes, that's what I want, my sweet." He kissed her on the forehead. "I have a much brighter career move to offer you."

"And you don't want to tell me now?" She smiled.

Ganston kissed her forehead again. "There is a time and a place for everything. I love you, my child." He turned and left.

Treva stood among the throng. Was her uncle going to offer her a position at Stone Braide? She didn't want to leave the Mountain before the Landers were freed. Well, she'd worry about that later. Right now her focus was to find Glade's daughter. She moved toward the security area.

Suddenly a hand grabbed her arm and whipped her around. Adrenaline rushed to her chest as she stood face-to-face with Stemple.

"What do you think you're doing?" His voice boomed, bouncing from the wall.

Treva wrestled her arm free and raised a fist. "This is the second time. Don't put your hands on me again. I may look like a lightweight, but I assure you, Mr. Touchy, I can lay you out on this floor for manhandling me." She'd have yelled for security, but that wasn't the kind of attention she wanted right now.

Stemple threw up both hands. "I'm sorry. I didn't mean for it to feel like an attack. But you have to know that if Everling ever saw the display of affection you just demonstrated with Ganston, you'd be out of a job in two seconds flat."

"What is it with the two of them? Uncle feels the same way about Everling."

Stemple shook his head. "The rivalry goes back too far for me to care. What are you doing down here? This is the last place I expected to find you."

Treva needed a plausible explanation. She chastised herself. Why hadn't she thought of that sooner? "I-I . . ." Her eyes darted over his shoulder as she looked to invent a reason. "I was looking for a merchant."

Stemple stared at her. "What do you need with an outside merchant?"

Her mind raced as her glance crossed the pallet of snake skins. "I was interested in studying the cellular biology of the large predator snakes from down south, and I remembered seeing those-size skins come in with the merchants." She gestured to the pallet.

Stemple eyed the pallet but seemed satisfied. She breathed a silent sigh of relief.

"I would say that you have too much work in the lab to be here looking for additional work to study. Did you get the data correlated I sent you this morning?"

Treva glanced down the corridor. She'd never make it to the holding cells with Stemple around. "Um, no. I was taking a little break. What are you doing down in this area?"

He straightened. "The biometric log-in triggered an alert in the lab that there might be a Lander present. Everling wasn't in my area, so I came down to check out the details."

She faked what she hoped looked like surprise. "Wow. Do you need me to go with you?"

"No. I'd be more comfortable if you were back in the lab, doing the work I assigned. I need those results later on this afternoon, and I don't want my own work languishing because yours isn't complete."

Treva intertwined her fingers as her shoulders dropped. There wasn't much chance of getting around him. How was she going to get to the holding cells? And what was she going to do if he got there first?

"Are you listening to me?" he asked.

Treva jerked. "I'm sorry. My mind seems so preoccupied lately. Yes, I'll get on it right away. Sorry to keep you waiting." Her mind raced, searching for options. She needed a minute to think. Where could she go so he wouldn't see her?

Treva stepped back against the wall to allow three merchants with large bundles slung over their shoulders to pass. *Think.*

"So I can expect your report before you leave today?" Stemple was getting impatient with her. She could tell by his tone it was time for her to vacate his line of sight.

"Yes, I'm going now," Treva said with a wave of her hand. She started slowly back up the long corridor. She couldn't leave. She'd promised Glade. If Stemple corralled his daughter, there was no telling what would happen. He seemed upset at the idea of dismantling the project, but she couldn't be sure of his intentions.

Her heart thumped with the speed of her steps, and her stomach churned. She reached the end of the security section and turned corridors twice. There was no chance of Stemple seeing her from here. Leaning against the wall, she closed her eyes and ran through all the available options. Her eyes flew open.

The holding area end of the security station opened into an area connected with a Jet Trans pod. She could get in that way, or at least observe from there. The loop of connecting streets would take her out into the Mountain community, and she could circle back around Science Consortium structures. It would take about four minutes. Would they still be there?

Treva took off at a dead run.

20

Ganston seethed as he watched Stemple manhandle Treva. Her father had died days before her second Birth Remembrance, and a month later Ganston had vowed to her mother, on her deathbed, that he would protect Treva to his last breath. After what he'd just witnessed, that time might be now.

Ganston waited for Treva to turn the second corner on her way out of the security station before he confronted Stemple. He didn't want her involved in his tirades. She'd probably know soon enough.

Stemple moved farther into the station toward the holding cells. That seemed odd in itself, but Ganston disregarded it as he wove among the merchants. Stemple stopped at the security station. The officers were both occupied with other tasks, so he waited, allowing Ganston to catch up to him.

"Stemple, I want to talk to you about the way you touched my niece," Ganston said in a loud voice.

The man turned slowly to face him with disdain. "What are you talking about, old man?"

Ganston frowned. "Your behavior was rude. It seems you only act civil when you're around Everling."

"I act civil when the gesture is reciprocated. You seem to have an overly active relationship with one of our key researchers, and I'm sure Dr. Everling would find it a cause for concern."

Was he trying to intimidate by threatening Treva's job?

"I couldn't care less what Everling worries about, but I do worry about the display I witnessed. I don't want you putting your hands on my niece again." Ganston glared at Stemple, who moved closer.

"You need new glasses, old man. I didn't hurt Treva in any way. The discussion about her work requirements and what she needs to do to accomplish them was very civil."

At that moment the officer who'd brought Ganston the tablet to sign for the chip procurement spotted him and approached. "Mr. Ganston, can I be of further service to you?"

Ganston sputtered a resounding no and waved the man off. He looked in the direction of the containment cells. The walls were no longer transparent, so he couldn't tell if the subjects had been released, and he dare not ask. He needed to leave before the guard chose to call him back with any other questions about the detainees. It wouldn't do to have to explain to one of Everling's stooges why he was giving payment chips to merchants.

He turned to Stemple and leaned in close. "You just stay out of my way."

✦

Everling stood between two of the check-in stations at the near end of the security station, watching Stemple and Ganston. He'd hurried down here because of the alert code for interlopers. Or at least he thought that was why he came down. Was that today? Or yesterday? His vision blurred and he shook his head. The days were running together.

No overly excited guards. Everything seemed normal. He lost interest and turned his attention to his assistant and his enemy.

Both Ganston and Stemple had walked past him without noticing. The noisy crowd congregated in the area helped, but the dramatic change in his looks took center stage for his open-faced deception.

The regression had continued. In the last twenty-four hours he'd lopped off at least another ten years from his appearance. Not bad. But he'd begun to worry. The shots he'd administered to himself and Bethany were designed to slow down the process but didn't seem to be working fast enough. Or maybe they were. His thinking was muddled. Anger surged. Was it because he couldn't remember details or because he was seeing the men colluding?

Stemple and Ganston stood with their heads together, deep in conversation. He wasn't stupid. He knew what they were up to—taking control of the Mountain from him. How long had they planned an overthrow? How many others had they convinced? Maybe Bethany? No, never Bethany. His mind raced with thoughts of betrayal.

A sharp twinge coursed through his side. Everling flinched and pressed his fist into the spot. He backed into the singular security room between the stations.

The guard looked up at him. "Sir?"

Everling held his breath at the pain. He ran his ComTex over the security scanner, which registered his name and level of clearance. The guard didn't know him by sight. He looked at the screen and nodded.

Everling managed a few words. "I need to use the section office."

The guard hit a switch and Everling heard the door unlock. As he lurched toward the door, sweat poured from his brow, soaking his collar. Breathing hard, he closed the door and leaned against it. He rummaged in his pocket for the vial and needle, then pulled off the cap with his teeth. With shaking hands he filled the syringe with pale yellow liquid, the elixir of life responsible for slowing down the process. A laugh pushed from his lips. What should he call aging in reverse—*unaging*?

He flicked the cylinder and pressed the plunger to remove the air. A squirt of the precious liquid jetted from the tip of the needle. He pushed up a sleeve. Tremors wracked his hands, but he remained steady enough to plunge the needle into the muscle of his arm.

The liquid pulsing through his muscle tissue felt like a searing knife cutting through flesh. Everling leaned back against the wall and took a deep breath. Steadiness returned to his hands and the wobble left his legs. Fresh and renewed once again, he rose to his full height. It was time to take care of Ganston and Stemple once and for all. He would put them both to death if they wanted to thwart his programs. Perfectly logical and acceptable. Anything or anyone defying his authority would be squashed.

Everling opened the door and walked through the small security room without acknowledging the guard. He looked to the place where Ganston and Stemple had been conspiring against him. Ganston was nowhere in sight, and Stemple was talking to a guard in the area of the containment cells. Everling strolled in that direction. He would have to be cunning and sharp to catch a prey such as Stemple. The man was very good at hiding his game face, the one that colluded with Ganston.

He walked up behind Stemple. "Why are you here and not working on the important task I gave you to complete?"

Stemple swung to face Everling and flinched. He stared into the man's enraged eyes. Fear and wonder fought to overtake the top spot in his brain. Everling had clearly regressed further in the aging process. His fresh younger features were unrecognizable as the older man who had been his boss just a week ago.

"Answer me!" Everling shouted. Spittle formed at the corners of his mouth, and his eyes darted wildly like fleas dancing on a dog.

"I-I'm sorry, sir. I'm not sure what you're asking me," Stemple said in a calm tone, trying not to elevate the man's reaction any further.

"Do you think I didn't see you talking to Charles Ganston? I suppose now you think it's time to move on to greener pastures."

Stemple frowned. *What is he talking about?*

"Oh, that. I was talking to him about T—" He stopped.

If he let it slip Treva was the man's niece, his career would be over.

"What? Talking about what? Helping him to take over the Company?" Everling turned, pacing from side to side in the hall. "So he thinks he's found the chink in my armor that will allow him to wheedle his way in like the burrowing insect he is." He screwed his index finger into the air to illustrate.

Stemple's heart pounded as though trying to get out. He wanted to crawl inside himself to avoid this madman. Everling was clearly having a psychotic break. Maybe it was a reaction to the new drug cocktail to slow the biological change.

He glanced around. Everling's voice was beginning to attract attention. He needed to get him back to the lab where he could do tests and review the latest findings of the tox panel he'd started running before he came down to security.

"Uh, sir." No response. "Dr. Everling." Stemple touched his arm.

Everling swung around with hands raised. Stemple grabbed Everling's fist before it connected with his face.

"Doctor, take it easy. It's me, Drace Stemple."

A moment of clarity registered on Everling's face. It was quickly masked by the wild-eyed slobbering wreck of the younger man he had become.

Stemple took him by the arm. "Sir, we need to go back to the lab."

"Yes, yes we do. I have some very important business to take care of right away," Everling said with a gleeful sneer. His steps faltered.

Stemple reached out and steadied him. Everling brushed away his hand. He searched the doctor's face. There was no recognizable ounce of Everling. Not appearance or attitude. Stemple steered him through the merchants. He needed to find Bethany. Maybe she was in better shape and she could help him. He hoped he could find something to alleviate the man's stress.

Stemple cringed as he listened to Everling's ramblings. The stress was beginning to take its toll on his stomach. Bile rose in his throat as they approached the lab. The more the old man's—well, to be precise, the younger-looking old man's—rhetoric intensified, the more Stemple regretted his part in the program. Why had it taken him so long to see the error in his judgment?

They stopped at the entrance. Everling's hands waved about in jerky movements as though he were conducting an orchestra. He'd expounded on every conspiracy theory he'd ever thought of, going back to the debacles at the time of the Sorrows. By the time he'd exhausted his speech, the words were beginning to slur.

Stemple's concern heightened as Everling coded the door twice and got it wrong both times.

"Dr. Everling, maybe you should think about taking the rest of the day off. You could go home and enjoy a restful evening with Bethany." Where had that woman gone? Lately she'd been hovering everywhere. Now that he needed her, she'd disappeared.

Everling swung around with eyes ablaze and came within an inch of Stemple's nose.

"The world decreased so we can increase. We are the new world that will rise from the ashes to claim immortality!"

Another filament of bile snaked up Stemple's throat. This

was the second time the doctor had spoken like that in the last few days. Was it symptomatic of a psychosis? Were there hallucinations involved? This could become dangerous.

Stemple smelled a fruity sweetness on the deranged man's breath. It appeared his body was trying to get rid of excess acetone. It must be ketoacidosis. His body functions were out of whack, so the psychosis could just be a chemical imbalance. Stemple needed to get him inside and start testing.

He went through the motions to get them into the lab. Everling watched with disdain.

"You do that all so easily, as though you're entering your own lab. What about me? Nobody cares that I've dedicated my whole life to this Mountain. Even you! You've always wanted my job and my position in this community. I've always known what you were striving toward."

Stemple ignored the ranting and led Everling toward his section of the lab. Everling pulled free and strode quickly toward Lab Section Ten. Stemple dropped his head in resignation. He'd have to follow the man around until he could guide him in the right direction.

Two more tries and Everling accessed the lab. He staggered and Stemple lurched to catch him, but the doctor turned on him with a demonic growl. He backed off.

Everling lunged for the control console. Stemple glanced toward the containment cells and did a double take.

The normally opaque wall stood transparent. Glade Rishon's cell was empty. Stemple hurried to the cell's open door. Logic said he could see there was no one in there but he ran inside anyway. Looking around the empty space, he turned to face Everling.

The door slammed shut. Stemple rushed to the clear partition. "Dr. Everling, what happened? What have you done? What did you do to Glade? Open the door."

Everling's eyes danced. "You thought you could outsmart me, didn't you? Don't act so surprised. I see what you're trying to do. I've decided I'll just have to take care of things myself."

"What I'm trying to do? What are you talking about? Open the door. We need to discuss—"

"No more discussion!" Everling screamed. His hands moved across the control panel. "You thought you could destroy my work. Well, I'm smarter than that. You have to get up pretty early in the morning to get ahead of me." His words slurred as his hand missed the controls.

Stemple's throat tightened. A madman stood in front of him. What had Everling done with Glade? Where was Bethany? Did he do something to her too? "Please, sir, you need to open the door and let me out of here. Let's talk to your wife. Where's Bethany?"

Everling ignored him. No reaction to anything he said. If all else failed he'd have to wait until Treva showed up. She should be back any minute. But then how was he going to handle Everling? There weren't many checks and balances in the Mountain to control him.

The motor on the wall units cycled on. Stemple looked behind him. The wall screen lifted into the ceiling and the panel closed. The wall unit slid open and the furniture retreated into their holders.

Stemple's eyes widened. "Dr. Everling, what are you doing? Stop this madness and open the door."

"Madness?" Everling mimicked him. "Madness. Stop this

315

madness." He pointed at Stemple. "You should have thought of that before you disregarded my direct orders."

Stemple shook his head. He pounded on the clear wall with both hands. "No, no! This is a misunderstanding!"

Everling lifted the square crystal cover and smashed his fist onto the red button.

Jets of fire shot from every part of his prison. Stemple screamed. The walls, floor, and ceiling turned into blow-torches of death.

Stemple ignited. He flailed as though the movement would ward off the hungry flames that licked at him from every direction. The whooshing sound and pain lasted for agonizing seconds that felt like hours. The flames seared beyond the pain receptors. Flesh melted into his eyes. For a split second his head protected his brain . . . before it boiled in his skull.

Bethany tucked the halo-tablet under her arm as she raced into the Prison Control Center. She'd gotten an alert that the JetTrans patrol had returned. She practically salivated at the thought of starting the DNA splicing with Glade Rishon's child.

"What do they have for me?" Bethany asked as she leaned over a security console. Years ago Noah had created his own security center separate from Mountain security. At the time he didn't trust the way the operating Board was treating his father, and he felt having a security force loyal to only the Everlings was desirable. Over the years it had proved profitable.

The technician at the console looked past her to the next station. The next person turned away as though he didn't want to be involved.

Bethany snapped her fingers. "Hello! Are you going to answer me?"

The young man averted his eyes. "They don't have the subject, ma'am." He flinched as though expecting retribution.

Bethany straightened up. Her voice lowered. "Why not?" Her heart rate shot up twenty beats a minute. She reined in her composure, but she wanted to kick something, or someone.

"There is a complete AirStream and JetTrans grid from the Mountain to Dominion Borough. There are no bio-signatures matching the child," the tech said.

Bethany closed her eyes. "Technically it would seem impossible to miss a complete bio-reading. The only way I could see that happening would be if she was underground where our sensors couldn't reach her." She walked away from the console. "But since there are no great caves between here and there, I'd say it's just rank incompetence. The grid needs to be tightened." She turned and slammed her fist on the console.

The technician jumped and so did those at the next three stations.

"What JetTrans teams are available in the Mountain?" Bethany asked. She had to keep reminding herself to stay calm, but in the face of abject failure it felt daunting. At least one of these teams would produce the desired results, or she'd keep them out there indefinitely.

"There's only one team not on patrol at the moment. They are being interviewed about an altercation outside the Mountain with several interlopers."

"Forget interviews! People trying to break into the Mountain are not my problem. Get me that team in the air ASAP," she said through clenched teeth.

"But ma'am, their unit was damaged," the tech said.

"Does it fly?"

"Yes, ma'am."

Bethany glared at the tech. "They've got ten minutes to get in the air . . . or else."

21

Selah studied the people milling about in the corridor. No one looked menacing or confrontational. They were probably safe for the moment. She only felt a void, a nothingness. A block of some sort. But the question burning in her mind had nothing to do with anything outside the confines of this cell.

She turned to glare at Cleon. "You took money for bringing diseased rabbits here? Are you crazy? People could die from eating them." She was still angry, and seeing Cleon being paid only served to push her further over the edge. How could she have misjudged her own brothers so much? Willing to kill people for money?

"It wasn't me. It was Raza's doing. But you eat them, and you haven't died, so I'm beginning to think it was one of Father's lies just to make us eat only what he liked."

Selah shook her head. "No, he was right. Well, no he

wasn't, but . . ." She let her shoulders drop. "Okay, I admit it. There are rabbits that are safe to eat, but not all of them."

Cleon stared at her. "You never thought it was important enough to share the knowledge?"

"Well, you saw us eating them. And Mother asked you many times if you wanted to join us." Now it was her turn to be on the defensive. "Besides, I had reasons I kept the secret to myself."

"That sounds really selfish to me," Cleon said.

"Well, you boys treated me like dirt."

"I never treated you that way."

Selah backed off, closed her eyes, and ran her hand across her forehead. She couldn't stand to lose another brother. "I'm sorry. It always felt like it was you and Raza against me."

"Okay, you two, we need to figure a way out of here," Bodhi said.

"Ganston's security woman said after the pilot interviews we could go," Cleon said.

"We can't wait that long," Selah said. "Amaryllis is by herself out there."

"You seem to have forgotten why we came here in the first place," Bodhi said.

A young woman wearing a white lab coat hurried up to the transparent wall. She looked them over, making eye contact with each. She stood as if thinking, then squared her shoulders and strolled toward the security station.

Selah watched as the woman pointed back in their direction. Fear sparked her chest and she backed up. Had they been caught?

The woman again approached the containment cell, this time with the overweight guard scurrying at her heels. She gestured at the cell. "Open it!"

Beads of sweat appeared on the guard's brow. "But ma'am, I don't have the authority to turn these detainees over to you."

"Didn't I tell you I'm Dr. Everling's assistant?"

"Yes, ma'am, you did," the guard stammered.

"You checked my credentials?"

"Yes, ma'am, I did." His face flushed.

Selah thought if the situation hadn't been so serious, it would seem almost comical. The guard kept bowing without looking at the woman. Who was she?

"So what's the holdup?" She slapped her hand on the plascine wall. "I have work to do, and if I don't get these subjects to the lab in short order, you're going to have an extremely unpleasant boss breathing down your necks. Do you want that?"

"No, ma'am, I don't," the guard said. Sweat rolled down his temples, wetting the collar of his uniform.

Selah could see his hands trembling. It fascinated her that a young woman could have this level of authority. Men invariably were the bosses in the world she knew. But on the other hand it worried her. What kind of new situation were they getting into? Bodhi and Cleon gathered behind her to watch.

"What's she trying to do?" Cleon asked.

"I think she's trying to get us released to her custody. It could mean trouble," Selah said.

Bodhi stared at her. "No, I don't think so."

"Why not? Do you feel something?" Selah turned to face him.

He shook his head. "No, I think it's more in what I *don't* feel."

She opened her mouth to answer as the cell door opened.

The young woman stepped inside and looked at Selah. "Are these two with you?"

Selah nodded and pointed. "Cleon and Bodhi."

She motioned to them. "Follow me." She left the doorway. No one followed and she turned back. "I said follow me, now!"

Selah looked at Cleon and Bodhi. They shrugged. She turned back to the woman. "Why should we follow? Who are you?"

The woman stepped close to Selah's face. "My name is Treva Gilani and I'm the person who's going to save your hide. Is that good enough for you?"

Selah hesitated. There weren't many options for getting out on their own. Something about this woman registered safety. She nodded then stepped out behind Treva. Bodhi and Cleon followed.

Selah moved beside Treva. "I don't want to seem ungrateful, but where are you taking us?"

"There's no time to talk. I have to get you to your father. This is falling apart too fast."

Selah grabbed Treva by the arm. "How do you know who I am? Where is he?"

Treva jerked her arm free and trotted down the corridor. "I told you we don't have time for small talk. The insurrection is going to happen whether we're ready or not." She shook her head and waved a hand. "I knew rebellion would take over and there were going to be ones we couldn't control, but nooo, Glade wanted them all brought out of the fog at the same time."

Glade. Thunder pounded in her chest. Selah hadn't felt the rumble in a couple days. She scrambled to keep up as they turned down a narrow corridor. Her sense of direction told her they were moving farther into the Mountain. Was her heart racing because of fear or apprehension? She knew she could be fierce, but did that level of bravery include meeting her real father for the first time?

"Where are we going? This isn't the way out," Cleon said as he galloped to keep up.

"We have to get Glade first." Treva keyed in the code and opened a door.

"You know where my father is?" Selah dug her fingers into the woman's arm.

Treva pried herself loose and darted through the doorway. "If you keep slowing me down it could have dire consequences. The order has already been given."

Selah released her. "What order?"

Treva hurried on with no response.

Selah looked back at Bodhi. He was uncharacteristically quiet. Normally she'd expect him to ask more questions. Take control. She tried to commit the direction they were going to memory, but they were moving too fast.

"Hey, I know where we are. We came down a different corridor, but this is where I came with Raza to deliver the rabbits," Cleon said.

Treva skidded to a stop and they nearly ran over her. She grabbed Cleon by the shoulders. "What did you say? Rabbits? Who'd you deliver rabbits to in the Mountain?"

Cleon squirmed free of her grasp. "A man named Ganston."

At that moment the door to the area slid open and Ganston stepped out.

Cleon pointed. "Him! We sold them to him."

Treva launched in Ganston's direction. "What are you doing buying diseased rabbits from outside this Mountain? Why would you do something so reckless?"

Ganston backed up to the wall as his eyes darted among the three other people crowded around him, then back to Treva. "What are you doing with these people, and how did they get out of containment?"

"I got them out. We have a common goal to thwart one of Everling's plans." Treva fisted her hands on her hips. "But you haven't answered my questions."

"I-I need to explain to you alone, my sweet child." He offered a nervous smile. "This is not for strangers' ears."

She hesitated then grabbed his hands. "There's no time right now. Do you trust me?"

Ganston pulled back. "What kind of a strange question is that?"

Treva's feet danced several hesitant steps. "I'm asking because it's going to get dicey here in the next few hours and I need to know I've got help if I need you."

Ganston kept his eyes on Treva and smiled softly. "Of course, my child. I would do anything for you."

"Good." Treva strode away briskly but yelled back, "I'm going to hold you to that."

Ganston raised a hand. "What's going on?"

She never answered. Selah and the others hurried down the hall behind her.

Treva led them down two more corridors, turning left and then right at the next junction, and then another left. Selah felt like a rat in the mazes she used to see at market, where they baited the rodents with food to see how fast they could move.

They rushed around another corner, through a doorway, and up an angled walkway to a higher level. The woman keyed them into another area. Selah glanced around.

Her hand rose to her chest in an effort to contain the pounding of her heart. She rubbed the scar on her arm and blew out several short breaths to gain control of her shakes. This looked similar to a healer-unit area at home, with equipment, work benches, and gurneys. She'd seen this kind of equipment when someone was ill or dying. She flinched and the hairs rose on her arms.

Treva moved to the other side of the room and stopped in front of a sealed partition to the right of where they entered. She keyed in a code, put her eye up to an optical identification scanner, and the doorway slid open with a whoosh. Selah watched as the young woman peered around the immediate area inside the doorway and motioned them in. They crowded through the narrow doorway.

Treva moved toward a long circular control station to the left of the opening. She stopped short and gasped.

A man lay sprawled across the floor, facedown.

Treva rushed to his side. "Dr. Everling!" She knelt beside the body.

"Is he dead?" Selah asked. The second body in as many

days. It appalled her that she wasn't more upset at the sight. At home she'd have run behind Mother, shaking.

Treva felt for a pulse. "No, he has a strong pulse." She pried his fingers from the shaft of a syringe in his right hand and lifted the tube. The pale yellow substance glistened in the light. She threw the syringe to the side and it skittered under the console.

She shook her head. "He's taking some kind of experimental drugs. I can't help him right now. I need to find Stemple—he'll know what to do." She looked around, rose, and pushed a button. The door to a containment room slid open. "Help me put him in there. I'll find Stemple when we're done. This will keep him out of the way in the meantime."

Cleon and Bodhi grabbed his arms and legs to haul him into the room.

Selah wrung her hands. "What if he's sick, and putting him in there kills him?"

Treva shook her head, her eyes growing cold. "If I get time, I'll tell you about this man and what he's done. Right now we have more important things to do."

Bodhi and Cleon returned to the console. Treva keyed the controls and shut the door.

She smiled triumphantly at Selah and pressed a series of buttons, gesturing to a long blank wall. "I'd like you to meet your father."

The coloring in the wall dissolved to a transparent surface. Black soot mottled the walls, ceiling, and floor. They stared at burnt human remains.

Treva's hand flew to her mouth. She gagged, bent over the

console, and heaved up the contents of her stomach. Tears pooled in her eyes.

Selah looked from the cell to Treva. "I don't understand. What is this?"

Treva's mouth opened and closed a few times. Words came out as strangled sobs. "Your father, Glade Rishon, was in there when I left."

Selah shook her head and her stomach lurched. No, it couldn't be true . . . to come so far, and then nothing. She screamed and charged the wall, pounding on the transparent surface. It felt warm. The room was clear of smoke. "No, no! What have you done to my father?"

The charred remains, with flakes of what could only have been clothing spread crumbled on the floor, were kneeling, forever locked in position with arms reaching out. The composite surface was littered with ash. An outline had burned around the corpse in a macabre design, solid on the inside edges near the body but feathering out as it moved away from the scene, as though the flames had burned outward. She rubbed her hand along the glass, tracing the outline of the remains.

Her screams of anguish were drowned out by the angry yells of Cleon and Bodhi.

She slumped to the floor in a flood of tears. She couldn't bear it any longer. She turned away from the carnage, her back resting against the still warm wall.

"What kind of sick joke is this?" Cleon charged Treva, coming nose to nose with her.

She backed up, looking bewildered. "I swear, he was fine when I left."

Bodhi grabbed her by the arm. "Who is responsible for this murder?"

The word *murder* stabbed at Selah's heart.

Treva struggled to get away but he held fast. "I don't know. Dr. Everling ordered the program dismantled and the subjects destroyed. I just didn't realize he—"

"What program?" a deep male voice asked.

22

Ganston stood leisurely in the open doorway, hands in pockets. He strolled in to stand among the group as they spun to face him. He'd watched out for Treva since she was a baby. Now was not the time to stop. He wanted to know what these outsiders had gotten her into.

Treva wrestled her arm free from Bodhi and ran to his side. "You can't be here. This is Dr. Everling's private lab."

Ganston peered over his glasses at the three other people. "I think that Neanderthal would have a bigger problem with outlanders being in here than me, but that's another issue entirely. What program?"

Treva's shoulders slumped. "There's no use hiding it now." Her arms waved in the air as a tear rolled down her cheek. "The purge has begun."

Cleon helped Selah from the floor. She rested her forehead against the glass. "Rest in peace, my father. I never knew you, but I felt your love reaching for me." She sniffed and walked on stilted legs to Treva and Ganston. "Tell me how this happened. Who murdered my father?"

Treva looked on the verge of tears herself. "I can't be sure who did this, but with Glade gone, there is going to be mass carnage down below. He was the only control over them."

Bodhi crowded in. "There are others. I feel them. Take us to them."

Treva shook her head. "You can't go there. I couldn't get you in without proper authority."

"I have the authority to go anywhere in this Mountain," Ganston said.

They wheeled to face him.

Treva took his hand. "Uncle, I'm not sure you realize what's going on, but there is danger involved here. Everling is not going to let these subjects go willingly, and we've lost the person controlling them."

Ganston clenched his teeth and pursed his lips. "Unfortunately, I do know what's going on. I've known all along and I never did anything to stop it."

Treva took him by the arm and pulled him away from the outlanders.

"Do you know what you're saying?" Treva's eyes grew large.

Ganston nodded. "Yes, I do. That's why I created Stone Braide."

Treva furrowed her brow. "What did you do? I thought that was just in development."

"We're ready to go in the next couple weeks. I've gathered a large group of like-minded people . . ." Ganston sighed and took off his glasses. "We leaving the Mountain and taking technology and knowledge to the outside world."

Treva ran a hand across her forehead. "This is huge. How did you keep it secret for so long?" She started to pace. "Why am I asking you that? Of course you have the ability keep it secret *and* do something on a grand scale. You've hated this place forever." She shook her head. "I'm hoping you were going to take me with you."

Ganston smiled. "Of course, my child. I would never leave you behind without giving you the opportunity to join me."

Treva's eyes widened. "Did you create a security force as part of your plan?"

"Yes." He put his glasses back on.

"I need to free the Landers below in the Prison Unit. Everling is going to have them all put to death. I think this was an example of his handiwork." She pointed to the burnt and scarred containment unit.

He glanced at the torched room and grimaced. "He never ceases to amaze me with the level of barbarism he aspires to attain. What person could ever think up such evil?"

Ganston stared at the jet openings in the walls, floor, and ceiling. It was clear from the soot trails just how closely this resembled a crematorium. He shuddered at the thought of what the poor man trapped in that room had gone through being burned alive. Thinking on the scenario steeled his resolve.

"Leaving here will burn all our bridges." He grinned at the thought of driving Everling into a rage over so many leaving the Mountain en masse.

"I'm not sure how much trouble you'll have. Everling's in that room over there."

Ganston's eyes opened wide. "Where? You have Noah locked in a room?"

Treva motioned him to the control panel. She pushed the button to transform the plascine wall to clear. The younger-looking Everling lay motionless on the floor.

"Who is that?" Ganston asked, staring at the full head of dark hair. He moved closer to the wall.

"That's Dr. Everling. He's been taking drug therapies to regress his age."

Ganston bent down to stare at the unconscious man's face. "I haven't seen him look this young in thirty years. Is he dead?"

"No. He's breathing, but he's been using untested drugs. I'm torn between calling medics—Everling would rage because no one knows about these drugs—or just leaving him there until I can find Drace Stemple. He'd be the only one Everling would allow to treat him." Treva smacked the button to turn the wall back to opaque. "This is a convenient time for him to be out of the loop, though. We need to be finished before he comes to."

Ganston smiled broadly. "I never thought I'd see the day, but now that it's here, I'm savoring the moment."

Treva waved her hand in a counterclockwise motion. "Okay, are we done with your moment? We need some help, and there's no time to spare."

Ganston lifted his ComTex, pushed a few keys, and Mojica's face filled the small screen.

"I need you. My office, ten minutes. You have an expert security team in training, yes?"

Mojica cracked a smile. "Yes. Why? Do you need a demonstration?"

Ganston pursed his lips. "A live demonstration, yes. Put

them in readiness, and we'll discuss this exercise when you get to my office."

"Can you tell me what kind of *exercise* you have in mind?" She knit her brows together.

"Let's just say your troops are going to engage in facilitating a mass escape." He held up a finger and turned to Treva. "How many people are we setting free?"

Treva shrugged. "I don't have a clue. I've never been down to that department. I'd say up to twenty maybe."

Ganston turned back to his com screen. "Twenty people."

Mojica raised an eyebrow. "Now you've got my attention. I'll be right there." The screen went blank.

Ganston led the four young people back to his section, where they'd be less noticeable. They reached his office as Mojica arrived.

She presented a commanding figure dressed head to toe in military combat gear. The weapon strapped to her right thigh was one of the most advanced laser weapons the Mountain had recently developed. Ganston wondered how much this equipment was costing him.

As he led them into his conference room, he decided whatever the cost, if it took him to the top and kept him there, it was worth it. "How many men do you have in this elite force?"

Mojica repositioned her weapon on her thigh to avoid rubbing the chair arm and sat down. "What makes you think my troops are just men?"

Ganston raised an eyebrow. "I didn't mean to insult your choices. I just didn't realize there were women of exceptional combat caliber in this Mountain."

"I'm of that caliber."

He nodded. "Touché. How many troops do you have ready?"

"How many do you need?"

Ganston's jaw set, his temper flaring. He didn't like playing word games, especially the "answer my question with a question" one. "Are you deliberately being evasive with me?"

Mojica straightened and leaned forward. "Of course not. I'm just saying whatever you need done and however many combat personnel you need to accomplish it, I can deliver. Just tell me what you want."

"Assess the situation. You decide." He stared at her. He would see how she did on this, since it was basically training to him and not a requirement for his new community.

"First tell me who we're setting free, and from what area of the Mountain?" Mojica drummed on the arms of her chair.

Ganston smiled. "You're going into Noah Everling's Level Three Confinement area and setting free the Landers."

Mojica's eyebrows raised, forcing her forehead into wrinkles. "And you think Everling isn't going to object?"

"At this point he's out of commission," Ganston said.

"And locked up," Treva added.

Mojica glanced between the two of them. "Should I ask how you know this, or is it better left unsaid?"

Ganston rubbed his chin. "Better left unsaid. He's definitely incapacitated, and Treva can't find his assistant Drace Stemple. There are no others to interfere. The rest are just workers."

"Don't forget his wife Bethany. She's become a force to be reckoned with since she woke from her coma. Wait until you see her age regression," Treva said.

"Where is she?" Mojica asked.

"I don't know. I haven't seen her in the lab today." Treva seated herself next to Cleon and gave him a sideways smile.

Ganston followed her movement. He knew that look. Whether she realized it or not, Treva had an attraction to Cleon. He marveled how young people could be in such dire straits but still emotionally involved elsewhere.

He cleared his throat to get their attention. "Treva, even though it's part of Everling's secret operations, do you know anything about the security in Level Three Confinement?"

She shook her head. "All I know are comm extensions, and I don't think they'll help."

"They might." Mojica raised a finger. "I don't know Everling's operation because guards have to sign a specific nondisclosure with his Science Consortium. But as head of security, I know the layout of the area and how many guards are on duty. Having comm channels might help us pinpoint where guards are at the moment of our incursion and extraction." Mojica rose from her seat, fingering her ComTex. She walked to the other end of the conference room and spoke into the device in hushed tones, then returned to her seat and leaned back, looking satisfied.

"How soon can we get them out?" Treva moved to the edge of her seat. Her hand brushed Cleon's and they both blushed.

"I'll leave that up to Mojica." Ganston raised an eyebrow at their interaction. He remembered being young. Stressful situations made strange associations.

"What part are these people to play in the operation?" Mojica waved a hand at the group.

"None," Ganston said. He didn't want Treva in danger or these outsiders running around in his Mountain.

"Oh no you don't," Treva said. "I'm going. I've been giving the Landers shots to bring them out of the slumber, and they've bonded with me. You go in there with a bunch of strangers and no Glade, no matter how well meaning, and it could cause a disaster."

"Who's Glade?" Mojica asked.

Ganston looked at her. "He was one of the Landers. There's a badly burnt corpse in his cell in Everling's lab, where we just came from." He gestured toward Treva. "She makes a valid point. But it's up to you."

Mojica raised an eyebrow and shrugged her shoulders. He nodded reluctantly.

"I can communicate with them telepathically to help keep them calm," Bodhi said.

Mojica gave Bodhi a look that Ganston couldn't interpret.

"How can you do that?" He furrowed his brow. How many other things about this operation didn't he know?

"Landers have telepathic abilities among themselves. Everling never quite guessed, but he put them on a drug cocktail to suppress their abilities before he understood how huge that could become," Treva said.

Ganston sat forward. "So you're telling me he's a Lander?"

Bodhi and Treva nodded.

"And I came here looking for my father, Glade Rishon. Since Everling killed him, I have a right and a need to help free those of my people who are trapped here," Selah said.

Ganston leaned on his desk and put his hand to his forehead. "So you're a Lander too?" What was he doing helping these people? He could think of so many ways that this could go wrong. He could spend the rest of his life in prison for this kind of insurrection.

Cleon turned to Selah. "Your people? I'm your people. You didn't know any of this stuff last week, and now you're joining a military operation to free people you've never met. What about me?"

Selah shrugged. "You can come too."

"Wait a minute. I haven't said any of you can go *anywhere* yet," Mojica said.

"Uncle!" Treva said. All four started arguing with Mojica.

Ganston raised a hand. Everyone ignored him. He slapped the desk. "Hey!"

The room went silent.

"Thank you," he said. "I hesitate to say this, but I think each of you has earned a right to go. You've been through a lot to get to this point." He especially didn't want any pushback from Cleon. In a perfect world the young man would die in the conflict and he could wash his hands of the whole mess.

Mojica shrugged. "Suit yourself. This is not going to be fun and games. Those guards will be using live ammo and so will we. You've all been warned." Her ComTex beeped. She answered it and replied with a curt, "ASAP. Wait for my command!"

Mojica rose and walked behind Ganston's desk. He looked up as she stepped in beside him.

"May I?" She gestured at his halo-screen controls.

He pursed his lips and leaned away from the desk. "Help yourself."

She keyed in her personal security code and the building

schematic appeared on the large wall screen to their left. She fingered through the pages until she came to the third sub-floor level. "This is the layout of the area we're going into."

The schematic showed a large rectangular area divided into four separate sections with corridors around them. Each section had a hallway running down the center with different size rooms on either side. One section was labeled and divided up as working lab areas, another was labeled as cells, and two were unmarked.

Ganston used a laser pointer and motioned to a section that was grayed out. "What is that?"

Mojica smiled. "That is the success of this operation. Apparently Everling's idea for this secret lab was to put it in an obscure location where no one would ever question its function. He chose an old section of the hovercraft factory. After we switched to JetTrans about twenty years ago, the space went idle. That grayed-out area is the old ramp from the area up to the present JetTrans terminal."

"There was a terminal off to the left side of the gate where we came in," Cleon said. "That's how we got caught. The JetTrans went that way and the pilots snuck back around and caught us."

Mojica nodded. "That's the only terminal on this end of the Mountain. I can get you all out of here in between security shifts and you can disappear into the forest."

Selah looked at the halo-screen. "Can it really be this easy?"

"Normally, no, but with Everling incapacitated and with Stemple missing, they have no command structure. The guards are good at keeping their subjects from escaping, but they've never been trained to prevent forces from getting in." Mojica looked over the group. "I think you all need to change. Your light-colored clothing makes a great target."

Cleon looked at Selah and Bodhi. "These are all we have." He pretended not to look at Treva, but Ganston noticed his side glance in her direction.

"I can take care of that." Mojica looked at her ComTex. "It's late evening. The guards will be settling down for the night." She looked at Bodhi. "Can you communicate with the prisoners and tell them we're mounting an operation to free them? They must remain quiet."

"Yes, I can do that, but it will take awhile to build up strength to get through to all of them."

Mojica raised a hand. "Well, hold off for now. I'm taking you to our staging area. While everyone is getting geared up, you can do whatever it is you do."

She rose and the four young people scrambled to follow. She turned to Ganston. "Any last words?"

He feared this operation would end in disaster, and he wasn't willing to sacrifice Treva for people he didn't know. He looked at her as his fingers tapped his chin. "Don't go."

23

Bethany glanced at her ComTex as she charged down the hall to Lab Section Ten. She'd left four messages. Where was Noah? He'd been erratic for the last two days. She'd tried to convince him to stop injections and let the serum dissipate. She hadn't taken additional shots and the tests showed she'd stabilized. But he wouldn't listen. She feared he was falling into psychosis and prepared herself to confine him if necessary. She had garnered support from top-level executive members who felt he'd grown distracted.

She keyed her way into the lab. "Noah!" No response. She walked toward the console as she scanned the area. All confinement cell walls were opaque. He wouldn't be here without leaving a transparent wall. She turned to leave and her foot kicked something. It slid out from the other side of the console. Bethany walked around.

The hair lifted at the nape of her neck. She reached down with trembling fingers and picked up the syringe, gripping it so tight her knuckles turned white. He'd been here, and he'd never have dropped this. Not if he was in his right mind.

A moan.

Bethany flinched at the sound. Her eyes darted around. Where was the sound coming from? She charged behind the console and slapped each of the buttons to turn the cells transparent. An involuntary scream rose from her chest as the charred remains came into view. "Noah, what have you done?" She anguished over the lost Lander. But where . . .

The second cell wall cleared. "Noah!" Bethany screamed. She pressed the button to open the door and ran to her husband. She shook him. Another moan. Her trembling hand felt for a pulse, and she started counting.

Her fingers turned to ice as she ran the light diode of her ComTex across his eyes. Both pupils were fixed and dilated. She squeezed her own eyes shut as her shoulders slumped. Their time together had come to an end. "Why didn't you listen to me?"

Bethany knelt beside his body, her head resting in her hands. She rocked and cried until no more tears came.

Eventually she lifted her head, sniffed, and wiped her nose. She fingered in a number to her ComTex. "Situation Alpha. Lab Section Ten. I'll also need intubation and ventilation ASAP."

She slipped Noah's ComTex from his wrist, punched in a code, and slid it on her own wrist after removing hers and shoving it in her lab pocket. She squared her shoulders and stood up straight. This changing of the guard was inevitable. She loved him, but Noah had lost his original focus of enhancing the DNA of Mountain dwellers. Now she was in charge. She hoped for a better solution.

⬩

Treva exited the locker area where the women in Mojica's forces were changing into black combat uniforms. They were rough and seasoned. She wasn't all that small, but they were six feet and taller, dwarfing her with their size. She felt they saw her as a kid.

She carried her lab coat, plain silk top, linen pants, and crepe-soled slippers in her hand. Her normal clothing seemed such a far cry from this uniform. She looked down at herself. All black! She'd never worn black clothing in her entire life, let along big clunky boots with rubber soles. She didn't even know how to fasten them, so she clopped along with flaps waving until she found an empty place to sit on the benches lining the walls of the staging area.

Cleon strutted over to join her. "This is some operation." He sat down beside her and dropped his regular clothes to the floor. "I've never worn boots that feel this good on my feet." He stood up and bounced in them a couple times. "It's as though they're a part of me. I think I could run a couple miles in these."

"That's because the soles are specially formulated rubber created for endurance," Mojica said as she walked toward them. "Not only do they conform to the shape of your feet, but as the latching is complete, they seal thermally to your limbs. The boot is a composite that both breathes and is virtually indestructible." She stooped in front of Treva to show her how to close the latches, then moved on to check on others down the line.

Treva sheepishly mimicked Mojica's movements to close the rest of the latches. Cleon knelt in front of her. As he locked the boots onto her legs, she experienced the strangest sensation. The weight had disappeared. She looked closer. The boots were still there.

Cleon looked up at her. "So how long have you been involved with Landers?"

Treva pulled back. Fear zipped down both arms, creating a strange sensation. How should she take the question? She'd never talked with an outlander before. Was he fishing for information or trying to prove some kind of duplicity?

Cleon finished latching her boots. "You didn't answer."

She shook her head. "I don't know what you want me to say."

He shrugged. "I was making conversation. I heard you say you were giving them shots to bring them out of the sleep fog. I was curious how you knew the chemical stuff." His warm smile went right to her heart and the chocolate brown of his eyes mesmerized her. She'd never met anyone with eyes that color. Most people in the Mountain had blue, green, or faded brown eyes.

Treva looked down at her hands, playing with her fingers. "I've been doing my own research for quite a while."

Cleon chuckled and moved to sit beside her. "You don't look old enough."

"Excuse me?" Treva set her jaw. How could she tell someone she'd just met about her secrets?

"I meant learning chemicals and stuff takes a lot of years

of schooling," he stammered. "You don't look much older than I am."

"I'm twenty, and I started university studies when I was . . . twelve," she said. *Someday, Cleon . . . if I learn to trust you.*

He raised an eyebrow. "You must be very smart."

She watched him looking at Selah. "Is that your girlfriend or something?"

"Her?" He motioned toward Selah. "That's my sister."

Treva's heart fluttered. She relaxed. "Your sister? Well, that's good to know." She regretted saying it as soon as the words were out of her mouth. It made her look interested.

She wanted to change the subject. She fiddled with her hands, suddenly conscious of his body next to her. His hip kept brushing hers, sending little shocks of electricity through her thigh. She wanted to move away, but then again she didn't.

"Are you scared?" she asked, biting her bottom lip.

Cleon puffed up his chest. "Nah, I've been in worse situations and I didn't have a security force to back me up."

He put his hand on hers. Their eyes met. They both quickly looked away and Treva pulled back her hand.

⟨⟩

Selah approached Cleon and Treva. "Are we ready?"

Bodhi followed. The all-black, form-fitting uniform combined with his muscular physique made him formidable . . . and appealing, as Selah had noted twice so far. The first time was when he bent in front of her to help latch her boots. She'd watched how to do it but having him bent down in front of her was too much to resist.

Selah liked the feel of the uniform, the way it conformed to her body. It made her feel different, almost like a warrior.

Cleon stood. "Are we going to get weapons?"

"I don't think they'll supply them. They don't know us," Selah said. She looked at Bodhi, who shrugged.

Panic flashed across Treva's face. "I'm not going to carry a weapon. I thought we were just going to release prisoners."

"Do you think the security guards are just going to release them?" Selah asked.

Treva gulped. "Well, I didn't think—"

"Just like a girl not to think," Bodhi said, smiling wryly.

Cleon matched Bodhi's look with a complementary snicker.

Selah and Treva stared daggers at them. Over the boys' shoulders Selah watched Mojica moving up the hall. She talked with her team and handed off some black material to each of them, then strode over to Selah's group.

"These hoods will mask your identity," she said. She handed them out.

Selah turned the piece over in her hand. "How do we breathe or see?"

"It's the latest technology. Intuitive fiber. It will create holes where your eyes, nose, and mouth are. Try it."

Cleon held it out. "I don't think this will fit over my head."

"It will expand as it feels the structure of your skull. Start from the top like this." Mojica used her hands to gather the length of the tube onto her thumbs.

Cleon got both thumbs in the end of the narrow tube and raised his hands over his head. As the fiber touched his head it expanded, molding itself to his skull as he pulled it down. The fabric separated and both eyes appeared in openings, as did his nose and mouth. The hood continued to mold to the rest of his head and neck, leaving no skin uncovered.

He stared at them, wide-eyed. "This is the strangest sensation I've ever felt. I know I have a hood on but I don't feel it."

"Now get ready for this." Mojica keyed a new appliance resting on her wrist right above her ComTex.

"Whoa!" Cleon jumped back.

The group flinched. Selah reached to steady him.

He groped in front of him, trying to touch something no one else could see. "How are you doing this?" he asked.

"Doing what?" Selah pivoted between Cleon and Mojica.

Mojica nodded. "The navigation technology. Good, I'm glad it works with outlanders. I wasn't sure it could recognize the subtle environmental differences in our DNA."

"Is someone going to answer me?" Selah fisted her hands on her hips.

Mojica grinned and gestured at the hood hanging from Selah's hand. "Put it on."

Selah stared at it for a few seconds. Could she do it? Her heart rate was already spiking just thinking about it. She held her breath and scrambled to get it on.

Treva and Bodhi also fumbled with the material but eventually got the hoods on.

Selah clutched her face as the fabric molded to her structure. "I can't breathe. I'm going to die in here." She was smothering. She ripped it off her head, her hands shaking.

Cleon put his hand to her shoulder. "It's all right." He turned to the others. "She's afraid of things covering her face."

Selah let out a small gasp. Tears formed in her eyes.

"The bio-structure of this material masks all Mountain technology from getting identification, a retinal scan, or even a vocal lock on the wearer. She can't go without a hood. Mountain facial recognition would imprint her and she'd be hunted forever," Mojica said.

"She's a Lander's child. They'll chase her anyhow," Treva said.

"I agree, but we don't need to make it any easier for them." Mojica ran her tongue around the inside of her cheek. She looked at each of the group, then back to Selah. "Do you need me to give you something so you're calm until you get used to the mask? Some of our strongest guys feel the same trepidation at the beginning. It doesn't reflect on you. It's just a phobia of confined space."

The words *baby* and *sissy* kept running through Selah's head. She bit down on her lip, wincing. "Do you think it will work?"

Mojica nodded. She turned and looked down the hall. "Tiller!"

One of the men straddling a bench looked up. "Ma'am!"

"Go juice!"

"Yes, ma'am!" Tiller trotted toward them and pulled a small vial from a pack on his hip. He handed it to Mojica and retreated back down the hall.

Mojica snapped the vial in half. "Hold out your hand."

Selah's hand trembled as she forced it out. Mojica tapped the back of her hand with the small cylinder, then threw the empty container into a receptacle next to the wall.

Selah looked confused. "Was that it?"

Mojica smiled. "That's all. Try the hood now."

She trembled as her fingers gathered up the material. She took a deep breath and worked the hood down over her head. She breathed in and out several times. Her shoulders began to relax.

Bodhi watched. "Are you going to make it?"

Selah's breathing came long and hard. "Yes, I think so. I don't feel the material anymore. Is it still there?" She rubbed her head, feeling the smooth fiber covering her face. The oddness subsided and she peered out. She could breathe through her nose and mouth. The tremble left her hands.

"I'm turning on your face screen. Don't be afraid," Mojica said as she keyed the appliance.

Selah jerked. "Yikes! This is unbelievable."

"It's face navigation technology." She keyed in something else. "What you're seeing now is the map layout of Level Three Confinement. You don't have to remember directions, just follow the map. My team is the green active dots. Guards will be red dots and the Landers will be blue dots. Unknowns are black dots."

"What about us?" Selah asked.

"Since you're not part of my system, I've keyed you four as black dots." She tapped the appliance. "Okay, everyone. This is a look at this group."

Facial navigations flicked on. Mojica showed up as a green dot encircled by four black dots.

"I'm a Lander. Why don't I show up as a blue dot?" Bodhi asked.

Mojica grinned. "These suits have special blockers. The wearers are invisible to the Mountain systems, and I code in our group so each individual gets the specific signal I want them to show. It's people not wearing these suits the systems will pick up."

"With these masks on, how are we going to be able to tell who is who?" Selah could tell Treva, Bodhi, and Cleon by their shapes and heights, and Mojica's team towered over them. She just needed the security of knowing where they were.

Mojica shrugged. "Transponders, and you'll remain in a group within sight of one another." She pointed at Bodhi. "I need you to contact the individuals we're extracting. Tell them to be ready to go and not to make any undue movements. We don't want to alert the guards that anything is out of the ordinary."

Bodhi walked to the other side of the wall, dropped his mask, and seated himself on the floor with his legs crossed, hands resting on his knees. He closed his eyes. Glistening moisture formed on his brow as he leaned his head back against the wall.

"How long will this take?" Mojica asked. She gestured to the meditating Bodhi.

Selah chewed her lip. "Not sure. He's only been here a week and the Landers he's trying to contact have been drugged for years."

"I've done the best I could to bring them out of it," Treva said. "I haven't been able to do any testing of synaptic—"

"That's more than I need to know," Mojica said, raising a hand. "Just tell me how long."

"To touch all of them, maybe a half hour." Selah shrugged. "Maybe less."

"Synchronize the time for thirty minutes. It will be a go."

Mojica hustled off in the other direction, leaving the group standing there.

"What did we get into?" Treva asked, noticeable fear in her voice.

Cleon moved to her side and put his hand on her arm. She smiled weakly.

"I came to find my father. Unfortunately, freeing his countrymen will have to suffice," Selah said with a note of sadness.

"Can you do it too?" Cleon asked, looking at Selah. "Contact the Landers using your mind?"

"My link is still weak. I only get random impressions." Selah rubbed at her chest. "I still get rumblings, like the feeling you get when thunder sounds. It hurts, but I think it scares me more than anything. I don't understand the emotions yet. They're different from the way we express things. If I tried to help Bodhi, I might confuse the Landers and make it worse."

At that moment a low moan punctuated the air.

Selah spun to face Bodhi.

His hands clutched at his head. He slumped back against the wall and slowly slid over sideways to the floor.

She pulled off her mask and dropped to her knees in front of him, reaching to touch his shoulder. The contact brought a surge of power shooting up her arm and across her chest. She jerked back. "What's that?"

Bodhi shook his head violently from side to side. He clawed at the wall, trying to gain control. "Too many. Reaching out all at once. Scared." He snatched Selah's arm in a viselike grip. "I need you to help me with them, but we have to bond first."

She tried to pull away from the energy streaming through her body. It frightened her, or maybe it made her feel she'd

351

never be the same again. Either way, she steeled herself and focused on his eyes.

Concentrate. Bodhi's thoughts flooded her head. *Feel where I am and join with me.*

Selah whimpered. *I'm afraid. It feels like I'm going to explode.* She wrestled the expanding waves. Sweat poured from her brow, stinging her eyes. She threw her head back and clenched her eyes tight.

Relax into the wave. Bodhi focused his eyes on Selah. *Let it carry you to me.*

Hair matted her wet face. Selah gasped. *I'm trying. It's so strong. I feel you reaching for me.* She could sense Bodhi smoothing the noise, allowing her to feel their base emotions.

Finish the connection the way I taught you.

Selah took Bodhi's left wrist with her right hand, then gripped her right wrist with her left hand. Bodhi held his right wrist with his left hand, and his right hand held her left wrist. As they created the power grid, a surge of white energy encompassed the two of them. *We did it!*

Selah felt the flood wash over her. Being linked mentally with Bodhi blossomed nerve endings in her mind that had been trying to connect for the past few days. A warmth radiated from the connection. *I feel like I'm floating.* Her body relaxed into the energy flow as the sensations turned from random stabs and poundings to an even hum of activity.

We've secured the bond. Bodhi's features relaxed. He took a deep breath and reached to hold her hand. *It will be easier to focus on personal communications between just the two of us, now that we're linked. We have no time to waste. Can you feel that?*

24

Selah and Bodhi became a voice of reason in the darkness. The only way she could describe it was like standing in a pitch-black room and calling to this mass of voices all talking at once. They argued for the better part of a half hour. Several of the stronger Landers wanted to overpower the guards.

You must be patient. Bodhi sounded authoritative. *We are coming very soon.*

Landers recovering from the brain fog were agitated. *We've been patient long enough. We've become strong again. We want out. We are not slaves to this world. We are immortals.*

Selah tried to soothe them. *We will get you out. I promise. We have a whole team.*

Promises don't mean anything in this world. All are lies.

Bodhi spent a lot of time quelling what amounted to an uprising. *Give us one hour. I give you my word.* He motioned

353

to Selah that she could break the connection and let him handle the rest.

She pressed her fingers to tight lips and backed away from the connection. The feeling of so many voices overwhelmed her. She rubbed at her temples and rose to walk to the other side of the hall. She didn't know if Bodhi could convince the Landers to remain calm.

She grabbed something to eat from the nearby table and paced the area. Past midnight. *Please let this start soon.* The compressed protein bar sat in her stomach like a logjam that industrious beavers would make on the pond back home. Acid backed up in her throat.

Her immediate concern—Amaryllis. Yes, the child was capable of taking care of herself, but that didn't cause Selah any less worry. She wanted to kick herself for not having made a plan if they got separated. Where was Rylla? Had she run back to her home or was she still waiting outside?

She reached for water, gulping it to push down her queasiness and her fears. The hum of the security team interactions echoed along the walls of the corridor, adding to her unease. She recognized one of their weapons, the pulse disruptors. They were similar to the model Raza had used in the forest. Weapons like that signified death. Fear.

Mojica verified that they wouldn't get weapons but each would be assigned a competent watcher. The guys balked at not getting to act like warriors, but Selah and Treva were relieved not to sport weapons.

Mojica marched up the hallway with her team. She motioned each of their watchers into position. With everyone's masks in place, Selah could see only their eyes. Her watcher was about six feet tall and had kind eyes. Confident he was male by his sturdy build and the way his belt slung on his square hips, Selah had a moment of levity picturing herself addressing him as a man only to find out the person was a woman.

"Everyone, facial navigation on," Mojica said. She keyed the face displays for Selah's group. The rest of the team controlled their own.

Selah glanced behind her to find Cleon and Bodhi. Treva stuck close to Cleon, but Bodhi was being kept at arm's length by Selah's watcher. She heard him huff once or twice, figuring he was jockeying the man for position and losing.

The optical screens were fine when she was standing still, but as she walked they proved a distraction. She nearly walked into a wall while concentrating on the movement of the dots before her eyes. Her watcher redirected her with a slight nudge.

She marveled at the silence as the group of twenty moved through the buildings. They turned onto several corridors and traveled down numerous ramps to get to Level Three Confinement. The only plus of the long trip was that she could orient herself to ignore the map and not careen down the hall like a drunken merchant at a spirit tasting.

Mojica signaled with her hands and the group halted. Selah started to ask a question but her watcher motioned for silence. He whispered that they were at their destination.

Selah's throat tightened. *Are you ready, Bodhi? Can I be scared?*

He soothed her nerves. *It's going to be fine. I'm here.*

It was wonderful and a bit strange, communicating with

thought. She had the hang of it now. She wondered how Cleon was handling this. He didn't have a reason to like or help Landers. He only did this for her, and now she was one of them.

A technician moved forward, applying a laser appliance to the door's security panel. Mojica had explained earlier that instead of using door codes, they'd hack access. There'd be plausible deniability when Everling started searching for offending parties.

Selah watched as the door swished open. The team rushed in as a wave of black uniforms. They fanned out. First stop—the station inside the door.

The guard had fallen asleep with the remnants of his dinner spread out before him, and the takedown happened fast and easy. His face registered shock as he woke to black-clothed and hooded interlopers in his domain. Swiftly rendered inoperable, he was trussed like a chicken ready for the roasting spit and was dumped into the closet behind his station.

Selah's heart ramped up as she peered down the wide hall. The area looked similar to the office in the Borough building back home. *Are you still there?*

Bodhi chuckled. *Where did you think I'd be?*

Just checking.

Tables and chairs, desks, and cabinets filled the space with only an uninterrupted aisle down the center. This didn't look like the facial navigation plans in front of Selah's eyes. Confusion filled her.

Entry teams on both sides of the hall used laser appliances to open doors, ignoring the obvious differences on the facial navigation. At least she could see dots signifying friendlies.

Suddenly a bright flash, a sharp percussion, and a yell. Selah's watcher pushed her to the floor, shielding her body with his own. She struggled to see around him. *Bodhi, what happened?*

Can't talk, came his curt reply. Farther down the area, guards armed with laser darts poured from an open doorway, firing rapid volleys. Points of energy struck the walls and floors, leaving an ozone smell. The security team fired back with pulse disruptors. The silent weapons gave off a docile, shimmering waveform that slammed into the guards with the force of a boulder, throwing them about like twigs.

Mojica ducked behind a desk and returned fire. A guard dove for cover, shooting under the legs of the desk as he slid across the floor. The laser dart ricocheted off the rocrete floor about a foot from Mojica, striking the appliance on her wrist. As her arm bounced up, her shoulder slammed into the floor. She rolled and fired, striking the guard full in the chest. With arms and legs splayed, he slammed against the wall. Mouth open, he slid to the floor.

"Stay here and keep your head down!" Selah's watcher yelled. He scrambled forward to give Mojica backup from the onslaught.

Bodhi, where are you? No answer. Selah's stomach turned to rock. The facial navigation system had gone down when Mojica's arm was struck. No dots, no hallways. Heart pounding, she tried to alert her watcher. He was engaged in a firefight with two guards who'd slipped past the advance force. Selah scoured the team to find Cleon and Bodhi. Only a sea of black amid the clouds of disruptor and laser fire. The smell burned her nose. *Bodhi, help!*

A laser scanner attached to the first room on the right continued to cycle access codes. Selah crept to the appliance with shaking limbs. It beeped and the door clicked open. Laser darts slammed into the wall near her. She ducked, muffled a scream, and crawled into the room, pushing the door shut behind her.

She leaned against the wall, pulling in jerky, fearful breaths. The light sensor activated. The layout of this room didn't match the floor plan she remembered, and her spirits dropped.

Bodhi, where are you? I'm in a room alone. No answer. Selah looked around. An hour ago she couldn't have imagined herself with a weapon, but now, in a moment of abject fear, she couldn't picture herself without one. Seeing a weapons locker against the back wall, she ran to the case and snatched up a laser dart. She held the piece, molding her fingers to the grip in an effort to convince herself she could shoot someone.

A scrambling sound on her right. Before Selah could react, the door flew open. She was face-to-face with a large, aged security guard buttoning up his uniform. He reached for his weapon but his holster was empty. He turned back toward her and she darted away.

Adrenaline pumped her arms and legs. No time to decide where to go. The first open door offered refuge, so she scrambled inside and smacked the lock. Leaning against the door, she groped for a light switch.

The guard crashed into the door repeatedly, bouncing her away from it, but the lock held. *Help! Bodhi, where are you? Why aren't you answering me? I need help!* Selah found the switch and flicked it on. She was in some kind of storeroom full of rows of crates and boxes. She pulled in a couple deep breaths to steady herself and peered down. Her hand still held the laser dart. Could she really shoot someone?

A blast against the door sounded like gunpowder exploding. She flinched and sprinted down one of the aisles, shoving herself between two metal crates at the back. The loud banging continued. She put trembling hands over her ears to muffle the sound. *Please, please, please help.*

Another blast blew the door open. Hanging from one hinge, warped and twisted, the door squealed to a halt as it hung up on the rocrete composite floor. The light circuit was tripped, plunging the room into darkness.

Selah opened and closed her mouth to relieve the pressure in her ears. Ringing bounced around in her head. Could she hear Bodhi if he called out? Peeking around the crates, she froze. The outline of a hulking man obscured most of the light in the doorway.

"Come out here and give yourself up," he yelled in a deep voice.

Selah jerked her head back. Where was everyone? Were they captured? Would he hurt her if she gave herself up? Or would he hurt her if she made him hunt her? She bit down on her lip, tasting the copper of blood. No one had discussed what to do in case of capture.

She felt the weapon in her hand. Maybe if she showed him she was armed he'd let her go. The fighting still raged full force in the main room. She shut her eyes and pleaded, *Someone come find me. I'm scared.* There, she'd thought it. She. Was. Scared.

She raised her hand and it trembled viciously. She used

both hands to steady the weapon. Maybe if he saw she was just a girl he wouldn't be so angry.

He held up an illuminator. A wide beam of subdued light washed the room, casting her shadow across the wall behind the crates. She tried to move away but he must have seen the movement. He walked toward her.

Selah sucked in a gulp of air. Nowhere to go. She moved into the open and came face-to-face with the man. Pointing the laser dart, she raised it at him. He scowled, moving closer.

"I see where you picked up that weapon. They're in for repair. It doesn't work," he said with a sneer.

She knew that look. Raza had subjected her to the same disdain whenever she told Mother he was throwing boomerangs at her or pushing her off the dunes.

He aimed his weapon. "Go ahead, pull the trigger."

Selah's hands trembled. She moved her finger from the trigger, fearing she would accidently fire.

"Shoot me!" he screamed. "Or I'm going to shoot you!"

Selah squeezed her eyes shut. Fear coursed through her limbs. Her throat tightened as she pulled the trigger. Nothing happened. She opened her eyes and pulled it again. Nothing. She pulled the trigger two more times in rapid succession. Fear weakened her.

She threw the weapon at the guard's head. He ducked, then threw back his head and laughed. "At least one of you is going to suffer the consequences of breaking into this area. Drop the weapon and get on your knees."

A strangled sob welled in Selah's throat. She pushed it down. She refused to show weakness to a man laughing at her. She could only hope cooperation would give her a chance for the others to find her. *Help me.*

"On your knees!" the man shouted.

She dropped to her knees, wincing in pain at contact with the unyielding surface.

He strode to her. "Well, let's see what we have here." He snatched her hood but also got a handful of hair.

Selah screamed and grabbed at her head to wrench it free.

"Well, by the voice I guess I have a female. Let's see what you look like." He grabbed the neck of the hood. Selah tried to spin away from him, but he ripped the hood from her head and held it up like a trophy.

Selah tried to move away. He reached out with his other hand and grabbed her hair, yanking her back. Pain stabbed her scalp like hot needles, tearing her eyes.

He spun her around to face him and lifted the light, trying to train the glow on her face. "Let's see who you are."

Fear scurried up her spine like runaway spiders. She pulled back and threw up her hands, hyperventilating. Her head spun from lack of oxygen. She couldn't last long.

He took two steps forward and she steeled herself for more pain.

25

Selah watched the guard's sneer evaporate into a blank stare. He crashed facedown on the floor. The light skidded off to the side and illuminated the doorway.

A tall silhouette replaced the fallen guard in the doorway as a person walked forward into the light. Bodhi!

"Are you hurt?" He reached out a hand.

Selah dissolved into tears as she rushed into his arms. "No, just my dignity for being so stupid to run into a dead-end room. I couldn't find you."

His trembling hand pulled her head into his chest. The strength of his arms made her feel safe.

Don't scare me like that again. I don't know what I'd do if I lost you.

Startled by his thought, she looked into his eyes.

Weapons fired. She disengaged, grabbed up her hood, and slid it back on. She needed to think about what he'd just said. But not now.

"If you stayed where the watcher left you, there would have been no danger." He ushered her out of the room and forced the door shut as they exited.

Selah turned. "I'm sorry. I panicked. Are Cleon and Treva safe?"

"Your brother's been injured—"

Selah scrambled from the room. Her watcher stood guard at the door. He led her into the entrance hall with Bodhi following. Weapon fire rang out again. The fighting had moved down a corridor out of sight.

She spun, surveying the wounded. At first glance they all looked the same in head-to-toe black. Bodhi pointed out Cleon. The slight female figure beside him had to be Treva. She stood with hands to her mask, sobbing.

Selah darted to their position. "How did this happen? Where is your watcher?"

Cleon shook his head and pointed to tube-shaped bags in a short pile against the wall. "He didn't make it. He took a shot for me, but the laser bounced off him and got me in the shoulder. It's just a flesh wound. I'll be fine."

Selah could tell his attempt at bravado was fake—his eyes spoke differently. He was just trying to impress Treva. A bandage was evident through the hole in his combat suit.

Selah turned to Bodhi. "Fix him!"

Bodhi tipped his head. "I don't understand."

She grabbed his arm. "Fix him like you fixed Amaryllis after the snake attack."

Cleon raised his good arm. "I'm not sure what mumbo jumbo you're talking about, but I'm fine. I don't need help from a Lander."

Selah noticed a hurt and fearful look come over Treva at his words. She'd have to explore that later. Right now she wanted Cleon healed.

Bodhi shook his head. "My abilities don't work for treating actual wounds. I can only do cellular reorganization—"

"I said I don't want anything from him." Cleon struggled to get up. Treva hurried to help him.

The medic nearby packed up his kit. "I've used Cell-Gel on him. He'll be good as new in an hour or so."

Selah looked from Bodhi to Cleon, shrugged, and turned to the medic. "I know this probably isn't the time to ask, but what's Cell-Gel? Won't he bleed out if he moves around?"

"The product is an artificial version of extracellular matrix. It creates connective tissue as it dries and heals the wound." The medic slung his pack, clipping it back to his waist.

Selah's watcher put his hand on her shoulder. "We have to move forward. Commander Mojica is ready to infiltrate the Prison Unit. We'll need Bodhi to reassure them."

"Are we going to get shot at again?" Cleon asked. He grimaced as he tested his shoulder. "I'd really like a weapon to defend myself, especially since I lost a watcher."

"We've had more casualties than we expected. There are exponentially more guards here than we knew were in service. Everyone has been pulled forward to battle," the watcher said.

"So what does that mean?" Selah asked. She had failed with her father, but she didn't want to fail the rest of his people. "Are we going to be able to free the Landers?"

The watcher nodded. "The team trained for this kind of mission. There's obviously more going on here than people know about, but they can handle it."

Treva leaned forward. "Common Mountain people don't know there is such a thing as a Lander. Only security, the Science Consortium, and the executives know of their existence. But I agree. Nothing we thought was going on here would warrant this level of active security presence."

Selah's heart sank. "What are we missing?"

Treva wrapped her arms across her chest and shook her head.

The watcher's ComTex chirped. He looked down at it. "We're being summoned to the infiltration force in the Prison Unit. They need Bodhi." Glancing around, he pointed at a laser dart under a desk. He motioned to Cleon. "Pick that up. I'll pretend I didn't see you with it."

Cleon scooted under the desk to retrieve the weapon.

Selah grimaced as she watched Cleon swell with pride. He used other weapons at home, so his handling it didn't worry her. It was just that now it made her brother more of a target.

Bethany stormed into the large triangular Prison Control Center. "What do you mean there's been a breakout in the Lander section? Who's in charge down there?"

From the doorway, the room fanned out and was staggered with work stations as it sloped downward to the large data screens covering the front wall. She pushed the guard away from the first console and began flipping switches on the right-hand wall section, which was divided into prison pod areas.

As a teenager, she'd spent a lot of time at consoles like these when she followed her father around, and he'd given her mock assignments to prepare her for the future she never wound up following. She could still run this operation with her eyes closed.

"I don't know, sir—uh, ma'am," the rattled guard sputtered. "No report from the section station. The incursion came out of nowhere. There has to be at least two dozen of them from the images we got before communications went down."

Bethany banged at the terminal. If those Landers got free, the rest of the Mountain might find out what was actually going on right under their noses. The guards had been issued her extermination order—maybe it had been completed before this started.

No ComTex. No visual feeds, just white static. She raged at the console. "Why can't I see anything?"

"They're jamming communications."

"Work around it!" she yelled. "If they get out of this Mountain, I'll have your heads."

The control room went silent. Eight men stared at one another before scrambling to meet the demands of their new boss.

Bethany pulled up a schematic of the area and pointed at the map. "Get me a squadron of guards at the northern section of the prison wing to block their exit."

Bodhi fell into step beside Selah. He wouldn't be leaving her side again until they were safely out of this place. They hurried to catch up with the security team, who'd forced the guards into retreating to the northern section of the wing.

They wove their way through the overturned furniture,

around several dead guards, and over piles of digital file storage containers from an overturned data bin. The sounds of fighting grew closer.

Selah's watcher moved out in front with Cleon beside him. He looked back at Bodhi. "Can you tell which side of the section they're on? Without facial navigation to find hot bodies, we're working blind here."

Bodhi stopped. He opened his mind, traveling on the air currents that carried the luminescence and clouds of smoke, winding through the halls at the speed of sound to the minds of his own people. Hovering over them like a feather in a breeze, he lowered himself to tap the first one. He made contact. This one was closing himself off . . . hiding . . . trying to get away from the confusion. But he couldn't. He was locked in a cell. Fearful.

"I found them," Bodhi said. He pointed to the next section of hallways off to the left. "They're in there. Both sides of the room. It's two long rows of cells."

The watcher spoke into his ComTex, then turned back to the group. "Commander Mojica wants you four to stay back until they've pushed the guards past the next section."

Bodhi winced and grabbed his head. "Fear. Several are trying to talk to me at once. I think they're trying to say a guard is killing Landers." All the voices talking at once overwhelmed him, like crabs climbing over one another in a barrel.

"We can't let that happen. Not now when we're so close." Selah stormed into the hall with Cleon and Treva right beside her.

Bodhi motioned for the watcher to follow. The man was speaking into his ComTex again.

Bodhi fumed. Selah needed protection. The watcher had

neglected to stick with her before and she'd almost died. Whether he wanted to admit it or not, he was falling for her and he wasn't going to take a chance on losing her now.

He dashed into the prison section. The mechanical scream of laser shots rang out. Inside the door, facedown, lay the black uniform–clad body of one of their team. He couldn't tell whether it was a man or woman as he bent to feel for a pulse. Whoever it was, the person was dead. He darted into a wide corridor and screeched to a halt.

Twenty feet down the hall on the left, Selah, Treva, and Cleon hid behind a partition jutting from the main wall. Another twenty feet or so beyond stood a Lander. The shaggy, dark-haired man in white tunic and pants was being held hostage by a guard, who had him tightly around the neck with a laser dart at his head. Bodhi cringed. He could see the man's mark. The first sight of another in this land and he was about to be extinguished.

"Throw down your weapon and you won't be hurt!" Cleon yelled. He took aim.

"I'll kill him if you come any closer," the guard said, his eyes darting wildly.

Selah started to move into the open.

Bodhi wanted to run to her position to shield her, but he feared moving closer and scaring the guard into firing. Cleon pushed her back without taking his eyes from the guard. Bodhi breathed relief.

"There's no way out. If you kill him, you won't have a shield and I'll shoot you," Cleon said.

Bodhi stared at him. Could Cleon really kill someone after what had just happened to his brother?

Thunder

The watcher snuck into the doorway beside Bodhi.

"I've called for help. There'll be reinforcements overrunning this place in short order," the guard said. He tried to back away with the struggling Lander.

Bodhi stared at the captive Lander, trying to make contact. The man finally turned his eyes to stare at Bodhi.

"No, you didn't call for help. We jammed communications before we entered this section," the watcher said. "Now let the prisoner go!"

At that moment a cell door across the way flew open and another Lander dove at the guard. The guard fired three shots at him. The Lander dropped, crimson invading the front of his tunic.

Bodhi passed a thought to the captive Lander. *Pretend you're passing out and drop to the floor. Now!*

The Lander relaxed his body and slipped from the guard's arm to the floor.

The watcher rushed in. His footfalls caused Cleon to turn in his direction. The guard took aim at Cleon's exposed back.

Grab his legs! Bodhi yelled to the Lander.

The Lander tackled the guard as he fired. The laser shot sliced into the ceiling. The guard went down.

The watcher disarmed him and handed Cleon restraints from his hip pouch. "We'll leave him for his people to find."

Cleon secured the guard while Selah and Treva ran to the shot Lander. They turned away. Bodhi could see that half his head had been blown off.

There's another guard hiding here, the voice permeating Bodhi's head said.

Where is he? Bodhi asked.

I'm not sure, but there were two of them a few minutes ago, came the response.

"A voice is telling—" Bodhi began.

Two cells down, another door flew open and an armed guard charged out. Treva fled and the guard turned to fire at her. Cleon hurtled himself at Treva, dropping her to the ground. The shot missed.

The watcher took aim and shot the guard. The man slammed into the open door and slid to the floor, leaving a trail of blood and bone fragments on the door frame.

Bodhi checked and disarmed the dead guard, then approached Cleon. He patted him on his good shoulder. "That was really brave. Are you all right?"

"No. Owww! Now my shoulder hurts," Cleon said. The girls doted on him as he sat up.

Bodhi glanced around nervously. They needed to keep moving and free Landers from the cells. He looked down the hall. At the other end, the corridor turned off to the right. The flashes of light told him the immediate fighting was going on down there. His hope was fading. He wasn't sure how they were going to get everyone out of the line of fire.

He systematically began opening doors. The Lander who'd feigned unconsciousness helped. Shaggy-haired Landers filtered into the hall, all in white linen, some with bare feet. They clung to one another. Several stood by themselves as though ready to run. They stared at the rescue team as though they were the enemy, their voices growing louder.

The watcher raised his hands for silence.

Selah helped Cleon to his feet. Bodhi watched as she scanned the faces of the Landers.

"Hold on." She touched the watcher's arm. "They're afraid of our masks. Imagine how you'd feel looking at people dressed in all black with hoods." She reached up to take hers off. "There's nothing—"

"Wait!" The watcher pulled her hand away from her mask and came in close to whisper, "We are not to take off our covers in this environment. We don't know if there are cameras we've missed. It would be putting your life in jeopardy. They'd have your picture and it could lead to others being caught."

Selah balked. "They're scared. What can we do? We need them to trust us."

Bodhi stepped forward, putting his hand on the small of her back. She turned and looked up at him. He smiled softly. "Let me do it." He walked forward with both hands raised. *I'm the one who's been talking to you. We're here to give you freedom.*

The sudden barrage of fifteen minds at one time drove Bodhi to his knees. He clutched at the sides of his head and wailed in pain.

"Stop!" Selah screamed at the group. "You're going to kill him."

The intensity in their eyes faded. They backed off.

Bodhi's head pounded. He propped himself up on one knee. Selah reached down, wrapped her arm under his armpit, and helped him up. He staggered a few steps before regaining his composure. Flinching, he said, "Let's try this another way. Do you have a spokesman among you?"

All eyes turned to a man standing off to the side by himself. He looked at each of them in turn. Bodhi felt the conversations, but since they weren't directed at him he couldn't hear.

The man stepped forward. He probed Bodhi's mind.

Why do you seem foreign to us? the man asked.

I've only been in this country a few days. I'm not completely acclimated, Bodhi said.

How can you understand our fears and the torture we've been through?

I know some of it through the Lander child.

The man's eyes widened. *There is one of our children here?*

Bodhi turned and motioned Selah forward. She hesitated but stepped up beside him. He wrapped his arm around her waist. *Her father was Glade Rishon. She is novarium.*

The man looked around at the others, then back at Bodhi. *Was? What do you mean?*

Bodhi felt the nearness of Selah's pain. He pulled her tightly to his side. She glanced at him with questions in her eyes. He passed a calm feeling to her and she relaxed.

Bodhi straightened. *Her father was killed by Dr. Everling earlier today.*

The man tipped his head, glancing around again, confusion on his face. Murmurs passed through the group. They were closing Bodhi off from the conversation. He'd never had anyone do that before. With the status he'd enjoyed at home, it bordered on being rude.

The man turned back to Bodhi. *She is a true heir.*

Selah touched Bodhi's arm. "What's going on?"

"They recognize you as novarium," Bodhi answered.

The watcher interrupted. "We need to get out of here. The fighting has moved to the next section. Commander Mojica says they can hold them off till we get out on the old ramp up to the JetTrans terminal. Her team cut a hole in the fencing around the area to make it look like you broke into the Mountain there. It will afford you an escape route into the forest."

⟁

Selah smiled at each of the Landers. Their expressions had seemed to soften when Bodhi announced she was novarium. She needed to find someone with a better explanation of the term when they got out of here. She felt like a lamb going to slaughter and everyone was waiting for the meal.

She marveled at so many marked people. They were all tall, at least six feet. Some were blond, others dark-haired, but all shaggy from long confinement. The mark stood out on the left side of each temple and forehead. All marks looked the same, no matter the shape or size of the head or their apparent age differences. She'd have to remember to ask Bodhi how the age thing worked. How long did it take to show age? He still looked twenty.

The watcher finished another call to Mojica and turned to them. "We need to get moving. We're going to the ramp. Everyone, follow this way." He started toward the corridor opposite the fighting, then looked back at Bodhi and Cleon. "I need one or two of you in the back of the group with weapons, just in case."

Bodhi picked up the weapon from the first dead guard and handed Selah the one from the guard who'd charged out the doorway. She handled it like it was a dead rodent. He knew the last thing she wanted was a weapon.

One of the Landers in the front of the group stopped them. "What about the others?"

Movement came to a grinding halt. Bodhi hurried back.

"What others?" The Landers murmured and he grabbed the man's tunic. "What others?"

An older-looking Lander gently removed Bodhi's hand from the man's clothing. "The ones they keep in the corridor behind us. We know they're there but they've never broken rank to communicate with us."

A barefoot Lander farther back piped up. "They ignore us. We've tried to make contact with them, but we've only seen one and he ignores us. Acts like we aren't here even when he's looking right at us."

The watcher, Bodhi, and Selah looked at each other in confusion.

Selah shook her head. "We didn't come this far to leave anyone. We have to get them."

"Since that's in the opposite direction, how about we leave Cleon and Treva here with these and we go?" Bodhi looked down the corridor they needed to traverse for access behind this cell block.

The watcher agreed.

Cleon already held a weapon, so Treva rushed back to the entrance and retrieved one from the body of a downed team member.

⬧

Bethany stormed around the Prison Control Center wearing a communication headset. Every few seconds she tapped a link on her ComTex to connect to another unit on standby. Fighting inside was fierce, and casualties were mounting. She didn't understand how insurgents could have been so well prepared.

"Ma'am, once units go inside the area, we have no communication with them. We can only talk to those who remain outside the perimeter. Don't you think it's time to contact Mountain security?"

Bethany spun to face the man. "If you contact them I'll break your hands."

The man pulled away from the console and put his hands in his lap.

"The Prison Unit is autonomous. We do not allow security inside for any reason. We have enough of our own guards and air support without bothering them," Bethany said. Noah had always felt Mountain security was compromised. He didn't trust the people in charge. Too many of them reported to the executives.

"I want JetTrans units ready on this side of the Mountain, and get me contact with Control for the laser cannons. I want them ready and waiting. I don't know how these people intend to get out of there, but they are not getting away with this. Not in my unit."

Selah stuck near Bodhi as they hurried down the far corridor to cells on the other side of the wall. Slinking in with weapons drawn, they peered over counters and around doorways for hidden guards who hadn't joined in the fight but would defend their own territory. None were found.

Bodhi and the watcher tried cell doors. Unlike on the Lander side, these doors didn't automatically open. They were discussing explosive charges to open the doors.

Selah noticed the guard had forgotten to secure the keypad.

"Guys, maybe this will help." She reached over the counter and pushed on the button. One by one the four heavy cell doors clicked.

She hurried over as they pulled open the first door and peered inside. Light filtered into the cell from behind them. She ran back to the console and flipped illumination switches, and light inside the cell spilled out the doorway.

Bodhi stared. Selah gasped. The watcher stumbled back against the doorway.

26

Selah blinked several times, trying to force her brain to register what she was seeing. Twenty identical male children, maybe twelve or thirteen years old, sat one to a bed in the long, narrow room of end-to-end bunk beds. They were dressed in identical white tunics and baggy pants, each with a Lander tattoo on the right side of his face.

"How is this even possible?" Bodhi asked.

The watcher tipped his head. "It isn't possible." He pointed. "I've never seen a Lander of such young age."

"I've only ever known adults." Bodhi scratched his head.

Selah shook her head. "Well, gentlemen, you've missed the obvious. They are all the same person, or at least identical to the same person, whichever one that is. Would the real boy please stand up?" She rolled her eyes and waved a hand dismissively as several of them stood up in response. The question was rhetorical, but she suspected they were too young to understand.

The watcher walked away and engaged his ComTex. Selah figured he was asking Mojica for advice. The only logical option was to get out of here and sort this out later.

Bodhi moved to her side. "Have you ever seen anything like this?"

Selah grimaced. "I've never seen a puppy litter this big, let alone a matching set of kids."

"How could this happen?"

She shook her head. "I don't know. They're your people, not mine. Well, no offense meant, I don't—"

"I understand what you mean. I'd better see if there are any more in other cells." He marched down the aisle, opening the three other doors. From where she stood, Selah could see more bunk beds, but thankfully, no more people.

She continued to stare. The boys sat or stood patiently, looking down at their hands folded in front of them. What was off besides their sheer numbers?

Bodhi strode to her side. "No others."

"They're such a sickly pasty white." With their shoulder-length dark hair, the stark contrast of their pale skin made Selah wonder what was wrong with them.

"Let's try asking," Bodhi said. He walked in among them. They scrambled to the far corner of their beds. He turned to Selah. "Am I that scary?"

"The mask is probably not the best way to make friends with children. Let me try." Selah moved in with a soothing tone. "Don't be afraid. We've come to take you out of here."

She moved toward the nearest one. He whimpered and pulled his legs underneath him. She remembered this kind of behavior from Amaryllis, and suddenly felt guilty for not having thought about the girl's whereabouts in the last few hours.

Bodhi coaxed one boy out of hiding. He timidly approached and reached to take hold of Bodhi's hand. Bodhi pulled back and the boy looked hurt.

Bodhi sighed deeply enough that it made Selah smile. He reached out his hand. The boy eagerly took hold, and with that, the other boys streamed off the bunks to surround Bodhi.

Selah was bypassed. She stood, hands on hips. "Well, I guess you've become the shepherd to this flock of identical sheep."

He grimaced.

The watcher strode into the doorway. Selah noticed the look of delight in his eyes at Bodhi surrounded by children. Actually, it tickled her too. He'd been so standoffish with Amaryllis. There was hope for his cold heart yet.

"Commander Mojica said to round them up and bring them out. We'll sort this out later."

Selah gasped. "I've got it! I know what's wrong."

Bodhi and the watcher stared, waiting for her to finish.

She grinned broadly. "Their mark. It's on the wrong side!"

Bodhi looked at them. Selah could tell that look. He was trying to contact them.

"Well, what do they say?"

He looked worried. "Nothing."

"You mean they won't talk to you?"

"No, I mean, I get nothing. As though they're not here," he said.

Selah looked around the group for some kind of subversion. "Could they be blocking you?"

"No, I'd know if it was a block—it's like hitting a wall. There's nothing here."

The watcher looked nervous. "Listen, we have to get out of here now."

Selah helped Bodhi herd the boys out into the group of Landers. It couldn't have been more of a surprise if they'd brought back a crate of snakes. The original Landers parted in the middle as the boys scurried forward, staying in a huddle around Bodhi.

The Landers stared at the boys. Selah couldn't blame them. She wanted to stare too. Not only were they odd, but they were quiet. Not one sound since they'd found them. Cleon and Treva tried talking to them, but the boys clung to Bodhi, refusing to look at anyone else.

Selah bit her lip. Poor Bodhi looked so uncomfortable surrounded by children. She noted they continually touched each other—holding a hand, patting an arm or a shoulder. When left to their own devices, they moved as a single group, never straying far from the core focus of Bodhi.

The order was set. Selah and the watcher were out front, then the boys with Bodhi, the Landers, and Cleon and Treva as the rear guards.

"If we get forty people out of here without incident, this is going to be an operation for the books," the watcher said. "Commander Mojica said she never fathomed an operation this large or with this much resistance. They're holding the line so we can get out, but she doesn't understand how it's working so well."

"Let's hurry then." Selah picked up the pace. The walls and floors were scorched from battle. Farther down the hall they turned left at the T. There appeared to be a body or two blocking the aisle in the other direction, or maybe it was furniture. Selah opted to think it was an inanimate object rather than a fallen person.

She remembered this area from the facial navigation. On the map it turned again to the left, and there was a long ramp that angled up to the JetTrans terminal—and freedom.

They turned left at the end of the short hall and ran into a solid wall—no ramp. Everyone skidded to a halt.

"Where did this come from?" Selah asked. "It wasn't on the map."

The watcher moved to the wall and felt the surface. "I was hoping it was a halo-projection and not really there."

"What do we do now?" Bodhi walked with boys hanging on both arms.

Cleon threaded his way through the group. "What's the holdup?" He stopped and looked at all four corners of the wall. "Where'd that come from?"

Selah glanced at him. "Well, if we knew, we wouldn't be standing here, would we?" She immediately felt bad for being snippy, but she was bone-tired and still worried about Rylla.

Cleon touched the surface of the wall, tapped on it in a few places, and turned with a smile. "I think it's just a false wall to block the corridor to the ramp."

Selah furrowed her brow. "How does that help us? A wall is a wall, isn't it?"

"No," Cleon said. "I mean, it's not a full composite wall. We should be able to break through it."

He stood near the end where the wall joined the corridor. He faced away from the wall, leaned back against it, and gave a sharp backward kick with his boot. The wall held. He grimaced.

"What now?" Selah asked.

Cleon held up a hand. "Patience, my dear sister, patience."

Now he was pacifying her. She figured she deserved it after her comment, but she couldn't see this working. They needed to find another way out.

Cleon moved three feet closer to the center of the wall and kicked again. Nothing. It didn't even make a dent. Selah shuddered. They had to move on.

Bodhi turned to thread the boys back through the group. The watcher spoke into his ComTex.

Selah heard Cleon kick the wall a third time. This time it sounded funny, like his foot went though. She turned. Cleon was leaning on the wall with both hands, kicking with all his might to enlarge the hole he'd made.

Selah ran back to him. "Stop. Let me look." She bent and peered through the hole. Her heart leapt. She could see the ramp. Morning light filtered through the terminal gates to the outside. "He got through!"

The retreating group turned back to the wall.

Landers helped to pull out hunks of wallboard until the area was about five feet wide and seven feet tall. The corridor filled with the white chalky dust of demolition. The hovering dust burned Selah's eyes and made her cough, but thinking of freedom made it worthwhile.

⬧

Cleon cleared the rubble on the floor, pushing it back with his boot. His chest puffed up as a slight grin crept across his face. He'd made an important contribution to the operation.

The group filtered through the hole and charged up the ramp to the top doors. The morning sun streamed into the cavernous opening as the sliding doors were pulled back.

The watcher tried to stop them, but people were charging into the outdoor enclosed area. "Commander Mojica will be—"

Suddenly a large craft descended from the sky, blocking out the sunlight. Everyone scattered. The watcher yelled and waved his hands, but to no avail. He couldn't be heard. Many scrambled through the hole in the fence. Selah helped herd the boys in that direction.

The watcher fought the downdraft and covered his eyes as the huge JetTrans set down in a great cloud of dust. Selah and the others stopped. The access panel of the pilot seat slid back and Mojica leaned out, motioning to them. The cargo door on the side facing the fence slid open, and several of the team jumped out with weapons drawn.

Cleon ran toward the Landers who were trying to escape through the fence. "Stop! Wait! These are our people."

The Landers seemed confused and the children terrified at the sight of armed forces. Selah and Treva tried to coax them back to the transport. The team shouted at them to come.

Selah pointed at the craft and yelled to Bodhi over the din, "Get them to go!"

Bodhi grabbed the closest boy around the waist and took off running toward the transport. The rest of the children followed. It was harder getting the Landers to come back.

Some had already passed through the fence and wouldn't come back.

There were more yells and then rockets exploded as heavily armed Prison Unit guards ran from the direction of the merchant gate. Pulse disruptors and laser darts fired rapidly. Grass exploded, trees shattered, and people ran.

Mojica's team fired back. The battle raged as Landers convinced of safety in the vessel tried to get aboard. Treva shoved a couple of hesitant ones toward the craft.

A Prison Unit guard hit a Lander with a shot from his disruptor. The man's chest exploded, showering blood and tissue in all directions, splattering the side of the transport. One of the team returned fire and killed the guard. Two more Landers were caught in the crossfire as they sprinted for the craft. The wounds were not ones to recover from.

Bodhi stood in the transport doorway, screaming for Selah to come. Surrounded by the children, he couldn't pry himself free.

Cleon pulled the last two Landers through the torn fence and turned to Selah, who was still on the other side near the trees. "Come on! We have to get out of here!"

Selah shook her head. "No. You go. I have to find Rylla! I know she's still nearby."

"No, you can't. She'll be all right on her own." His words were lost in the battle.

Selah sprinted into the woods.

Cleon raced after her. A team member grabbed him by the arm, dragging him toward the transport. He fought back, straining to get loose. Weapons fire exploded around them. A laser dart whizzed over his head. Cleon ducked, which

386

gave the team member the leverage he needed to pull him to the craft. A guard fired a pulse disruptor, hitting the open doorway. One of the children fell out dead, his head split open. The team member jerked Cleon, screaming and fighting, into the craft.

Bodhi tried to disengage from the children. They crawled over him in fear, like crabs trying to get out of a barrel. The transport rocked, trying to lift off. The last two team members lunged onto the platform as the transport rose.

"Selah!" Cleon screamed. She was gone. He turned to Bodhi. "Why didn't you watch her? Why did you leave her?"

"She was beside me when I ran!" Bodhi yelled over the din.

The watcher ignored both of them. He slid on a helmet fitted with a headset and long-range vision goggles, engaged a strap harness mechanism around himself, and hung out the door with his hand wrapped in a stationary hook.

Cleon could feel the transport traveling high. It swung around and moved back to the JetTrans station side of the Mountain. Two team members leaned out with laser-sighted guns, projectiles mounted on the ends. As they moved over the area, both fired. The ground below exploded with fire, a flash, and huge dust clouds.

The transport slowed its forward motion. Cleon was sure they were going to set down and get Selah. The watcher was yelling into his headset now.

The transport started to move off. The watcher slid the door closed and unhooked himself, throwing the helmet to the side.

Cleon grabbed him. "You can't leave her. They'll catch her."

The watcher pried himself free. "Not now." He charged

to the back of the transport. Cleon felt like beating the man to a pulp for leaving his sister behind. Bodhi too.

The watcher ran to the back side of the cargo bay, opened the latches holding a thick bulkhead door, and tossed the door aside like it didn't weigh the hundred pounds Cleon knew it did. The watcher grabbed a containment ring with both hands and guided a cable up and over the winch mounted above the open doorway.

27

"What? Why did you let that happen?" Bethany screamed into her mouthpiece. "Rank incompetence!" She ripped off the headset and flung it across the room. She turned to the tech manning the scanner. "Tell me what kind of vehicle just left the Mountain and get a laser cannon tracking its movement. It should be far enough from the Mountain in a few minutes to get a clear shot at it."

The scanner tech scrambled to assemble the info. "Ma'am, it was a JetTrans, but I don't have an identa-marker for it."

Bethany spun to face him. "All JetTrans have identa-markers. You must be mistaken."

"No, ma'am," the tech said as he pointed at the screen. Fear registered in his eyes.

Bethany stepped to the screen. The identa-marker box was blank. "Well, apparently we have a secret operation going on inside this Mountain. I will find those dogs later. Launch a prison JetTrans to bring that transport down."

The tech pointed at the screen again. "They just went dark. I don't know their direction."

Bethany seethed. "I repeat! Get one of ours in the air and find them!"

⟐

In the harness trailing behind the swift-moving transport, Selah clutched Amaryllis tightly to her chest. The force of the wind against her face stripped away every attempt to regain her breath after she'd run to catch the lowered harness. She buried her head in the child's hair, thankful the girl had been running toward all the noise rather than away from it.

She forced her head up. The doorway to the transport was almost within reach. The watcher reached out, hooked himself to their harness, and pulled them into the cargo bay.

Selah clung to Amaryllis as they moved away from the open door.

The girl jabbered like a magpie. "I knew it. I just knew you'd come out of that Mountain. I stayed close by the fence. And all that shooting scared me, but I knew it was you getting away. I knew it!"

Selah was so relieved to have found her swiftly that the nonstop talk was enjoyable. She needed time to thaw. So many things had happened so fast in the last week that her emotions were stunned into a frozen state other than immediate, instinctive responses. Being pulled through the sky at the end of a rope would hit her later.

She reached to hug Cleon and Treva. Cleon clutched her tightly, cutting off her air as he attempted to hide tears. Bodhi

390

extricated himself from the children. They let him move away but huddled together, staring at him.

Bodhi hugged her fiercely, then held her face gently in both hands and gave her a light kiss on the forehead before moving back to the children. It gave her pause. Then she noticed something else.

"Where's the other boy?" She swung around, counting heads in the open transport. All were visible from her position in the back.

Bodhi bit down on his bottom lip. She didn't understand. He mouthed, "Dead."

Selah gasped. Tears welled in her eyes. She looked at Cleon. "And the three missing Landers?"

He set his jaw, closed his eyes, and shook his head. The rest hung their heads. The children hid their faces against each other.

She collapsed back into the seat. Silent tears formed tracks down her cheeks. She tried to be brave and strong and act like she could handle everything, but she couldn't. The thaw had come. Amaryllis slid onto the seat beside her and rested her head against Selah's shoulder. The child's warmth comforted her broken heart.

Her head hurt from people probing it. Her heart hurt from the losses. Mother, Raza, her father, and now people she was trying to save—lost because of her. Maybe she didn't deserve to live, to come through this, to find the life Mother talked about.

If she'd listened to Mother and not gone to the beach, time would have passed her by like a wave slipping back into the ocean without getting her wet.

Tears clouded her vision.

Suddenly Bodhi was on her other side. He slid his arm around her shoulder, looked at her tenderly, and gave her a hug. She buried her head in his shoulder and sobbed.

"It's my fault they're dead," she murmured.

Bodhi tipped up her chin. "If it weren't for you and your tenacity, none of these people would have been saved."

"I should have saved them all. That poor boy, and those Landers. They lived through all this and I got them killed."

"Sometimes there are casualties of war." Bodhi rubbed her back.

Selah looked up at him. She rubbed the backs of her hands across her eyes. "What war?"

"The constant war of good against evil," he said. "I remember somewhere in your country's history it talked about man's inhumanity to man. There's nothing new under the sun."

Their watcher, who had moved forward to talk to Mojica, headed back to them. "Commander Mojica says we will be landing in a few minutes."

Selah tried to look out the side window over Amaryllis's head. All she saw was forest. "Where are we?"

"She'll explain when we land." The watcher grabbed the overhanging straps and threaded his way forward again.

"Did anyone tell you where we'd be dropped off?" Selah moved to the window, trying to get a bearing on the lands below.

"No," Bodhi said, looking down at himself. "I think we need other clothes. We can't go around in these uniforms without people getting suspicious."

"I was hoping we could take off these hoods by now, but I see the watcher still has his on. Maybe we'd better wait."

The transport slowed its forward movement. Selah felt it lurch as it moved toward the ground. The Landers and children became animated. It was curious to watch the children touch heads without words. Selah resigned herself to the beginning of a new life.

A soft thud announced the transport landing. The door slid open and team members hopped out and set up a perimeter. Selah hadn't liked their dark and brooding presence when the operation began, but now she felt a certain level of panic at being left without them.

Cleon and Treva scrambled down from the open side along with the Landers. Selah waited as Bodhi lifted Amaryllis down and herded the children out. The boys still moved as a single unit. They held hands and waited at the side of the transport until all were together before moving away.

Selah hopped down, taking in the scenery. This was a strange place. She could see forest in the distance, but this land had been deliberately cleared of trees. She recognized the work as something her father and brothers did often to make new pasture for the horses and cows.

Why would land be cleared here in the middle of nowhere? This wasn't that far from the Mountain. She wrung her hands and tried to finger her scar through the uniform.

Mojica came around the side of the transport, pulling her hood off as she walked. Her dark hair flowed freely, covering her shoulders and flowing down her back. She shook her head and agitated her hair with both hands, making her look more like a princess than a warrior.

Selah grinned. "We can take these hoods off now?"

"Yes, you're free from the covers," she said. She motioned

to one of her team, who hopped up in the transport and slid out a large canvas bag. "Here are your clothes. I'd appreciate getting our uniforms back so we can leave before we're spotted. Our unit is running in stealth mode, so as long as there are no visuals of us, we're back in the Mountain, home free."

Selah smiled. "Thank you for the foresight. I hadn't thought how we'd get out of these." She dropped to her knees, opened the bag, and fished out her stuff. Relief flooded her. A part of normal life reclaimed. She darted for cover in the trees while Bodhi and the others pulled out their clothing.

When she emerged, Mojica was leaning against the transport with one foot on the rail. Selah dropped the uniform on the deck of the transport and glanced around. Amaryllis moved to her side and took her hand. Selah noted how the child stayed close by since they'd been reunited. It made her smile.

"Where are we?" She looked at the sun's position, figuring which way was north.

Mojica swept her hand out across the view. "In the next few months this is going to become a community in exile of the Mountain. We've gathered from all areas of society to build this new life in the fresh air."

"You said 'we.' You're part of this?"

"Yes, I'll be the head of security and defense," Mojica said with a half smile. "Over there are the beginning phases of the town square." She pointed to the left.

Selah peered in the distance. About a thousand feet away, foundation stones created a rectangle shape jutting from the ground.

"Who's doing all this? I grew up to believe no one ever left the Mountain and very few ever came outside," Selah said.

Mojica pursed her lips. "Well, I guess you can know, since you won't be going back inside. This is the ground where Charles Ganston's going to make his mark in the world."

Treva walked up to the transport, uniform in hand. She added hers to Selah's. "Did I hear you right? This land belongs to my uncle?"

Mojica kicked at the dirt. "You can't repeat this when you go back inside."

"Don't worry. I'm not going back in," Treva said, her voice firm.

Selah let go of Amaryllis's hand and pivoted to face her. "Are you sure? Your whole life's in there. No one knew you were part of our operation. You could sneak back in with Mojica and no one would be the wiser. Don't you think you might regret leaving it and everything you owned?"

Bodhi and Cleon arrived. Bodhi looked at Selah and Treva. "Did something happen?"

Cleon approached Treva. "What'd we miss?"

"You missed her saying she's not going back in the Mountain," Selah said.

He looked at her and reached for her hand. "Are you sure? Your uncle is still in there. He's the only family you have."

Treva pursed her lips. "Hopefully Uncle Charles will be out soon. But the only things I'm giving up are the drugs and lies I've been using to cover up."

Bodhi slid his arm around Selah's waist. She found comfort in his embrace, but now she was worried about her new friend. Drugs? Did she have some kind of an addiction? Selah had heard about people with that kind of problem, but she'd never met any.

Cleon bit his lip. Selah knew that look. He was afraid to speak.

"Treva, what kind of drugs? Tell us what we can do to help." Although Selah didn't have any idea how to help someone on drugs. She decided she could at least be supportive. This girl had risked a lot to help them.

"Yes, you can help me," Treva said. "Help me learn how to deal with this." She reached for the neckline of her shirt and pulled it down enough to expose the wing imprinted below her collarbone.

Selah's legs gave way. Bodhi gripped her waist and for a second she was suspended in his arms. "I don't know what to say. How is this possible?"

Bodhi's mouth opened. "How come I couldn't feel you?"

"That's why I've been taking drugs. A few years ago I came up with the formula to effectively mask it." Treva looked at Selah. "Are you all right?"

Selah beamed from ear to ear. "All right! I'm ecstatic. I've got someone like me. We can learn together. The only thing better would have been if I'd gotten to meet my father." With Amaryllis, Cleon, and the rest, she would start a new family. She'd never forget the others, but this would help soothe her losses.

She saw Mojica nod to one of her men. She figured with their work finished, they'd go home. The uniformed group approached the transport, and she moved from the opening to get out of their way.

Mojica put her hand on Selah's shoulder. "I'm hoping

you'll forgive me for this, but it was the only way I could ensure your safety once I understood."

Selah furrowed her brow. "Why would I need to forgive you?"

Mojica pointed to her team. The men in the front separated and her watcher moved forward. As he pulled off his hood, Selah saw the mark on the left side of his temple and forehead. "He's a Lander! Why didn't we feel his presence?"

Treva's hand went to her mouth as she gasped out loud.

"Because I am the oldest among us, and I can block anyone from discerning my thoughts or presence," the Lander said.

Selah looked at Bodhi for clarity. He shrugged.

She turned back to Mojica. "I don't understand. Who is this?"

Mojica smiled. "Selah Rishon, I'd like you to meet your father, Glade Rishon."

Selah squeaked a scream as her legs went weak again. Bodhi braced her. She stared, taking in the man's features. Her mind reached out in shaking beats to make a connection, but then she pulled back, unsure. The facts didn't add up. Was this a trick?

Cleon moved to her side in defense mode. "How do we know this is really her father?"

Treva came forward, stood directly in front of Glade, and put her hand to his chest.

He embraced her hand, putting her fingers to his lips. "Thank you for giving me my life, and the lives of my fellow Landers, and for saving my child," he said. "I can never repay you."

Treva turned to face the group. "I've been taking care of

this man, and I'm the one who brought him out of the drug fog. This is Glade Rishon."

Selah fisted her hands on her hips. "Then why didn't you notice he was in our group?"

Treva cocked her head. "I've only known him a few days. Sorry that one out of twenty masked people didn't make an extra impression on me."

"But his eyes," Selah said. "You didn't recognize his eyes?"

Treva pursed her lips. "Please tell me how many of this group of combat forces you have actually stared at."

Selah stopped to think, then snapped to the present. "We saw him burnt to a crisp in that cell." She was afraid to accept the hope that her father really stood in front of her.

Mojica raised a finger. "I personally got Glade out of his cell while you were still in the security area. He can explain later. I don't know who was in that cell, but I'd venture to guess it was Drace Stemple. He's the only one missing so far."

Treva lowered her head. "That would make sense. I ran into him in security and he was on his way back up. It's just so sad. I'd made progress with him. He was beginning to doubt everything Everling stood for."

"That's probably what got him killed," Mojica said.

Selah took it all in. Fear of the unknown slid away before her eyes. Here was her chance at a happy future. She gained her footing and walked to Glade on shaky legs. "Father?"

Glade smiled. He touched his fingers to her cheek. "You look exactly like your mother. You have her eyes, and I've definitely seen her spirit in you."

Selah's bottom lip trembled. "You're really my father?"

Glade reached out gently and pulled her to his chest. "Yes,

my child. I am your father. I must confess I never dreamed this day would happen." He wrapped his arms around her and rested his chin on her head.

"Where have you been? Mother searched for you," Selah said between tears. She wrapped her arms around his waist and squeezed. She could feel him. He was real. Her father.

"I've been in the Mountain. It was my turn," Glade said. "How is your mother?"

"Mother is well. She never stopped loving you. But what do you mean about your turn?"

Glade glanced around, his brow furrowed. "I've always loved her. But I needed to protect you from . . . we'll talk about this later, privately."

Selah felt him trembling. The feeling was mutual. She lost the capacity for words. Tired. Overwhelmed. Stunned to silence. Just basking in his presence for a few minutes was enough. All the questions she'd thought of had died with the fire in that cell. She needed to start her list again. With her newfound knowledge, some of her questions would change. She glanced at Amaryllis standing to the side. The look on her face was one big question mark. Selah smiled for what felt like the millionth time in the last hour. This could take a lot of explaining.

Glade patted her arm. "I must get my things from the transport so they can leave." He moved to the open doorway and carried his clothing into the woods.

Mojica strode to the group and looked at Treva. "I have a data package here that Charles Ganston asked me to hand over if you decided not to return. I guess he knew there was a good chance you wouldn't be coming back."

Glade, dressed in a white linen tunic set like the others, emerged from the trees and hoisted his uniform onto the pile.

Mojica reached around him to a box mounted inside the transport, pressed her thumb to the scanner, and opened the lid. She handed Treva the package inside and signaled her team. "Mount up, boys and girls. We're going home."

The team scrambled back inside the transport. Mojica took her place in the pilot seat and the transport lifted off, stirring the landscape as it rose above the trees.

⊕

Mojica felt rejuvenated. The adrenaline rush of the past several hours had sent her to new heights. She swiftly moved away from the landing area and shot off toward the Mountain.

She turned to her navigator. "Scan the five miles to the Mountain. I want you looking for Prison Unit JetTrans." Still, she didn't think they'd chase a transport they couldn't get a transponder signal from. She'd been running stealth and no one saw what direction they'd taken.

They were already a mile closer. The navigator nodded and keyed several screens. "Uh, ma'am. We have a bogie at two o'clock, coming in hot."

Mojica swore under her breath and punched it, taking evasive maneuvers. "Everyone buckle down, we're going to take fire!" she shouted into her headset.

The PU JetTrans flew faster than Mountain units. Mojica wondered what else Everling had developed that no one knew about. It caught up to them in a matter of seconds, firing across their bow. A shot clipped the right flank, shuddering the transport.

Mojica rolled to the left. The next shots disappeared into the landscape. Her transport, powerful enough to carry eighty soldiers and still fly at sonic speed, showcased her skills. With a complement of only twenty on board, she could outfly anything in the sky.

"Check their comm link for chatter," she said with a smile. She darted and wove back and forth in the sky. The PU JetTrans fired at them repeatedly. Mojica didn't want to engage in a firefight and allow them time for backup, so she easily evaded shots with rolling and dropping sequences. She imagined the people they had just dropped off were getting quite a show. She'd keep the PU unit out here away from the Mountain until they could lose it.

"Ma'am!" the navigator yelled. "Since we have no transponder signal, they're tracking hot hulls. The PU is staying behind us so the cannon knows to target us as the lead unit. They've powered up a laser cannon, and they've got tone and lock on us."

Mojica called up all her skill. She lowered the cruise speed, watching the PU follow suit. "Give me the signal."

The navigator watched the instruments. "They fired!"

Mojica slammed both hands into the controls, reversing the thrusters. They slowed so fast the PU JetTrans overshot them, putting it in the lead. The laser cannon made contact with the lead unit, vaporizing it.

Mojica veered off to the right, banked low, and skirted the treetops to stay off the Prison Unit's radar as she navigated her way back to their secret entrance on the back side of the Mountain.

She smiled. Mission accomplished.

28

S elah watched as Glade gave advice to the group of Landers that wanted to leave right away. She had attempted to have a private conversation with him twice in the last few minutes, but there were too many people vying for his attention. She stood there staring. Was this another person who was going to rebuff her affection?

Bodhi walked up behind her. He slid his hand onto her shoulder. "I feel your sadness."

Selah didn't turn. "I'm beginning to feel like a loser that no father wants."

"Don't feel that way. Apparently Glade is the oldest and wisest among them and they all value his counsel," Bodhi said.

"But I'm his daughter." Her lip trembled. She bit down on it rather than show her distress.

"I don't know that he's ever experienced fatherhood. You may need to teach him." Bodhi gently turned her to face him and smiled. "Give him a little more leeway than an hour."

Selah sighed and looked around. Where were the children? They had been a little farther away but now the spot
was empty. The notes of a lilting melody drifted from the
trees, sounding almost like wind instruments. Cleon and
Treva walked toward the sound with Amaryllis between
them.

Selah walked beside Bodhi. They rounded a stand of trees
and headed toward the sound. The haunting melody, the most
beautiful song she'd ever heard, lent a feeling of anticipation.
A strange sense of peace. Bodhi reached for her hand. She
hesitated. Was this a knee-jerk reaction to all the emotions
they'd visited in the last few days? The look in his eyes melted
her fear, and she slipped her hand into his.

"Do you feel that?" he said softly, his voice expressing
wonder.

Prickles of excitement tapped on her chest. Strange. The
thunder had subsided. She felt the change, like when her
brothers had worked on a Sand Run. As they found the right
fuel mix, the idle went from rough and noisy to smooth and
purring.

Cleon and Treva stood off to the right with Amaryllis
hiding behind them. She had been reluctant to go near the
group of children, and Selah hadn't forced the issue. The
boys formed a circle, all nineteen of them holding hands.
The music emanated from them.

Bodhi looked at her for an explanation.

Selah knitted her brow. "I don't have a clue what's going
on."

They reached the circle. Bodhi touched the boy closest to
him. "The song is beautiful. What's it for?"

"We are summoning our salvation," the boy said softly.

Bodhi turned to Selah. "Do you know what that means?"

She grimaced. "I've never heard the term before."

The rest of the Landers were filtering into the area.

She tapped Bodhi. "We've got company."

"Do any one of you know what's going on?" Bodhi yelled to the Landers moving closer.

The one who'd been the guard's prisoner stepped forward. "It feels very familiar, but none of the others have ever heard it before."

Bodhi turned back to the children. "Please tell us what we can do to help."

The boy stared at the center of the circle. "You cannot help us. We do not belong here." The song continued.

"But you can stay with us. We are all the same." Selah pointed to the group of Landers.

"No, we are not the same," the boy said. "We are an abomination."

Selah looked at Bodhi. "What does that mean? Why would a child say that?"

"If you give us time I'm sure we could figure out a solution," Bodhi said.

Selah's hopes fell. Something was coming. She couldn't tell if it was good or bad. "You are Landers. You have the mark. I have the mark below my collarbone," she said.

Glade moved up behind her and touched her shoulder. Just his touch warmed her heart. "I sense we should probably move away," he said, looking sad.

"But Father, who would think precious children are an abomination? They are just children. They have the mark on the other side of their forehead. What's so bad about that? Mine is below my collarbone."

The music grew louder.

"We are not children," the boy said. "We are clones. Our mark is on the wrong side because we are mirror images of you. We are wrong for this world. We are not supposed to be here. Evil created us, not good."

The music took on more tones. A breeze drifted across the treetops, rustling the leaves in concert with the sound.

Treva rushed over. "We had a few of their bodies. I thought they were Landers but they had the same right-sided mark." Her eyes opened wide. "They all disintegrated into piles of dust. You'd better move away."

The breeze picked up. The wind began to push dirt and leaves around. Selah pushed the hair from her eyes. The song moved to a higher pitch.

She turned back to the children. "Please, stay with us. We can help you."

Bodhi took her by the arm. "I've had a moment of clarity. I'm beginning to understand. I think we need to move back."

Selah pried his hand from her arm. "No! They need us and we need them. We can make this work. They're only children. There must be people who will take them in." She thought of all the time Amaryllis had spent alone without a family.

"We must go," the boy said. "We are being summoned by—"

The last words were cut off by a howling wind. Bodhi's mouth opened in surprise. He stared as though trying to comprehend. His eyes widened and he fell to his knees, weeping.

A funnel cloud formed high in the sky over their position.

Glade took Selah's arm again. "We can't help them," he yelled over the roar of the wind. "They have no choice but to go back." He pulled her away from the circle.

"Back where?" Selah struggled against his grasp.

"I can't say. Not yet," Glade said. Bodhi scrambled from the ground to help him.

The boys turned and looked at them one last time. In unison, a smile crossed their faces as their bodies collapsed to the ground.

Selah tried to charge forward. Her father wrapped her in his arms to hold her back.

The fallen boys disintegrated into sparkling molecules of light that looped and swirled and dove together into one lustrous, multi-stranded ribbon of soft colors.

Selah screamed, clutching at the air. Her legs tried to catapult her into the swirl. Glade restrained her.

The funnel of wind, like a finger pointing toward the earth, reached out to touch the ribbon, sucking it inside.

"No, no! They were only children!" Selah collapsed to the ground and pulled herself into a ball as she rocked and cried softly at the lost lives.

The funnel retreated into the sky. The roar subsided and the wind died to a gentle breeze. The funnel swirled, passing above the clouds and out of sight as the sun returned.

⚛

Selah watched Amaryllis exploring the grounds around the building lots. The child seemed carefree and none the worse for wear after what they'd experienced. Even after watching the group of rescued children turn into dust and get sucked up by a tornado, she seemed to take it in stride. Selah, on the other hand, wasn't so indifferent. Maybe she would be later, after she discovered more explanations. Right now, no one could supply those.

She walked past Glade and Treva engrossed in the package of data her uncle had supplied. It would give the Landers safe routes to follow and help with making travel plans. Apparently Charles Ganston was a treasure trove of information because of his long association with Treva's parents and the secrets they had imparted to him.

For the first time in a week she didn't have a mission or purpose, and she felt disconnected.

The sounds of water lapping at the shore drew her attention. A large lake engulfed the area on the other side of the trees. She walked to the water's edge and stood watching birds swoop over the water, chasing bugs. It reminded her of home and the lake where the farm animals drank.

Suddenly a pair of arms slid around her waist. She jerked. "You almost scared the life out of me."

Bodhi playfully snuggled her neck. "There's enough life in you for three women, so there's no chance of that happening."

She turned in his embrace to face him. "You sure do have confidence that I want anything to do with you."

Bodhi feigned sorrow. "Are you turning me away? Let me see if I can remember. I think you called me a sea slug the first time we met, and then another time later. But you didn't turn away when I kissed you."

"That's what that was, huh? I'd say it was a pretty sorry excuse for a kiss." She moved her face closer to his.

Bodhi stared into her eyes. "You didn't really give me a good chance. I was afraid you were going to hit me, which, I will remind you, you did at various other times." He moved closer.

"Well, I'm not hitting you now," Selah said.

He brushed her lips with his. She felt a surge of electricity skitter up her back. She didn't resist. A dozen emotions pushed at her, but only one manifested. Her knees began to wobble.

Selah tenderly touched her lips to his.

Why was she kissing him? Because it felt right. It left her gasping for air.

He held her tighter and whispered in her ear, "Are you going to fall?"

"Um, I don't know. Are you going to let go of me?"

His breath caressed her cheek. "Never, and I really mean that."

Amaryllis ran through the trees, breathless. She stopped in front of them and fanned the air like kisses were contagious. "Glade wants you two to come back and hear the announcement from the Lander people!"

Selah and Bodhi strolled through the trees, holding hands.

Amaryllis, giggling like a normal child, ran to a stump where Cleon was setting up a game of pick-up sticks. Selah smiled. He'd spent a lot of time making games for their brother Dane, so this was right in line with his skill for entertaining kids.

The Landers sat cross-legged in a circle on the grass. Treva and Glade had walked to the construction area, pointing at places on a map. Selah wandered over to them while Bodhi joined the Landers.

Glade stopped at the cornerstone for the new government

building as Treva laid out the map. He searched around for a few seconds and then stepped inside the perimeter.

"What are you looking for, Father?" Selah got a rush when she called him *Father*. She longed for time they could spend alone, away from these present responsibilities. But she understood. Her mother used to say, "Short-term discomfort for long-term gain." Now Selah was beginning to understand the saying. If only her mother could be here.

Glade smiled softly at her. "I'm interested in the symbol Ganston has on the drawn image of this building. His notation called it an artifact."

He walked to a pile of construction materials, pushed back the heavy tarp protecting them from the elements, and reached to touch a large stone block. It looked ragged around the edges, as though it had been in a demolition. His fingers traced the circle superimposed over the three entwined ovals.

"What is that?" Selah peered around his shoulder at the old stone. Why did old people care about old stuff? Mother had seemed drawn to archeology too.

"I was not sure anything significant could have survived the Sorrows," Glade said.

Selah touched the granular surface. She would much rather take interest in the here and now and let this stuff go the way of the rusted building corpses on the shore in Dominion. Nature would reclaim them soon enough. "What's so important about a ragged piece of stone?"

Glade re-covered it and sat down on the edge of the pile. "It's a remnant of a very sad time in history. People went crazy back then. They destroyed many spiritual buildings and burned holy books, all in a rage for not getting what they thought they deserved. The depravity of man brought about the end of an age."

Selah sat beside him and leaned her head on his arm. This was the first time he'd sat still long enough for her to get close. She savored the moment before it was gone. "Did you see it? Were you here?"

"No, but I did arrive shortly after." Glade hung his head. "My shortcomings sent me here." He covered her hand with his.

"What do you mean?" Selah felt the kinship of his touch. Her real father. The reality started to sink in. She had done it. She had found him.

He rubbed his chin. "Someday I'll tell you, but for now I want you to know it was my deep sense of repentance that caused my capture. I needed to save you and your mother. I wasn't running away from my responsibilities but was finally running toward them." He rose, took her hand, and wrapped it around his arm.

Selah smiled and strolled with him back to the group. She glanced at the position of the sun. They'd been here about an hour. She'd been too excited for food, but now her stomach was beginning to growl. She and Amaryllis needed to make some weapons and do some hunting.

The Landers were on their feet and moving about.

Bodhi approached Selah and Glade. "They've decided they don't want to stay, and I'm not sure they'd be safe anyhow."

"Do they know where they're going?" Selah asked. "I've never known anyone to go farther than the Mountain."

One of the Landers spoke up. "Glade knows where we'll be. There are many large colonies in the north. It's just inhospitable country in the winter, very cold and a lot of snow."

Selah cringed. Intriguing. She'd heard of snow but had never seen any. "Do you have to leave so soon?"

Another Lander spoke. "We're only as far away as your thoughts."

"We're anxious to see what's left of our families. We must take our leave," another said.

"If we delay much longer, we will have to travel in the heat of the day, so I suggest we get started," one said, moving away from the group.

They all clasped arms. Selah had never seen the gesture before. Each man grabbed another's elbow with his right hand, so instead of holding hands they were clasping forearms. She liked it.

She watched them walk away, free for the first time in many years. Sadness overwhelmed her. She realized they weren't her blood, but they were her people. She belonged somewhere no one could take away.

They watched the group move off into the woods, heading north.

"I'm worried they have no food or weapons to hunt," Selah said.

Bodhi smiled. "You just can't turn off the mom part, can you?"

Selah shot him a glare. "My attention to detail has gotten me this far, bucko."

Glade laughed. "Ganston left us a map of the north. I showed them the communities where they could find sympathetic allies and procure weapons or supplies. They'll be fine. They're grown adults."

Treva grinned. "Yeah, really old adults."

Selah ran her hands through her hair. "Okay, I'll stop. So what are we going to do?"

The six of them sat down where Glade and Treva had the package open.

"We're welcome to stay here," Treva said. "My uncle has work crews coming daily. His community will leave the Mountain in about a month."

Selah looked at Glade. "I don't think it's safe for us to stay here."

"I agree with that assessment. It may be safe in the future, when this place gets established. I got the impression from Commander Mojica that there were Landers in the Mountain that no one knows anything about," Glade said.

Everyone sat up straight.

"What do you mean? More prisoners?" Selah asked.

"There were no others in the labs," Treva said.

Glade raised both hands. "I'm sorry I said that. It was just an impression I got from our conversation. Mojica told me she altered Selah's bio-signature in the system so the search fleet couldn't find her. And she also changed the report where Selah was questioned by a transport at one of the stations. "

Selah put a hand to her mouth. "I forgot all about that."

"It just seemed that she knew more about the situation than I would have expected. With her in command, I'm sure if there were other captives we'd have gotten them out also. Right now staying here might set us up for capture again. We'd do better to go north."

Selah looked at Bodhi and Cleon. "Do you guys agree?"

Cleon shrugged. "I'm the odd man out here. I'm the only

one who's not marked, so I have to go with what you all think is safe."

Amaryllis squeezed in next to Selah and looked at her with big eyes. "Do I get to go too?"

Selah hugged her. "Yes, you go wherever I go." She'd figure out this little sister thing later when they all had time to rest and regroup, but at least the child wouldn't be alone.

"Treva, what about you?" Selah asked, holding her breath. The girl had grown on her, and she saw her good influence on Cleon.

"I'd like to be here for my uncle when his community starts. He's carried a huge burden, and I love him for it. He wrote in my letter that he always knew my father was a Lander, and he's protected me from the very moment they died. He knew there was a possibility that I could acquire the mark, but he never wanted to ask me about it, in case it didn't happen."

"So does that mean you want to stay?" Cleon asked. His countenance fell as he slipped his hand into hers.

Selah knew he might elect to stay with her. How would she deal with leaving her brother behind?

Treva thought for a minute. "I guess we could come back after the town is built."

Cleon beamed from ear to ear. "Yes, I'm sure we could do that. Couldn't we?"

He looked at Bodhi and Selah. They nodded in agreement.

Glade raised a finger. "We should head northeast, to the original colony I came from before I went south twenty years ago. We should be safe there."

"Will the colony still be there?" Selah asked.

He reached to hug her. "Yes, the colony is called TicCity.

414

In the ancient world it was called Atlantic City, New Jersey. Unlike in the south below the Mountain, Landers are not hunted in the northern areas. There are large homogenized cities of Landers and normals just waiting . . ." His words drifted off.

"Waiting for what?" Selah pressed her forehead to his shoulder.

"Waiting for answers that I can't give them until I get back to my original work of searching for the old woman," he said.

Selah lifted her head to look at him. "An old woman? Excuse me for laughing, but after twenty years she may be dead."

Glade shook his head. "Not this old woman. She was among the first of us to come here. She's out there somewhere. I just need to get back to finding her. Besides, you'll get to be near the ocean again."

Selah pulled back to look at him. "How do you know about my ocean?"

Glade smiled broadly. "I couldn't be with you, my child, but I've taken pains to watch over you all these years."

She pursed her lips. "We really need to have a talk."

Her father tipped his head to touch hers. "Well, we've got about a week's travel from here to the coast and then north. That should make me a captive audience to your questions."

Selah's heart raced. A 150-year-old woman. What kind of journey would this new quest be? She dismissed the fear trying to creep in and allowed her emotions to soar. She had found her father and would get her ocean back too.

COMING
FALL 2015

LIGHTNING

BOOK 2 IN THE
Stone Braide Chronicles

1

A clipped sound echoed along the cavernous street as Selah Rishon raised her foot onto a stone bench. She jerked her head up to glance around the abandoned streetscape. This modern world of TicCity was strangely out of sync with the life she'd known in Dominion Borough. At home, the ancient cities were completely abandoned and mostly reclaimed by the environment, but up here in the north, the old and the new existed side by side, with the purposes sometimes overlapping. She was never quite sure what to expect.

A groan bounced from the facades.

Eyeing the landscape cautiously, she finished tightening her shoe and then stretched her calf muscle. She reminded herself that no matter how much she disliked exercise, it had a dual purpose—to rebuild the leg strength she'd found waning over the last few months of lounging here seaside, and to alleviate her current predicament. She had been informed early on that walking around TicCity with knives hidden in her pants legs was completely uncivilized, so this regiment of training seemed like a great alternative to carrying kapos. In reality, she had an ulterior motive for staying toned and lean—like love . . . regaining what had been lost.

She switched feet, tightened her other shoe, and stretched her calf as she squinted into the waning rays of the evening sun hanging low on the horizon. Dramatic shadows sliced across the building facades, creating elongated, one-dimensional bogeymen. She shivered. It reminded her of the tree-shadow soldiers in the field at home where the dead body probably was planted. She pushed off at a slow jog down the broken, weed-congested street.

A shadow slid to the edge of the surrounding darkness in a doorway two building cavities away on her side of the street.

Selah stopped. Her chest constricted and her heart rate ticked up, pushing blood-rush starbursts into her vision. She squinted at the different shades of black, attempting to distinguish a face among the sprinkled flashes. Her brain deciphered the outline of a short club protruding from an overly thick hand, probably gloved. Her mouth went dry. She sniffed at the air. She could almost distinguish the smell. Sweat and vegetation mixed with musk and dirt. A male.

The black-clad figure separated from the darkness and lunged onto the uneven sidewalk. She inhaled to draw in calm and studied the shape and posture of the figure. A little taller than her five foot six. Broad at the shoulders, rectangular stance between legs and hips. Yes, it had to be a man.

Her heart pounded a staccato rhythm against her rib cage, drowning out her thoughts. *Control your breathing.*

Bonnie S. Calhoun

She turned to run the other way. Adrenaline surged, prickling up the back of her neck and across her scalp. Another movement whispered in front of her.

A second figure emerged from one of the numerous doorways, blocking her retreat.

How did she miss him? Not paying attention could get her hurt.

She pivoted and her back faced the street. No! Bad move. Another attack angle unprotected. She spun, positioning her back against the building. One assailant stood to her left, the other approached from the right. If she let them get close at the same time, she'd be done. Her legs trembled. She steeled herself for an attack.

A squeak. An audible click. The man to her left flicked open an auto-blade. He brandished the knife and lunged. Selah jerked her wrist up to block the attack but over-swung. Her hand accidentally connected with her own chin and she bit into her lip. The taste of copper heightened her senses. Selah balled her fists tight to her chest and thrust out her left leg, planting her foot in the man's stomach.

He doubled over as air expelled from his lungs with a grunt. The knife flew from his hand and skittered across the broken street surface. He scrambled for the weapon. Selah bounced to a defensive stance. Pivoting her hips to the side, she kicked at his middle, connecting with his chest. He collapsed to the road, gasping.

Emboldened that she hadn't suffered a blow, she bolted in the other man's direction. He raised his club and she assumed a fighting posture. As he swung, she blocked the downward motion of his left wrist with an upward thrust of her right

421

forearm. It rocked her core, stinging her arm. An adrenaline rush absorbed the pain.

His right fist jabbed at her head. She pulled to the right side. Her left leg shot out in a low kick and connected with the outside of his knee, knocking him off balance. As he started to fold, she maneuvered a hefty jab, shoving her fist into his nose.

Spittle flew from his mouth.

The man grabbed his face. "My nose! Why, you . . ." He cursed and released the club. It clattered to the ground.

She sprinted down the street, crossing to the other side. Her core buzzed with the electricity of rapid-fire movements and precision strokes. Her speed felt fluid and natural.

Pay attention. Focus. Focus, she recited until her breathing leveled off.

Stinging. She shook her hand, blew on her fingers, and examined them. Tiny smears of blood dotted the back of her hand. She had skinned two knuckles but just now noticed.

White AirStream at three o'clock. Someone in the pilot's seat.

This time she wasn't taking chances. She dodged behind a tree and used the street-side refuse container to hide her advance. She sprang from her hiding place and ran to the AirStream, creeping along its length to the front. With her back against the sleek side, she reached across her chest with her left arm and snatched the occupant out by his tunic. As he exited the cockpit, she jammed her right hand between his left arm socket and shoulder blade. She felt his shoulder separate and he howled in pain.

Lowering the man's center of gravity to throw him off balance, she drove his face into the narrow grassy strip at the edge of the sidewalk and planted her knee on his neck.

"All right, all right! I'm down!" With his plea muffled by the grass, the man fell limp.

"Okay, Selah," boomed the speaker mounted high on the side of a nearby building. "Your session is done, and by the looks of it, so are my men." The head of TicCity security chuckled.

Selah looked up at the tiny visi-unit mounted on the street illuminator and smiled. "Okay, Taraji! I think I may have broken Arann's nose. He zigged when he should have zagged. And Hex needs to lubricate his auto-blade. His prop's got a serious squeak." She looked down the street and assessed her victims.

Arann, still holding his nose, raised his hand in a thumbs-up. Selah waved and jogged back to the training zone entrance.

A black-clad figure dropped in front of her. Selah recoiled as the hooded figure crouched like a jumping spider and charged. Selah blocked the charge and spun to the right, executing a roundhouse sweep. The figure jumped her leg and came in, fists flying. The two of them parried back and forth. Blow for blow, slice for slice, Selah felt her comfort level with the defensive moves increase with her speed and confidence.

A smile pulled at the corners of her lips. She felt exhilarated.

The spider figure lunged, rolled, and swept Selah's feet from under her with one fell swoop. Selah landed on her back with a grunt as the air rushed from her lungs. The figure scrambled over her and pressed a glove-covered fist to Selah's throat.

"Augh! I surrender." Selah threw up her hands.

The black-clad figure ripped off her hood. Taraji grinned at Selah. "Never let your opponent see your level of confidence, because they will use it against you every time."

Selah shook her head. "I really thought I had you."

Taraji held out a hand and yanked Selah back to her feet. "You would have if you hadn't stopped to grin at me. It made for a perfect break in your concentration. But your increase in speed is phenomenal. You're ready to move to the next level. I'll see you in tactical first thing in the morning."

Selah watched Taraji saunter back up the stairs leading to the catwalk connected to her office, thinking someday she'd be as agile and stealthy as her teacher. But today she'd settle for this new lesson.

Breathless and sweaty, Selah entered the staging area on the backside of the security team training center. Mindful that she didn't have to hide it here, she peeled off the vibrant blue top of her workout suit, exposing the mark hovering below her collarbone. Her narrow-strapped cotton undershirt offered welcome relief as the suit top trailed behind her on the trudge across the equipment area to the ultrasonic-showers. What a workout! This ancient form of martial arts called Krav Maga that Taraji recommended was the perfect form of self-defense. But then again everything Taraji suggested seemed to be the perfect advice for the situation.

The woman reminded her of Mojica, head of security in the Mountain, from their singular names to both of them being six feet tall, with muscular builds, long dark hair, and beautiful large eyes with heavy lashes. The only difference—

Taraji's complexion was dark like the honey Selah loved for dipping her morning bread. If Mother had met her, she'd have said the woman was smooth as silk but tough as nails.

Selah sighed at the recollection. If only she could find her missing mother.

Bonnie S. Calhoun teaches workshops on Facebook, Twitter, HTML, and social media at writers' conferences. In her everyday life she is a seamstress and clothing designer. Bonnie and her husband live in a log home in upstate New York with a dog and two cats who think she's waitstaff. *Thunder* is her first YA novel. Learn more at www.bonniescalhoun.com.

Don't Miss
TREMORS
the prequel to *THUNDER*

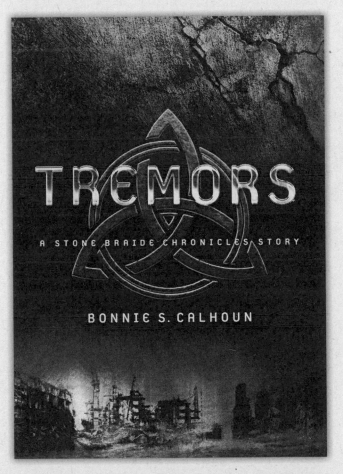

Find out what happened before the story of *Thunder* begins and discover the disturbing secrets and harrowing events that changed Selah's life forever.

• Available in Ebook Format Only •

Get to know

BONNIE S. CALHOUN!

◆ ◆ ◆

BonnieSCalhoun.com

STONE BRAIDE CHRONICLES △ 1

THUNDER

A NOVEL

BONNIE S. CALHOUN

Revell

a division of Baker Publishing Group
Grand Rapids, Michigan

© 2014 by Bonnie S. Calhoun

Published by Revell
a division of Baker Publishing Group
P.O. Box 6287, Grand Rapids, MI 49516-6287
www.revellbooks.com

Paperback edition published 2015
ISBN 978-0-8007-2445-0

Printed in the United States of America

All rights reserved. No part of this publication may be reproduced, stored in a retrieval
system, or transmitted in any form or by any means—for example, electronic, photocopy,
recording—without the prior written permission of the publisher. The only exception
is brief quotations in printed reviews.

The Library of Congress has cataloged the previous edition as follows:
Calhoun, Bonnie S.
    Thunder : a novel / Bonnie S. Calhoun.
        pages cm. — (The Stone Braide chronicles ; bk. 1)
    Summary: 150 years after a nuclear attack destroyed much of the United
States, Selah, just turned eighteen, learns that she is a hybrid of two surviving
factions and sets out from what was Norfolk, Virginia, to seek the father she
never knew, aided by her stepbrother Cleon and Bodhi, a Lander like her father.
    ISBN 978-0-8007-2376-7 (cloth)
    ISBN 978-0-8007-2416-0 (int'l trade paper)
    [1. Science fiction.] I. Title.
PZ7.C12745Thu 2014
[Fic]—dc23   2014016629

This book is a work of fiction. Names, characters, places, and incidents are the product
of the author's imagination or are used fictitiously. Any resemblance to actual events,
locales, or persons, living or dead, is coincidental.

15   16   17   18   19   20   21   7   6   5   4   3   2   1

I dedicate this book to my sister Robin.
She has always loved me, even though I tried to pull
her through the bars of my former crib when she was
a newborn and I cut her hair when she was three.

YA FIC
Calhoun, Bonnie S.
Thunder : a novel
c2015

Discarded by
Santa Maria Library

THUNDER